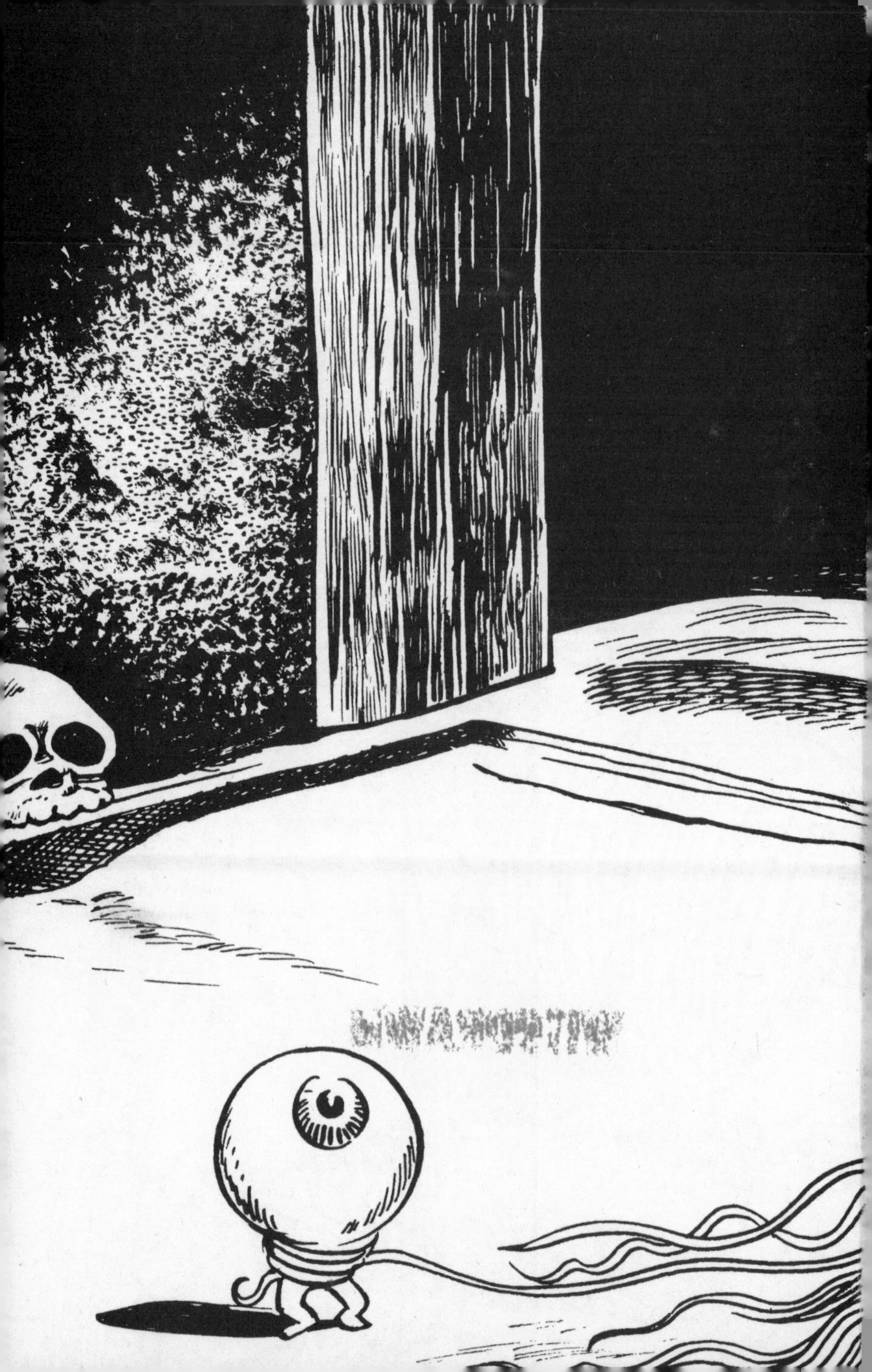

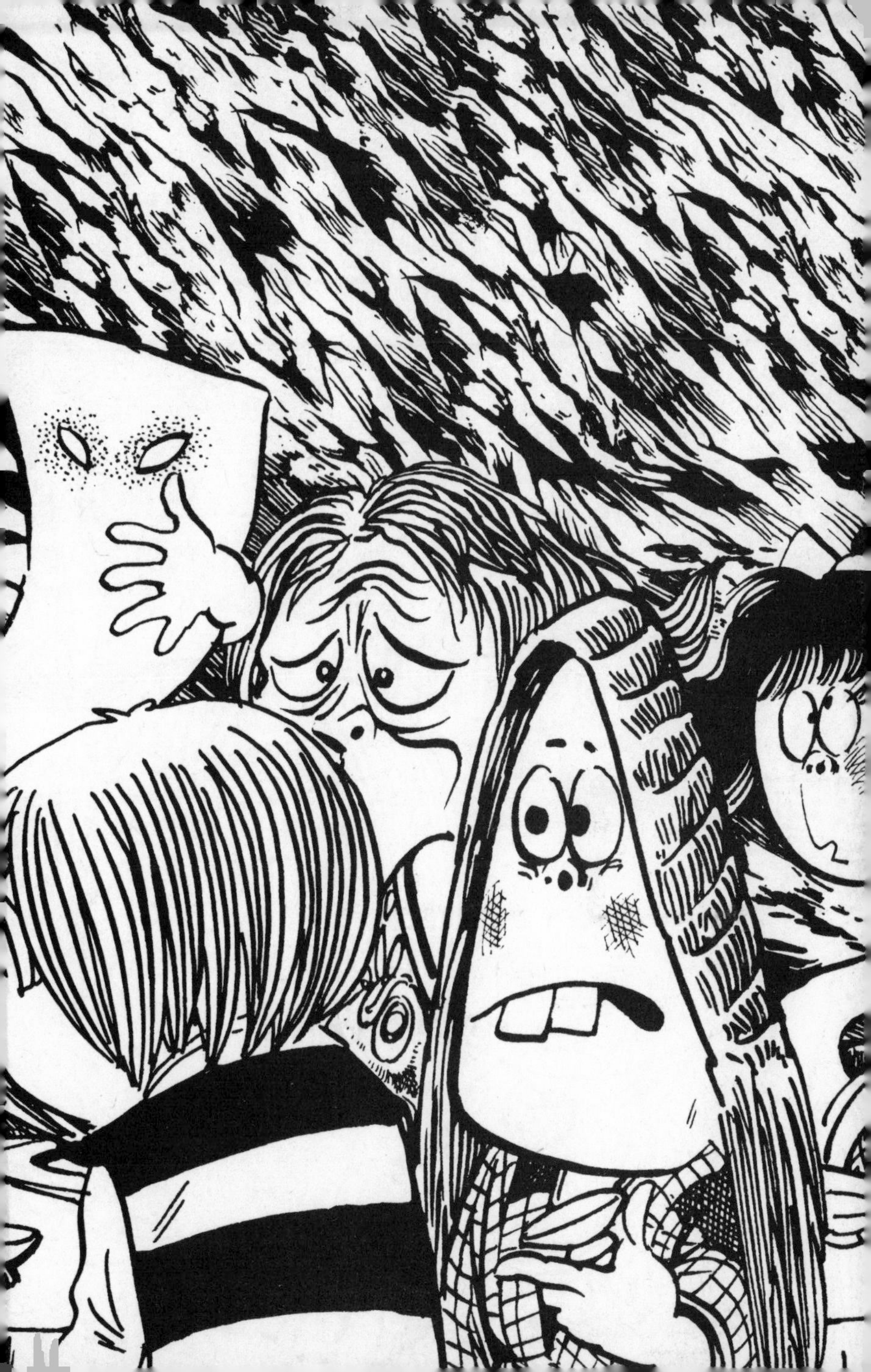

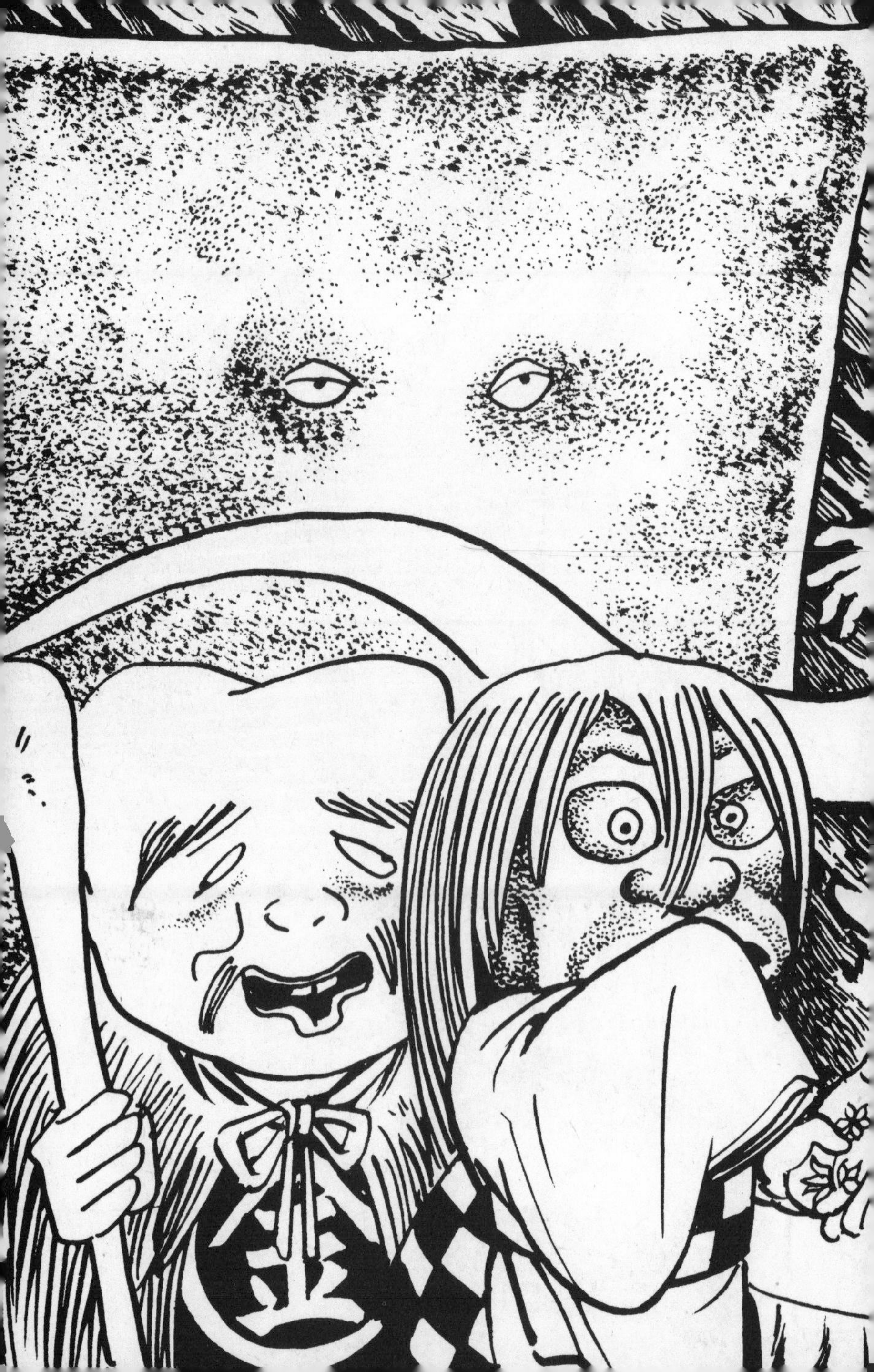

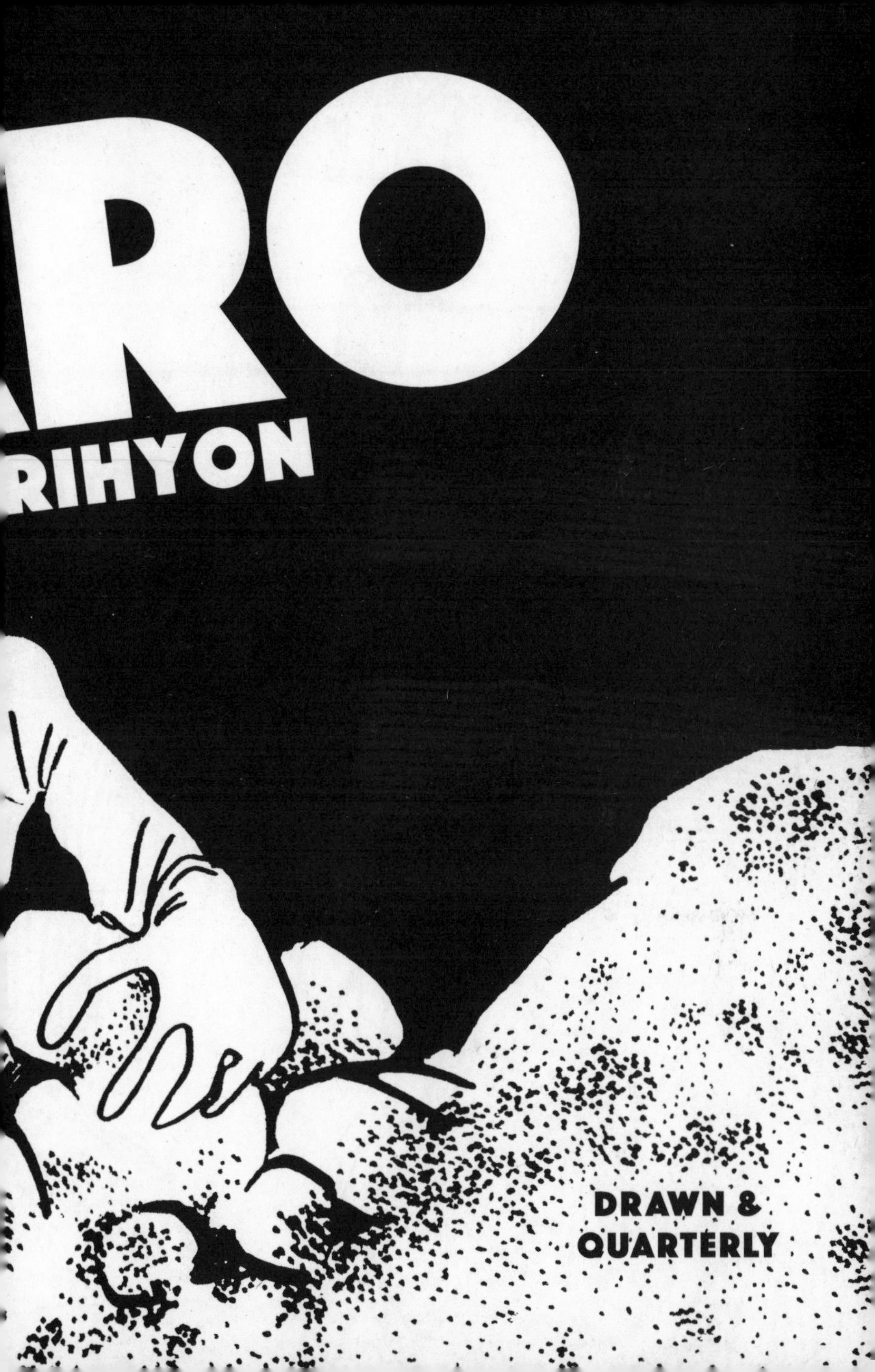

RO
RIHYON
DRAWN &
QUARTERLY

SHIGERU MIZUKI'S
KITA
KITARO MEETS NUR

TRANSLATED BY ZACK DAVISSON

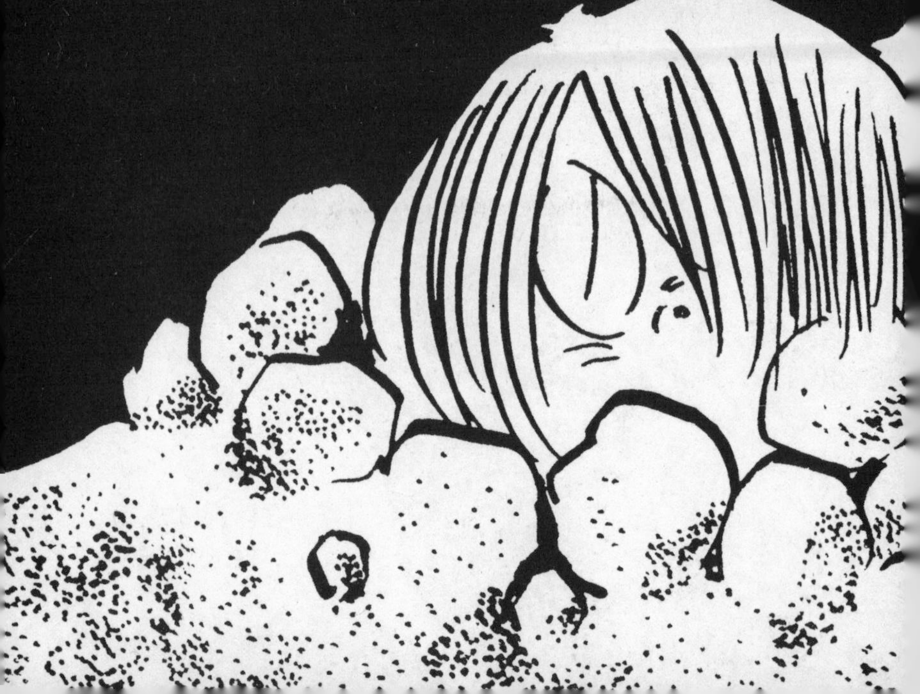

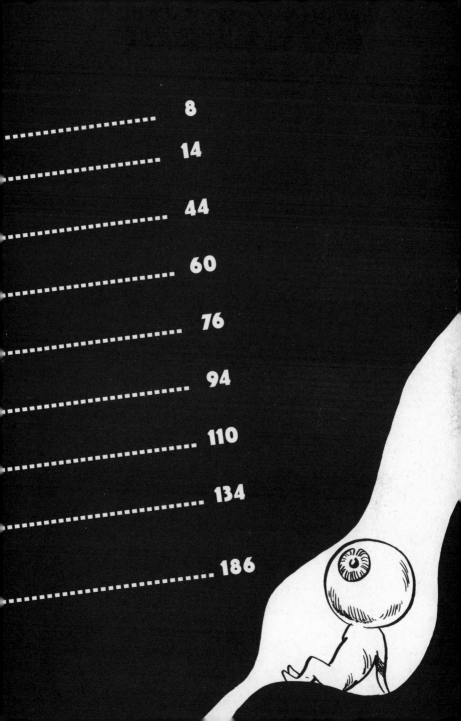

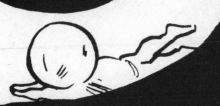

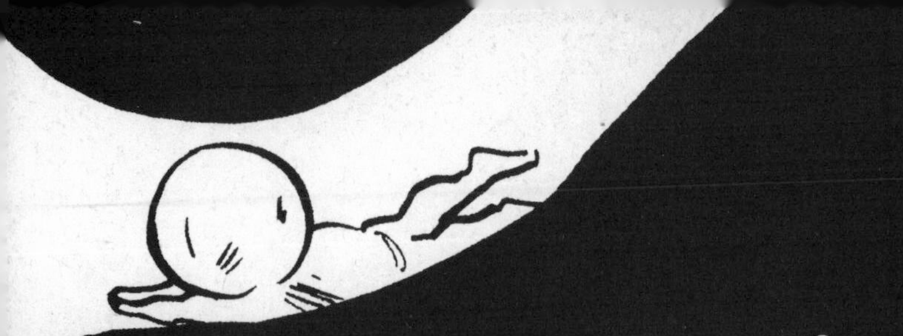

HISTORY OF
KITARO PART 2 ZACK
DAVISSON

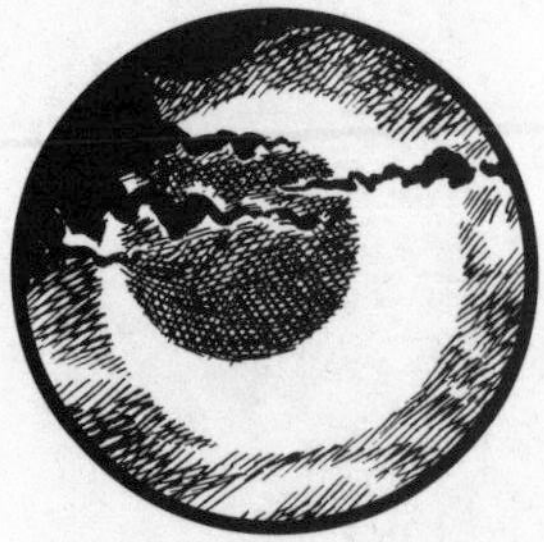

On March 8, 1922, Shigeru Mura was born in the city of Osaka. When he was young he couldn't say his own name; he stumbled on the "ge" in the middle and gave himself the nickname "Gege." While his childhood friends and family always called him Gege, the world would come to know him as something else. Under the name Shigeru Mizuki, he inherited Masami Ito and Kei Tatsumi's Hakaba Kitaro (Graveyard Kitaro) and transformed the deformed misfit into the popular character known and loved today—GeGeGe no Kitaro.

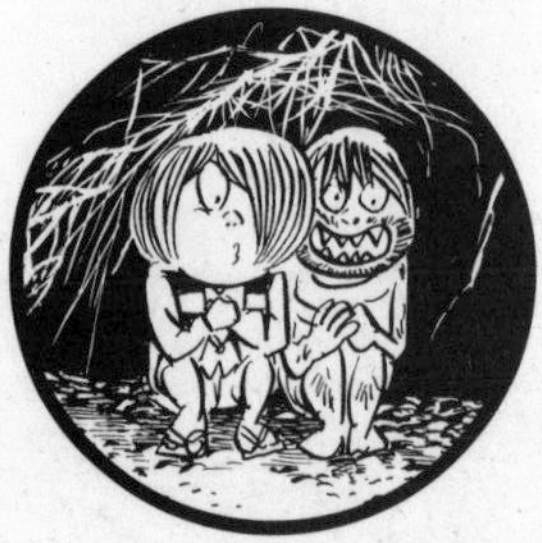

Although he was born in Osaka, little Gege didn't stay there for long. His parents soon brought their new son—the middle child of three brothers—home to Sakaiminato, in Tottori prefecture, where he would live for the next twenty-plus years. Sakaiminato was a rural fishing village. Unlike the urban metropolis of Osaka where he was born, Gege's hometown was isolated from modern Japan. While the rest of the country was seeing traditional beliefs and superstitions vanish before the wonders of electricity and technology, in Sakaiminato the legends and folktales of ancient times lived on. Gege grew up surrounded by nature and magic.

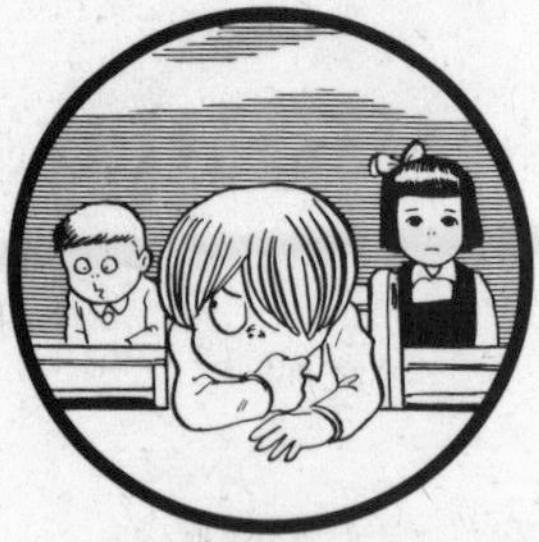

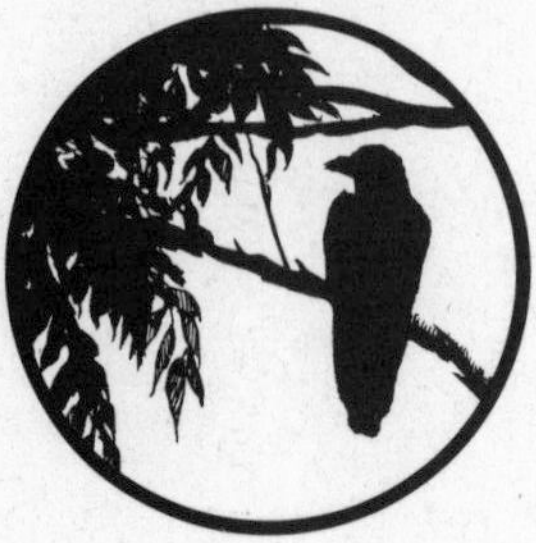

Gege's tour guide into these worlds of nature, magic, and yokai was an elderly nanny named Fusa Kageyama. Although often mistakenly referred to as his grandmother, she was not related to him by blood. She had been a servant of the Mura household when she was young, and when she grew up, she took care of the children. Gege had a nickname for

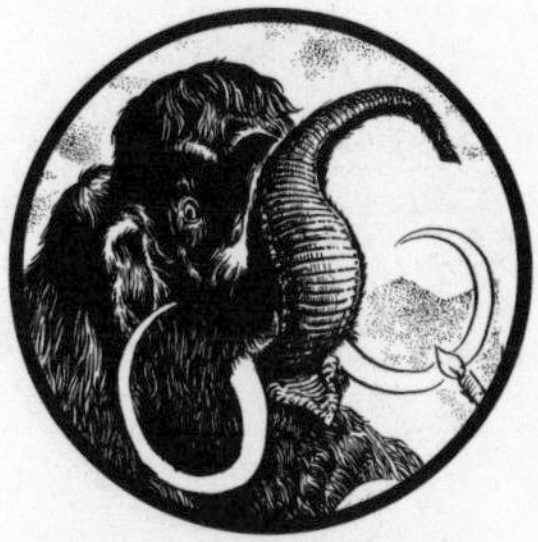

her too—he called her NonNonBa. She was old enough to remember all of the stories from before Japan became a modern country, and Gege liked nothing more than wandering with NonNonBa while she told tales of yokai and forest spirits. He never forgot their time together, and through him, NonNonBa's stories found their way into Japan's comic books—and eventually to the rest of the world.

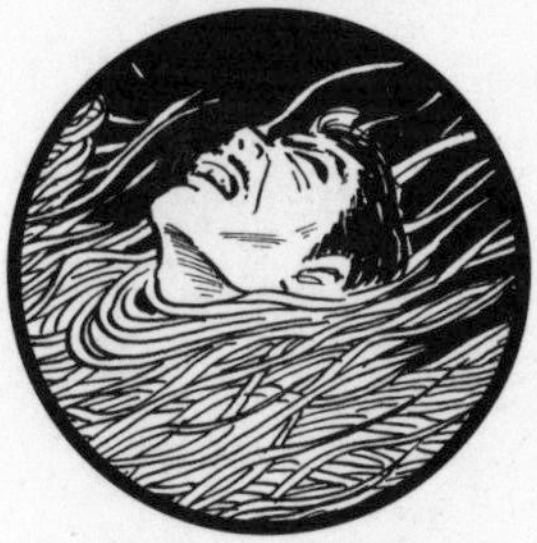

Aside from his love of old stories, what set Gege apart was his ability as an artist. He had an almost magical ability to draw and paint, even without any training. His teachers noticed his talent, and he was given his first solo exhibition show in elementary school. He was written about in the newspaper as an artistic prodigy. But Gege grew up eventually; in his mid-twenties he was drafted into World War II. Fighting on the island of Rabaul in Papua New Guinea, he lost an arm in an Allied bombing attack. When the war was over, he came back to Japan and had to adjust to his new circumstances.

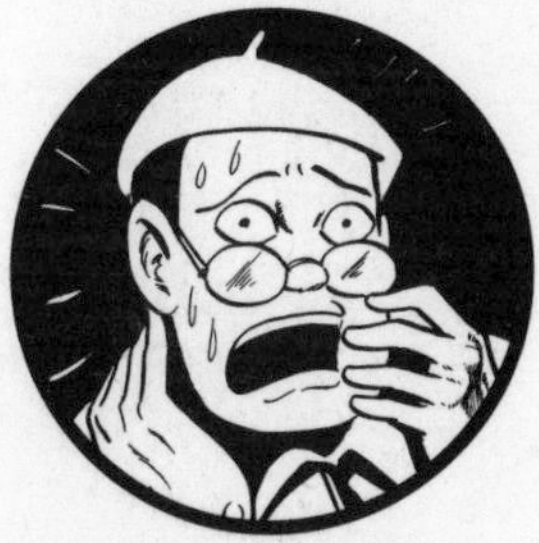

After trying a few different jobs, from fishmonger to pedicab driver, Gege—now called Shigeru Mura—borrowed money from his parents to buy an apartment building in Kobe named Mizuki Manor. He didn't make much money, but the apartment changed his destiny. One of his first renters was an artist who worked in the popular entertainment of *kamishibai* (meaning paper theater). Talking to him reignited Shigeru's artistic dreams. From his renter he got an introduction to kamishibai writer Katsumaru Suzuki who gave

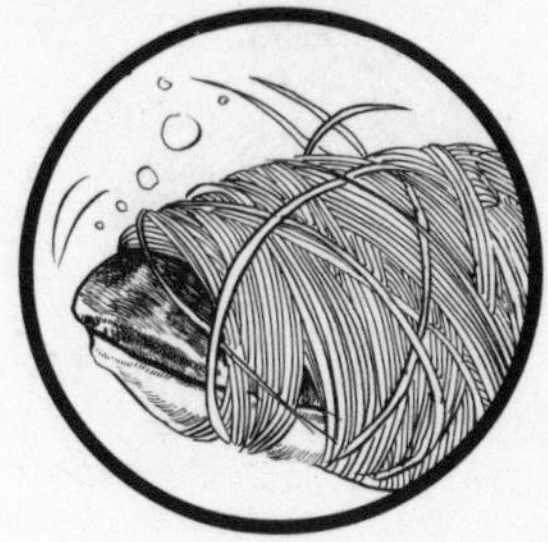

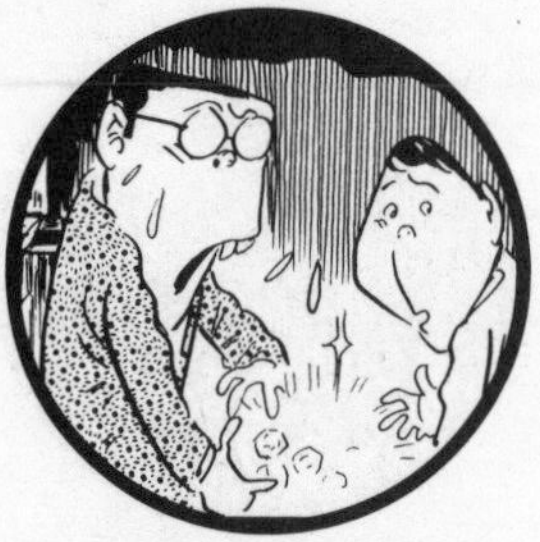

him an audition. He worked hard to produce ten paintings for a story Suzuki was developing. Suzuki liked the artwork and hired him. He advised Shigeru to use a pen name. On an impulse, Suzuki named himself after the apartment complex he owned, and so Shigeru Mizuki was born.

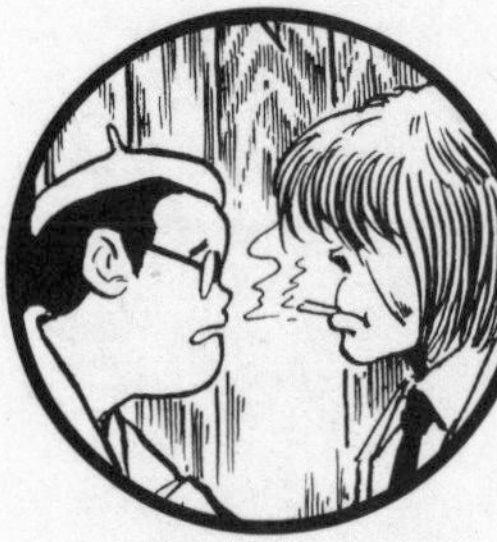

Through Suzuki he met Koji Kata, one of Japan's premier kamishibai artists, who guided him as a mentor. Mizuki worked on everything he could—he drew anything from action sci-fi adventures to romance. His own favorites were horror stories. He loved working on series like Neko Musume (Cat Daughter), where he was able to incorporate the old yokai stories and other legends he had learned from NonNonBa. He created some of his own series as well, like Sanpei the Kappa, a story about a schoolboy who got into all sorts of adventures because he looked like a kappa, a mythical water spirit. Some of his characters were hits, and some weren't. But he kept going, working as a landlord of Mizuki Manor apartments by day, and drawing kamishibai by night.

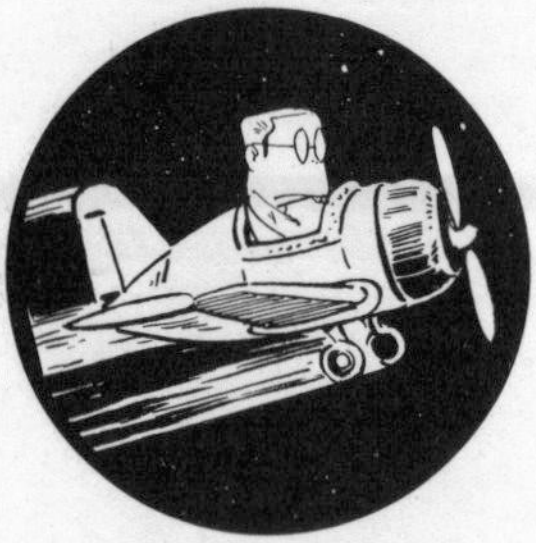

Inspired by his unique art style, Suzuki introduced Mizuki to the works of Masami Ito and Kei Tatsumi and their Hakaba Kitaro series. The series had been popular during the early Showa period in 1925, but was no longer active by the 1950s. Mizuki became obsessed with the story. He especially loved the main character Kitaro, and began to imitate the series. Mizuki created Hebi-jin (Snake Man), about a boy named Kitaro who was born from the belly of a snake and sought revenge against humanity.

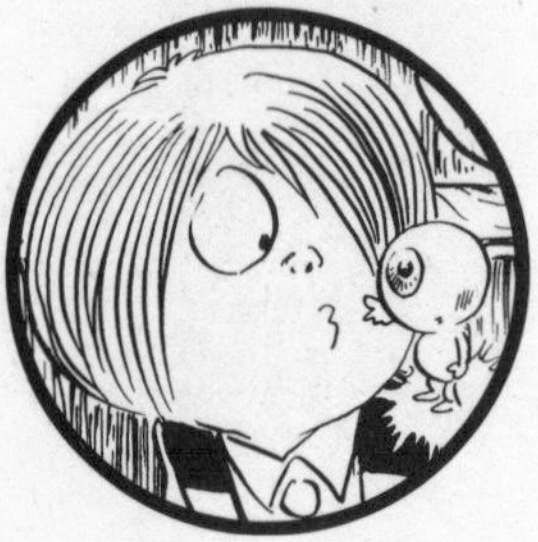

He also created a sports story called Karate Kitaro. Modeled after his older brother, Karate Kitaro showed a young man becoming skilled at karate through effort and training. With each version of Kitaro, Mizuki changed the character just a little, slowly making him his own.

In the middle of the 1950s, things like television, radio, and magazines started to replace kamishibai as a popular form of entertainment. Artists like Mizuki found it more and more difficult to earn a living. Struggling to find a hit, Mizuki finally convinced his publishers to take a shot at reviving Hakaba Kitaro. He got permission from Masami, who only asked that Mizuki change the kanji in the name "Kitaro" from 奇太郎 (Mystery Boy) to 鬼太郎 (Demon Boy) in order to differentiate the two versions.

Mizuki's Hakaba Kitaro was a success. They did over a hundred episodes with bizarre adventures like Kitaro battling a giant gorilla. But it was not enough to save the dying art form. Kamishibai was on its way out, and Mizuki had to figure out what to do for his future. He heard from the artist Kata about a new form of entertainment that was taking off in Tokyo. Comic stories were being bound together in books and either sold or rented in special shops. They called these comic books "manga." In 1957, when he was thirty-five years old, Mizuki sold his building, packed his bags, and headed to Tokyo to try and break into this new industry.

To be continued...

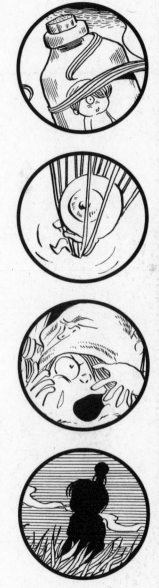

NURARIHYON

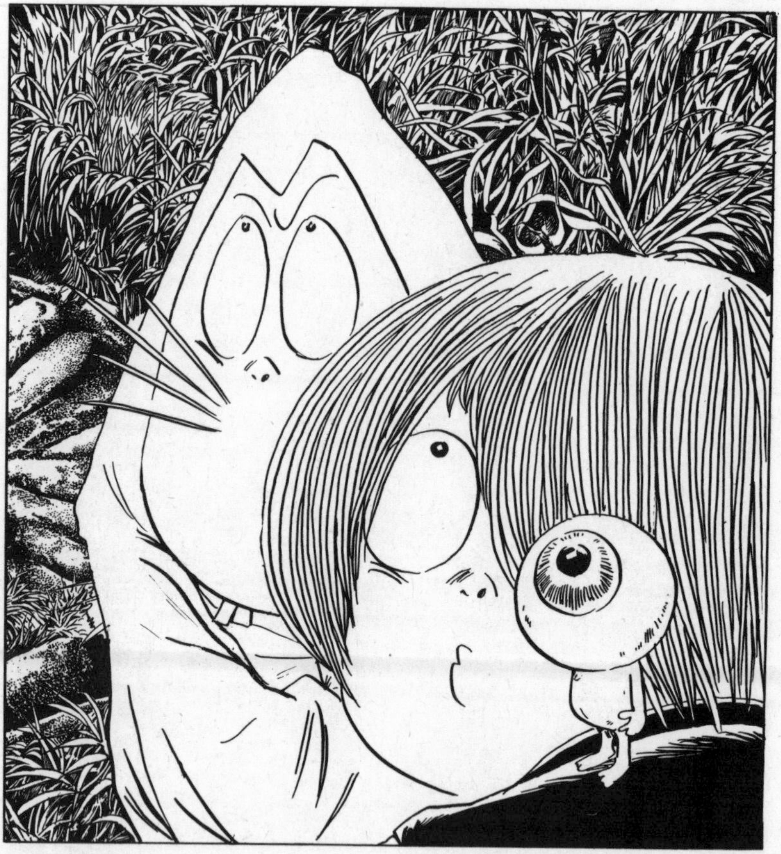

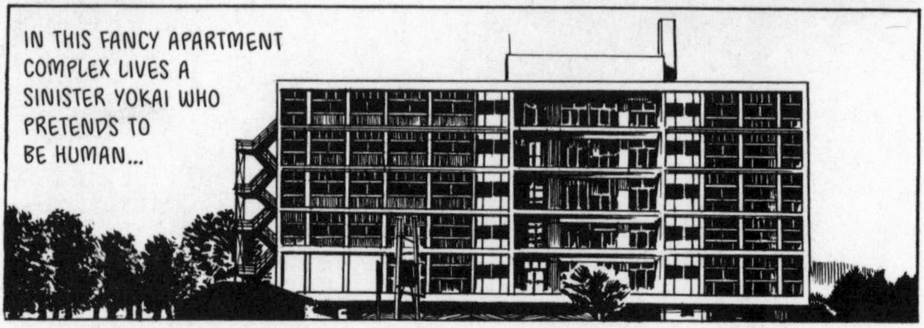
IN THIS FANCY APARTMENT COMPLEX LIVES A SINISTER YOKAI WHO PRETENDS TO BE HUMAN...

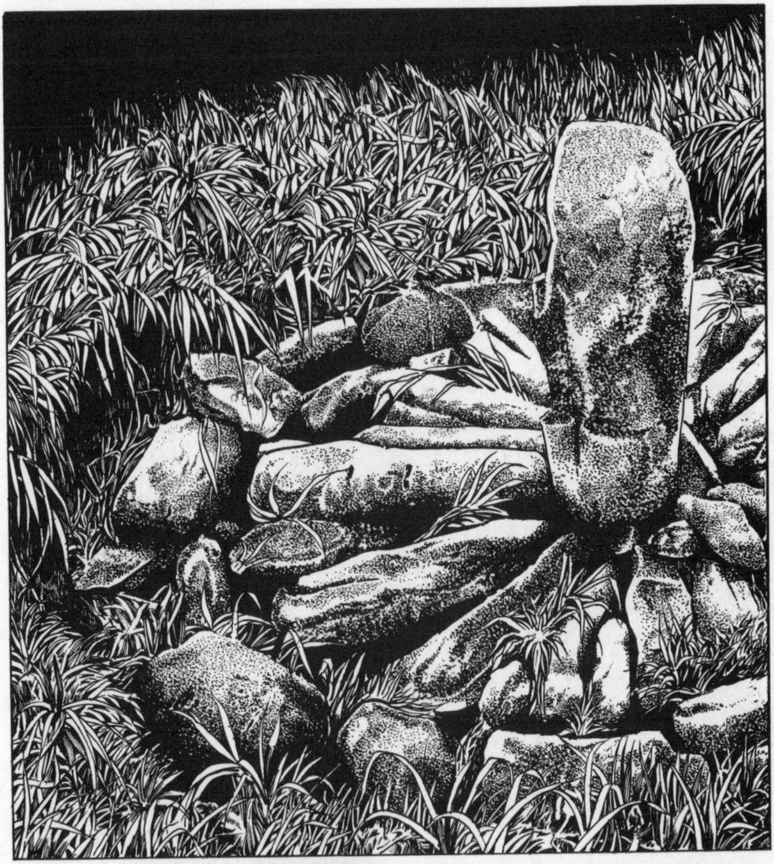

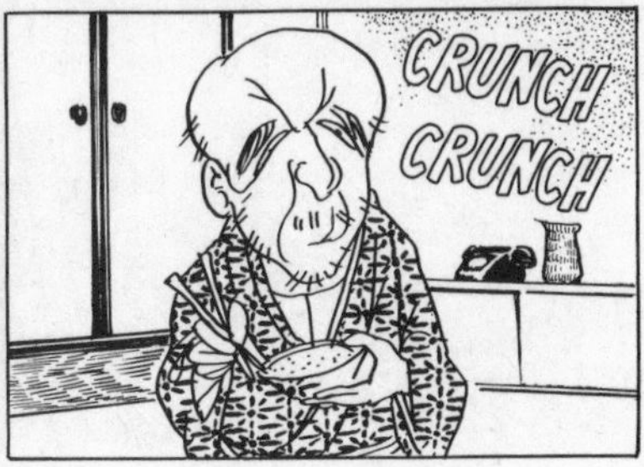
CRUNCH
CRUNCH

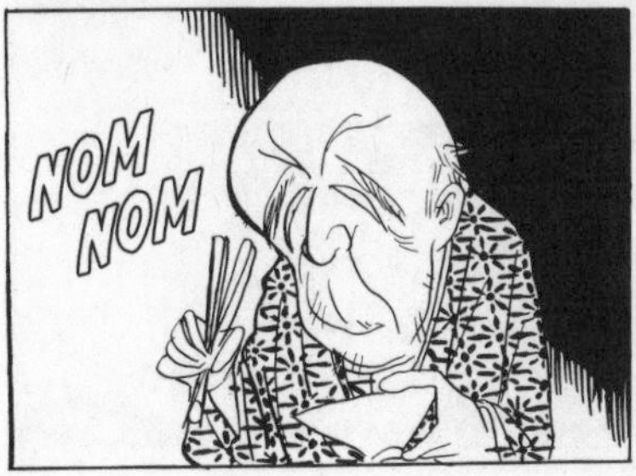
NOM
NOM

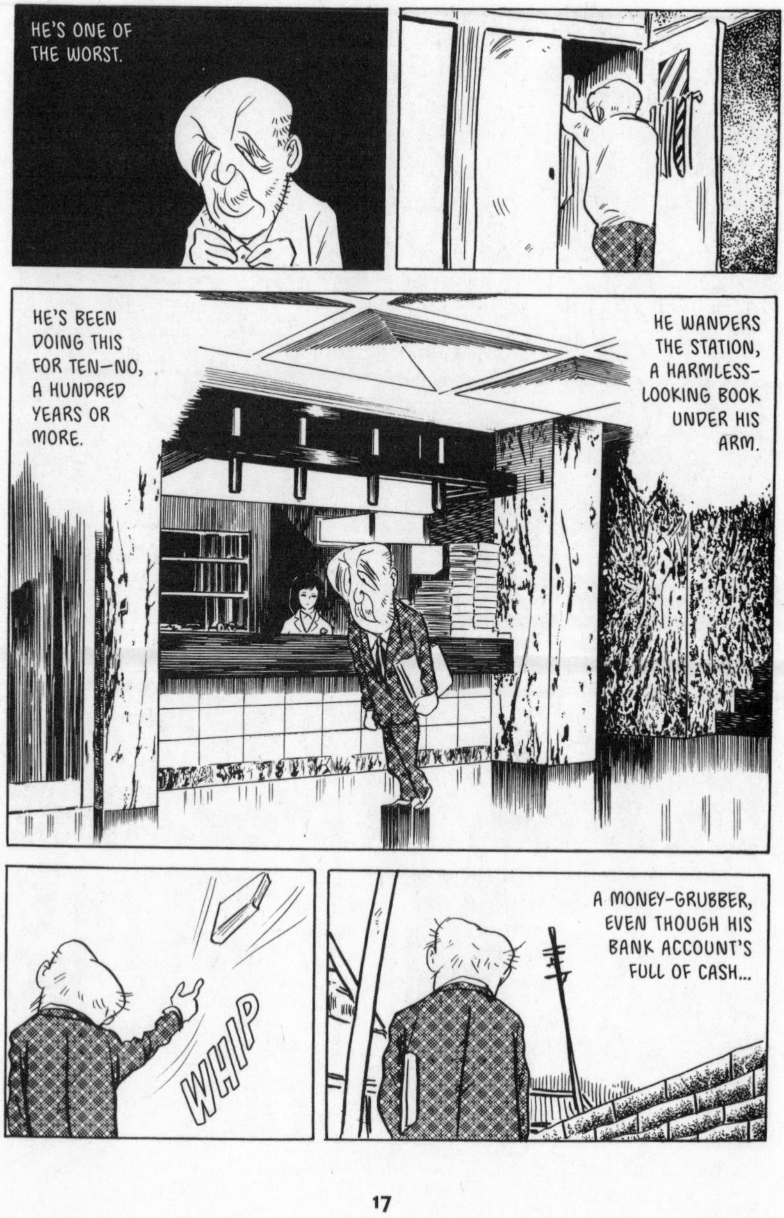
HE'S ONE OF THE WORST.
HE WANDERS THE STATION, A HARMLESS-LOOKING BOOK UNDER HIS ARM.
HE'S BEEN DOING THIS FOR TEN—NO, A HUNDRED YEARS OR MORE.
A MONEY-GRUBBER, EVEN THOUGH HIS BANK ACCOUNT'S FULL OF CASH...
WHIP

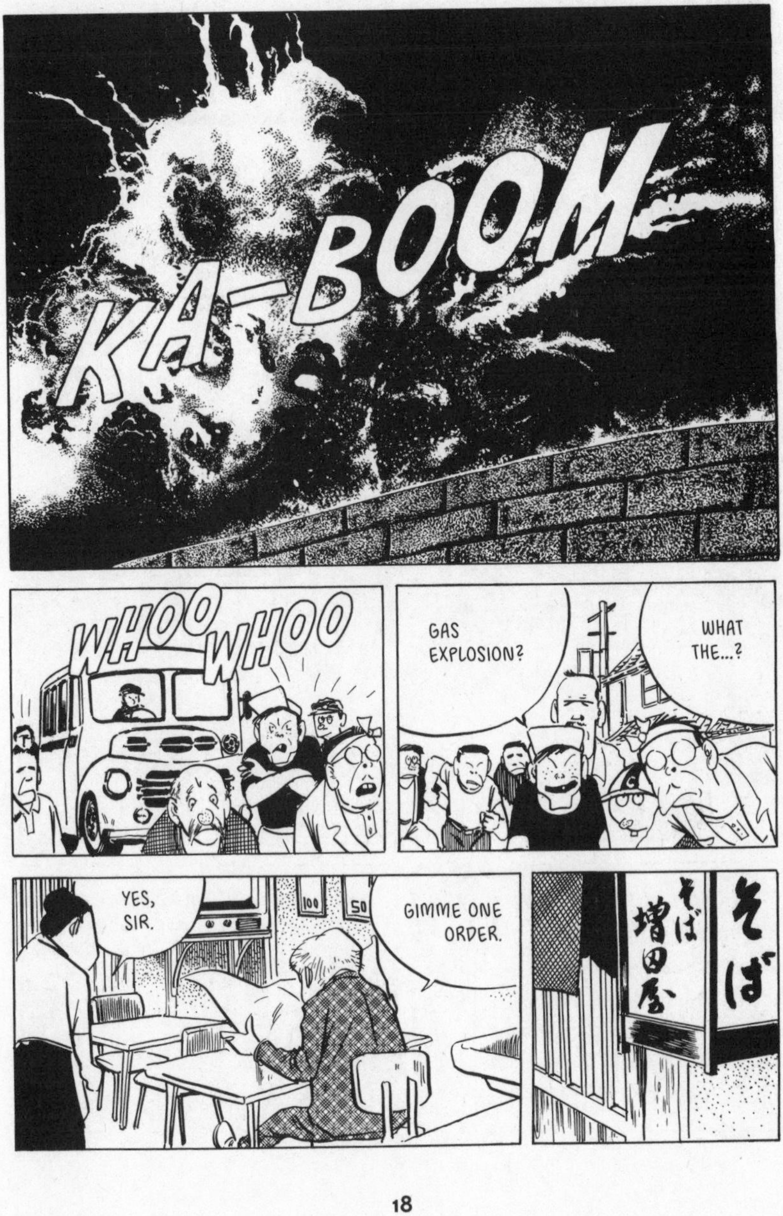
KA-BOOM
WHAT THE...?
GAS EXPLOSION?
WHOO WHOO
そば
そば
増田屋
GIMME ONE ORDER.
YES, SIR.

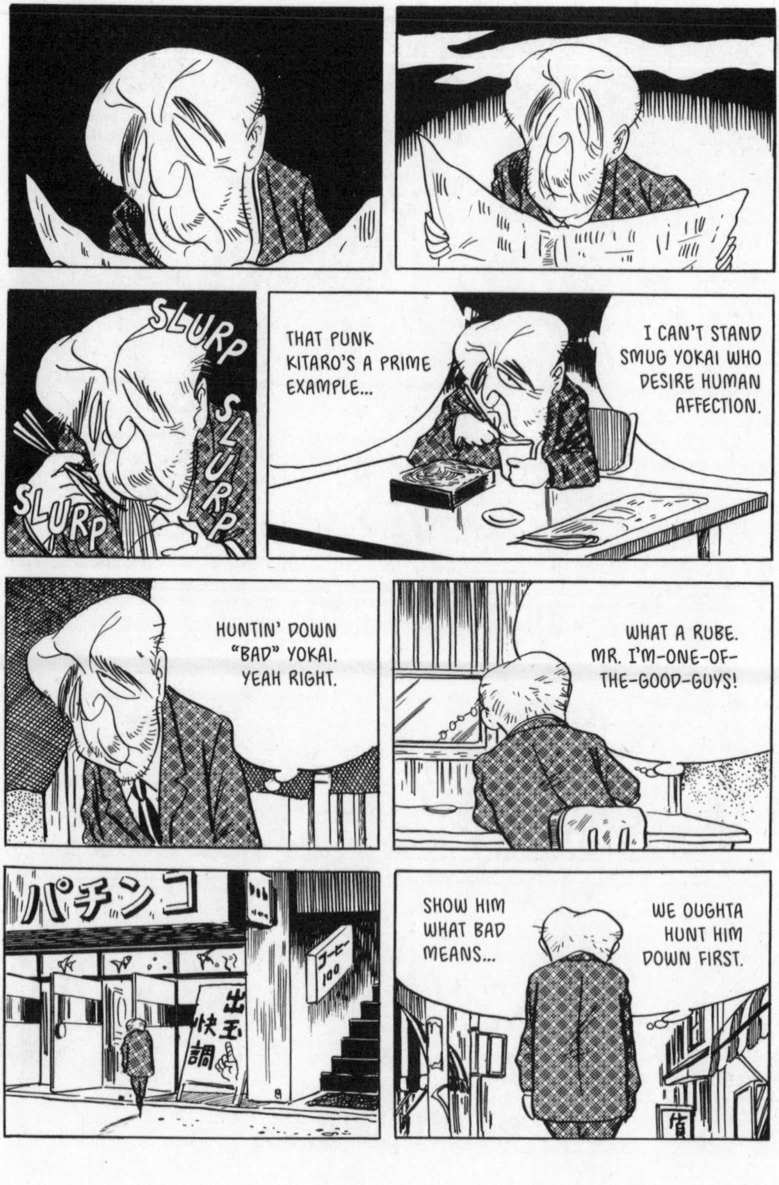
I CAN'T STAND SMUG YOKAI WHO DESIRE HUMAN AFFECTION.
THAT PUNK KITARO'S A PRIME EXAMPLE...
SLURP
SLURP
SLURP
WHAT A RUBE. MR. I'M-ONE-OF-THE-GOOD-GUYS!
HUNTIN' DOWN "BAD" YOKAI. YEAH RIGHT.
WE OUGHTA HUNT HIM DOWN FIRST.
SHOW HIM WHAT BAD MEANS...
パチンコ
コーヒー 100
出玉快調

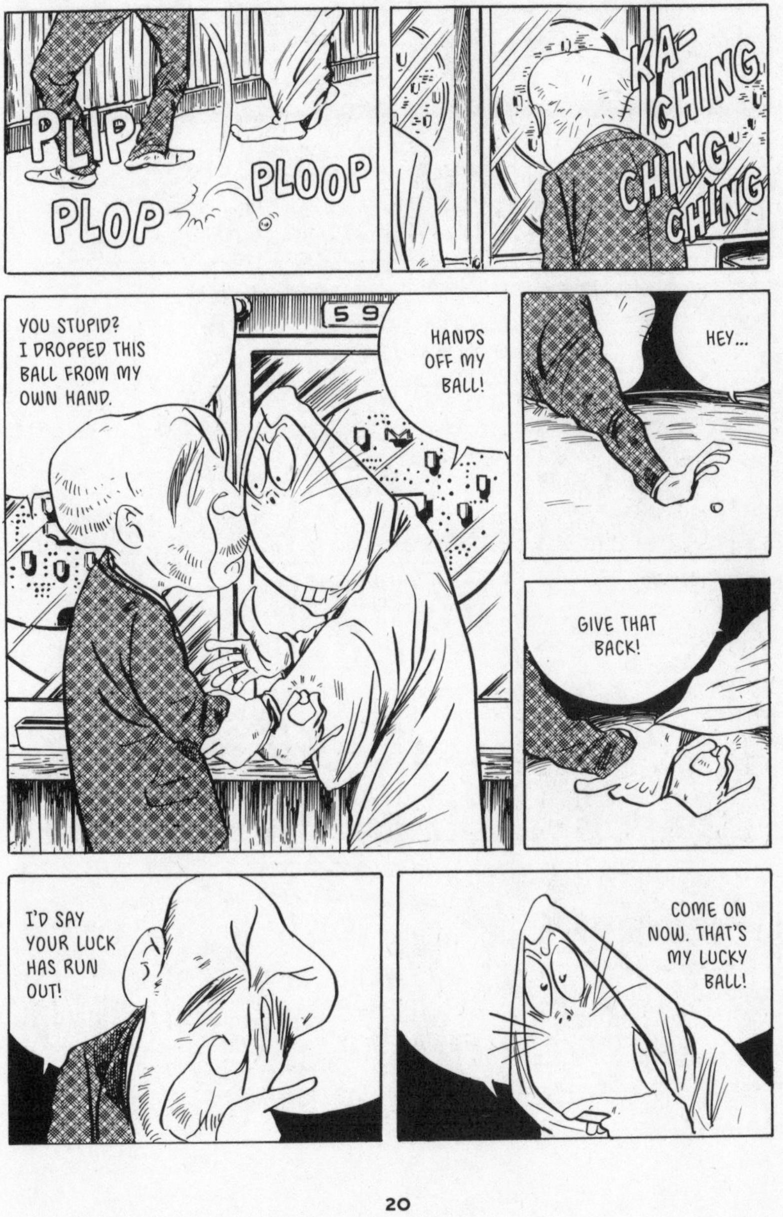
KA-CHING
CHING
CHING
PLIP
PLOOP
PLOP
HEY...
GIVE THAT BACK!
HANDS OFF MY BALL!
YOU STUPID? I DROPPED THIS BALL FROM MY OWN HAND.
COME ON NOW. THAT'S MY LUCKY BALL!
I'D SAY YOUR LUCK HAS RUN OUT!

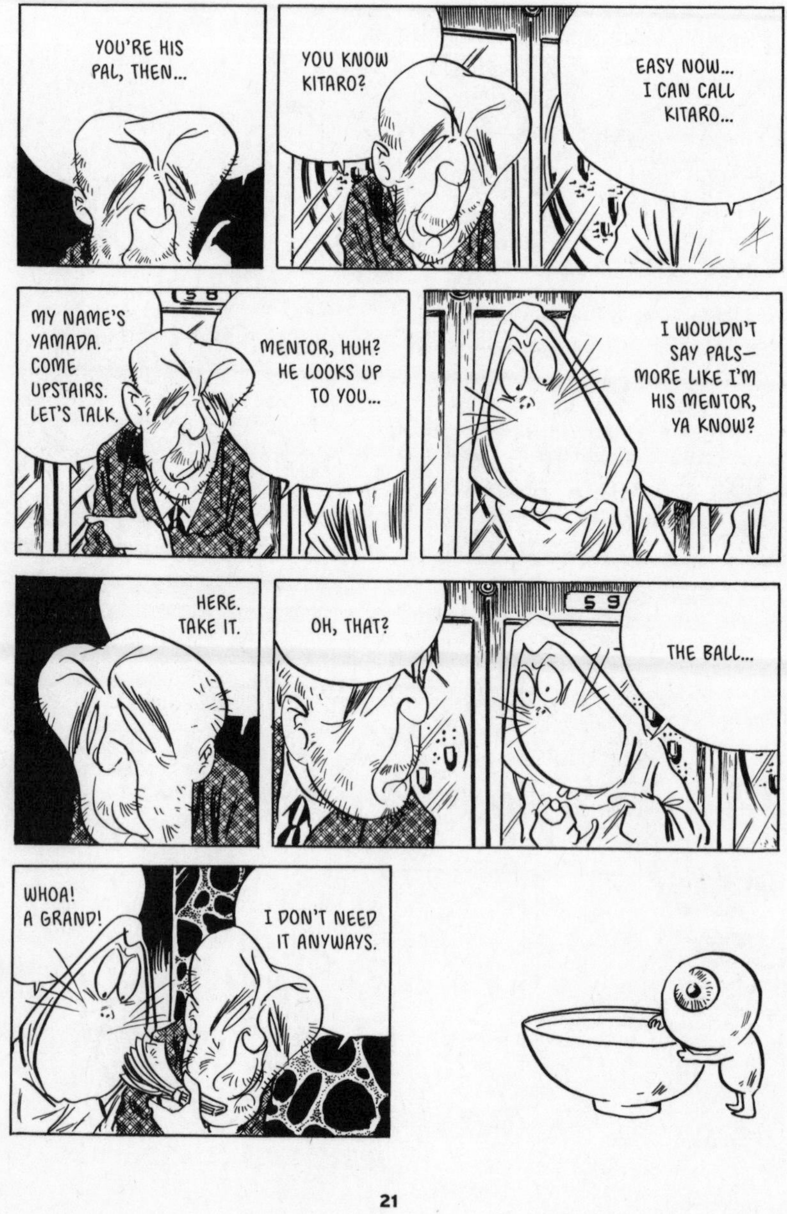
EASY NOW... I CAN CALL KITARO...
YOU KNOW KITARO?
YOU'RE HIS PAL, THEN...
I WOULDN'T SAY PALS— MORE LIKE I'M HIS MENTOR, YA KNOW?
MENTOR, HUH? HE LOOKS UP TO YOU...
MY NAME'S YAMADA. COME UPSTAIRS. LET'S TALK.
THE BALL...
OH, THAT?
HERE. TAKE IT.
I DON'T NEED IT ANYWAYS.
WHOA! A GRAND!

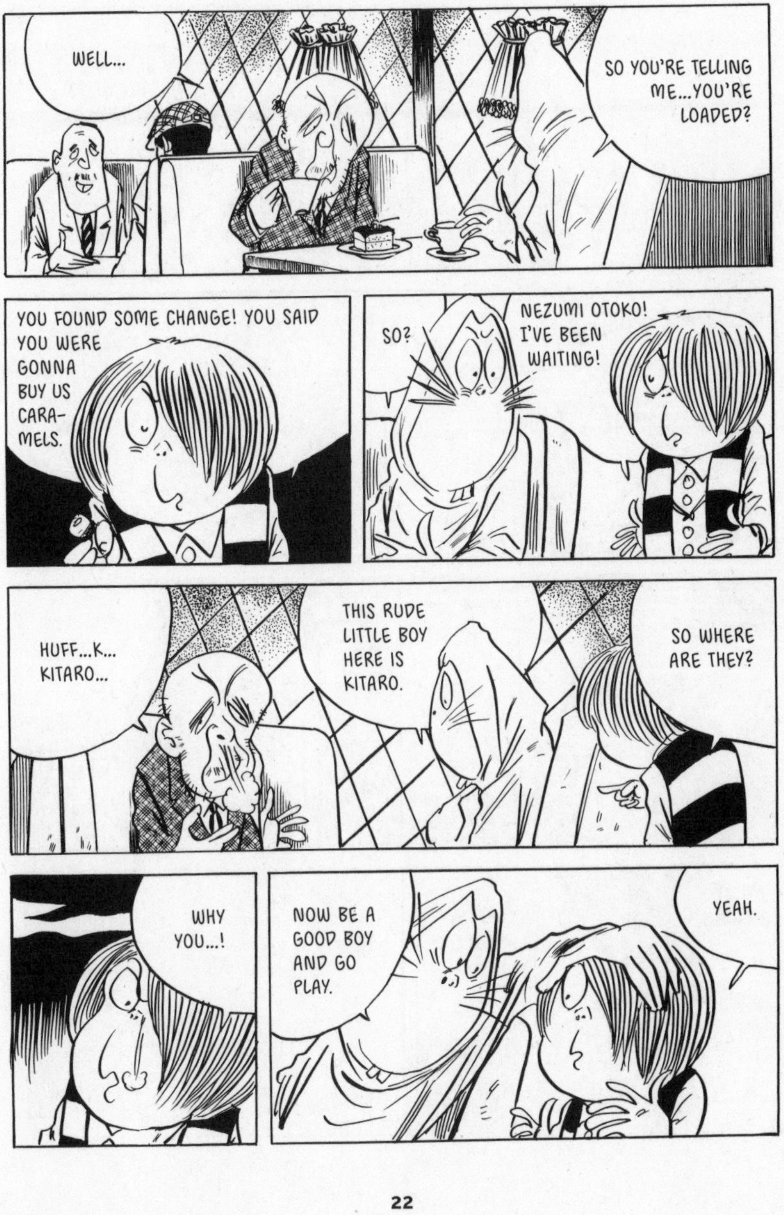
SO YOU'RE TELLING ME...YOU'RE LOADED?
WELL...
NEZUMI OTOKO! I'VE BEEN WAITING!
SO?
YOU FOUND SOME CHANGE! YOU SAID YOU WERE GONNA BUY US CARA-MELS.
SO WHERE ARE THEY?
THIS RUDE LITTLE BOY HERE IS KITARO.
HUFF...K... KITARO...
YEAH.
NOW BE A GOOD BOY AND GO PLAY.
WHY YOU...!

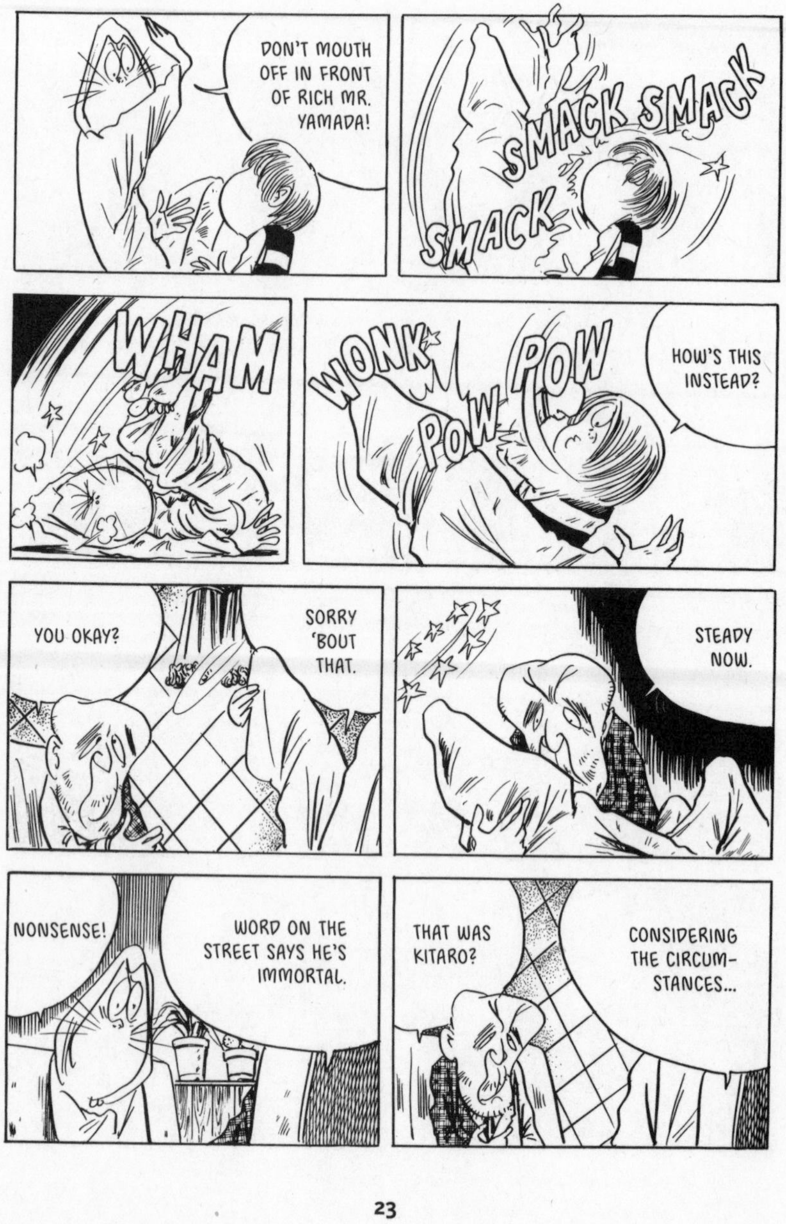
SMACK SMACK
SMACK
DON'T MOUTH OFF IN FRONT OF RICH MR. YAMADA!
HOW'S THIS INSTEAD?
POW
POW
POW
WONK
WHAM
STEADY NOW.
SORRY 'BOUT THAT.
YOU OKAY?
CONSIDERING THE CIRCUM-STANCES...
THAT WAS KITARO?
WORD ON THE STREET SAYS HE'S IMMORTAL.
NONSENSE!

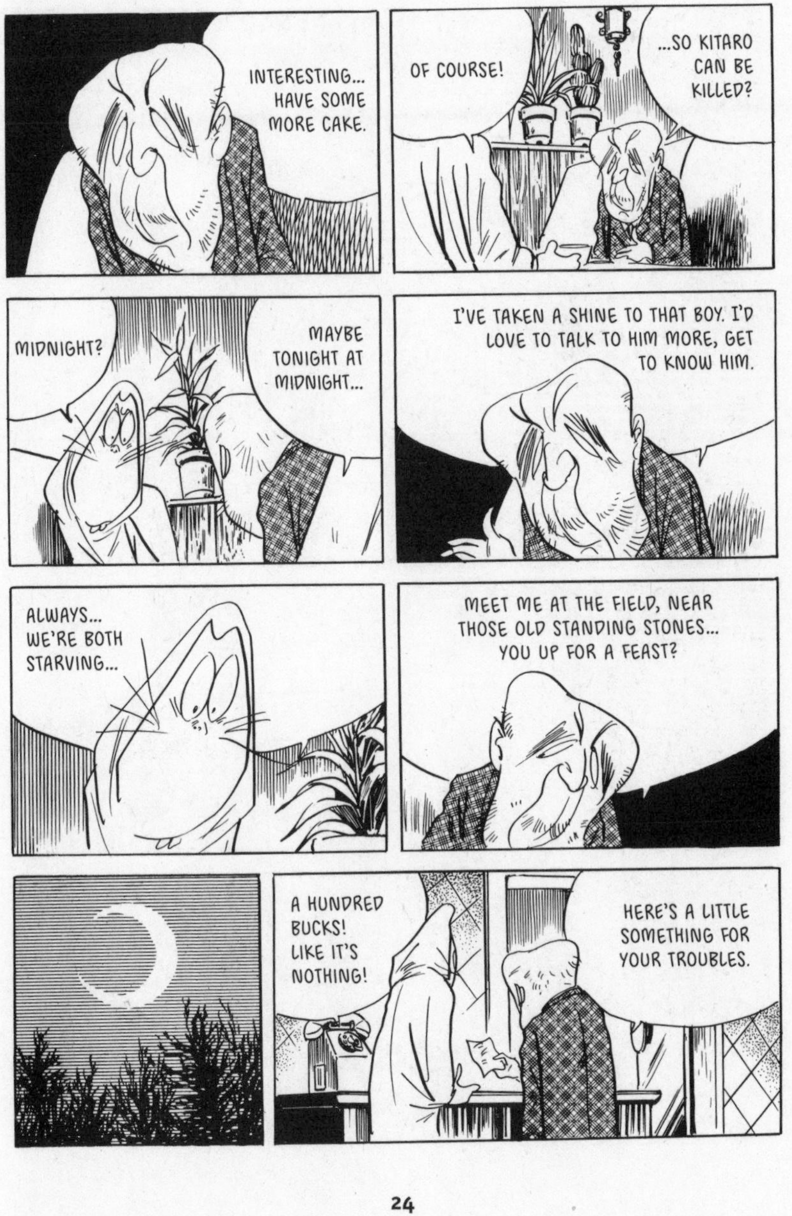
...SO KITARO CAN BE KILLED?
OF COURSE!
INTERESTING... HAVE SOME MORE CAKE.
I'VE TAKEN A SHINE TO THAT BOY. I'D LOVE TO TALK TO HIM MORE, GET TO KNOW HIM.
MAYBE TONIGHT AT MIDNIGHT...
MIDNIGHT?
MEET ME AT THE FIELD, NEAR THOSE OLD STANDING STONES... YOU UP FOR A FEAST?
ALWAYS... WE'RE BOTH STARVING...
HERE'S A LITTLE SOMETHING FOR YOUR TROUBLES.
A HUNDRED BUCKS! LIKE IT'S NOTHING!

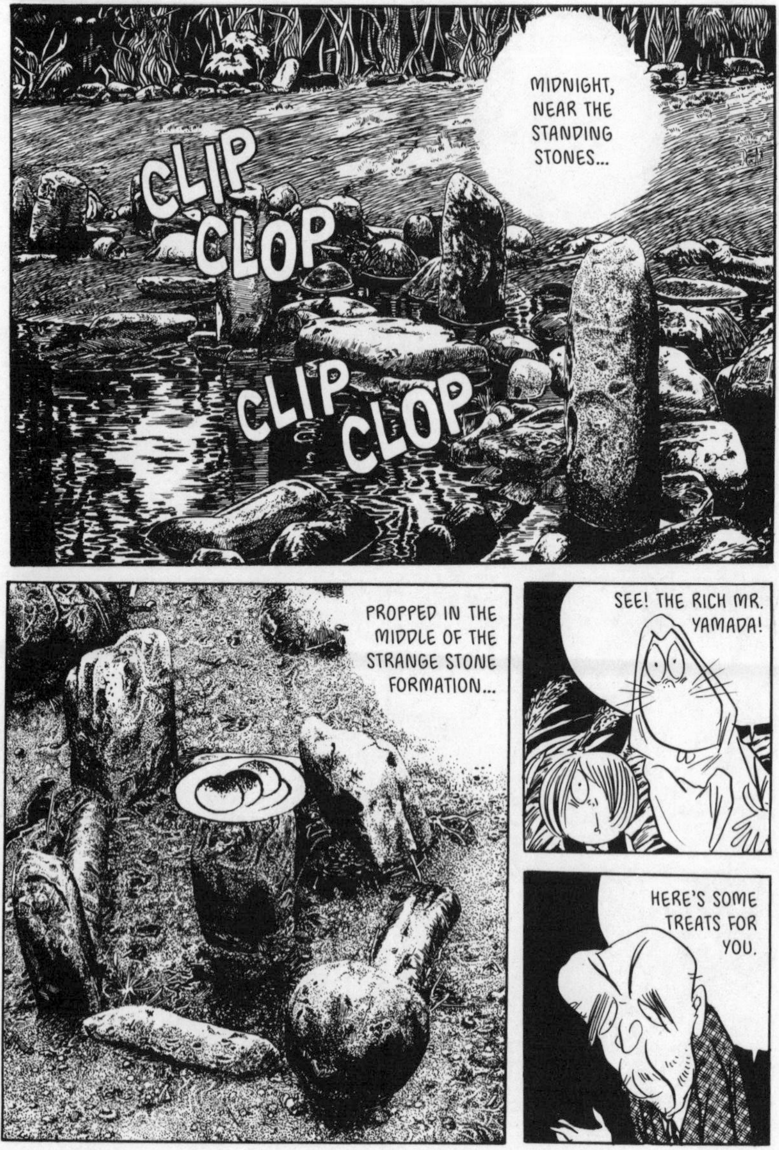
MIDNIGHT, NEAR THE STANDING STONES...
CLIP CLOP
CLIP CLOP
SEE! THE RICH MR. YAMADA!
HERE'S SOME TREATS FOR YOU.
PROPPED IN THE MIDDLE OF THE STRANGE STONE FORMATION...

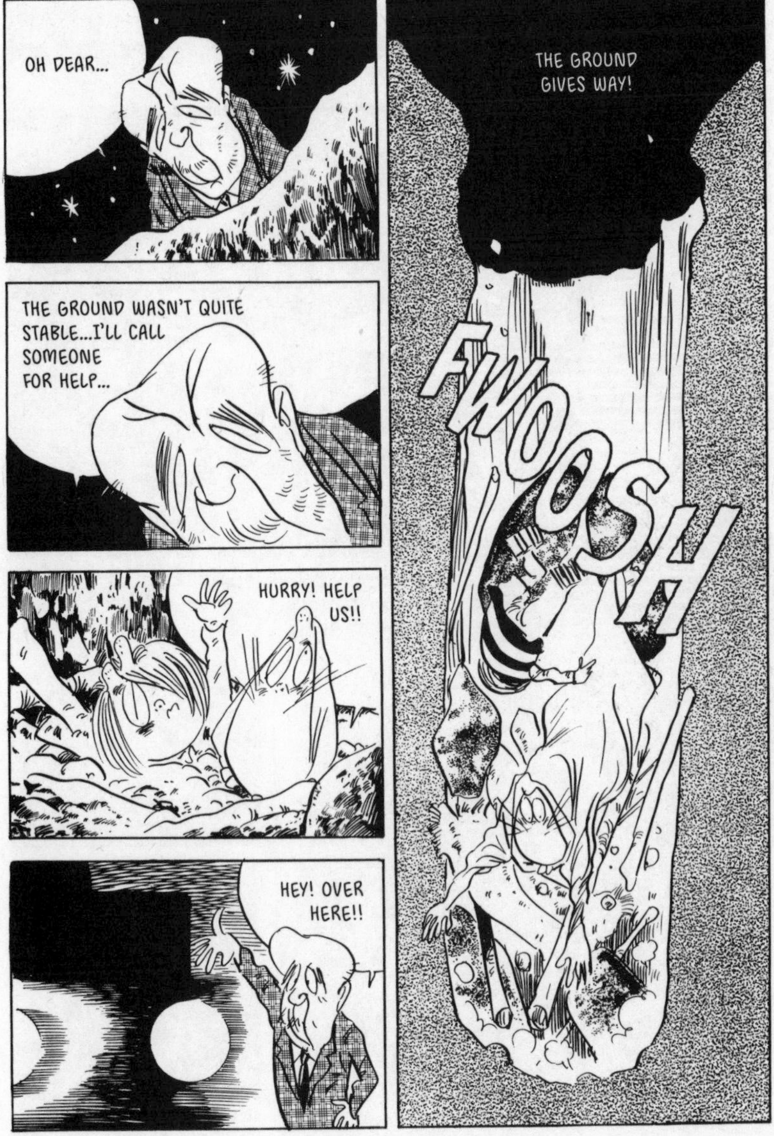
THE GROUND GIVES WAY!
FWOOSH
OH DEAR...
THE GROUND WASN'T QUITE STABLE...I'LL CALL SOMEONE FOR HELP...
HURRY! HELP US!!
HEY! OVER HERE!!

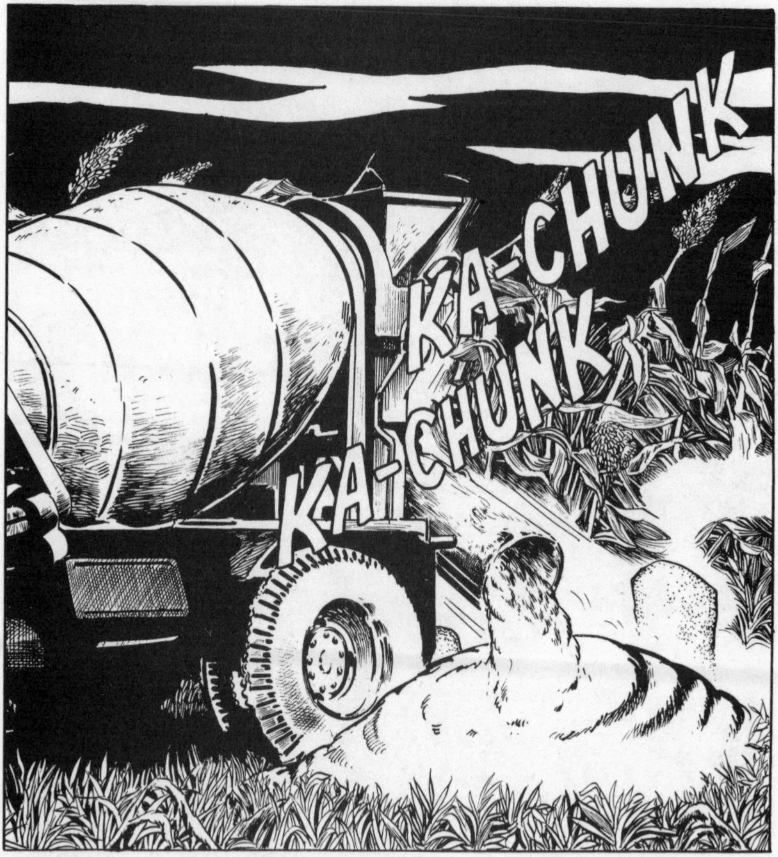
KA-CHUNK
KA-CHUNK

WHAT A CRUEL FATE FOR OUR HEROES... THE VILLAIN DUG THE HOLE IN ADVANCE AND RIGGED IT TO COLLAPSE. AND NOW, OF COURSE, HE'S SEALING THEM IN WITH CONCRETE.

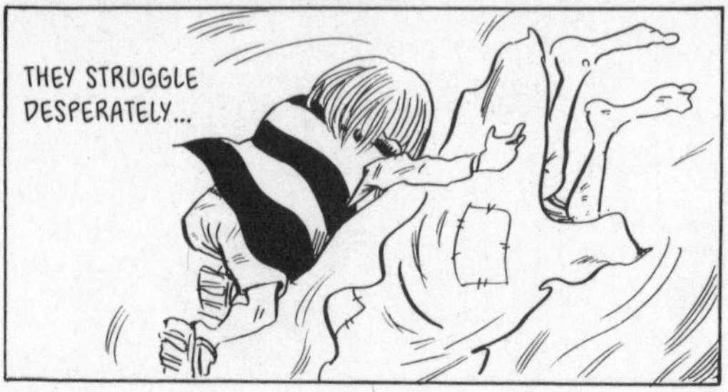
THEY STRUGGLE DESPERATELY...

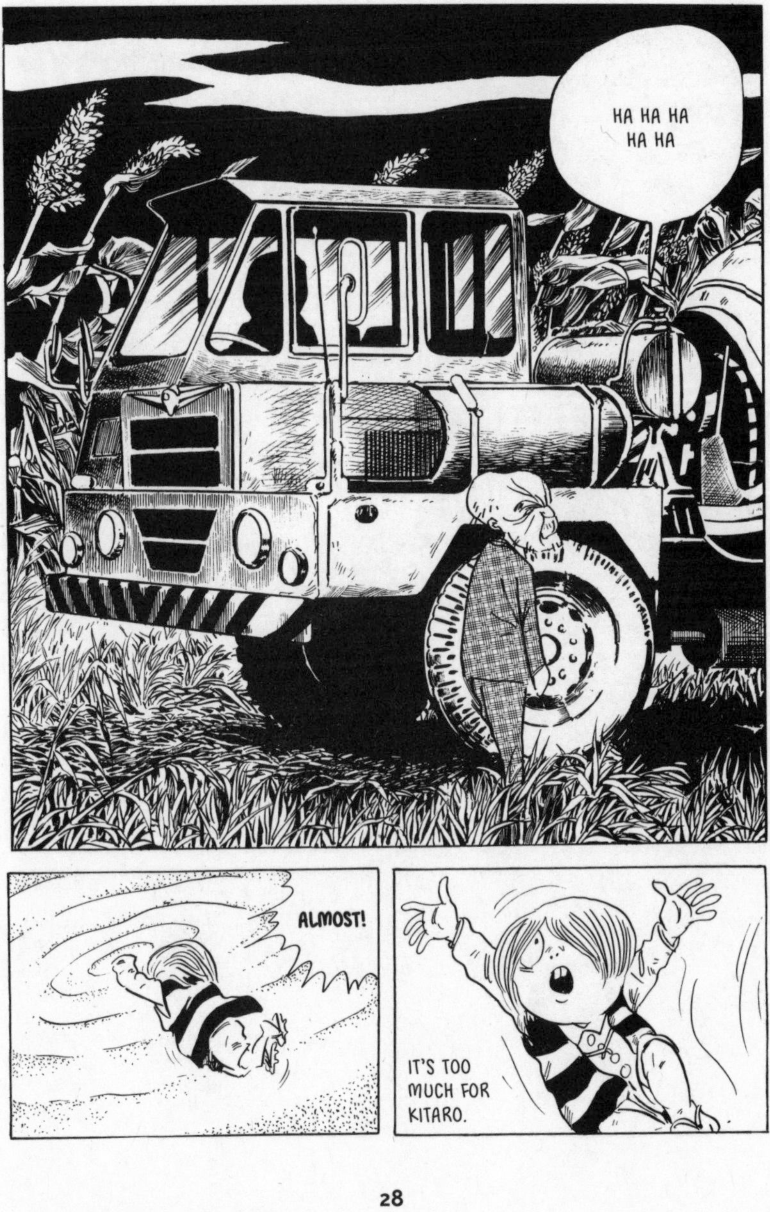
HA HA HA
HA HA
IT'S TOO
MUCH FOR
KITARO.
ALMOST!

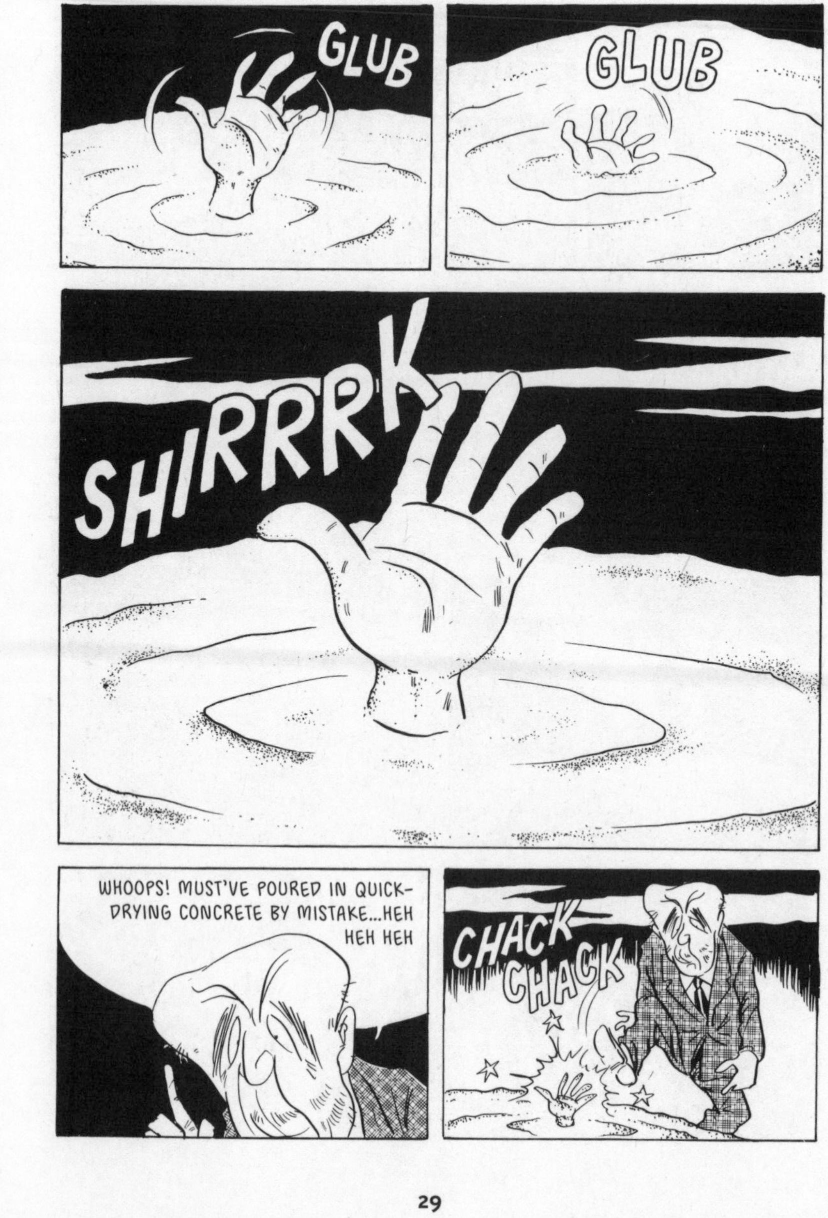
GLUB
GLUB
SHIRRRK
CHACK CHACK
WHOOPS! MUST'VE POURED IN QUICK-DRYING CONCRETE BY MISTAKE...HEH HEH HEH

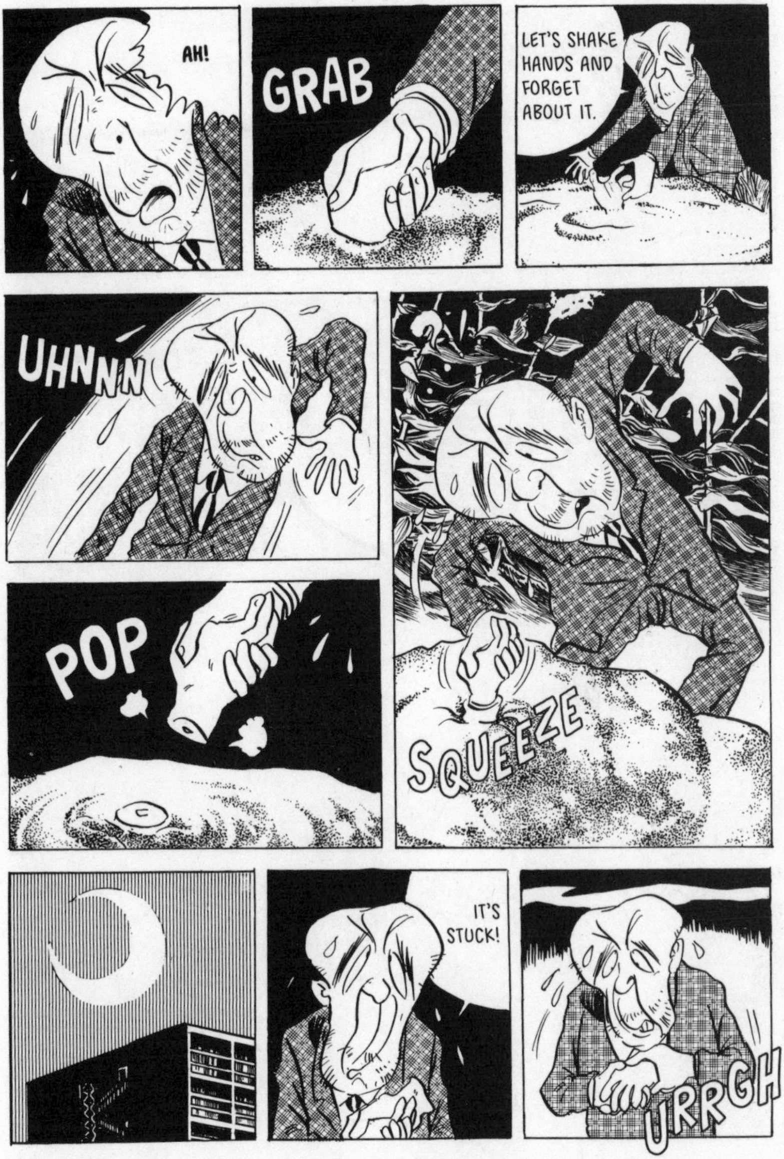
LET'S SHAKE HANDS AND FORGET ABOUT IT.
GRAB
AH!
SQUEEZE
UHNNN
POP
URRGH
IT'S STUCK!

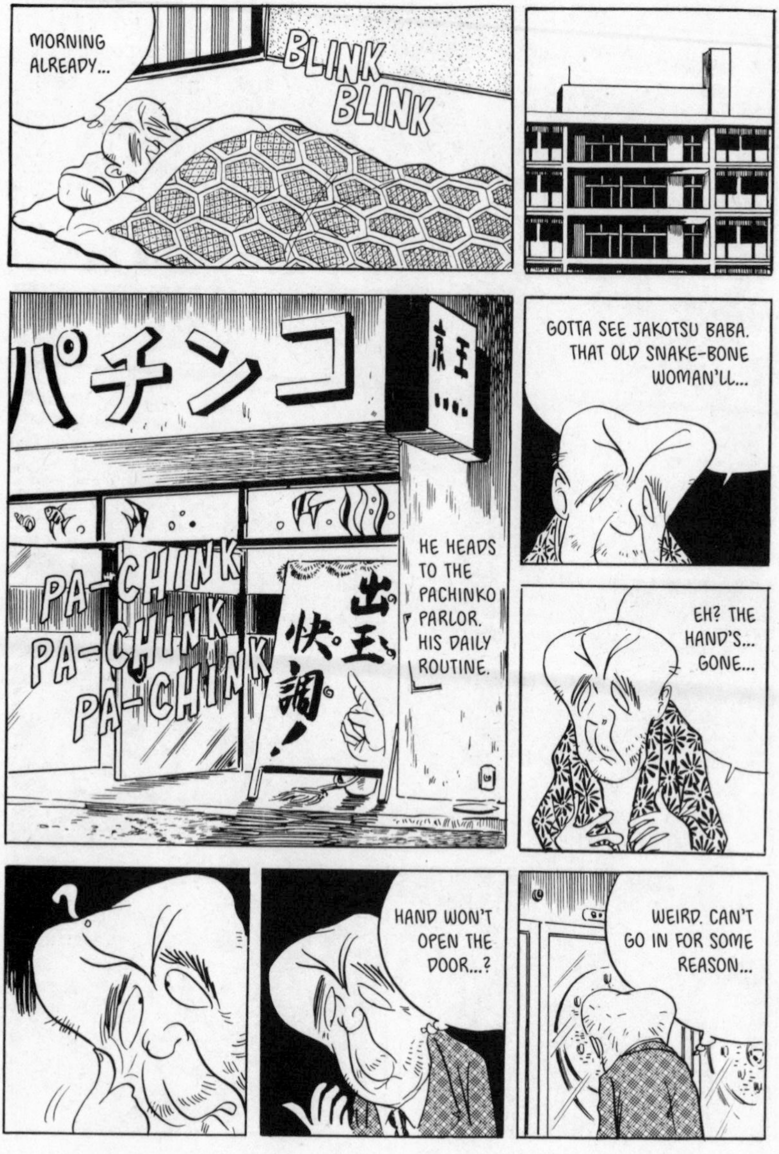
MORNING ALREADY...
BLINK BLINK
GOTTA SEE JAKOTSU BABA. THAT OLD SNAKE-BONE WOMAN'LL...
EH? THE HAND'S... GONE...
パチンコ
HE HEADS TO THE PACHINKO PARLOR. HIS DAILY ROUTINE.
出玉快調！
PA-CHINK PA-CHINK PA-CHINK
WEIRD. CAN'T GO IN FOR SOME REASON...
HAND WON'T OPEN THE DOOR...?
?

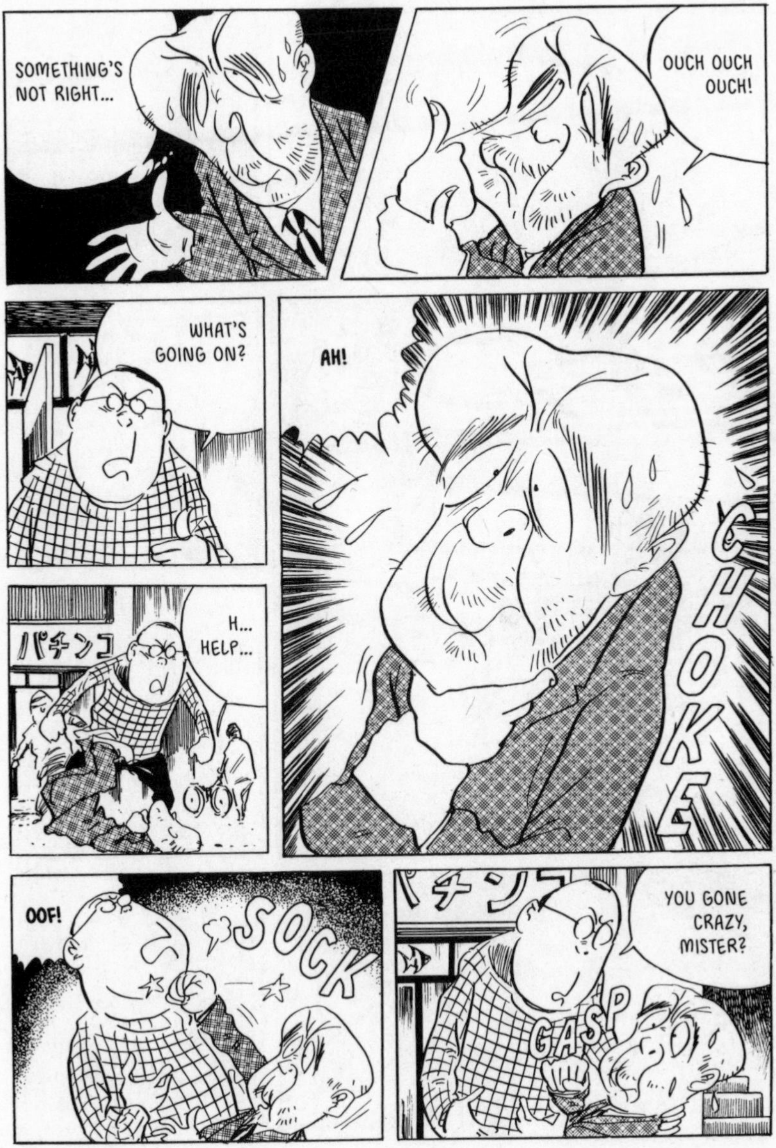
OUCH OUCH OUCH!
SOMETHING'S NOT RIGHT...
AH!
CHOKE
WHAT'S GOING ON?
パチンコ
H... HELP...
パチンコ
YOU GONE CRAZY, MISTER?
GASP
OOF!
SOCK

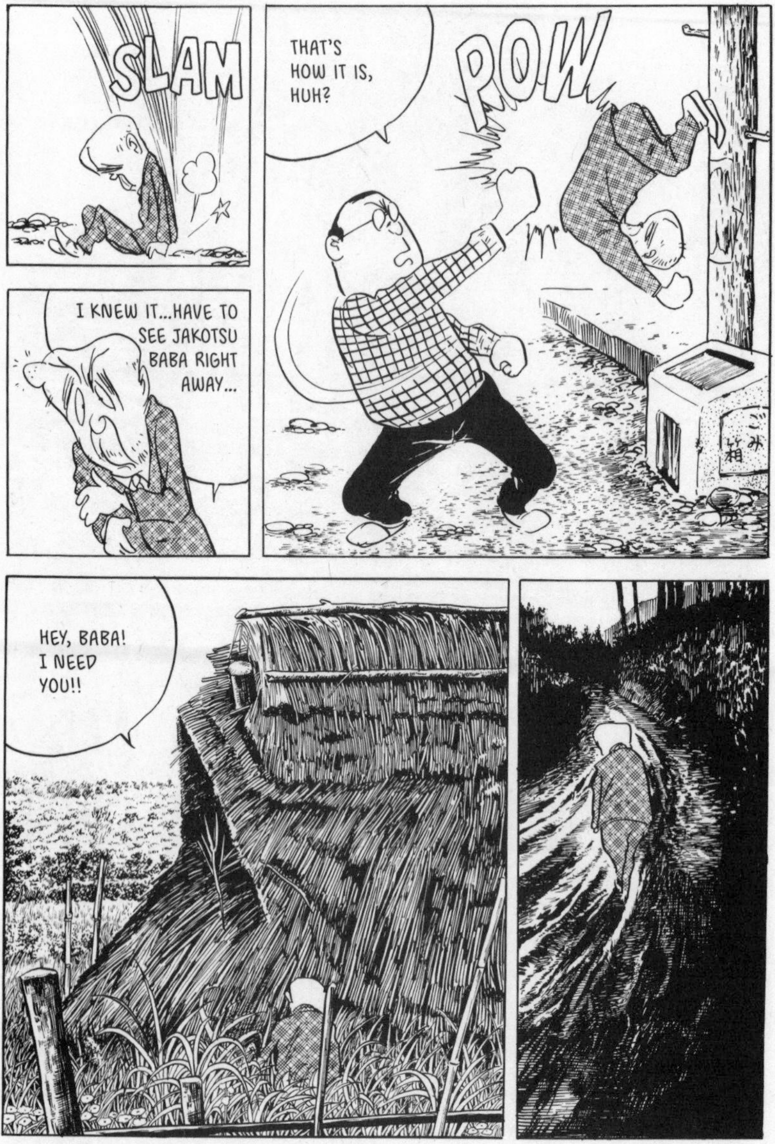
THAT'S HOW IT IS, HUH?
POW
SLAM
I KNEW IT...HAVE TO SEE JAKOTSU BABA RIGHT AWAY...
HEY, BABA! I NEED YOU!!

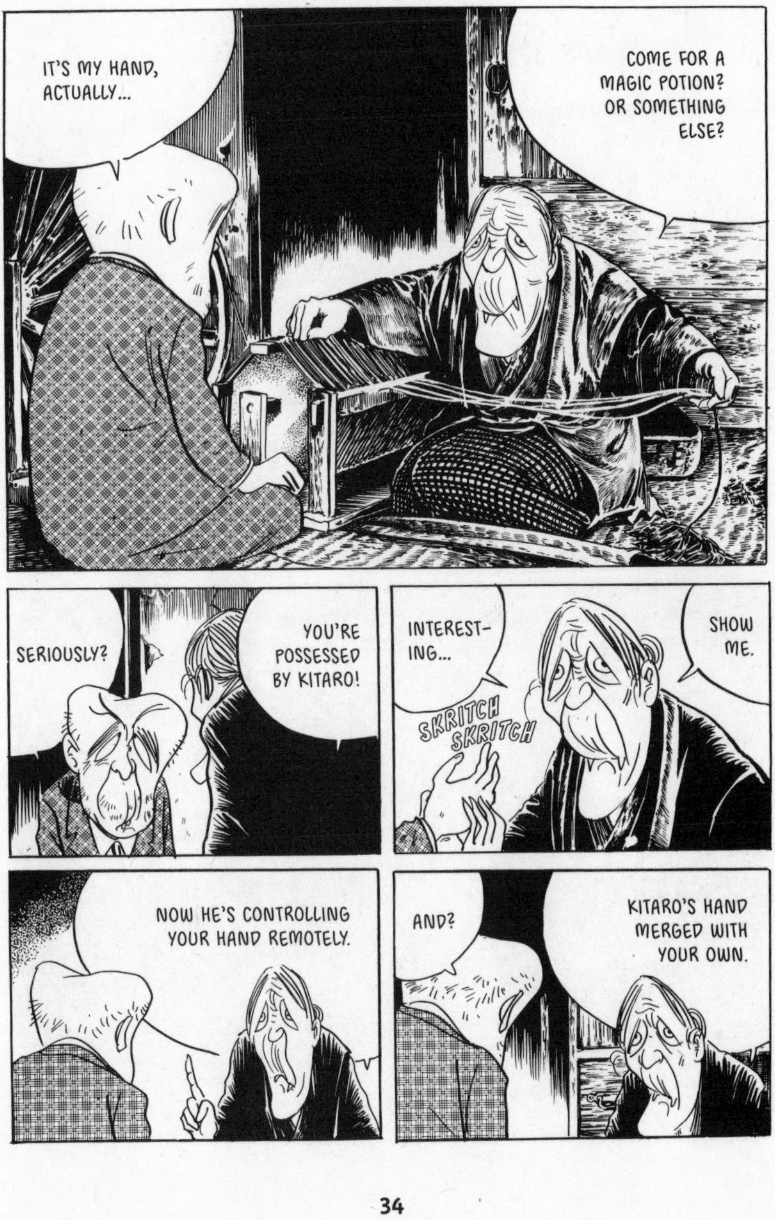
COME FOR A MAGIC POTION? OR SOMETHING ELSE?
IT'S MY HAND, ACTUALLY...
SHOW ME.
INTEREST-ING...
SKRITCH SKRITCH
YOU'RE POSSESSED BY KITARO!
SERIOUSLY?
KITARO'S HAND MERGED WITH YOUR OWN.
AND?
NOW HE'S CONTROLLING YOUR HAND REMOTELY.

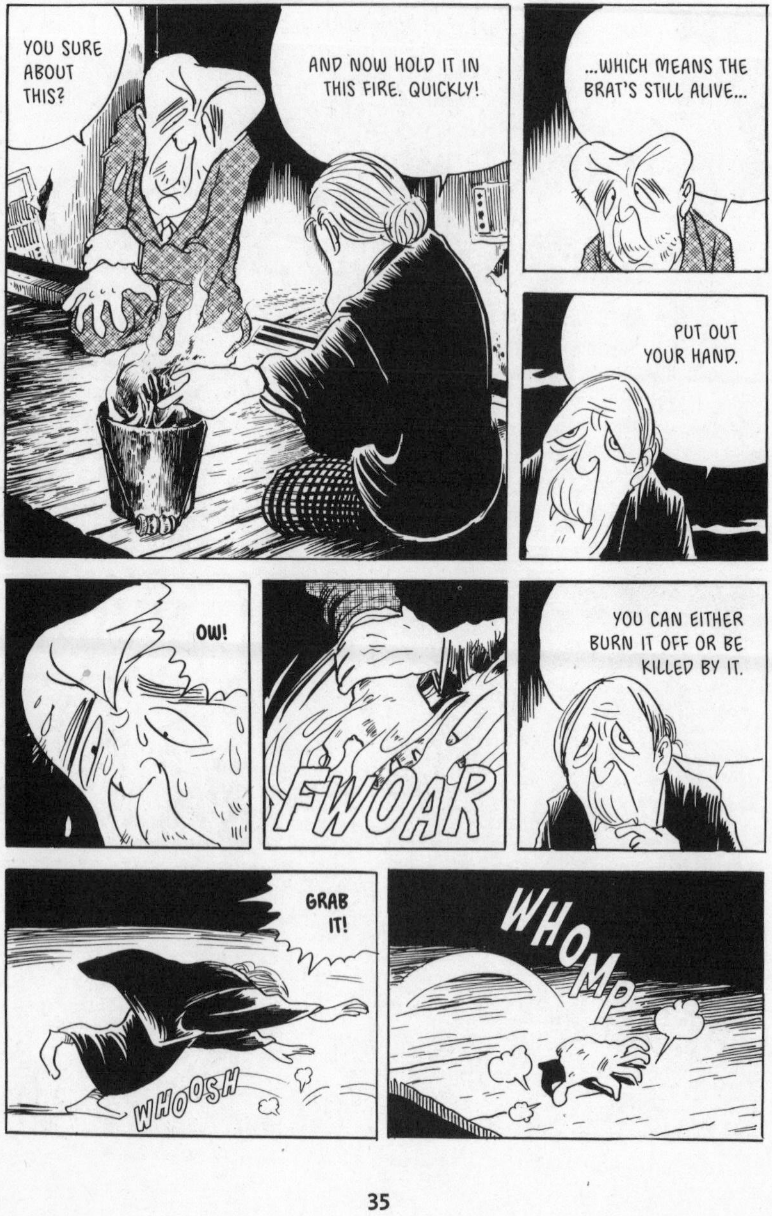
...WHICH MEANS THE BRAT'S STILL ALIVE...
PUT OUT YOUR HAND.
AND NOW HOLD IT IN THIS FIRE. QUICKLY!
YOU SURE ABOUT THIS?
YOU CAN EITHER BURN IT OFF OR BE KILLED BY IT.
FWOAR
OW!
WHOMP
GRAB IT!
WHOOSH

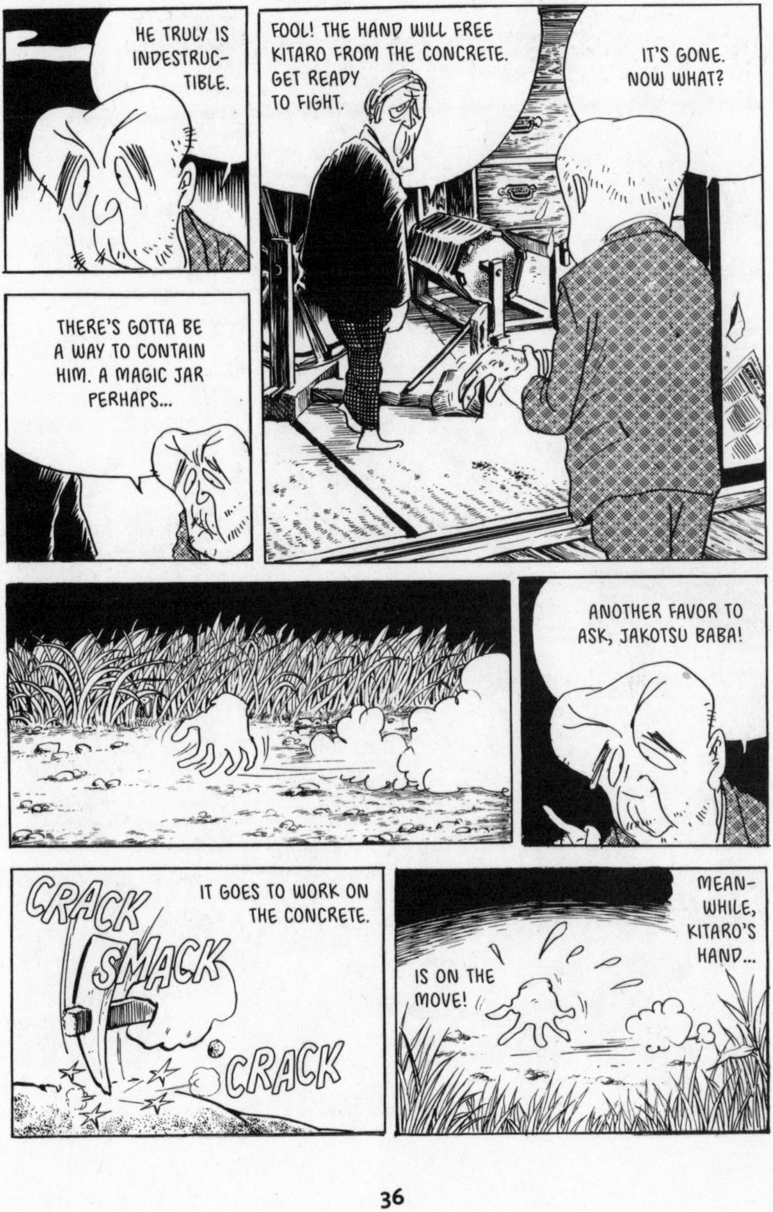
IT'S GONE. NOW WHAT?
FOOL! THE HAND WILL FREE KITARO FROM THE CONCRETE. GET READY TO FIGHT.
HE TRULY IS INDESTRUC-TIBLE.
THERE'S GOTTA BE A WAY TO CONTAIN HIM. A MAGIC JAR PERHAPS...
ANOTHER FAVOR TO ASK, JAKOTSU BABA!
MEAN-WHILE, KITARO'S HAND...
IS ON THE MOVE!
IT GOES TO WORK ON THE CONCRETE.
CRACK
SMACK
CRACK

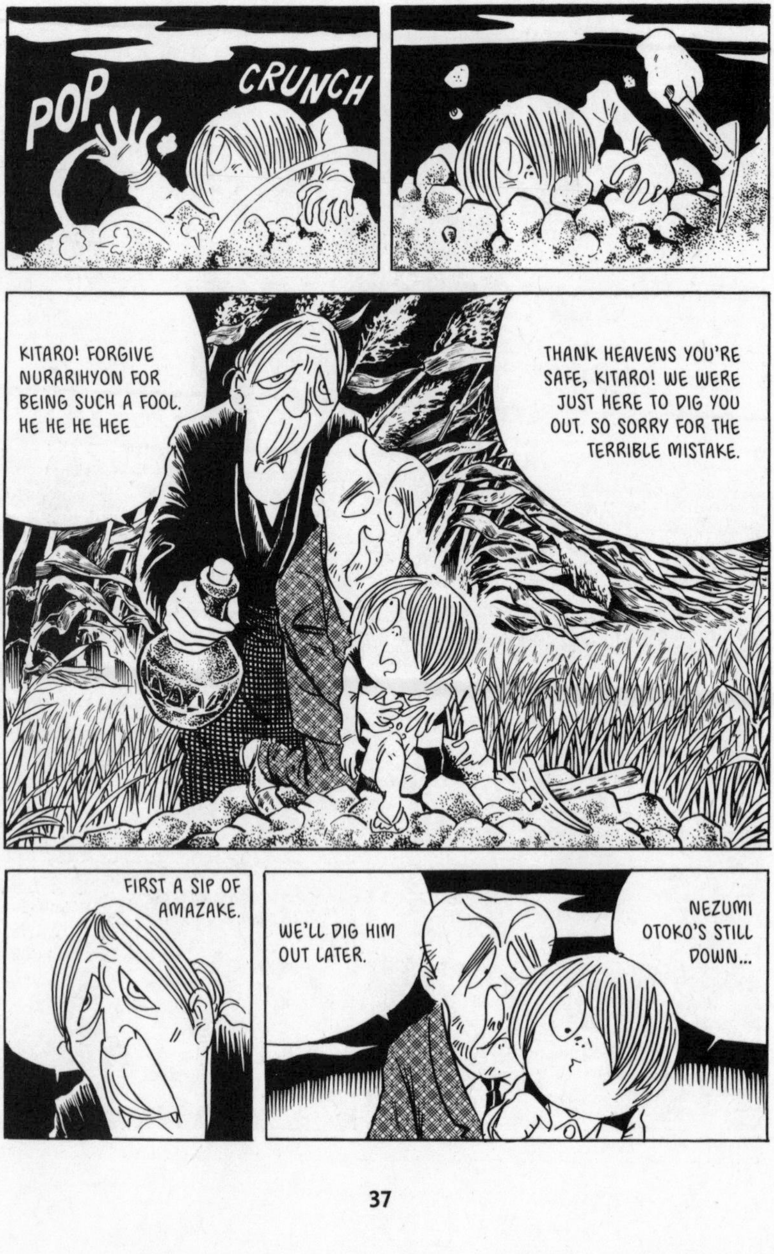
CRUNCH
POP
THANK HEAVENS YOU'RE SAFE, KITARO! WE WERE JUST HERE TO DIG YOU OUT. SO SORRY FOR THE TERRIBLE MISTAKE.
KITARO! FORGIVE NURARIHYON FOR BEING SUCH A FOOL. HE HE HE HEE
NEZUMI OTOKO'S STILL DOWN...
WE'LL DIG HIM OUT LATER.
FIRST A SIP OF AMAZAKE.

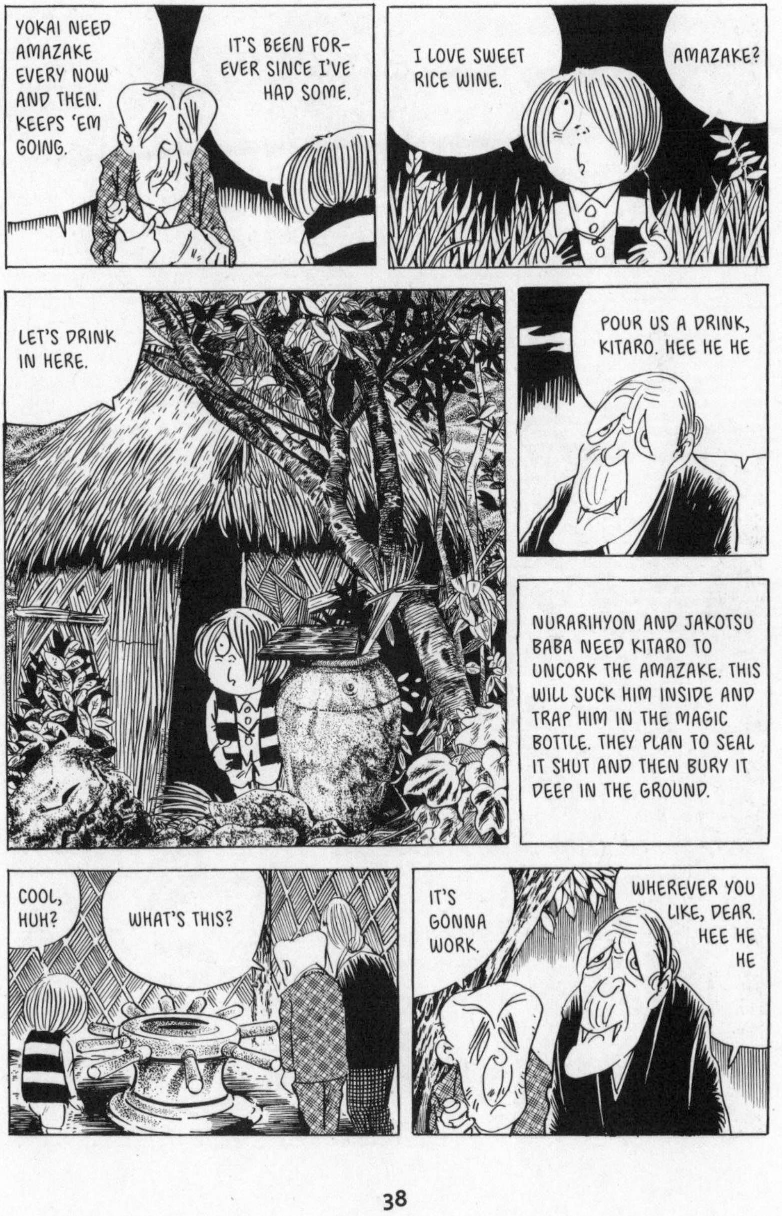
AMAZAKE?
I LOVE SWEET RICE WINE.
IT'S BEEN FOREVER SINCE I'VE HAD SOME.
YOKAI NEED AMAZAKE EVERY NOW AND THEN. KEEPS 'EM GOING.
POUR US A DRINK, KITARO. HEE HE HE
NURARIHYON AND JAKOTSU BABA NEED KITARO TO UNCORK THE AMAZAKE. THIS WILL SUCK HIM INSIDE AND TRAP HIM IN THE MAGIC BOTTLE. THEY PLAN TO SEAL IT SHUT AND THEN BURY IT DEEP IN THE GROUND.
LET'S DRINK IN HERE.
WHEREVER YOU LIKE, DEAR. HEE HE HE
IT'S GONNA WORK.
WHAT'S THIS?
COOL, HUH?

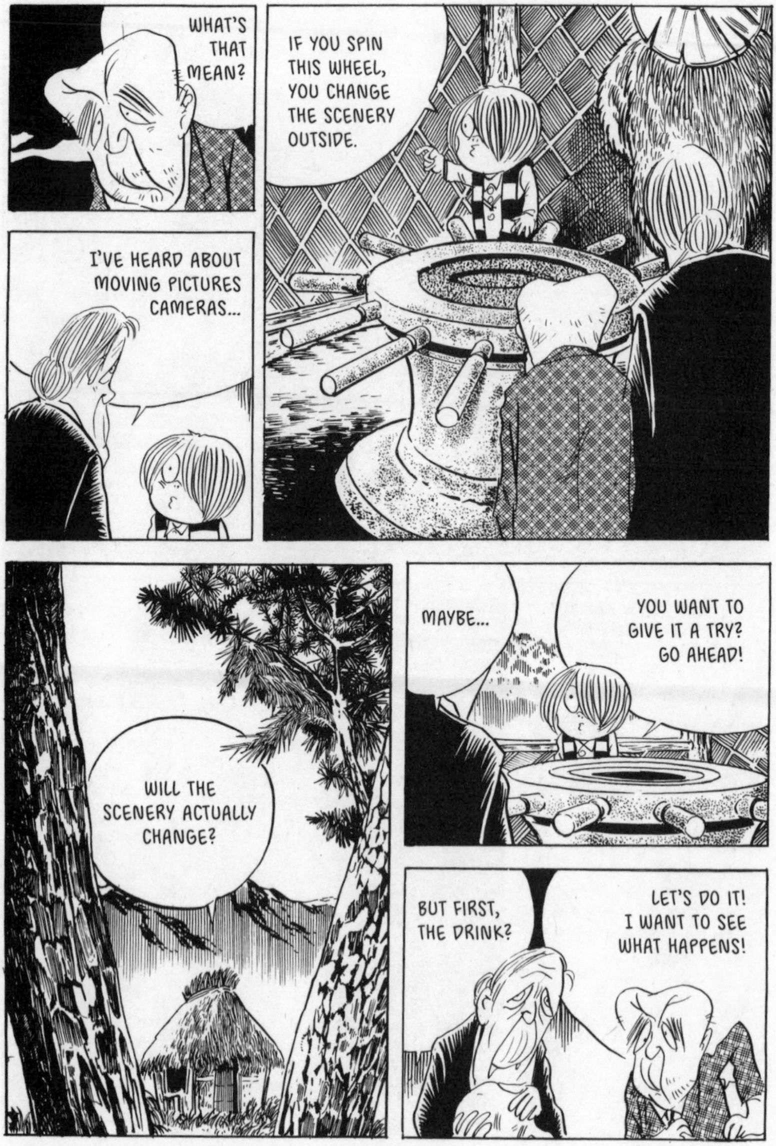
IF YOU SPIN THIS WHEEL, YOU CHANGE THE SCENERY OUTSIDE.
WHAT'S THAT MEAN?
I'VE HEARD ABOUT MOVING PICTURES CAMERAS...
YOU WANT TO GIVE IT A TRY? GO AHEAD!
MAYBE...
LET'S DO IT! I WANT TO SEE WHAT HAPPENS!
BUT FIRST, THE DRINK?
WILL THE SCENERY ACTUALLY CHANGE?

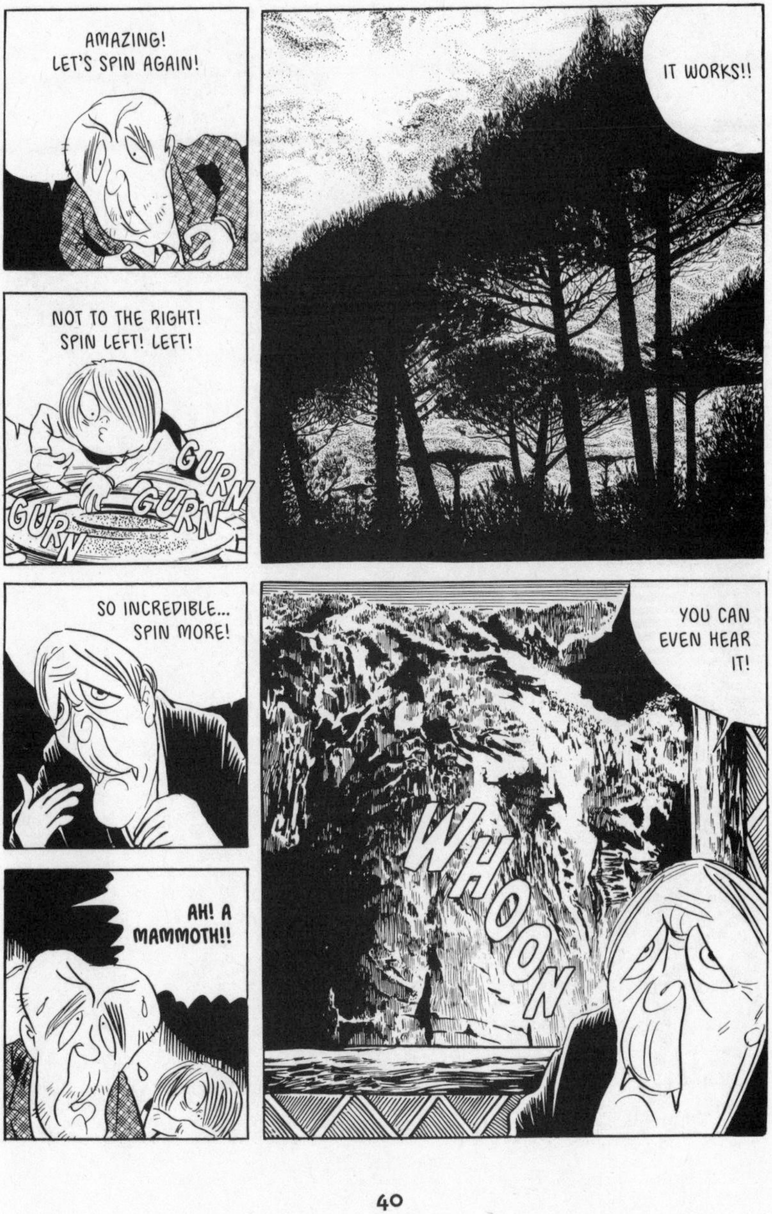
IT WORKS!!
AMAZING! LET'S SPIN AGAIN!
NOT TO THE RIGHT! SPIN LEFT! LEFT!
GURN GURN GURN
YOU CAN EVEN HEAR IT!
WHOON
SO INCREDIBLE... SPIN MORE!
AH! A MAMMOTH!!

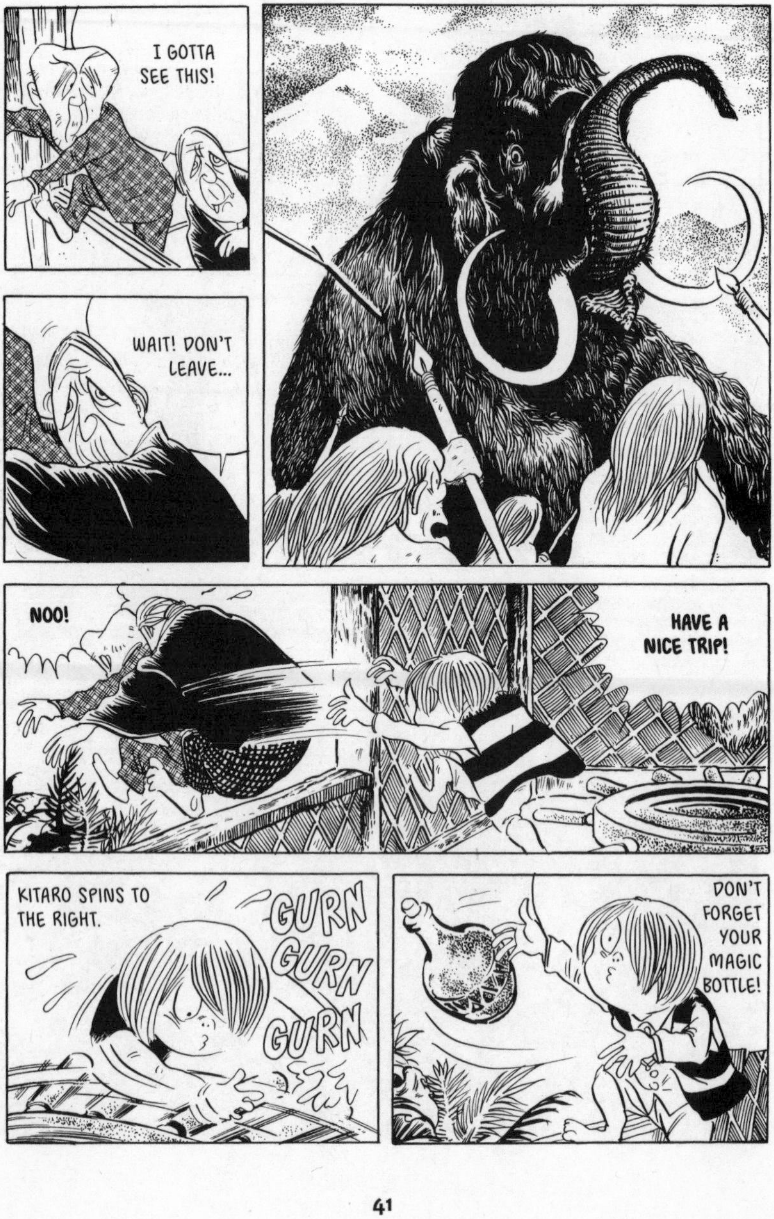
I GOTTA SEE THIS!
WAIT! DON'T LEAVE...
HAVE A NICE TRIP!
NOO!
DON'T FORGET YOUR MAGIC BOTTLE!
GURN GURN GURN
KITARO SPINS TO THE RIGHT.

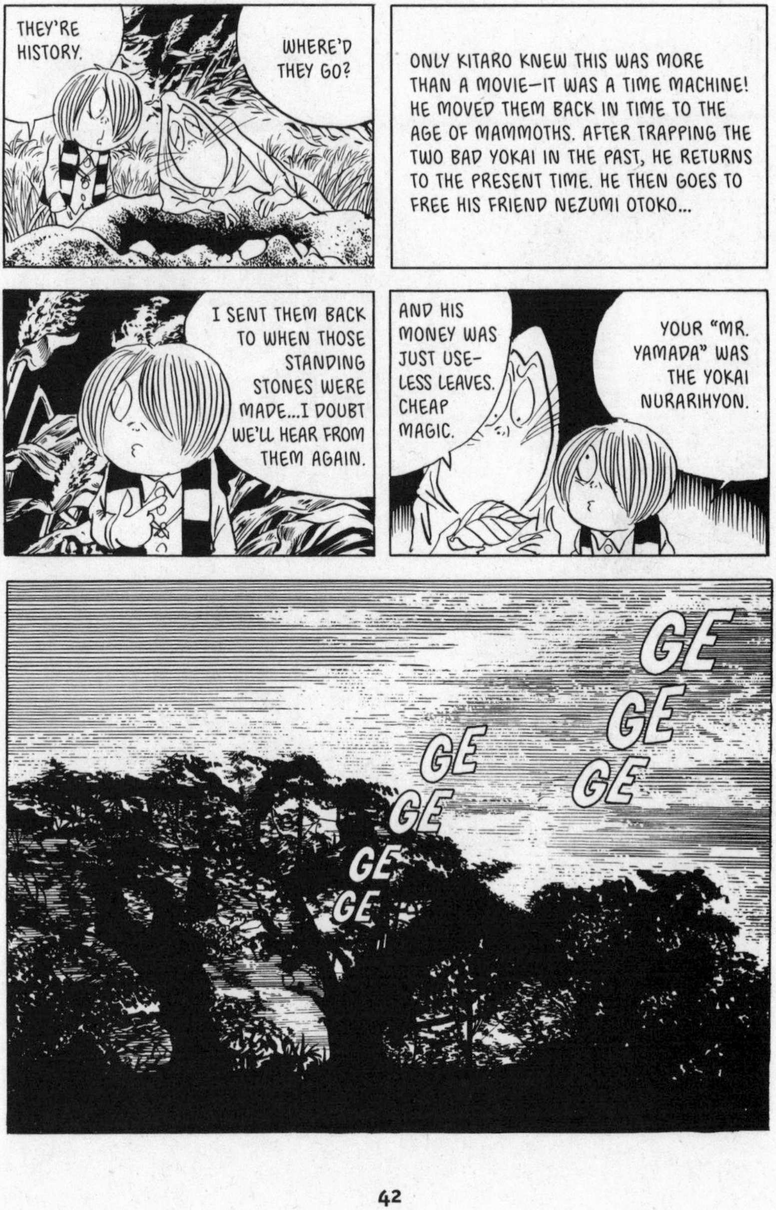
ONLY KITARO KNEW THIS WAS MORE THAN A MOVIE—IT WAS A TIME MACHINE! HE MOVED THEM BACK IN TIME TO THE AGE OF MAMMOTHS. AFTER TRAPPING THE TWO BAD YOKAI IN THE PAST, HE RETURNS TO THE PRESENT TIME. HE THEN GOES TO FREE HIS FRIEND NEZUMI OTOKO...
WHERE'D THEY GO?
THEY'RE HISTORY.
YOUR "MR. YAMADA" WAS THE YOKAI NURARIHYON.
AND HIS MONEY WAS JUST USE-LESS LEAVES. CHEAP MAGIC.
I SENT THEM BACK TO WHEN THOSE STANDING STONES WERE MADE...I DOUBT WE'LL HEAR FROM THEM AGAIN.
GE GE GE
GE GE GE GE

DATSUI BABA

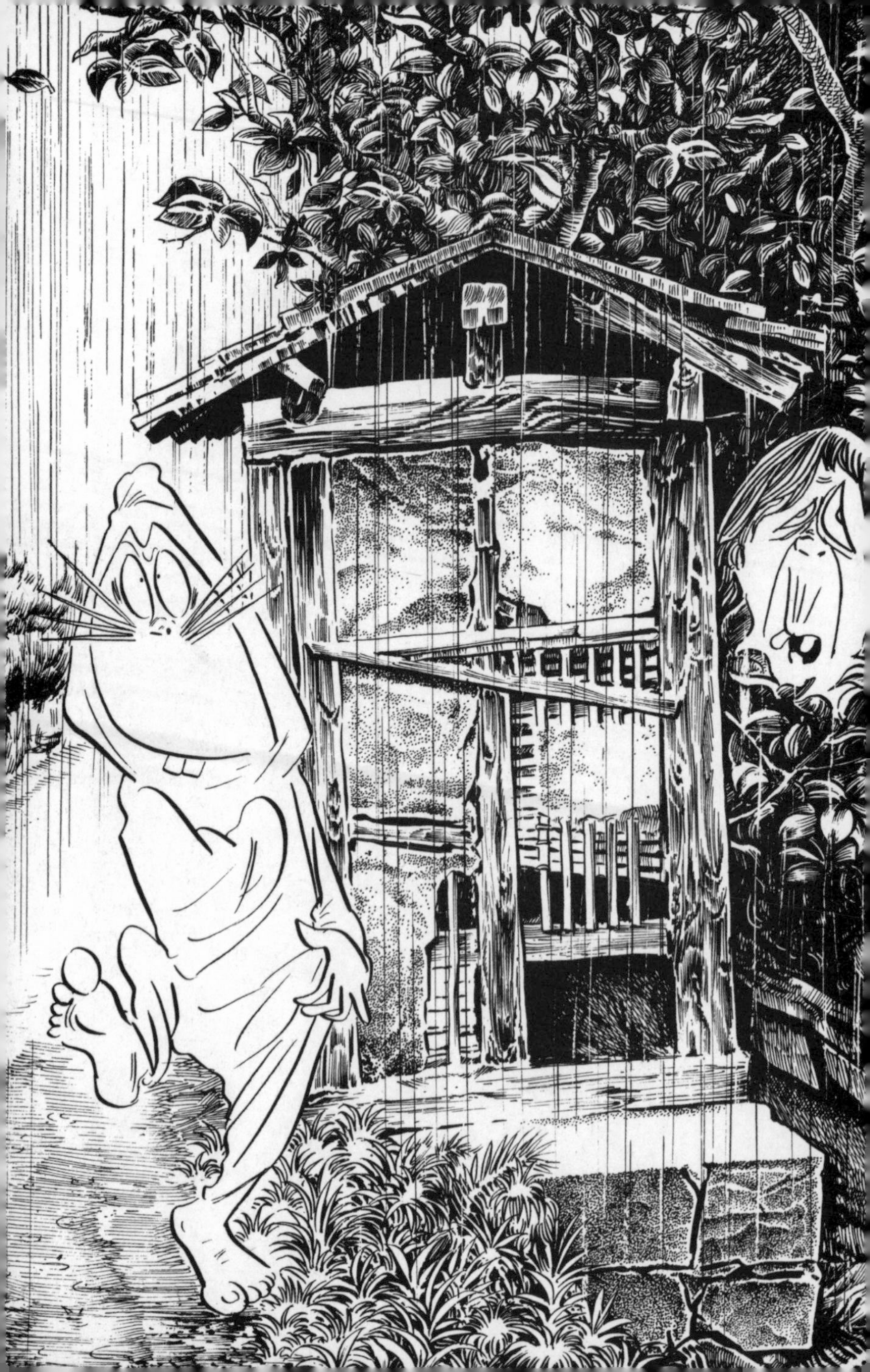

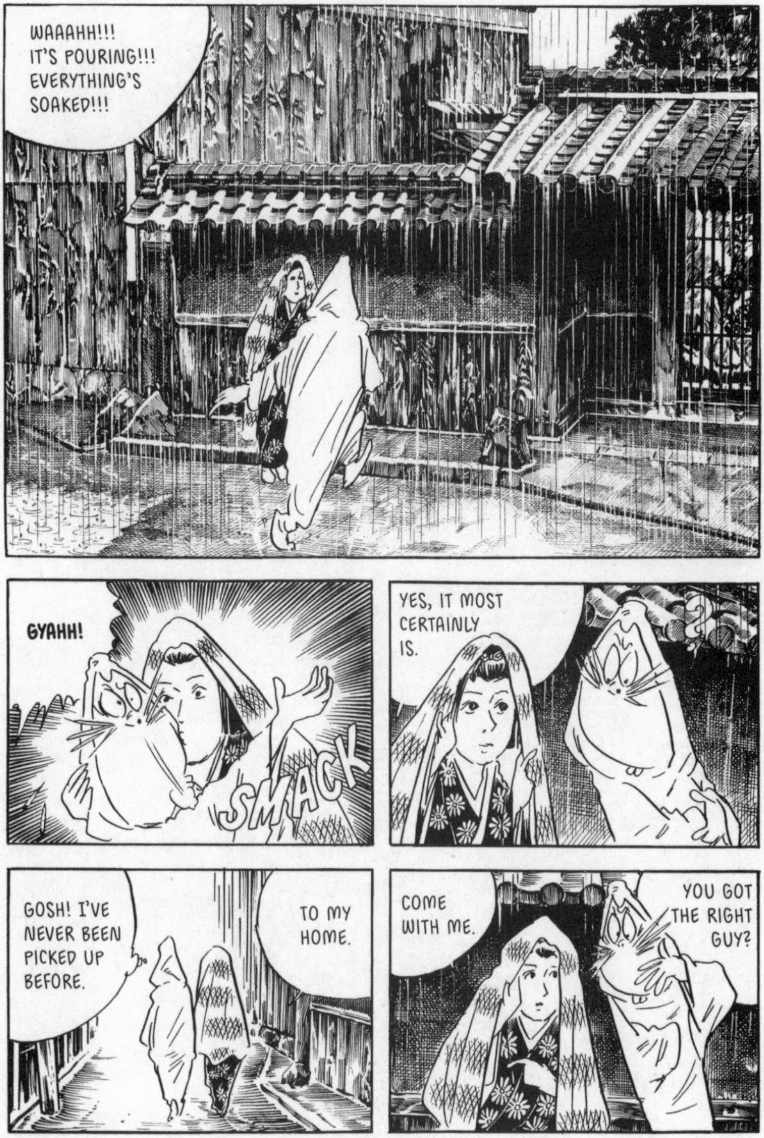
WAAAHH!!! IT'S POURING!!! EVERYTHING'S SOAKED!!!
YES, IT MOST CERTAINLY IS.
GYAHH!
SMACK
YOU GOT THE RIGHT GUY?
COME WITH ME.
TO MY HOME.
GOSH! I'VE NEVER BEEN PICKED UP BEFORE.

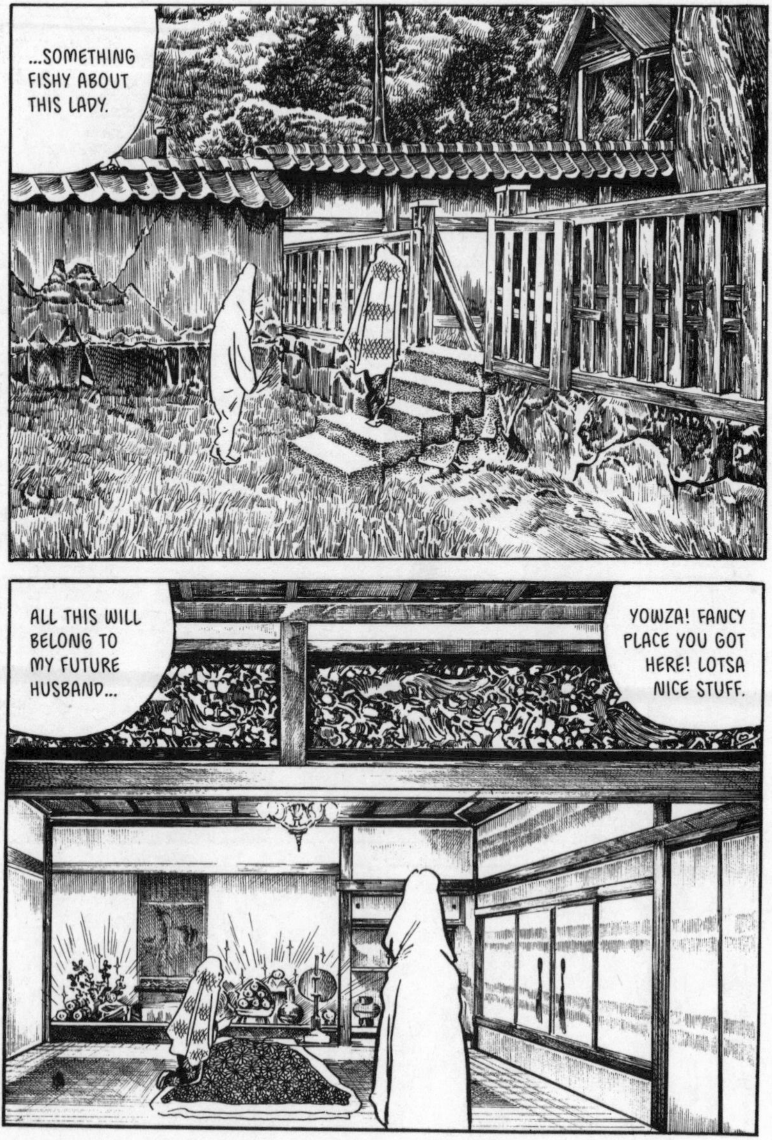
...SOMETHING FISHY ABOUT THIS LADY.
YOWZA! FANCY PLACE YOU GOT HERE! LOTSA NICE STUFF.
ALL THIS WILL BELONG TO MY FUTURE HUSBAND...

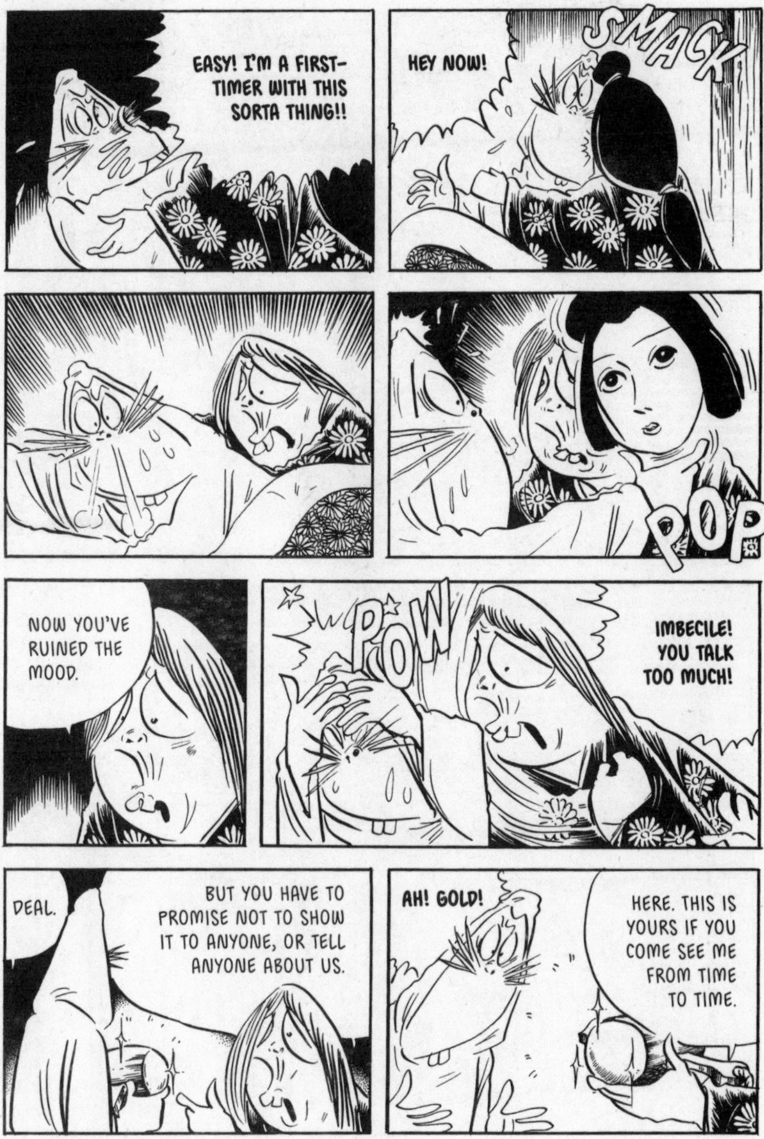
SMACK
HEY NOW!
EASY! I'M A FIRST-TIMER WITH THIS SORTA THING!!
POP
IMBECILE! YOU TALK TOO MUCH!
POW
NOW YOU'VE RUINED THE MOOD.
HERE. THIS IS YOURS IF YOU COME SEE ME FROM TIME TO TIME.
AH! GOLD!
BUT YOU HAVE TO PROMISE NOT TO SHOW IT TO ANYONE, OR TELL ANYONE ABOUT US.
DEAL.

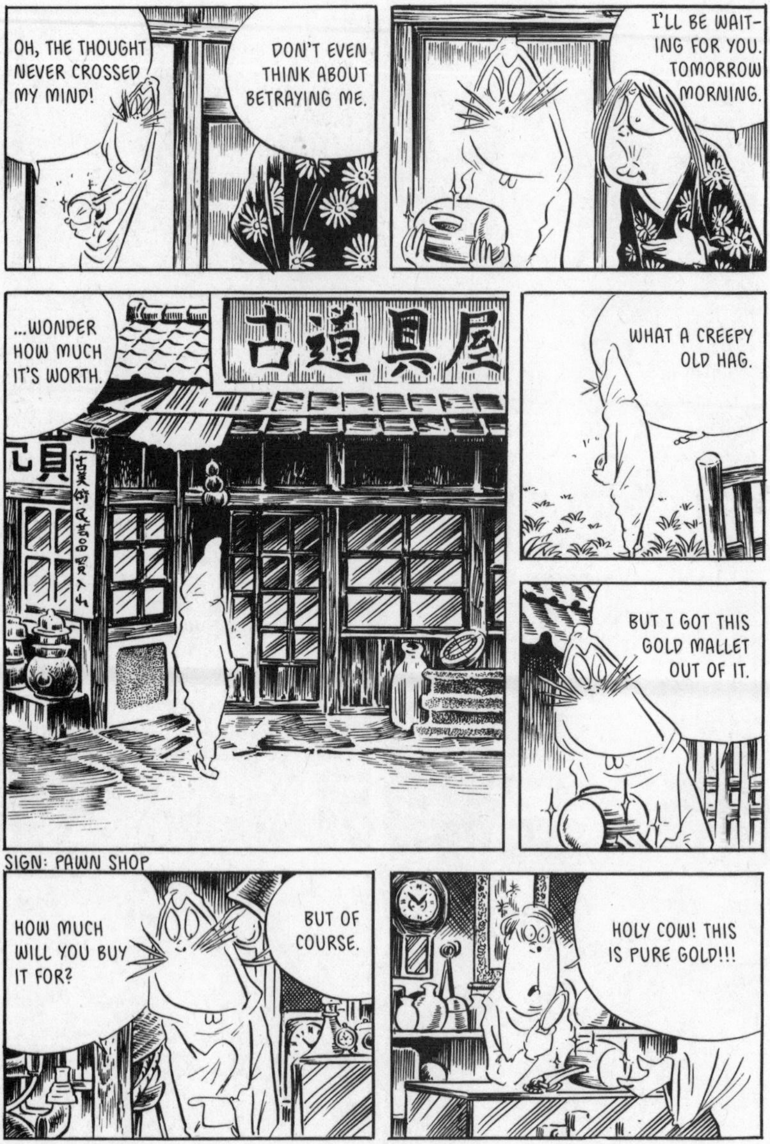
I'LL BE WAITING FOR YOU. TOMORROW MORNING.
DON'T EVEN THINK ABOUT BETRAYING ME.
OH, THE THOUGHT NEVER CROSSED MY MIND!
WHAT A CREEPY OLD HAG.
BUT I GOT THIS GOLD MALLET OUT OF IT.
...WONDER HOW MUCH IT'S WORTH.
古道具屋
SIGN: PAWN SHOP
HOLY COW! THIS IS PURE GOLD!!!
BUT OF COURSE.
HOW MUCH WILL YOU BUY IT FOR?

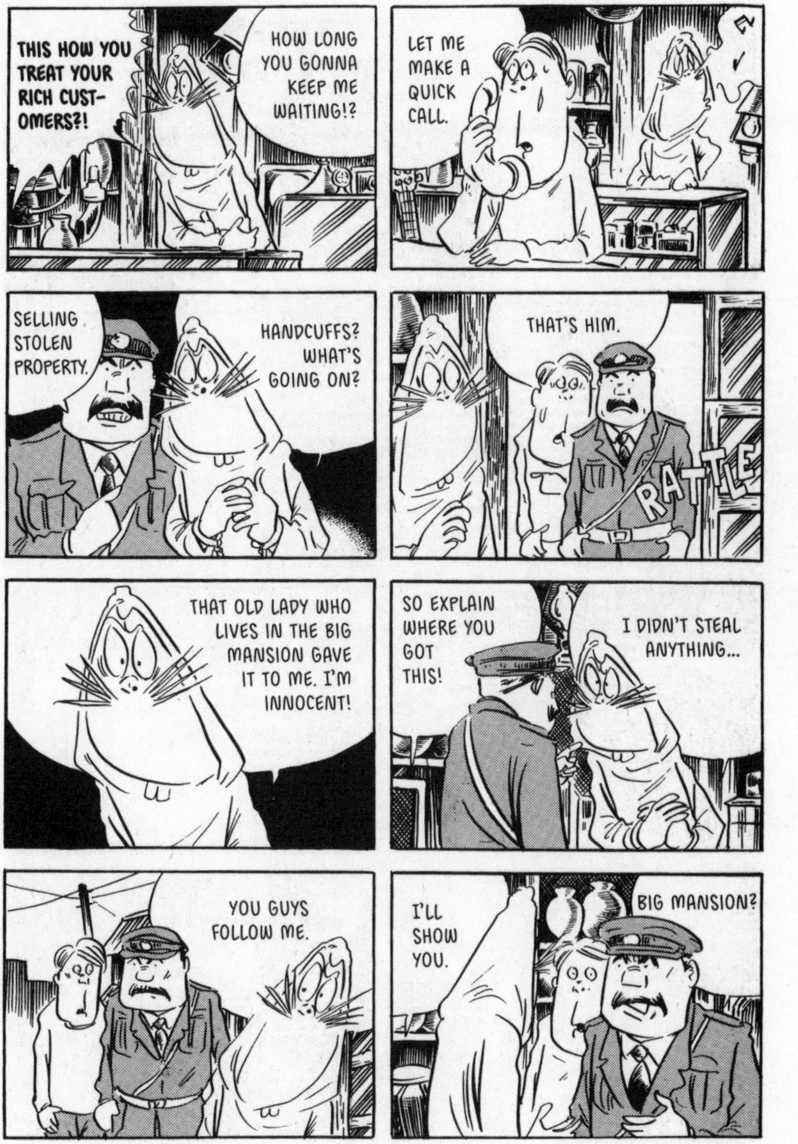
LET ME MAKE A QUICK CALL.
HOW LONG YOU GONNA KEEP ME WAITING!?
THIS HOW YOU TREAT YOUR RICH CUST-OMERS?!
THAT'S HIM.
RATTLE
HANDCUFFS? WHAT'S GOING ON?
SELLING STOLEN PROPERTY.
I DIDN'T STEAL ANYTHING...
SO EXPLAIN WHERE YOU GOT THIS!
THAT OLD LADY WHO LIVES IN THE BIG MANSION GAVE IT TO ME. I'M INNOCENT!
BIG MANSION?
I'LL SHOW YOU.
YOU GUYS FOLLOW ME.

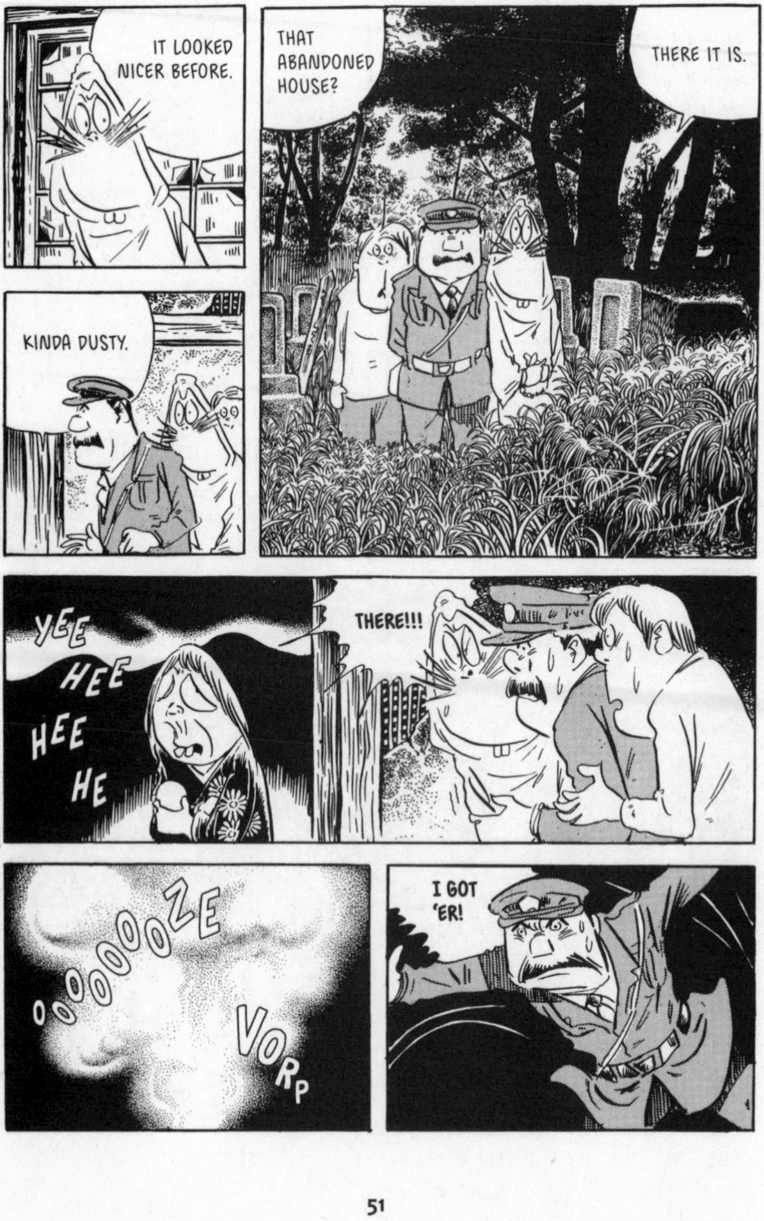
THERE IT IS.
THAT ABANDONED HOUSE?
IT LOOKED NICER BEFORE.
KINDA DUSTY.
THERE!!!
YEE HEE HEE HE
I GOT 'ER!
OOOOOOOZE
VORP

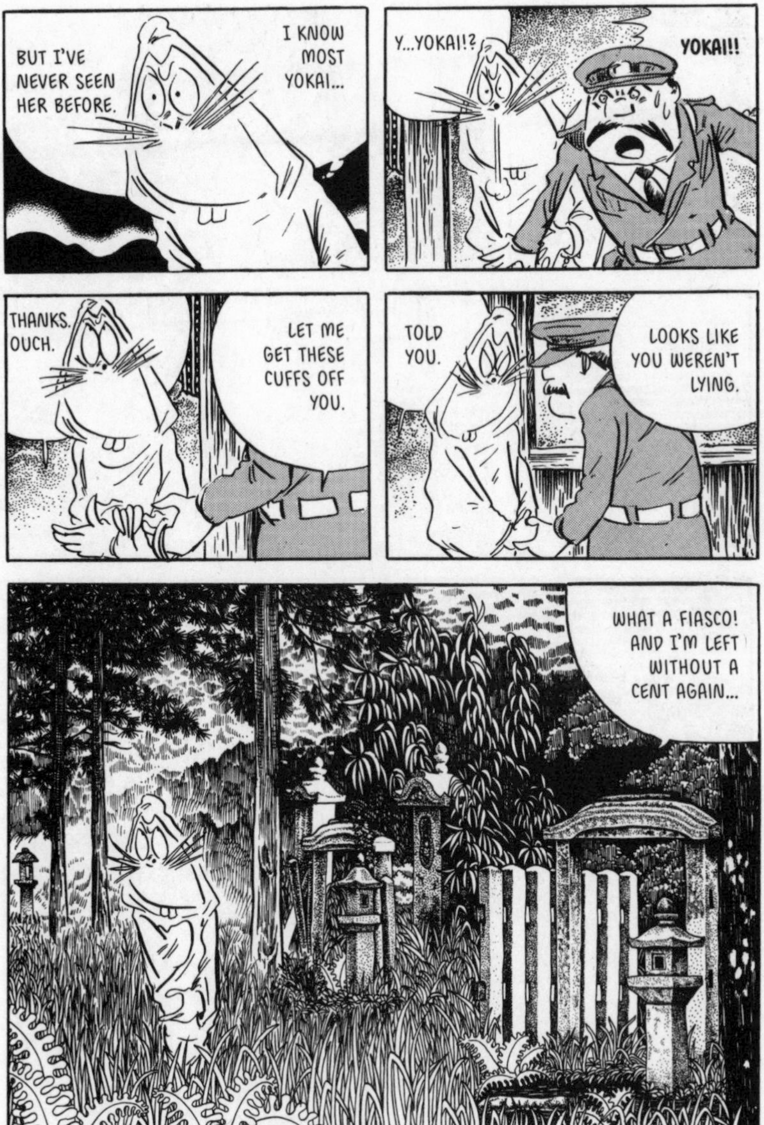
YOKAI!!
Y...YOKAI!?
I KNOW MOST YOKAI...
BUT I'VE NEVER SEEN HER BEFORE.
LOOKS LIKE YOU WEREN'T LYING.
TOLD YOU.
LET ME GET THESE CUFFS OFF YOU.
THANKS. OUCH.
WHAT A FIASCO! AND I'M LEFT WITHOUT A CENT AGAIN...

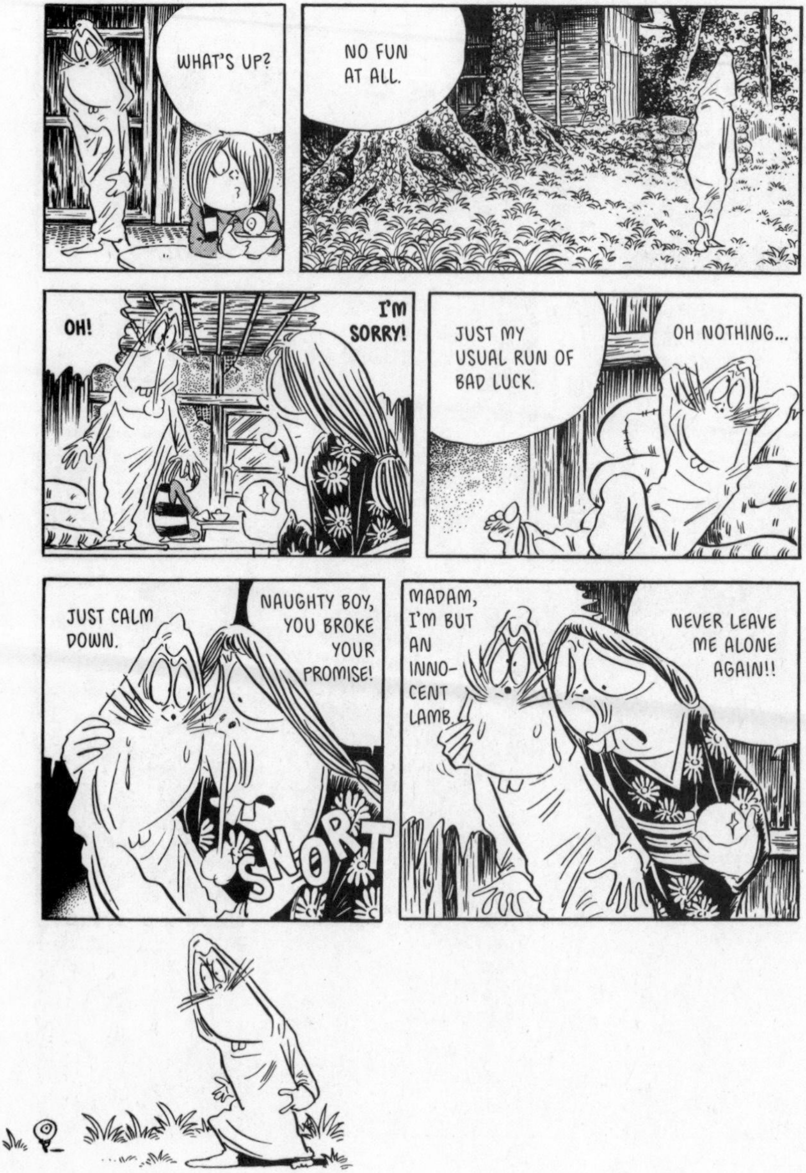
NO FUN
AT ALL.
WHAT'S UP?
OH NOTHING...
JUST MY USUAL RUN OF BAD LUCK.
I'M SORRY!
OH!
NEVER LEAVE ME ALONE AGAIN!!
MADAM, I'M BUT AN INNO-CENT LAMB.
NAUGHTY BOY, YOU BROKE YOUR PROMISE!
JUST CALM DOWN.
SNORT

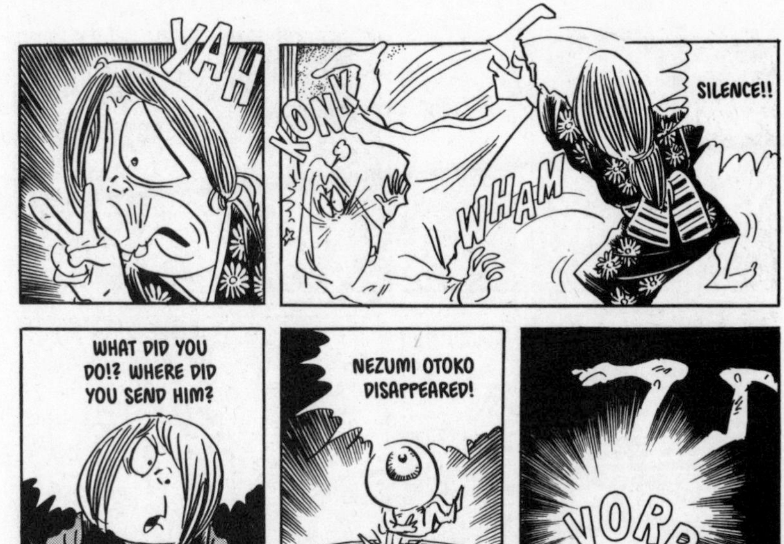
SILENCE!!
KONK
WHAM
YAH
VORP
NEZUMI OTOKO DISAPPEARED!
WHAT DID YOU DO!? WHERE DID YOU SEND HIM?
SILENCE!
YOU CAN'T SHUT ME UP THAT EASY.
I'LL DO MORE THAN THAT—!
YAH

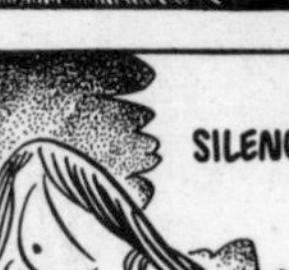

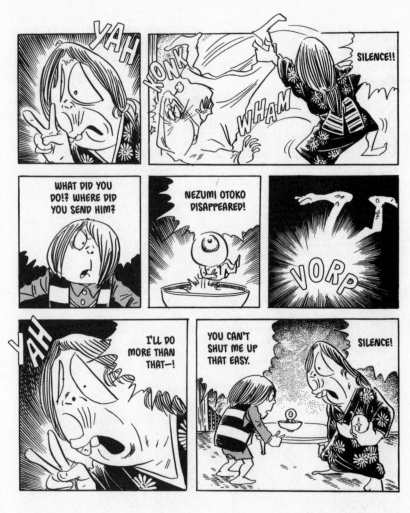

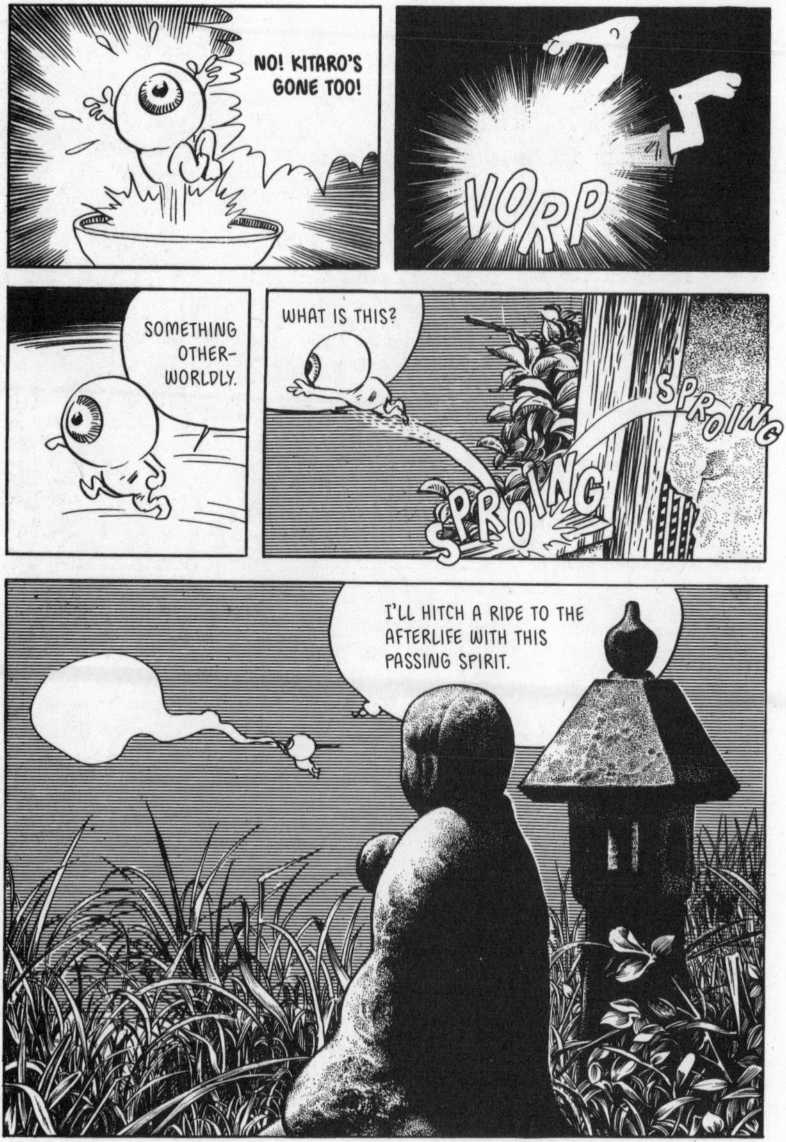
VORP
NO! KITARO'S GONE TOO!
WHAT IS THIS?
SPROING
SPROING
SOMETHING OTHER-WORLDLY.
I'LL HITCH A RIDE TO THE AFTERLIFE WITH THIS PASSING SPIRIT.

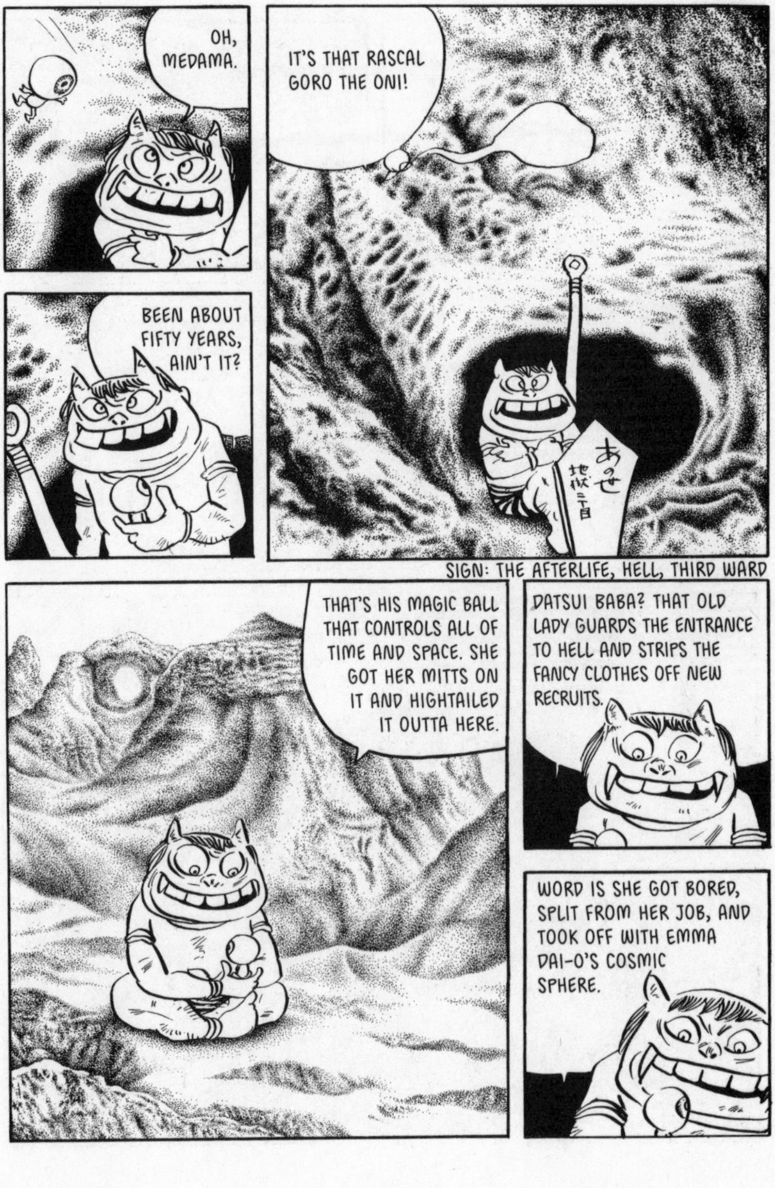
IT'S THAT RASCAL GORO THE ONI!
あの世 地獄三丁目
SIGN: THE AFTERLIFE, HELL, THIRD WARD
OH, MEDAMA.
BEEN ABOUT FIFTY YEARS, AIN'T IT?
DATSUI BABA? THAT OLD LADY GUARDS THE ENTRANCE TO HELL AND STRIPS THE FANCY CLOTHES OFF NEW RECRUITS.
WORD IS SHE GOT BORED, SPLIT FROM HER JOB, AND TOOK OFF WITH EMMA DAI-O'S COSMIC SPHERE.
THAT'S HIS MAGIC BALL THAT CONTROLS ALL OF TIME AND SPACE. SHE GOT HER MITTS ON IT AND HIGHTAILED IT OUTTA HERE.

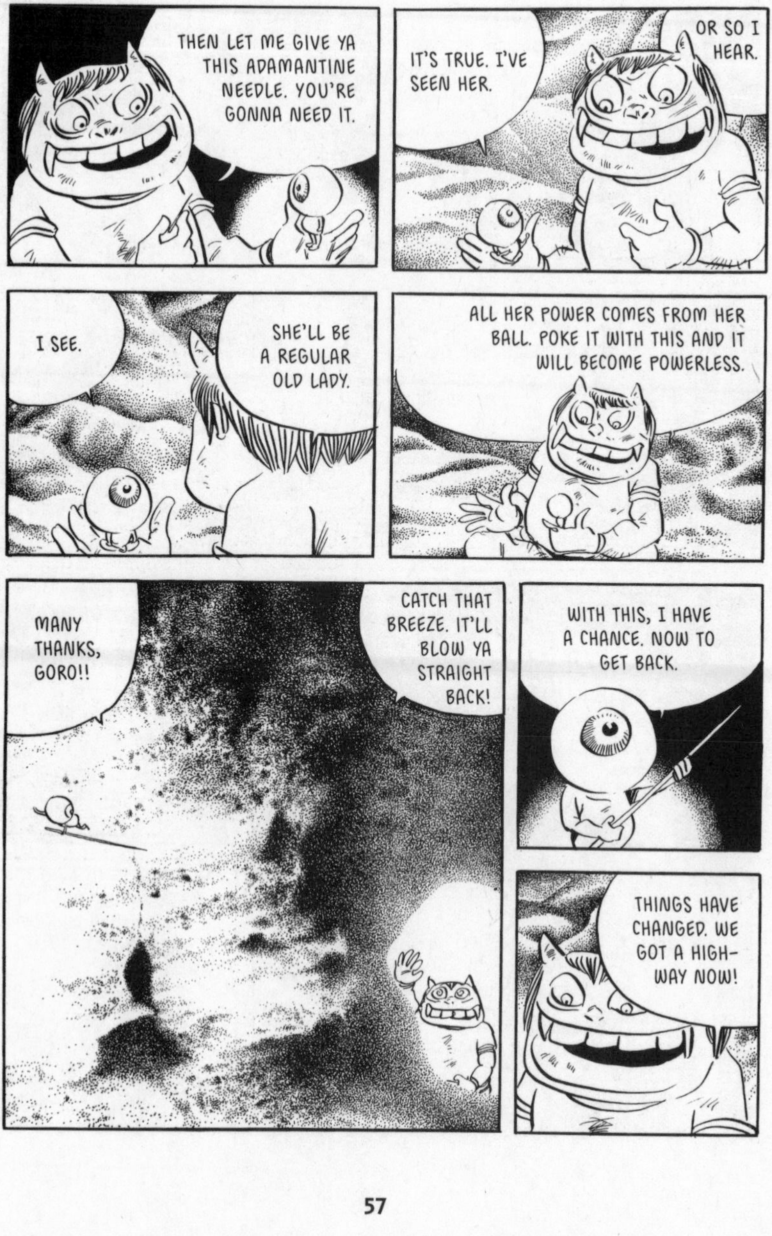
OR SO I HEAR.
IT'S TRUE. I'VE SEEN HER.
THEN LET ME GIVE YA THIS ADAMANTINE NEEDLE. YOU'RE GONNA NEED IT.
ALL HER POWER COMES FROM HER BALL. POKE IT WITH THIS AND IT WILL BECOME POWERLESS.
SHE'LL BE A REGULAR OLD LADY.
I SEE.
WITH THIS, I HAVE A CHANCE. NOW TO GET BACK.
THINGS HAVE CHANGED. WE GOT A HIGH-WAY NOW!
CATCH THAT BREEZE. IT'LL BLOW YA STRAIGHT BACK!
MANY THANKS, GORO!!

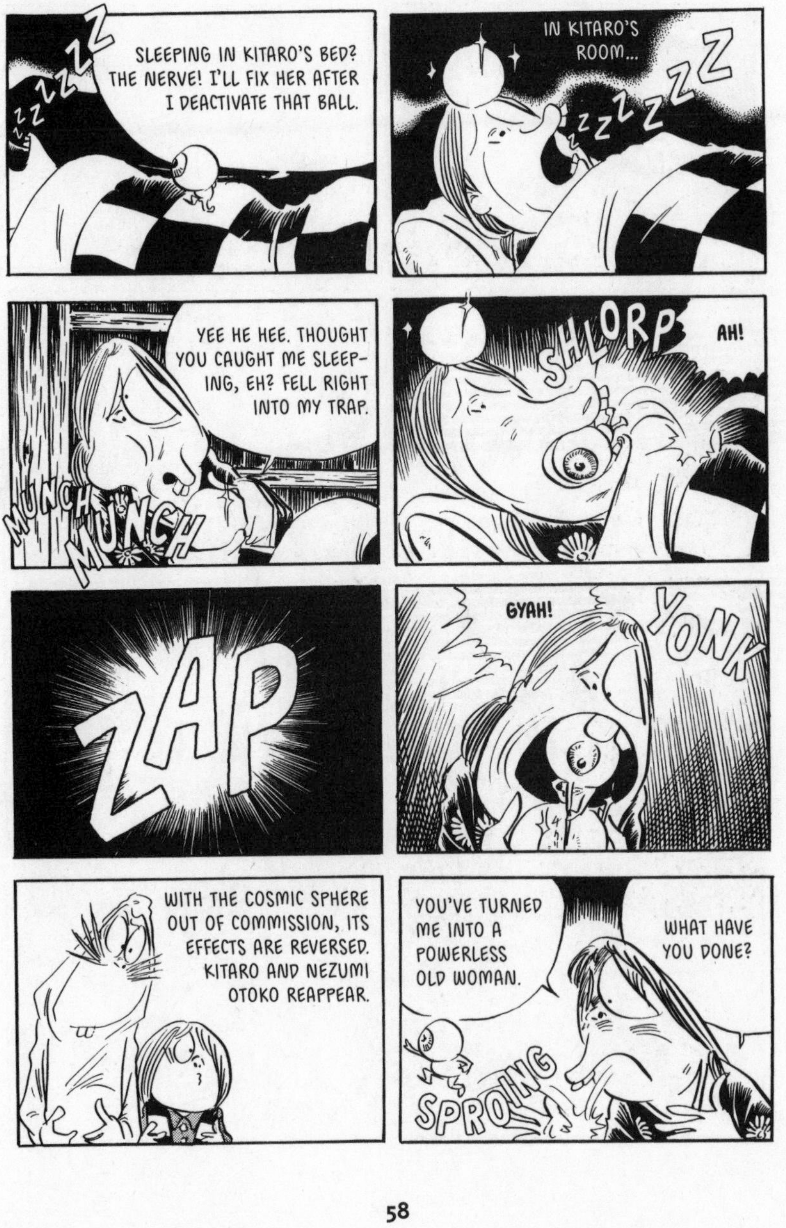
IN KITARO'S ROOM...
ZZZZZZZ
SLEEPING IN KITARO'S BED? THE NERVE! I'LL FIX HER AFTER I DEACTIVATE THAT BALL.
ZZZZZZZZ
AH!
SHLORP
YEE HE HEE. THOUGHT YOU CAUGHT ME SLEEPING, EH? FELL RIGHT INTO MY TRAP.
MUNCH MUNCH
YONK
GYAH!
ZAP
WHAT HAVE YOU DONE?
YOU'VE TURNED ME INTO A POWERLESS OLD WOMAN.
SPROING
WITH THE COSMIC SPHERE OUT OF COMMISSION, ITS EFFECTS ARE REVERSED. KITARO AND NEZUMI OTOKO REAPPEAR.

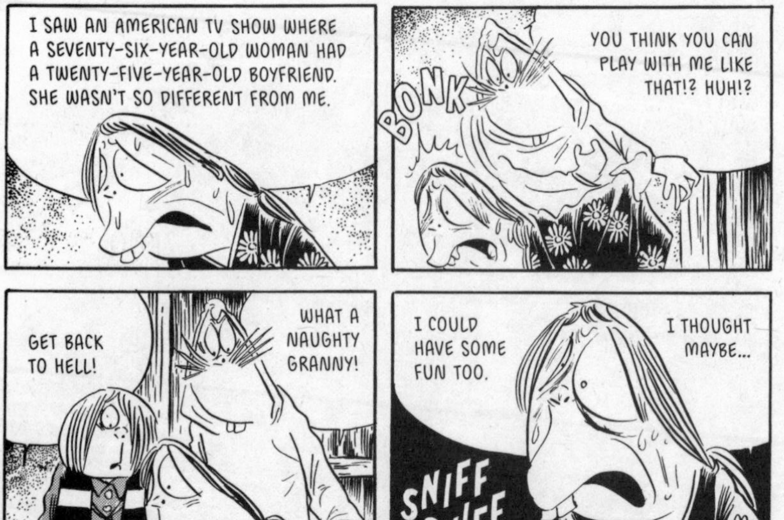
YOU THINK YOU CAN PLAY WITH ME LIKE THAT!? HUH!?
BONK
I SAW AN AMERICAN TV SHOW WHERE A SEVENTY-SIX-YEAR-OLD WOMAN HAD A TWENTY-FIVE-YEAR-OLD BOYFRIEND. SHE WASN'T SO DIFFERENT FROM ME.
I THOUGHT MAYBE...
I COULD HAVE SOME FUN TOO.
SNIFF SNIFF
WHAT A NAUGHTY GRANNY!
GET BACK TO HELL!
CAN'T I PLAY A LITTLE BIT MORE?
NO! NEZUMI OTOKO, YOU BETTER MAKE SURE SHE GETS BACK. TAKE THE HIGHWAY!
BONK
YOU SURE WERE A PAIN.

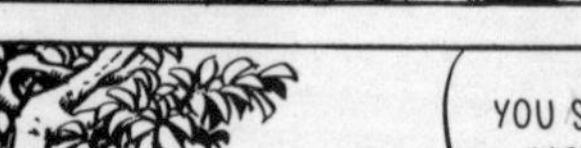

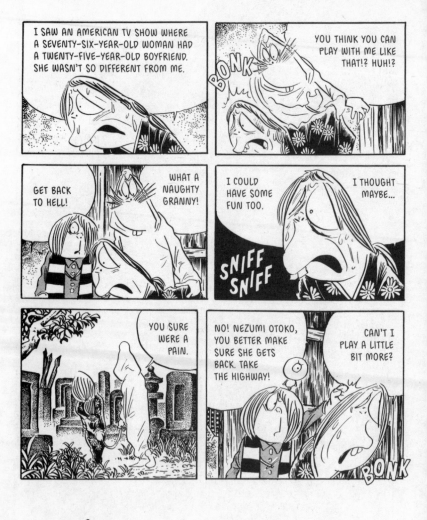

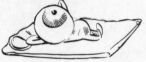

SARA KOZO

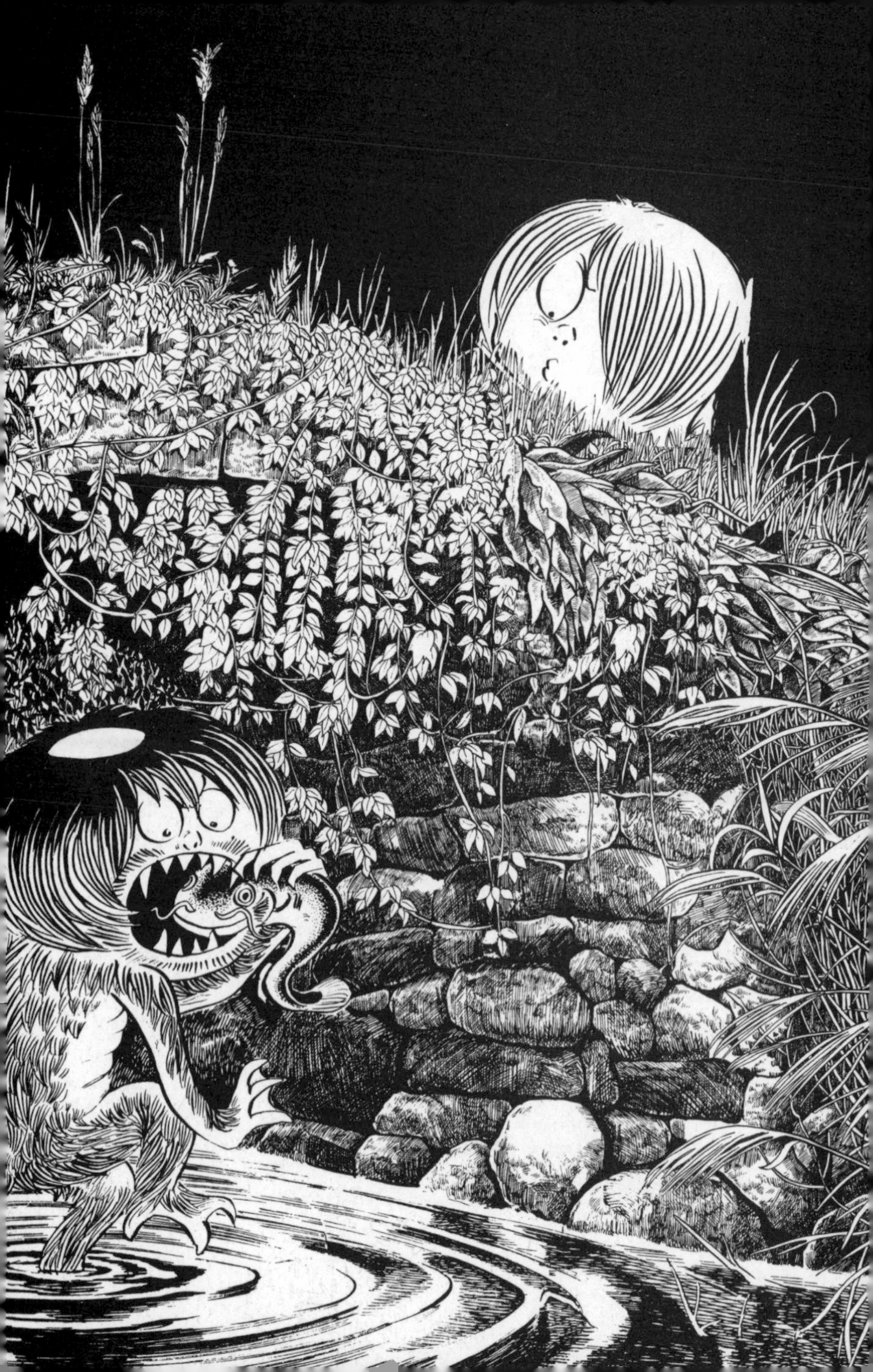

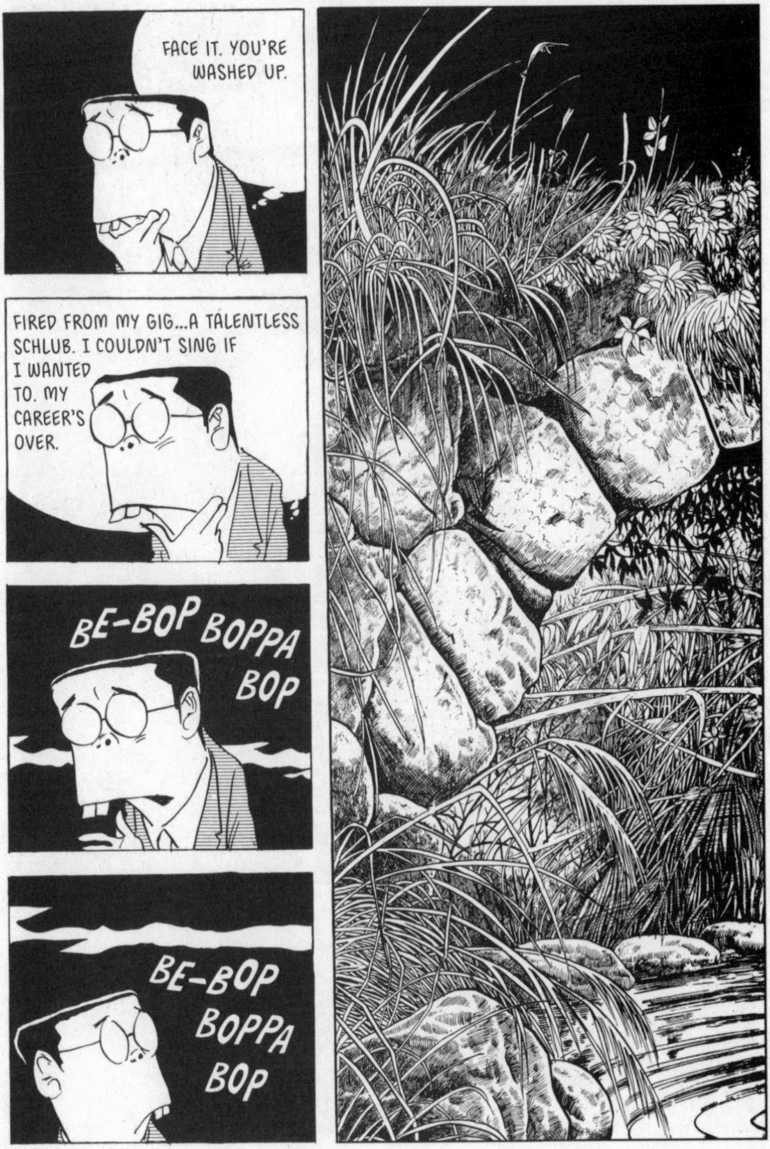
FACE IT. YOU'RE WASHED UP.
FIRED FROM MY GIG...A TALENTLESS SCHLUB. I COULDN'T SING IF I WANTED TO. MY CAREER'S OVER.
BE-BOP BOPPA BOP
BE-BOP BOPPA BOP

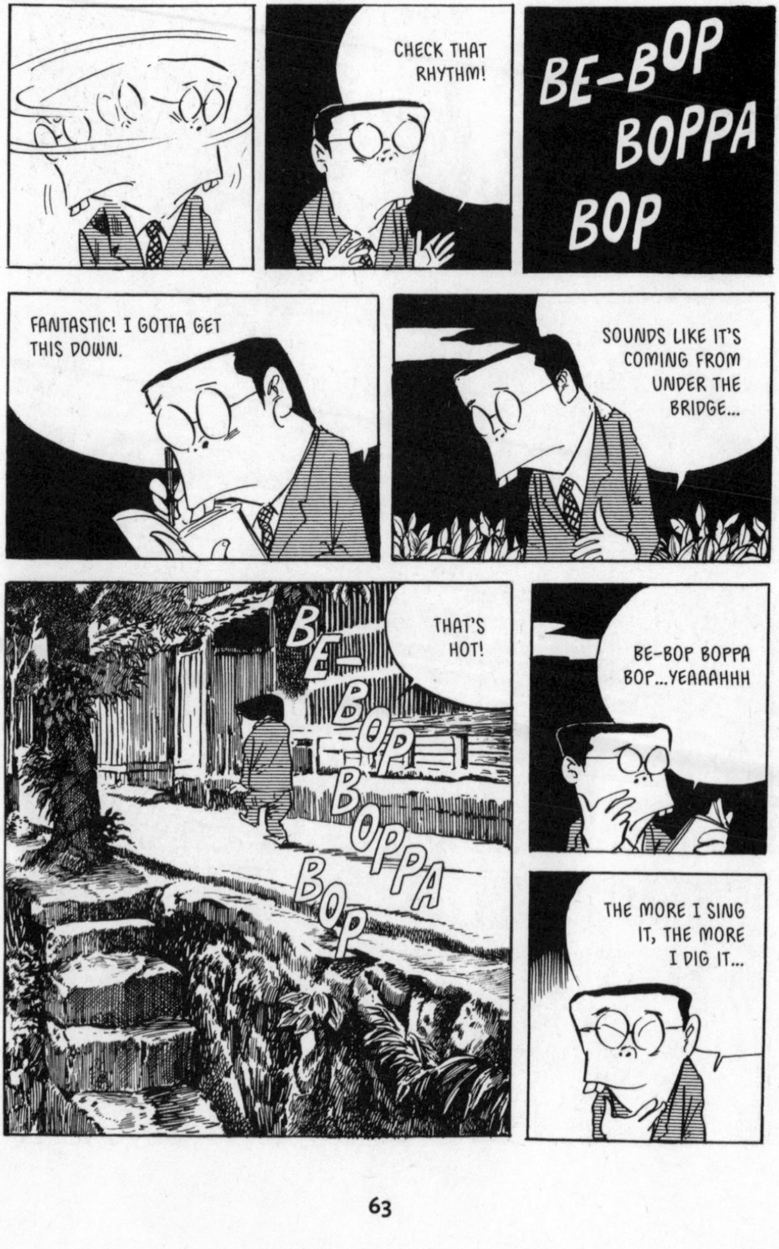
BE-BOP BOPPA BOP
CHECK THAT RHYTHM!
SOUNDS LIKE IT'S COMING FROM UNDER THE BRIDGE...
FANTASTIC! I GOTTA GET THIS DOWN.
BE-BOP BOPPA BOP...YEAAAHHH
THE MORE I SING IT, THE MORE I DIG IT...
THAT'S HOT!
BE-BOP BOPPA BOP

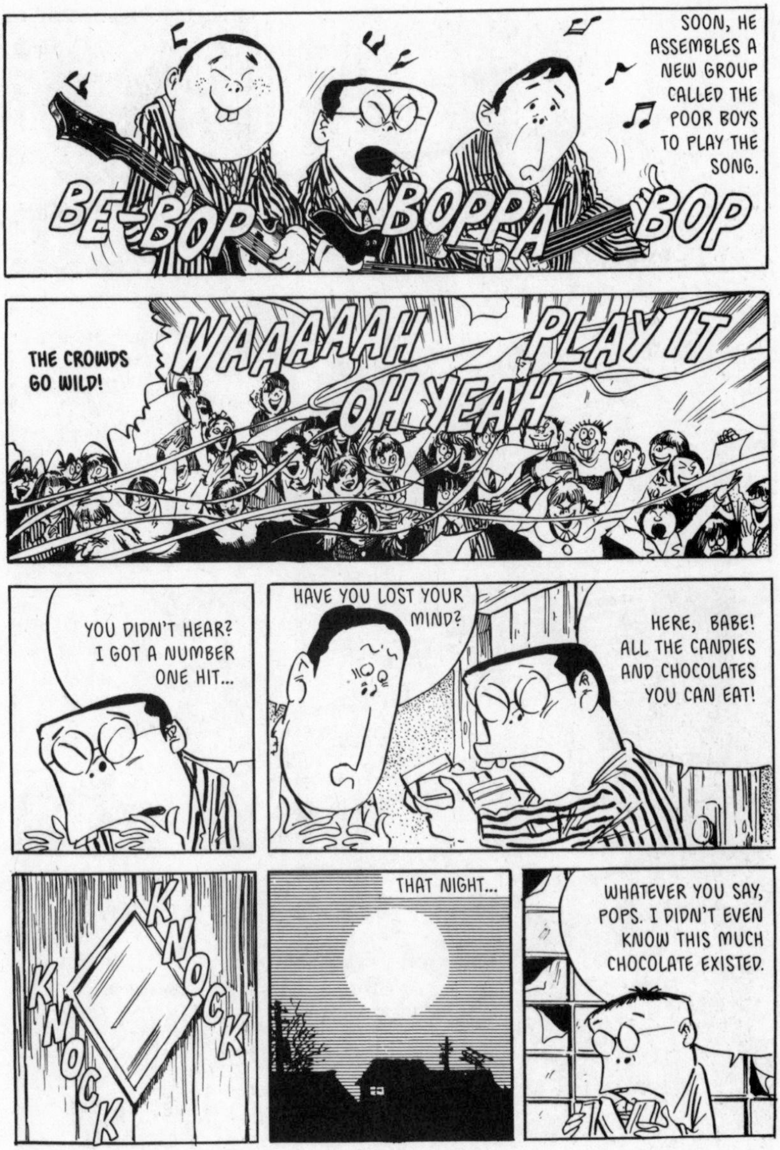
SOON, HE ASSEMBLES A NEW GROUP CALLED THE POOR BOYS TO PLAY THE SONG.
BE-BOP BOPPA BOP
PLAY IT
WAAAAAH
OH YEAH
THE CROWDS GO WILD!
HERE, BABE! ALL THE CANDIES AND CHOCOLATES YOU CAN EAT!
HAVE YOU LOST YOUR MIND?
YOU DIDN'T HEAR? I GOT A NUMBER ONE HIT...
WHATEVER YOU SAY, POPS. I DIDN'T EVEN KNOW THIS MUCH CHOCOLATE EXISTED.
THAT NIGHT...
KNOCK
KNOCK

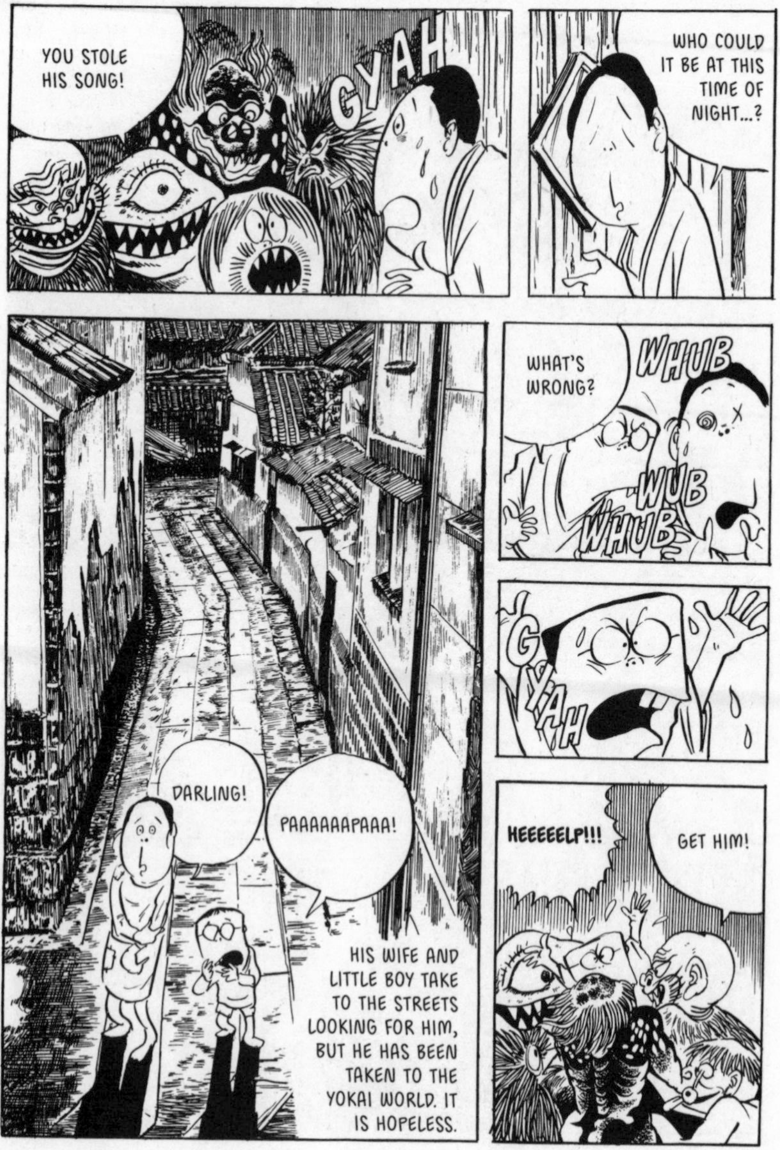
WHO COULD IT BE AT THIS TIME OF NIGHT...?
GYAH
YOU STOLE HIS SONG!
WHUB
WHAT'S WRONG?
WUB
WHUB
G
GYAH
GET HIM!
HEEEEELP!!!
DARLING!
PAAAAAAPAAA!
HIS WIFE AND LITTLE BOY TAKE TO THE STREETS LOOKING FOR HIM, BUT HE HAS BEEN TAKEN TO THE YOKAI WORLD. IT IS HOPELESS.

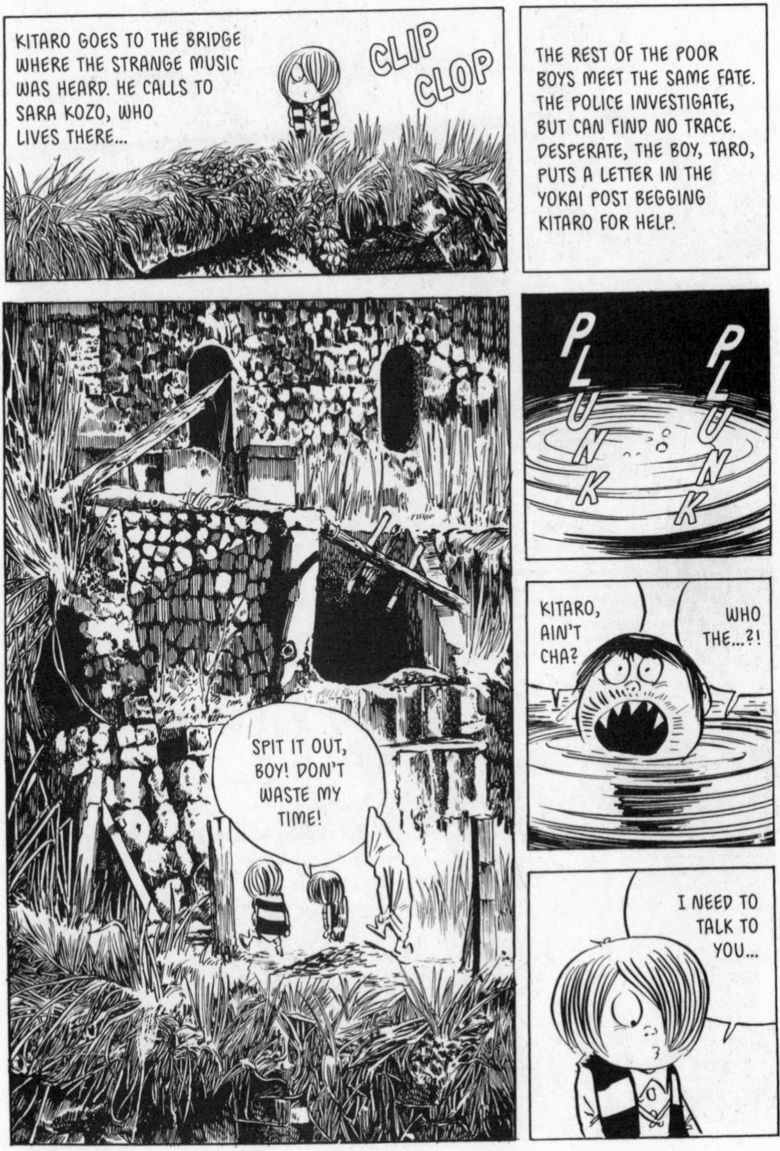
THE REST OF THE POOR BOYS MEET THE SAME FATE. THE POLICE INVESTIGATE, BUT CAN FIND NO TRACE. DESPERATE, THE BOY, TARO, PUTS A LETTER IN THE YOKAI POST BEGGING KITARO FOR HELP.
CLIP CLOP
KITARO GOES TO THE BRIDGE WHERE THE STRANGE MUSIC WAS HEARD. HE CALLS TO SARA KOZO, WHO LIVES THERE...
PLUNK
PLUNK
WHO THE...?!
KITARO, AIN'T CHA?
I NEED TO TALK TO YOU...
SPIT IT OUT, BOY! DON'T WASTE MY TIME!

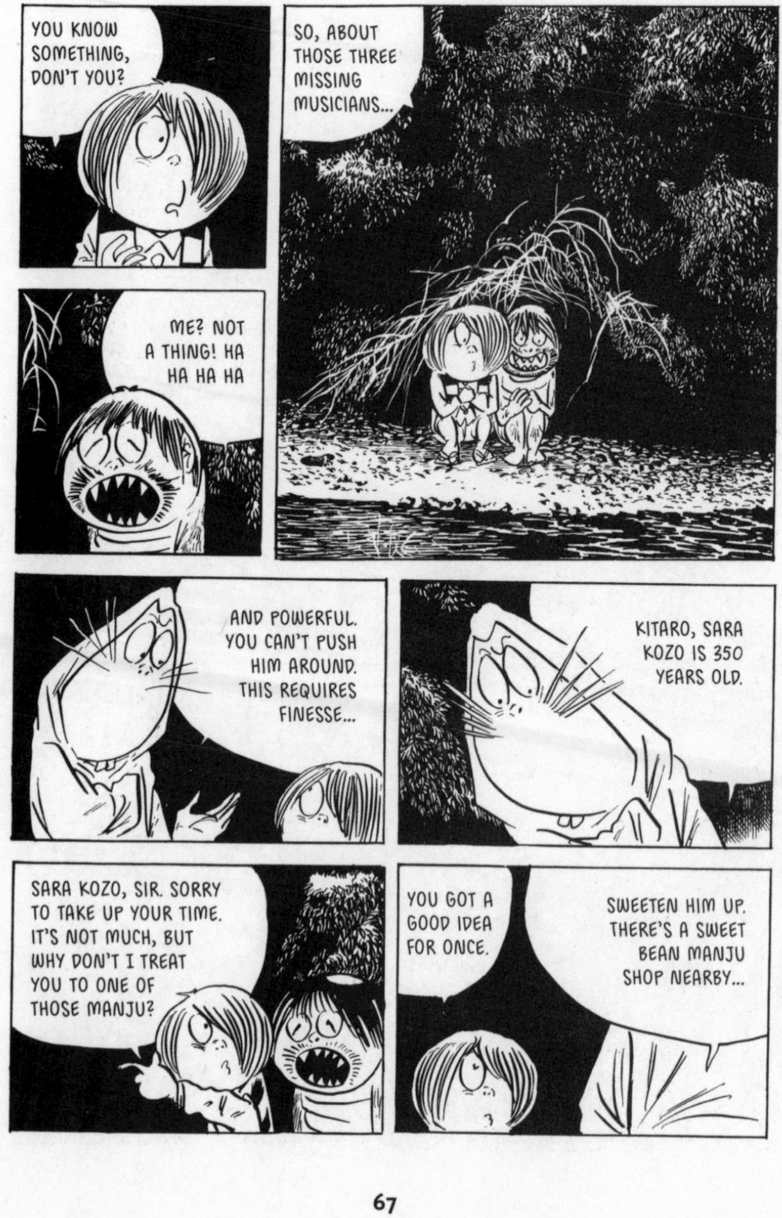
SO, ABOUT THOSE THREE MISSING MUSICIANS...
YOU KNOW SOMETHING, DON'T YOU?
ME? NOT A THING! HA HA HA HA
KITARO, SARA KOZO IS 350 YEARS OLD.
AND POWERFUL. YOU CAN'T PUSH HIM AROUND. THIS REQUIRES FINESSE...
SWEETEN HIM UP. THERE'S A SWEET BEAN MANJU SHOP NEARBY...
YOU GOT A GOOD IDEA FOR ONCE.
SARA KOZO, SIR. SORRY TO TAKE UP YOUR TIME. IT'S NOT MUCH, BUT WHY DON'T I TREAT YOU TO ONE OF THOSE MANJU?

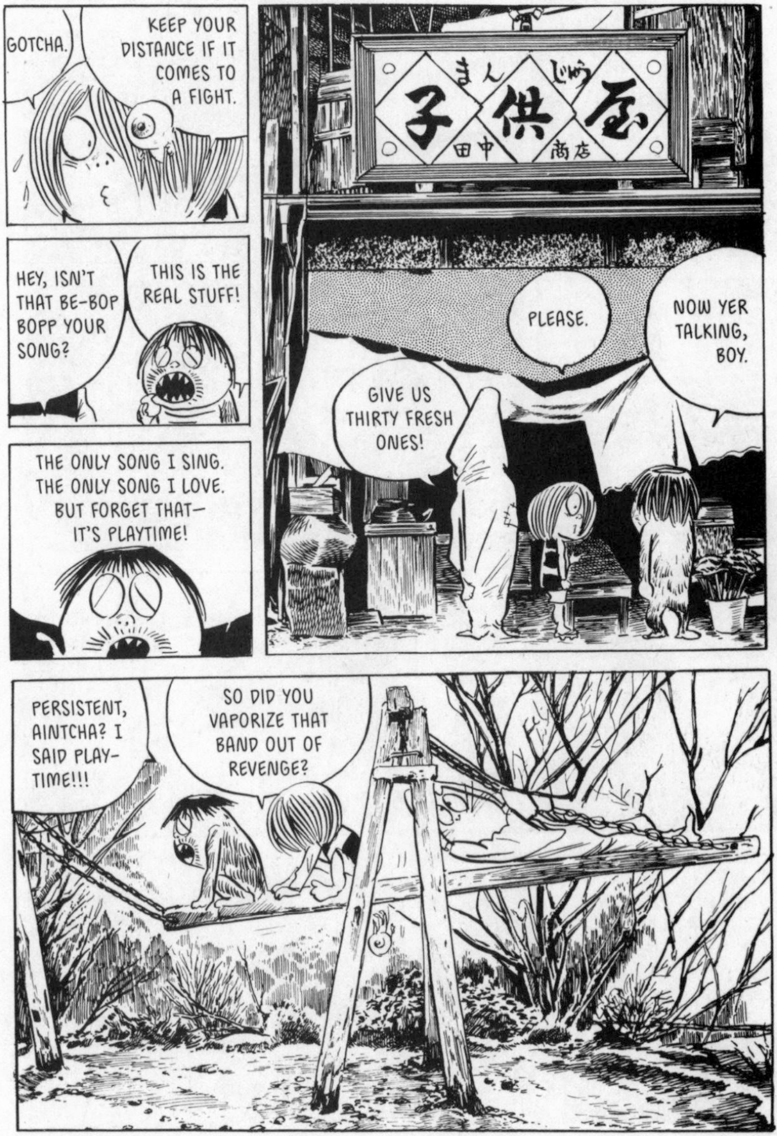
まんじゅう
子供屋
田中 商店
NOW YER TALKING, BOY.
PLEASE.
GIVE US THIRTY FRESH ONES!
KEEP YOUR DISTANCE IF IT COMES TO A FIGHT.
GOTCHA.
THIS IS THE REAL STUFF!
HEY, ISN'T THAT BE-BOP BOPP YOUR SONG?
THE ONLY SONG I SING. THE ONLY SONG I LOVE. BUT FORGET THAT— IT'S PLAYTIME!
SO DID YOU VAPORIZE THAT BAND OUT OF REVENGE?
PERSISTENT, AINTCHA? I SAID PLAY-TIME!!!

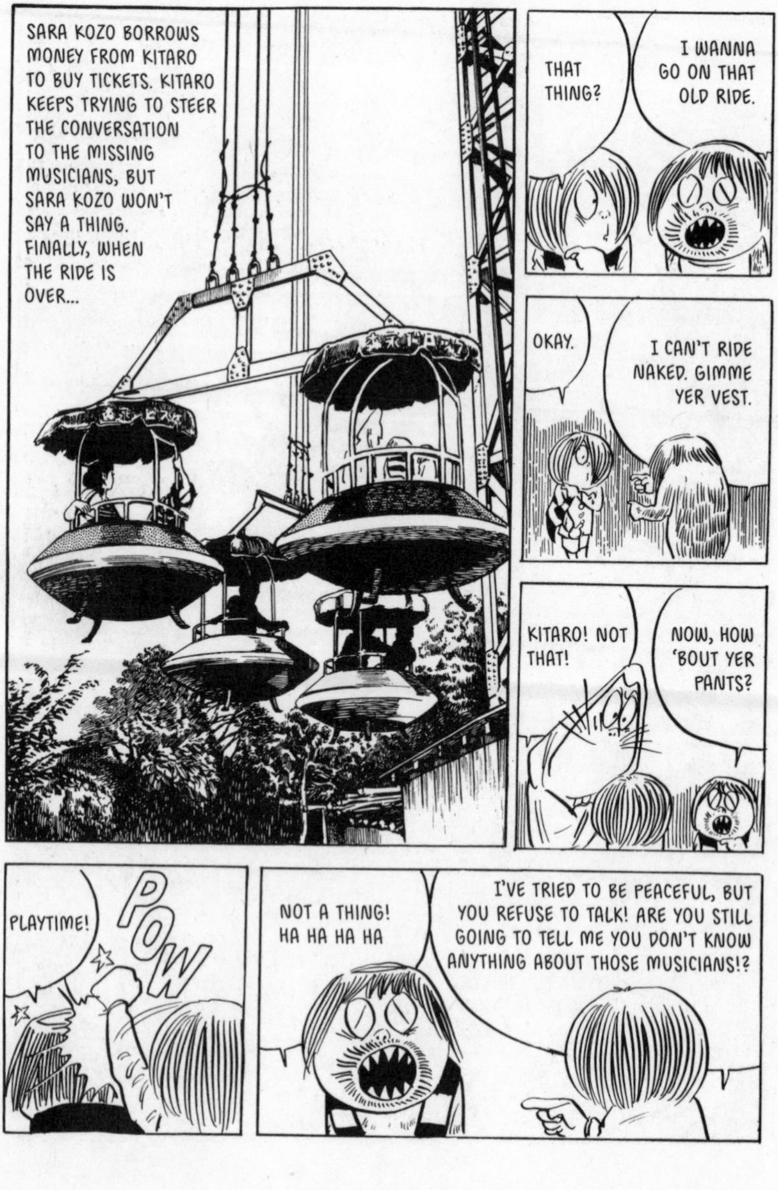
I WANNA GO ON THAT OLD RIDE.
THAT THING?
I CAN'T RIDE NAKED. GIMME YER VEST.
OKAY.
NOW, HOW 'BOUT YER PANTS?
KITARO! NOT THAT!
SARA KOZO BORROWS MONEY FROM KITARO TO BUY TICKETS. KITARO KEEPS TRYING TO STEER THE CONVERSATION TO THE MISSING MUSICIANS, BUT SARA KOZO WON'T SAY A THING. FINALLY, WHEN THE RIDE IS OVER...
I'VE TRIED TO BE PEACEFUL, BUT YOU REFUSE TO TALK! ARE YOU STILL GOING TO TELL ME YOU DON'T KNOW ANYTHING ABOUT THOSE MUSICIANS!?
NOT A THING! HA HA HA HA
POW
PLAYTIME!

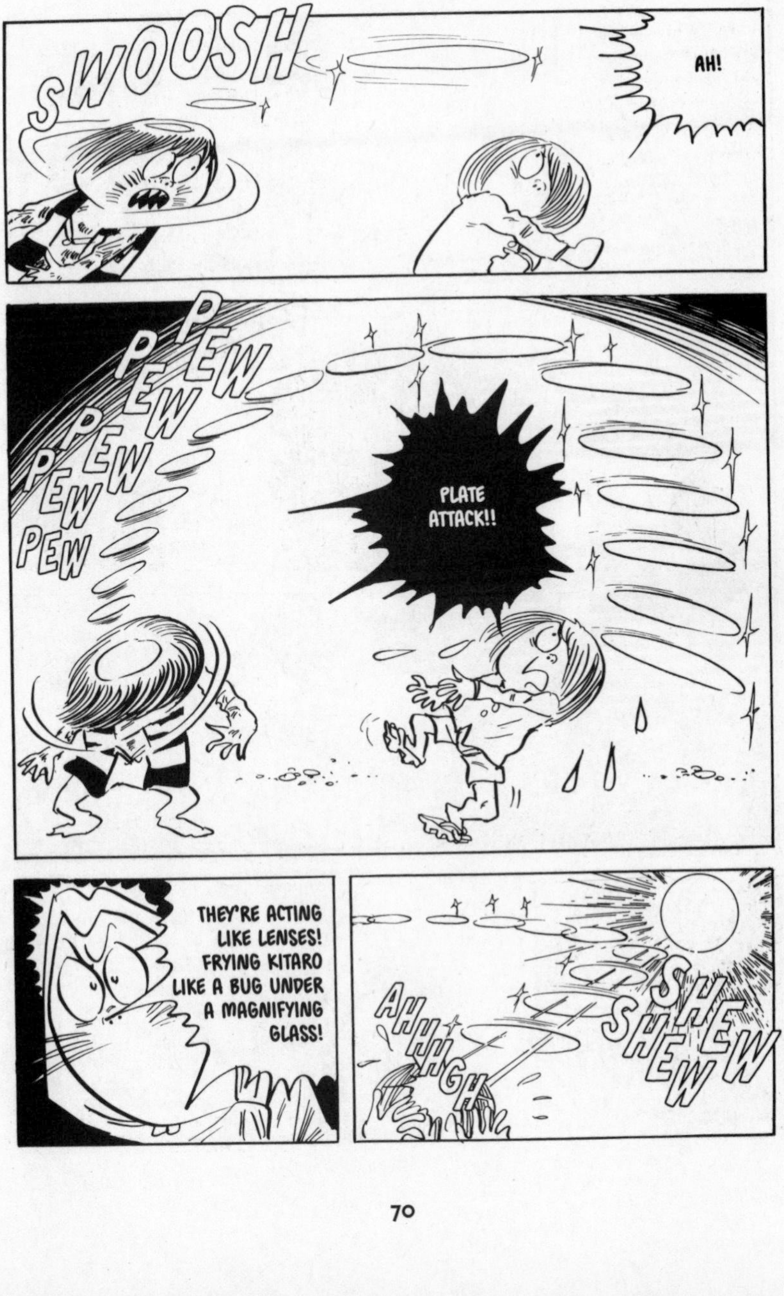
AH!
SWOOSH
PLATE ATTACK!!
PEW PEW PEW PEW PEW
SHEW SHEW
AHHHGH
THEY'RE ACTING LIKE LENSES! FRYING KITARO LIKE A BUG UNDER A MAGNIFYING GLASS!

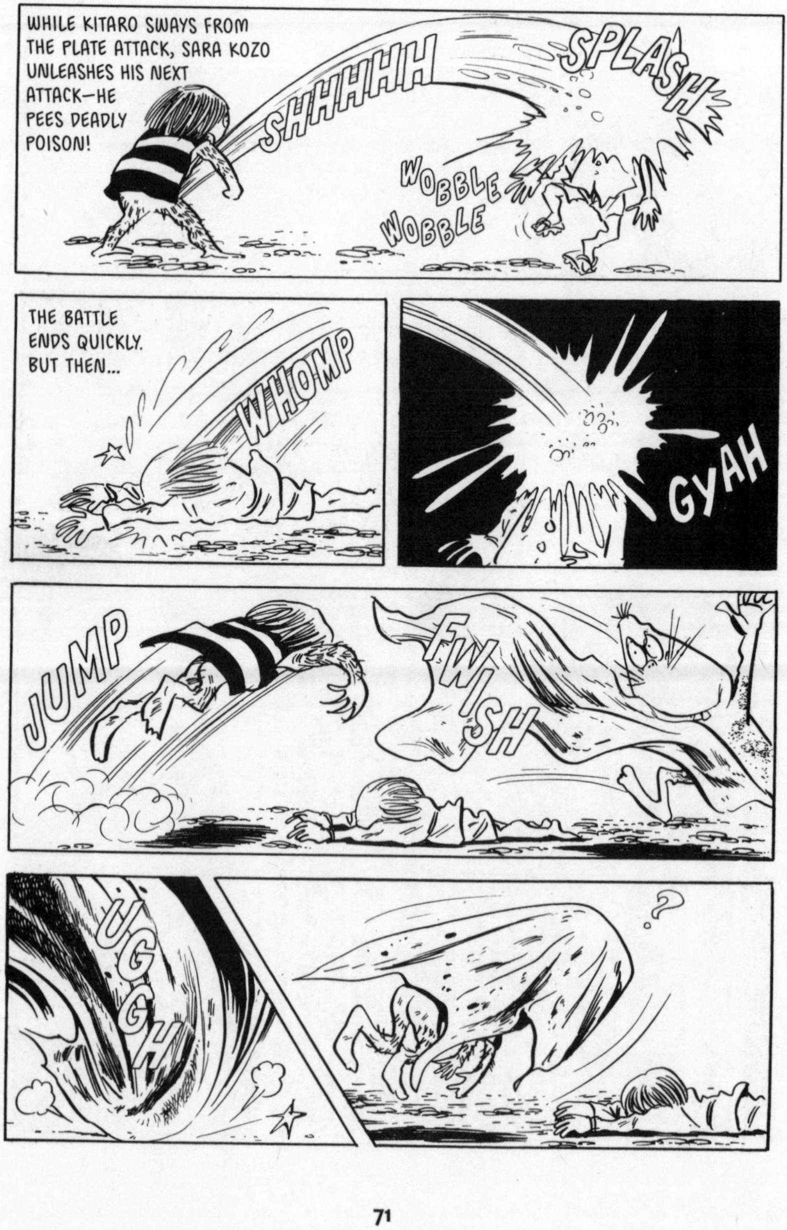
SPLASH
SHHHHHH
WHILE KITARO SWAYS FROM THE PLATE ATTACK, SARA KOZO UNLEASHES HIS NEXT ATTACK—HE PEES DEADLY POISON!
WOBBLE WOBBLE
GYAH
THE BATTLE ENDS QUICKLY. BUT THEN...
WHOMP
FWISH
JUMP
?
UGGH

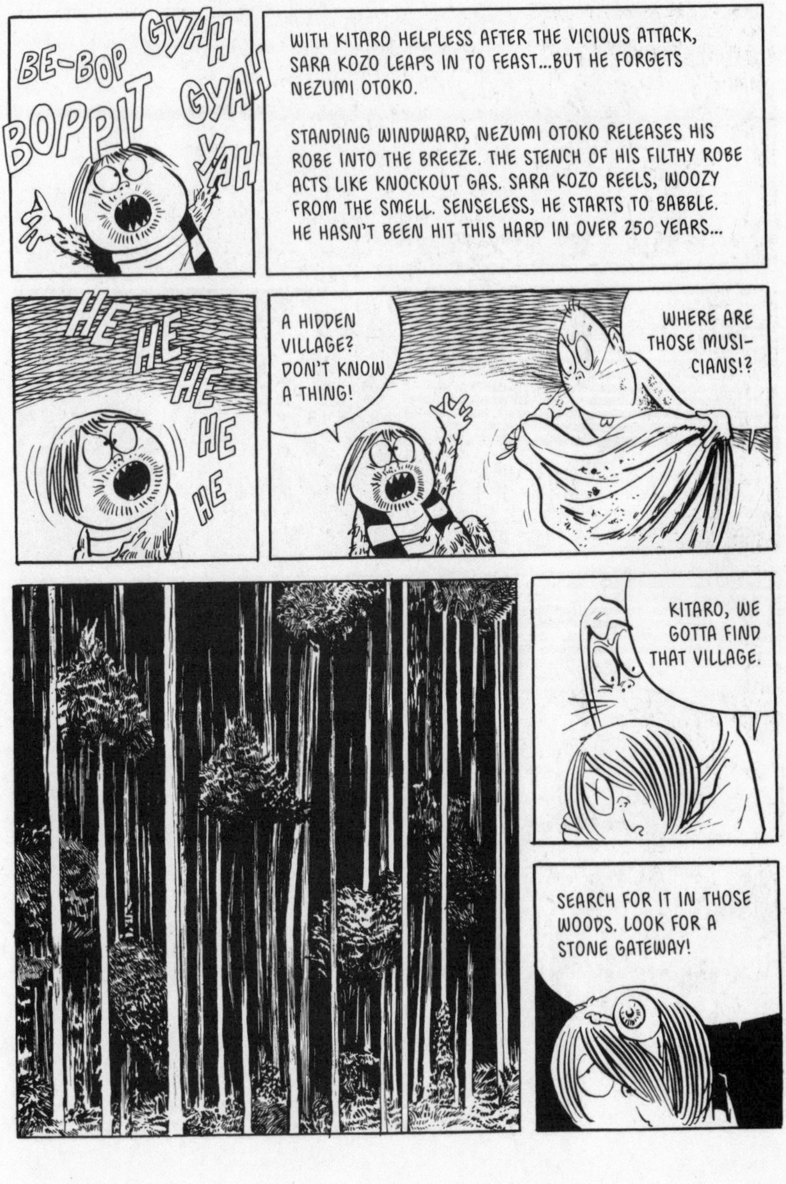
WITH KITARO HELPLESS AFTER THE VICIOUS ATTACK, SARA KOZO LEAPS IN TO FEAST...BUT HE FORGETS NEZUMI OTOKO.
STANDING WINDWARD, NEZUMI OTOKO RELEASES HIS ROBE INTO THE BREEZE. THE STENCH OF HIS FILTHY ROBE ACTS LIKE KNOCKOUT GAS. SARA KOZO REELS, WOOZY FROM THE SMELL. SENSELESS, HE STARTS TO BABBLE. HE HASN'T BEEN HIT THIS HARD IN OVER 250 YEARS...
GYAH
GYAH
YAH
BE-BOP
BOPPIT
WHERE ARE THOSE MUSICIANS!?
A HIDDEN VILLAGE? DON'T KNOW A THING!
HE HE HE HE HE
KITARO, WE GOTTA FIND THAT VILLAGE.
SEARCH FOR IT IN THOSE WOODS. LOOK FOR A STONE GATEWAY!

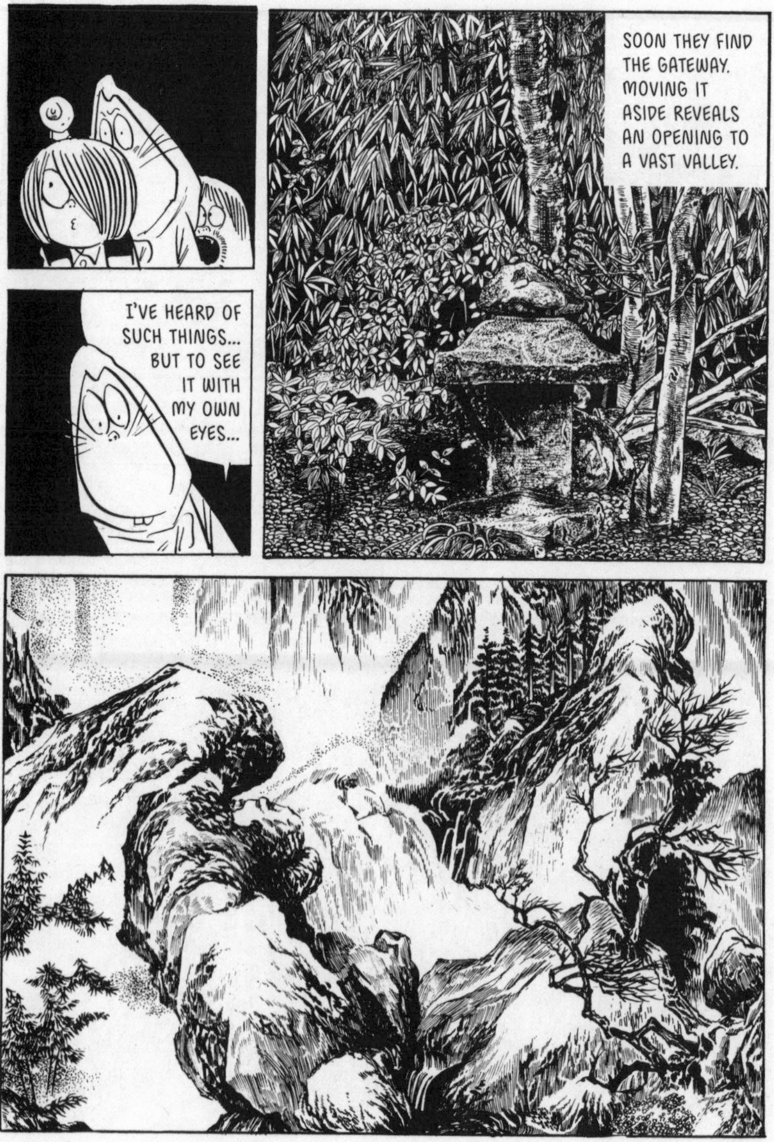
SOON THEY FIND THE GATEWAY. MOVING IT ASIDE REVEALS AN OPENING TO A VAST VALLEY.
I'VE HEARD OF SUCH THINGS... BUT TO SEE IT WITH MY OWN EYES...

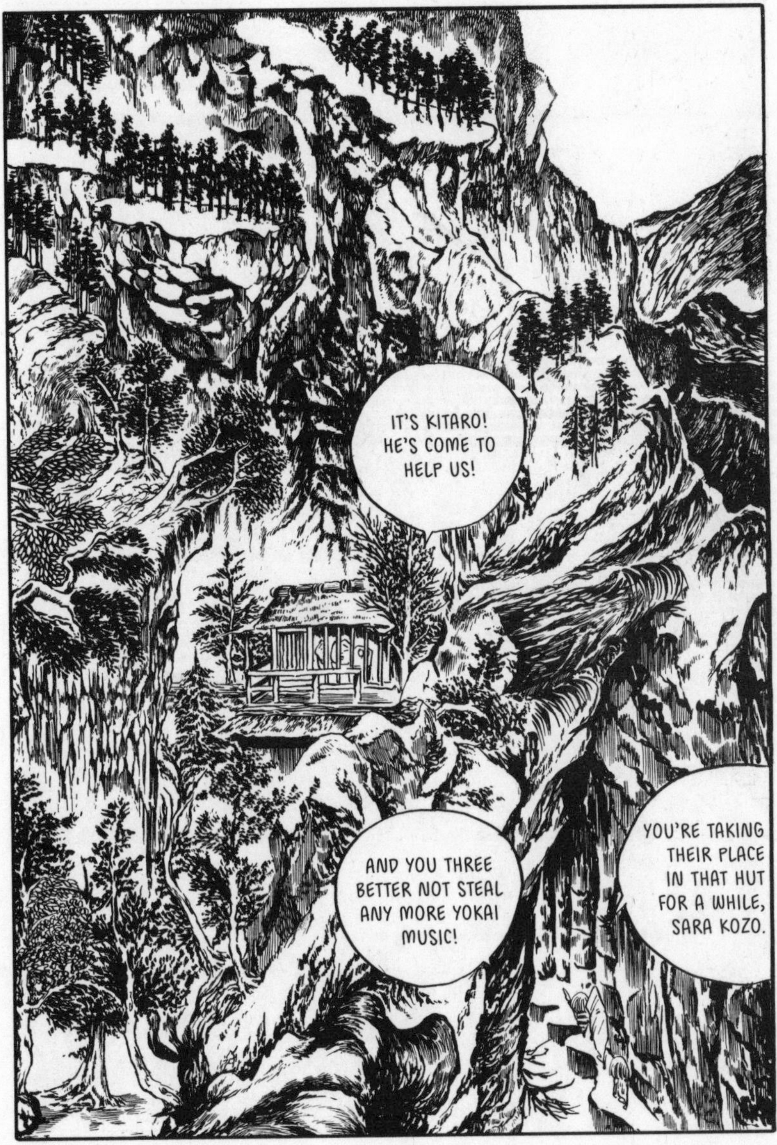
IT'S KITARO! HE'S COME TO HELP US!
YOU'RE TAKING THEIR PLACE IN THAT HUT FOR A WHILE, SARA KOZO.
AND YOU THREE BETTER NOT STEAL ANY MORE YOKAI MUSIC!

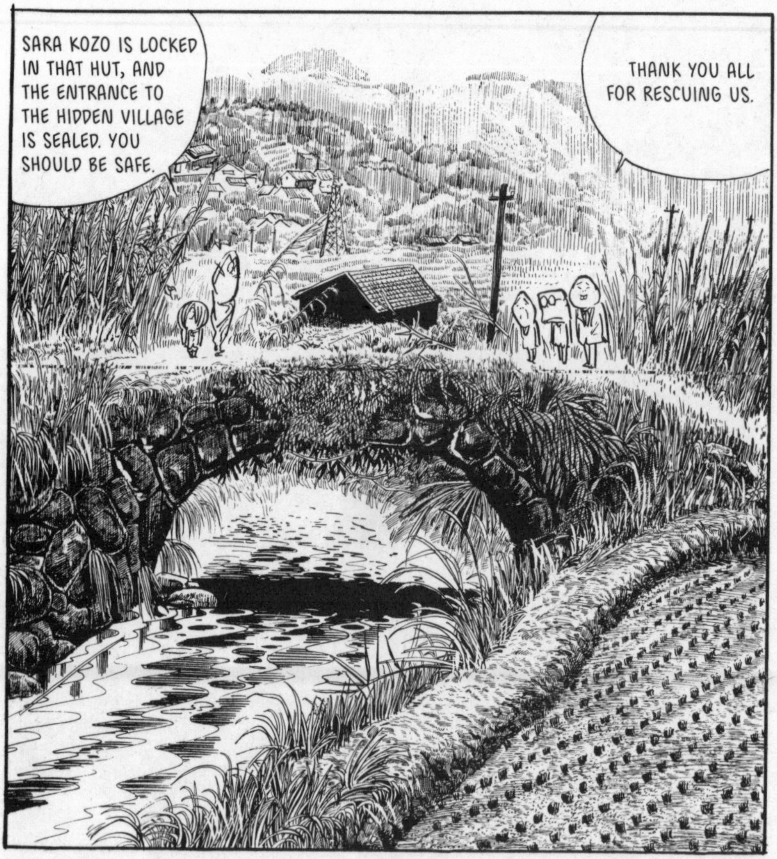
THANK YOU ALL FOR RESCUING US.
SARA KOZO IS LOCKED IN THAT HUT, AND THE ENTRANCE TO THE HIDDEN VILLAGE IS SEALED. YOU SHOULD BE SAFE.

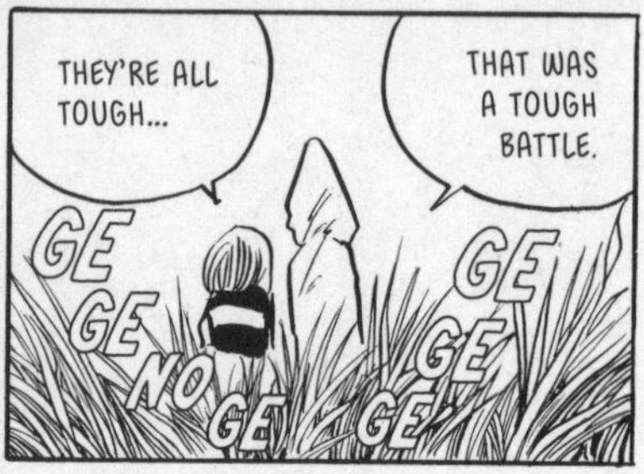
THAT WAS A TOUGH BATTLE.
THEY'RE ALL TOUGH...
GE GE GE
GE GE NO GE

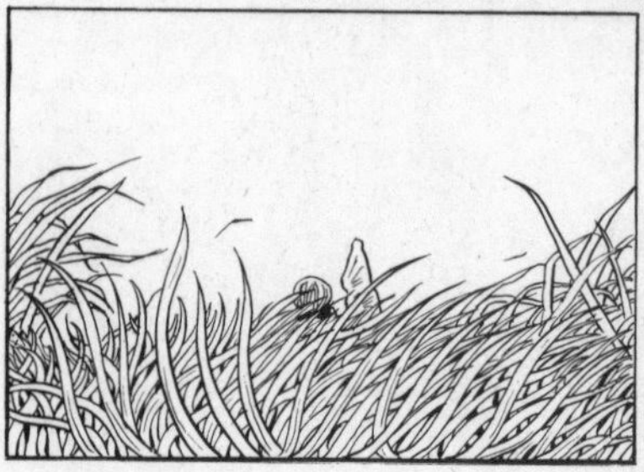

DIAMOND YOKAI

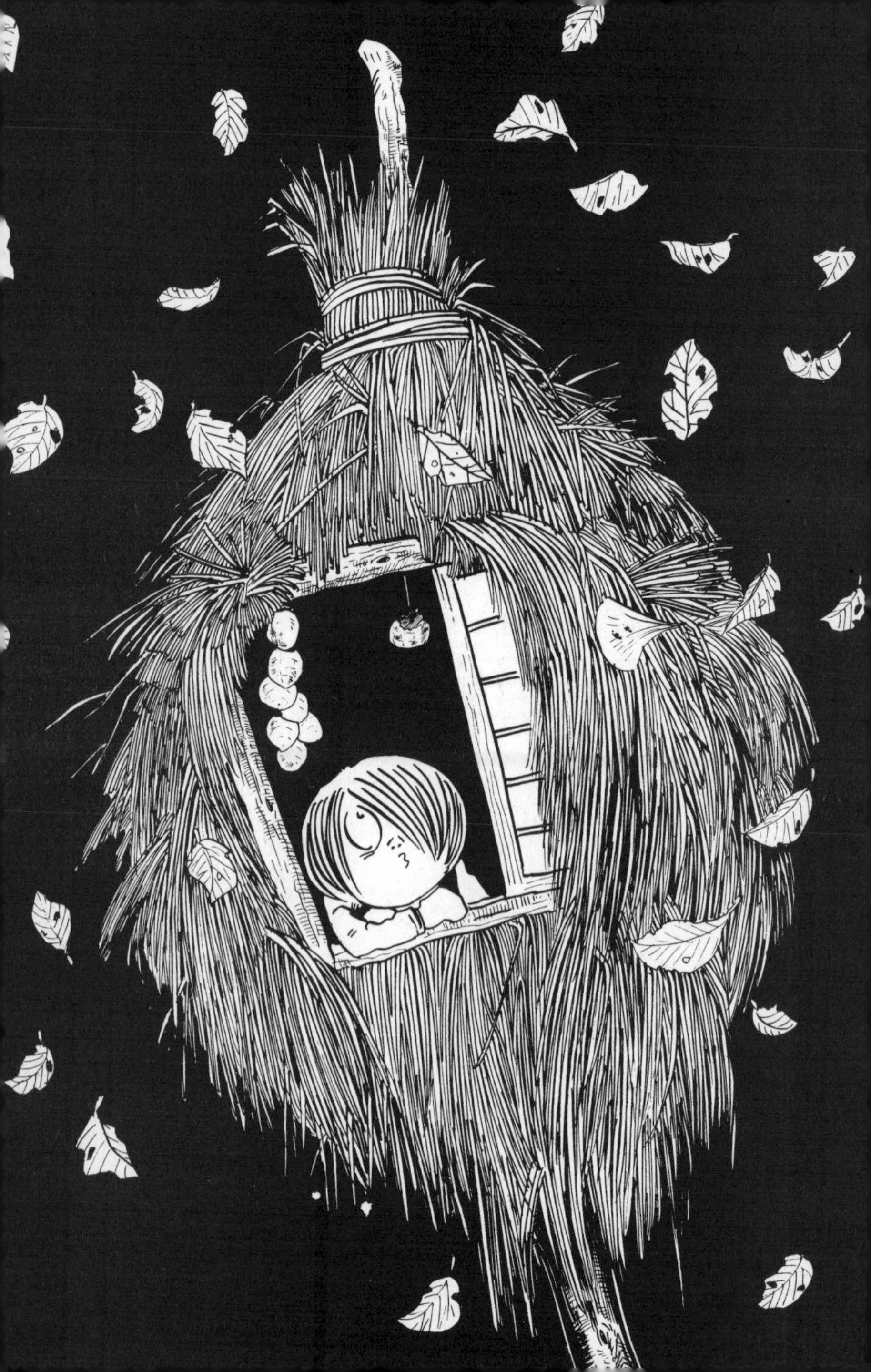

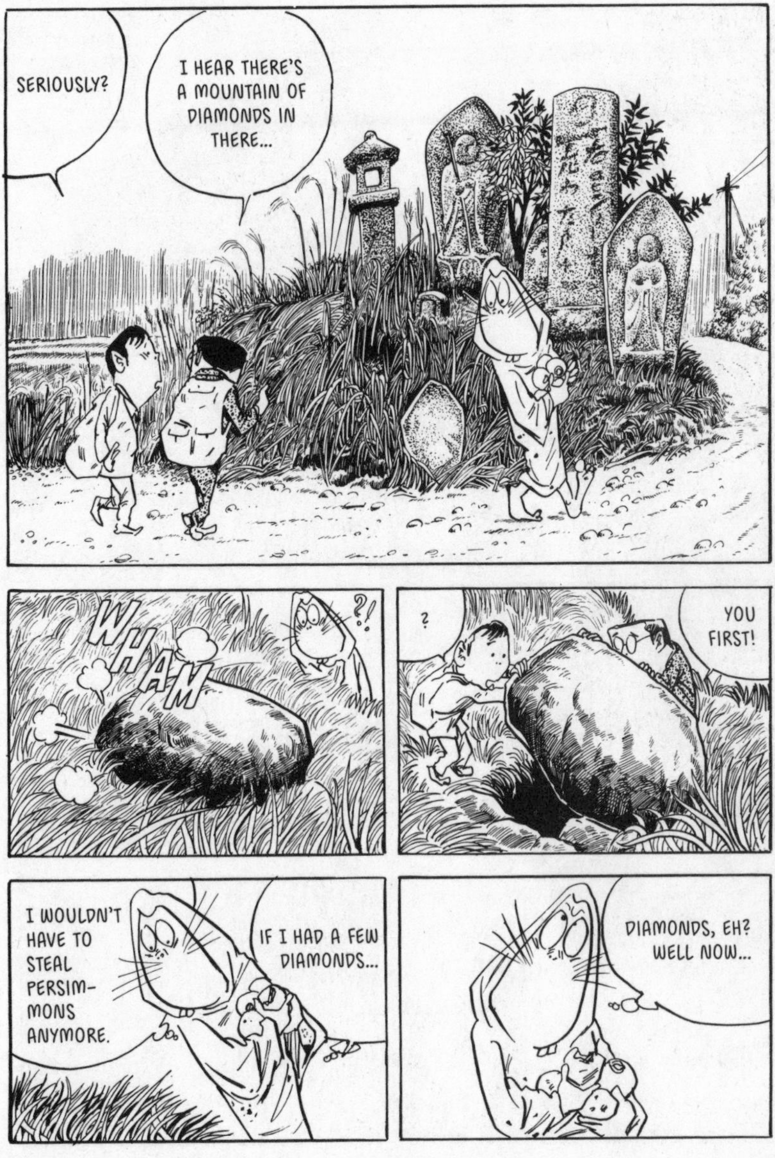
I HEAR THERE'S A MOUNTAIN OF DIAMONDS IN THERE...
SERIOUSLY?
YOU FIRST!
?
?!
WHAM
DIAMONDS, EH? WELL NOW...
IF I HAD A FEW DIAMONDS...
I WOULDN'T HAVE TO STEAL PERSIMMONS ANYMORE.

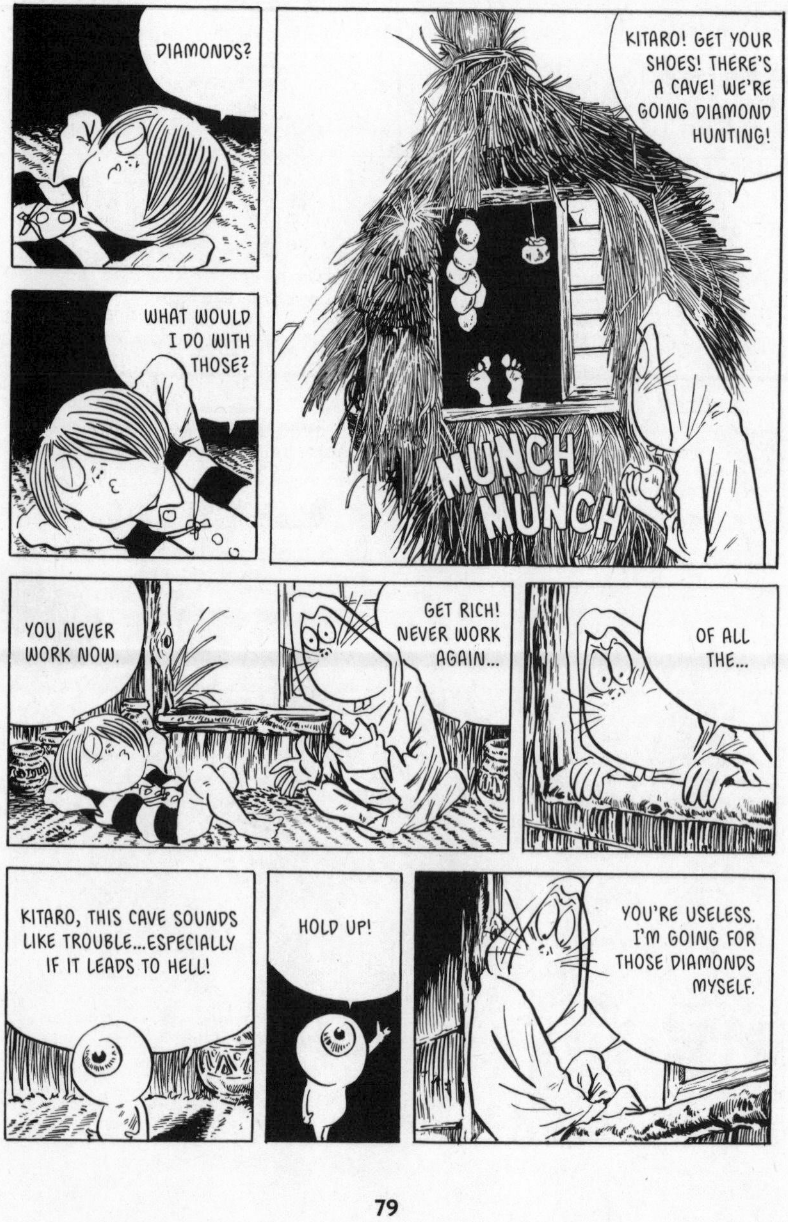
KITARO! GET YOUR SHOES! THERE'S A CAVE! WE'RE GOING DIAMOND HUNTING!
MUNCH MUNCH
DIAMONDS?
WHAT WOULD I DO WITH THOSE?
OF ALL THE...
GET RICH! NEVER WORK AGAIN...
YOU NEVER WORK NOW.
YOU'RE USELESS. I'M GOING FOR THOSE DIAMONDS MYSELF.
HOLD UP!
KITARO, THIS CAVE SOUNDS LIKE TROUBLE...ESPECIALLY IF IT LEADS TO HELL!

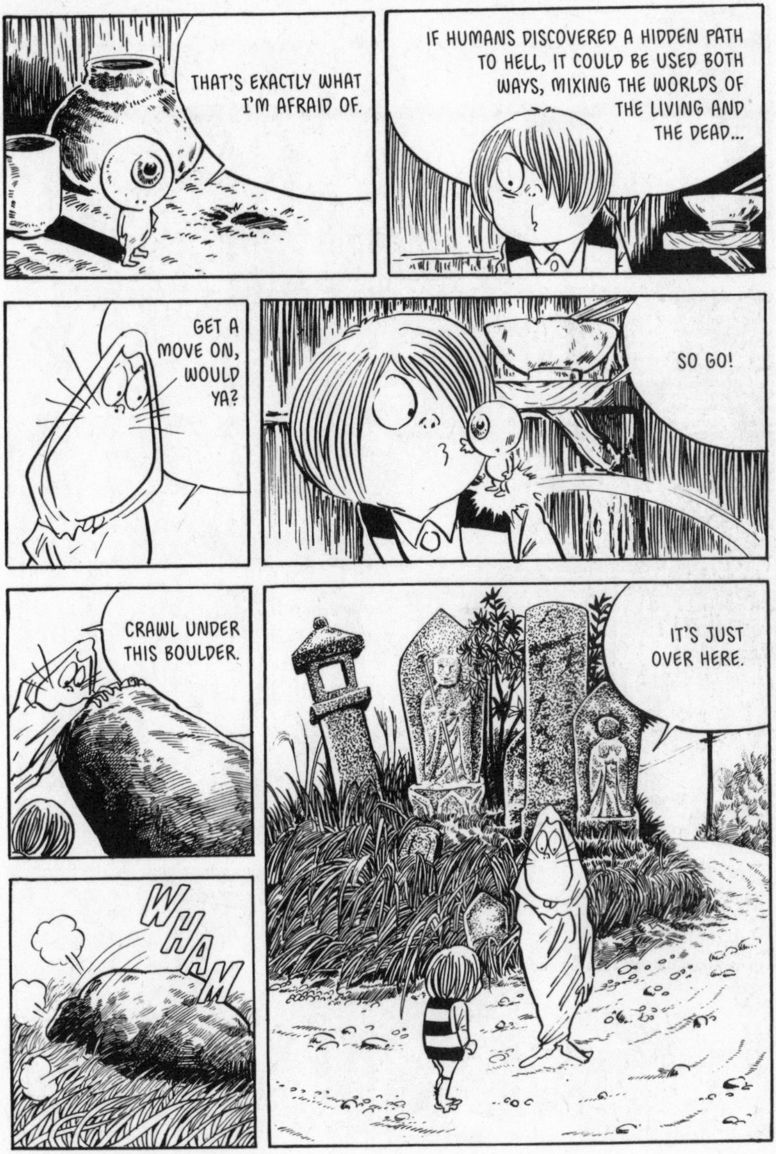
IF HUMANS DISCOVERED A HIDDEN PATH TO HELL, IT COULD BE USED BOTH WAYS, MIXING THE WORLDS OF THE LIVING AND THE DEAD...
THAT'S EXACTLY WHAT I'M AFRAID OF.
SO GO!
GET A MOVE ON, WOULD YA?
IT'S JUST OVER HERE.
CRAWL UNDER THIS BOULDER.
WHAM

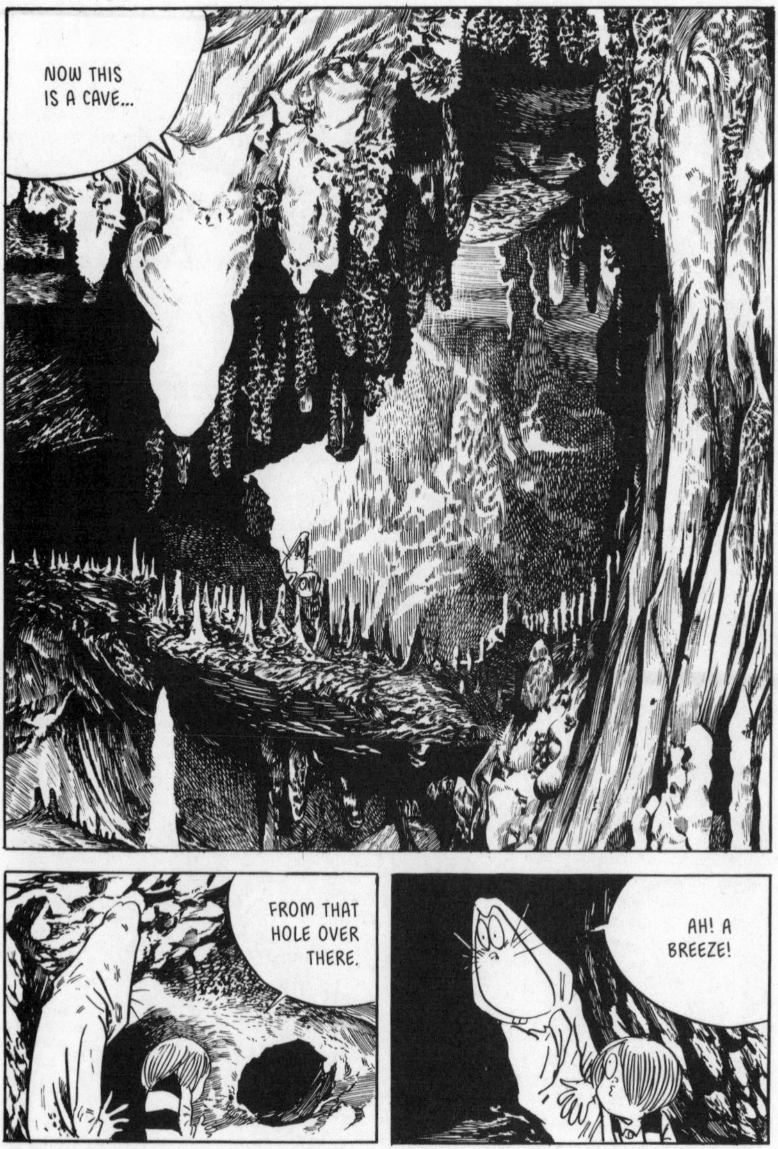
NOW THIS IS A CAVE...
AH! A BREEZE!
FROM THAT HOLE OVER THERE.

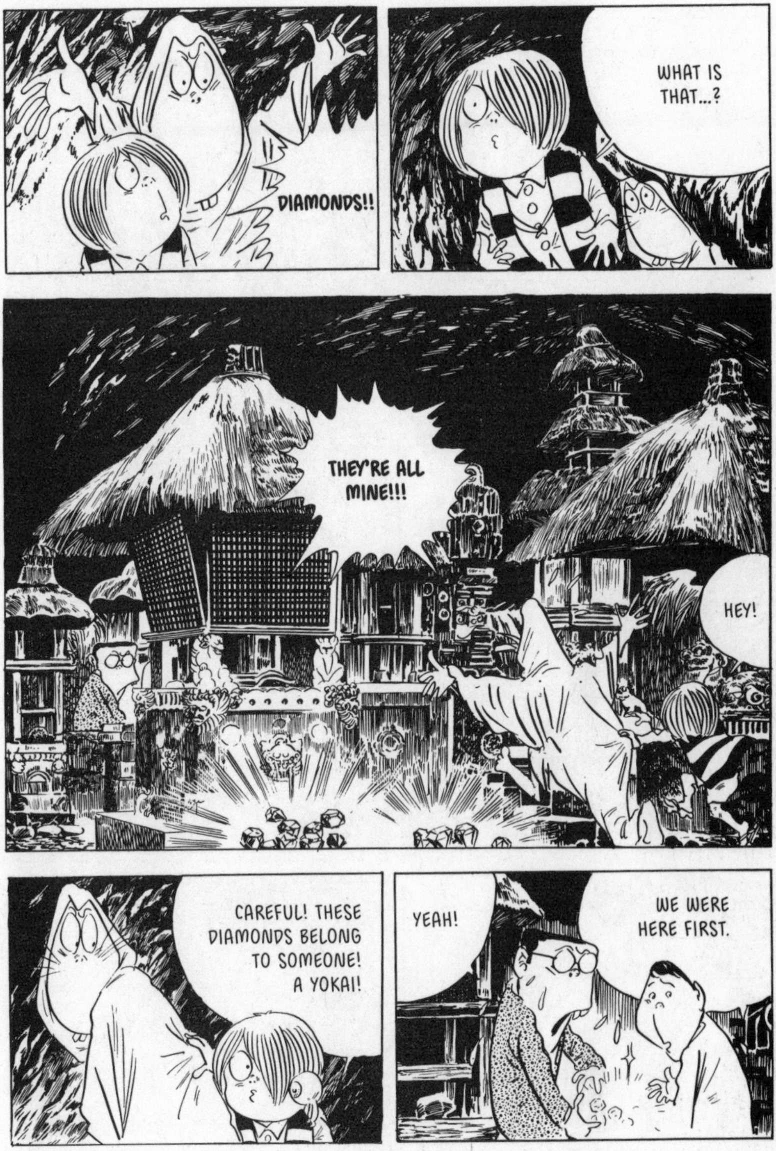
WHAT IS THAT...?
DIAMONDS!!
THEY'RE ALL MINE!!!
HEY!
WE WERE HERE FIRST.
YEAH!
CAREFUL! THESE DIAMONDS BELONG TO SOMEONE! A YOKAI!

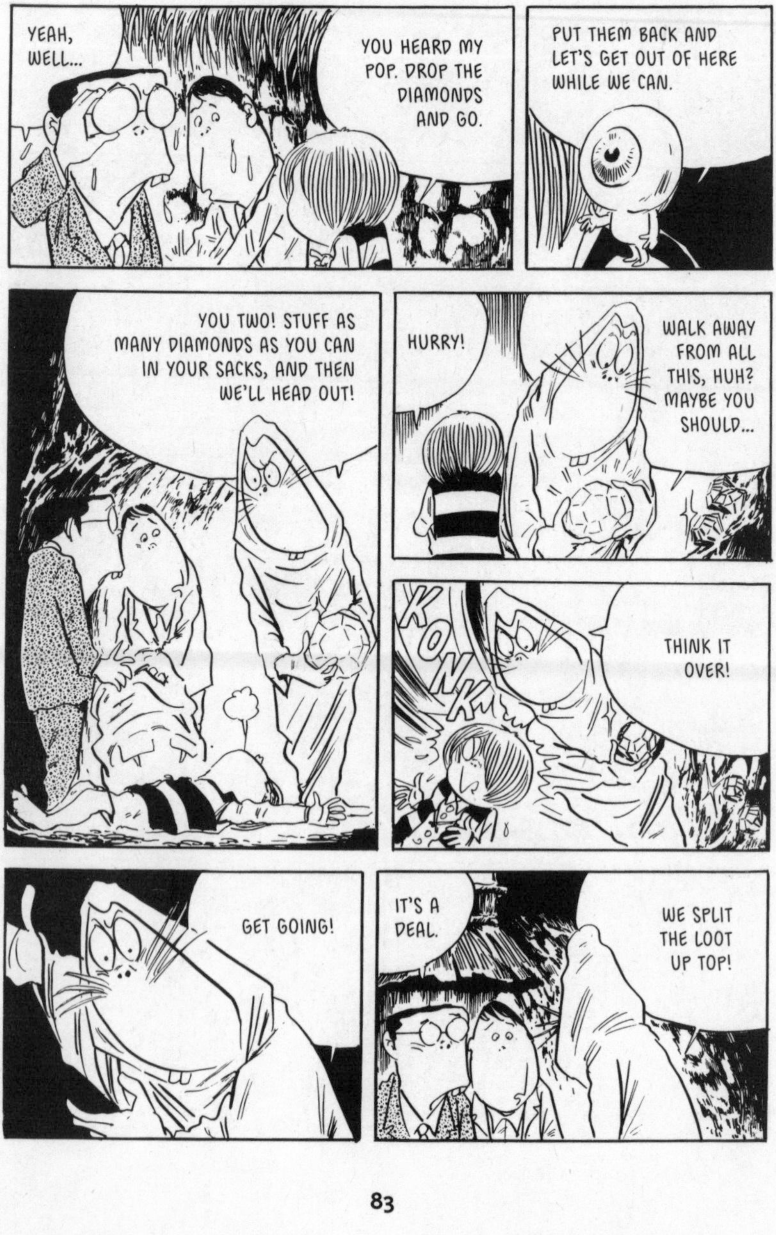
PUT THEM BACK AND LET'S GET OUT OF HERE WHILE WE CAN.
YOU HEARD MY POP. DROP THE DIAMONDS AND GO.
YEAH, WELL...
WALK AWAY FROM ALL THIS, HUH? MAYBE YOU SHOULD...
HURRY!
THINK IT OVER!
KONK
YOU TWO! STUFF AS MANY DIAMONDS AS YOU CAN IN YOUR SACKS, AND THEN WE'LL HEAD OUT!
WE SPLIT THE LOOT UP TOP!
IT'S A DEAL.
GET GOING!

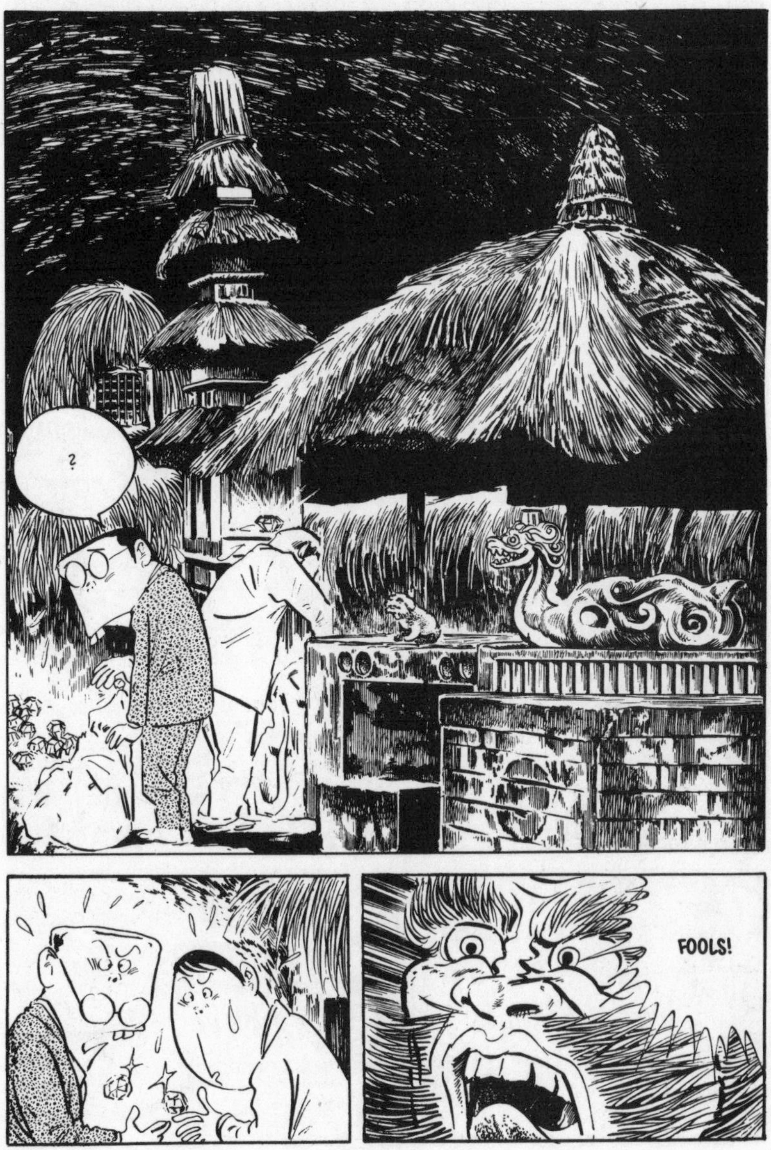
?
FOOLS!

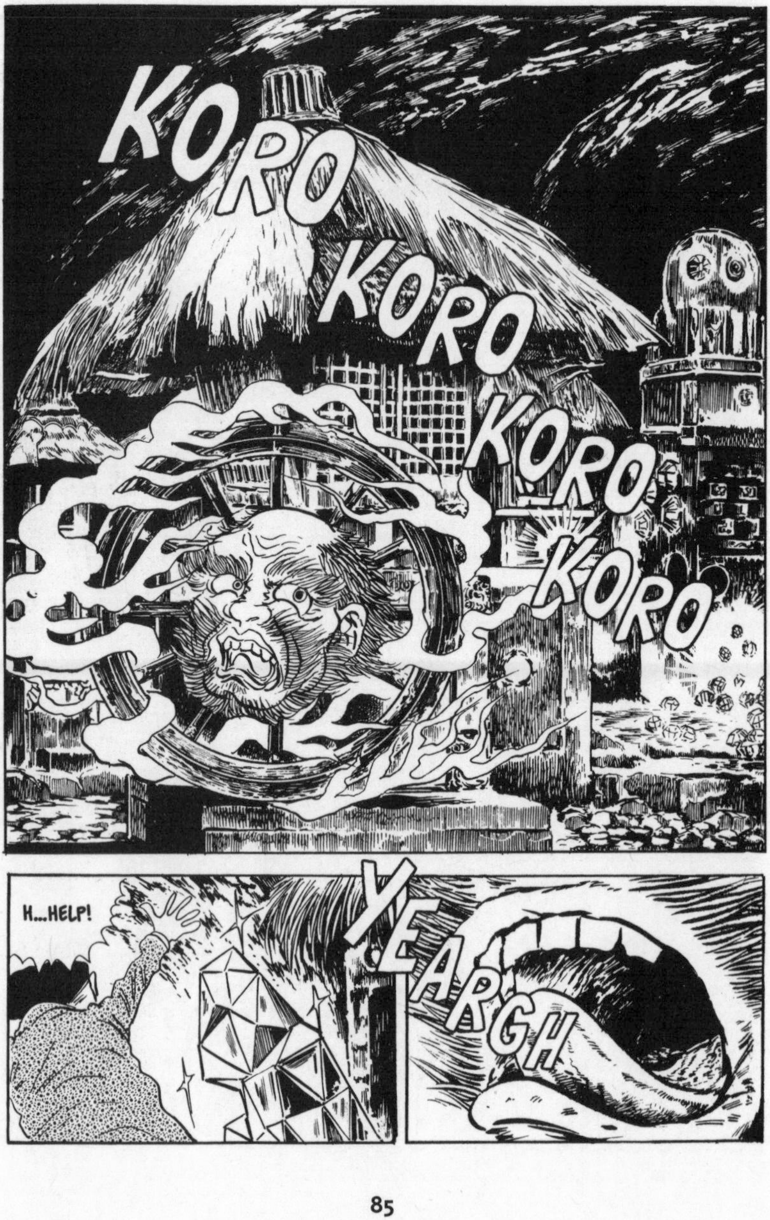
KORO
KORO
KORO
KORO
YEARGH
H...HELP!

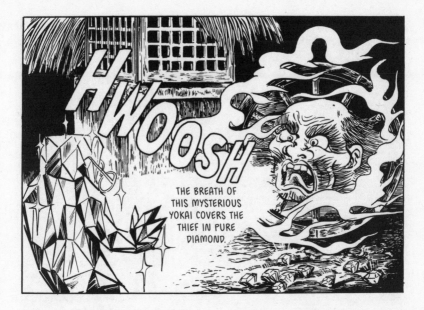

HWOOSH

THE BREATH OF
THIS MYSTERIOUS
YOKAI COVERS THE
THIEF IN PURE
DIAMOND.

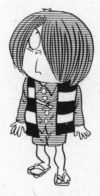

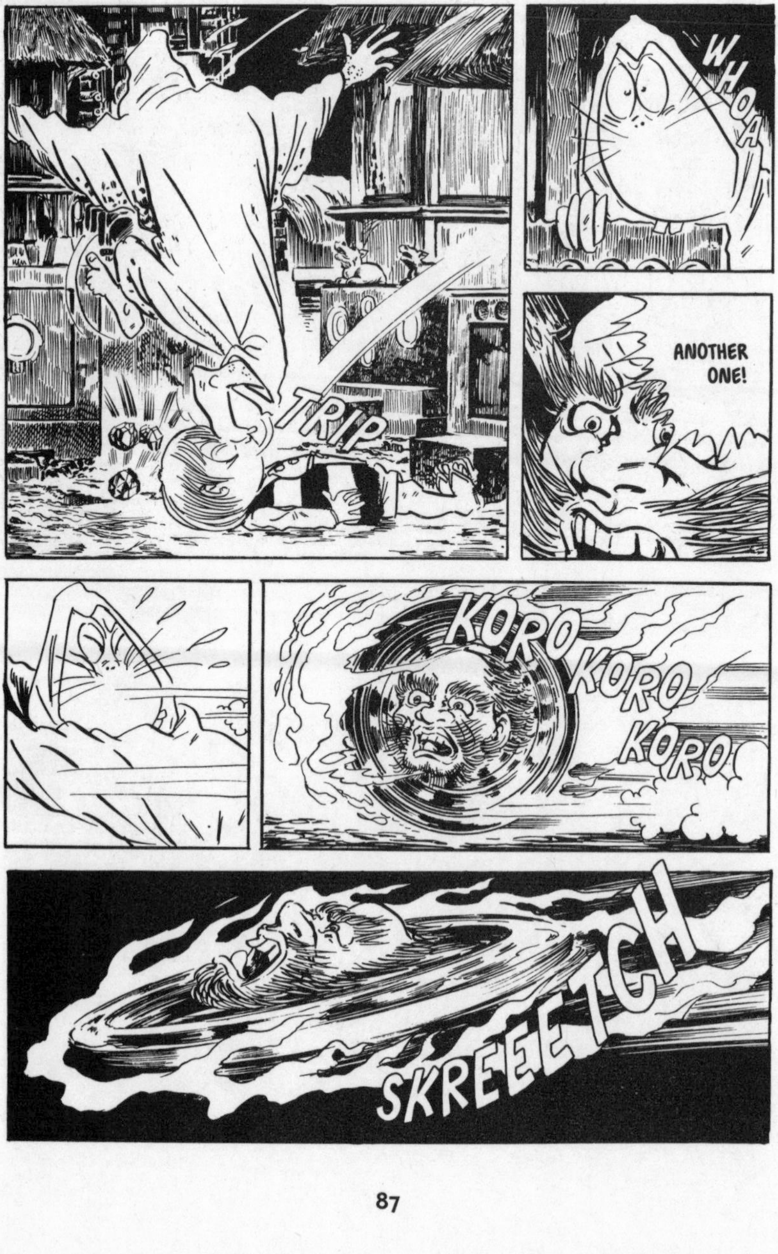
WHOA
ANOTHER ONE!
TRIP
KORO KORO KORO
SKREEETCH

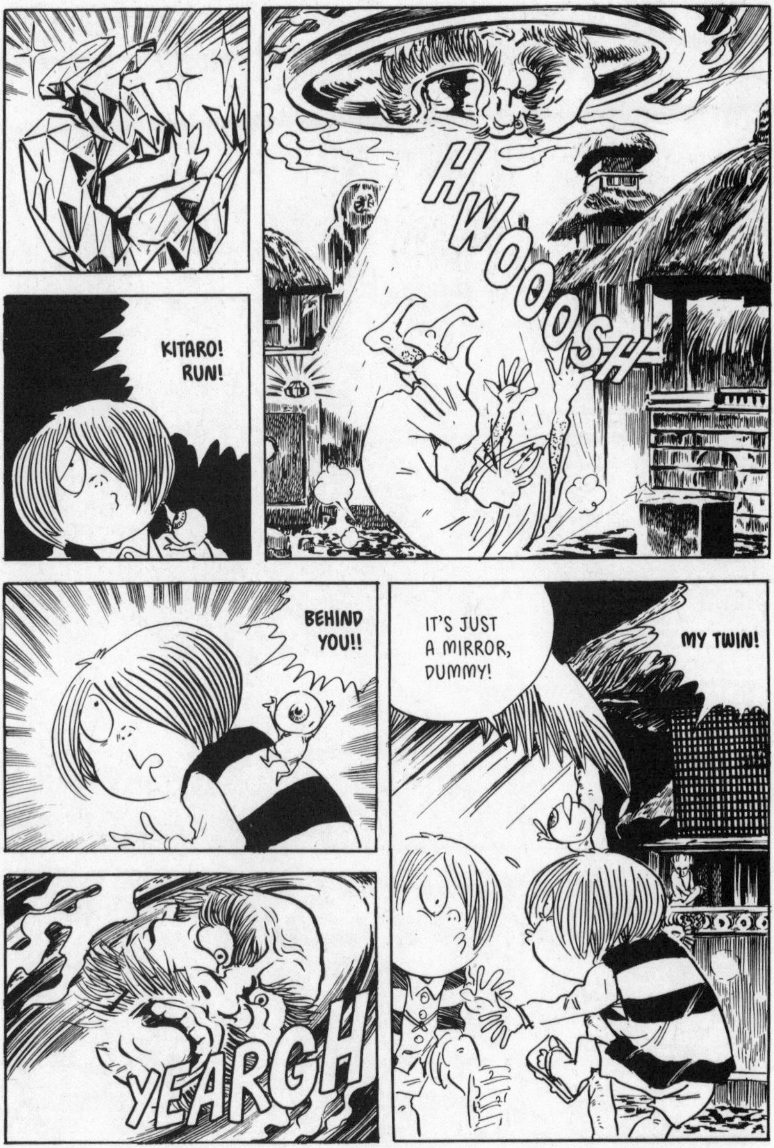
HWOOOSH
KITARO! RUN!
MY TWIN!
IT'S JUST A MIRROR, DUMMY!
BEHIND YOU!!
YEARGH

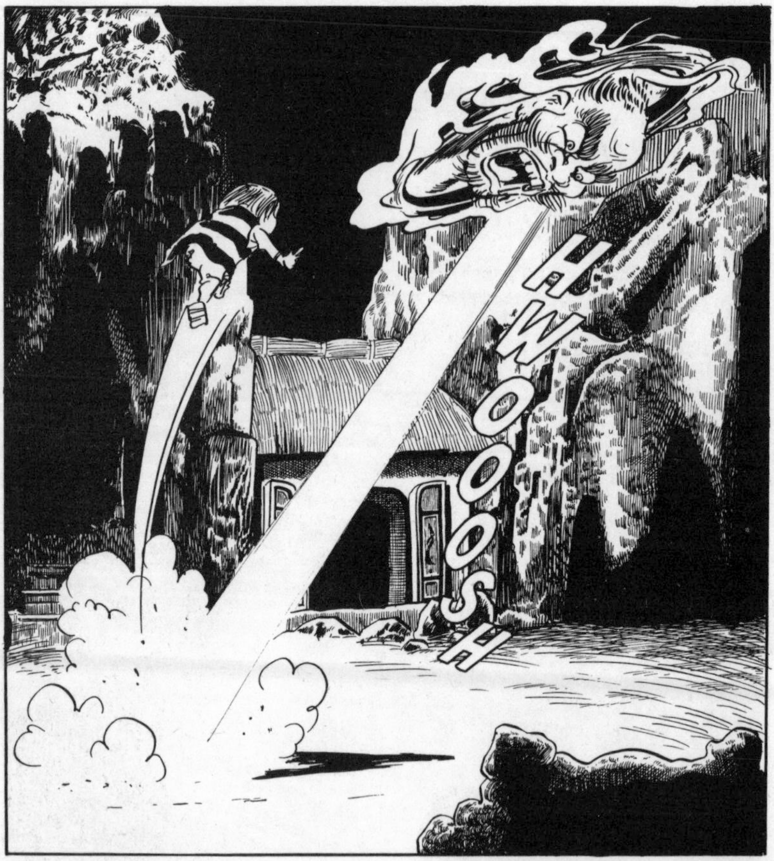
HWOOOSH

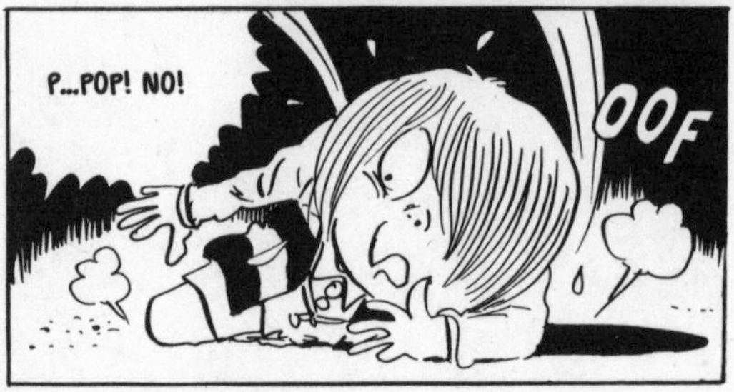
P...POP! NO!
OOF

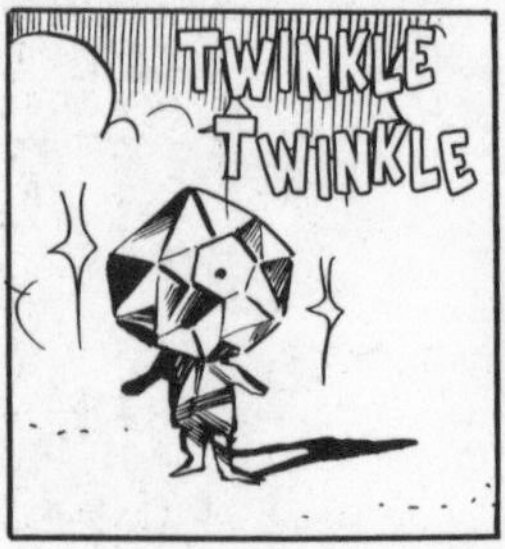
TWINKLE
TWINKLE

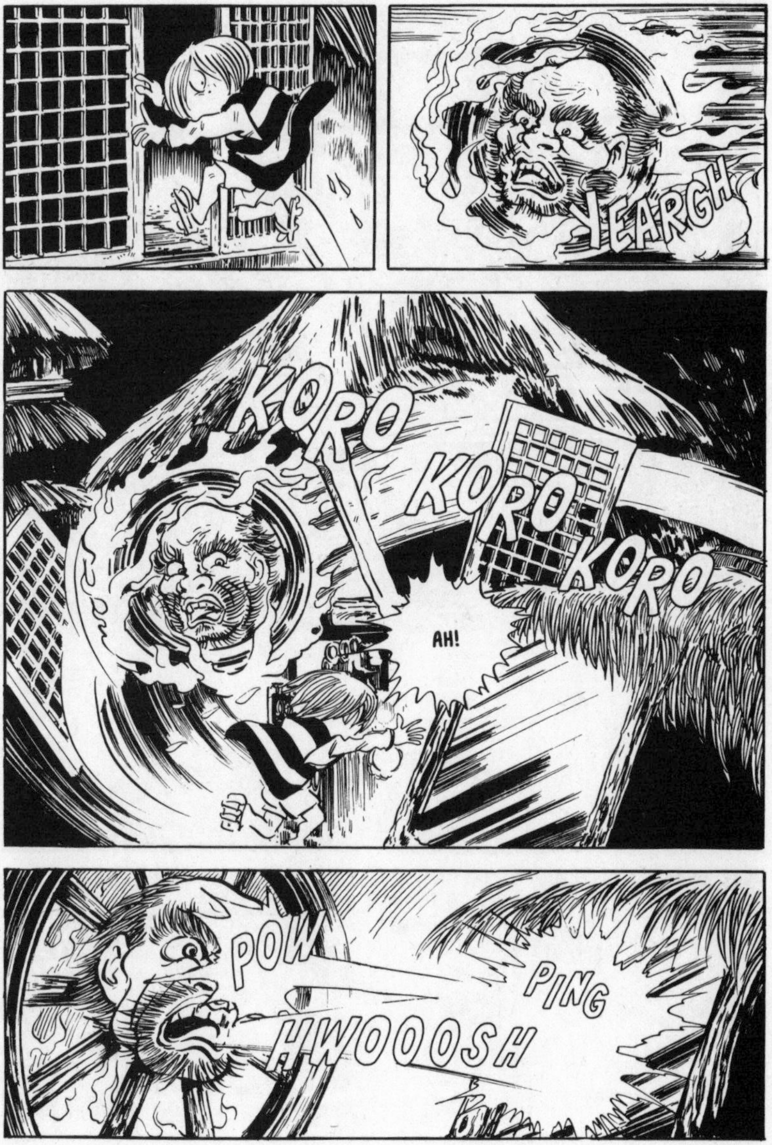
YEARGH
KORO
KORO
KORO
KORO
AH!
POW
PING
HWOOOSH

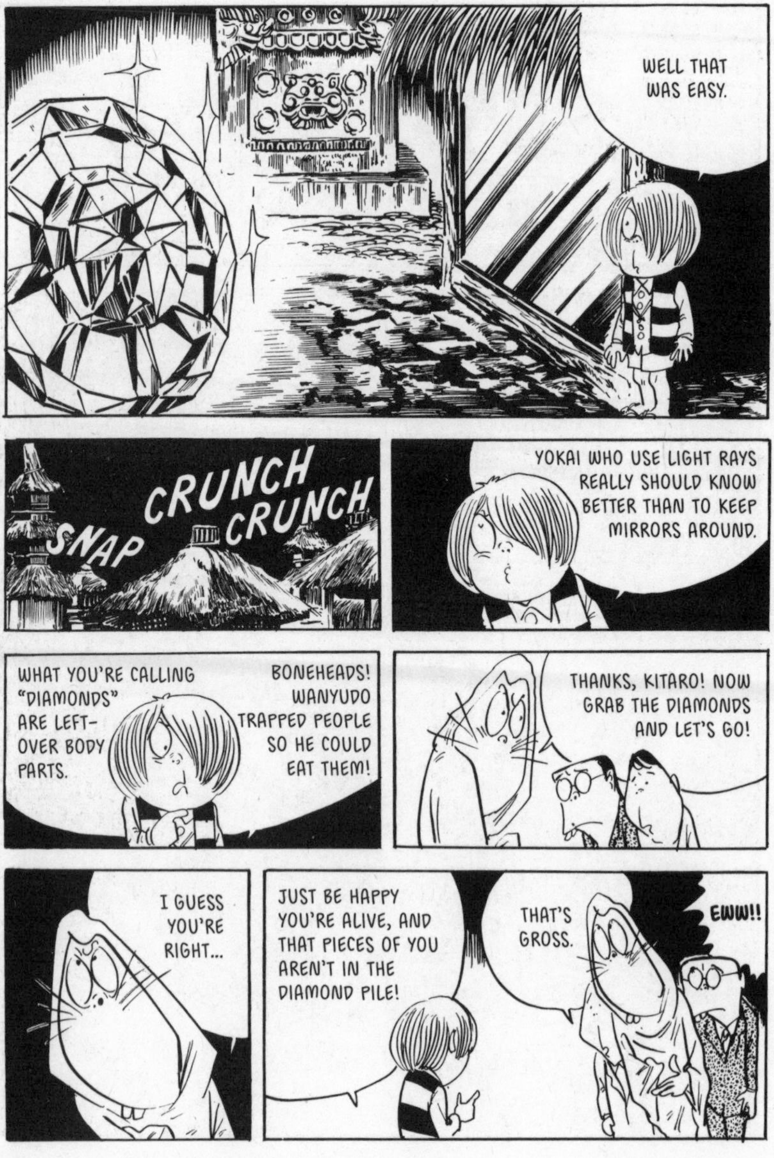
WELL THAT WAS EASY.
YOKAI WHO USE LIGHT RAYS REALLY SHOULD KNOW BETTER THAN TO KEEP MIRRORS AROUND.
CRUNCH
CRUNCH
SNAP
THANKS, KITARO! NOW GRAB THE DIAMONDS AND LET'S GO!
BONEHEADS! WANYUDO TRAPPED PEOPLE SO HE COULD EAT THEM!
WHAT YOU'RE CALLING "DIAMONDS" ARE LEFT-OVER BODY PARTS.
EWW!!
THAT'S GROSS.
JUST BE HAPPY YOU'RE ALIVE, AND THAT PIECES OF YOU AREN'T IN THE DIAMOND PILE!
I GUESS YOU'RE RIGHT...

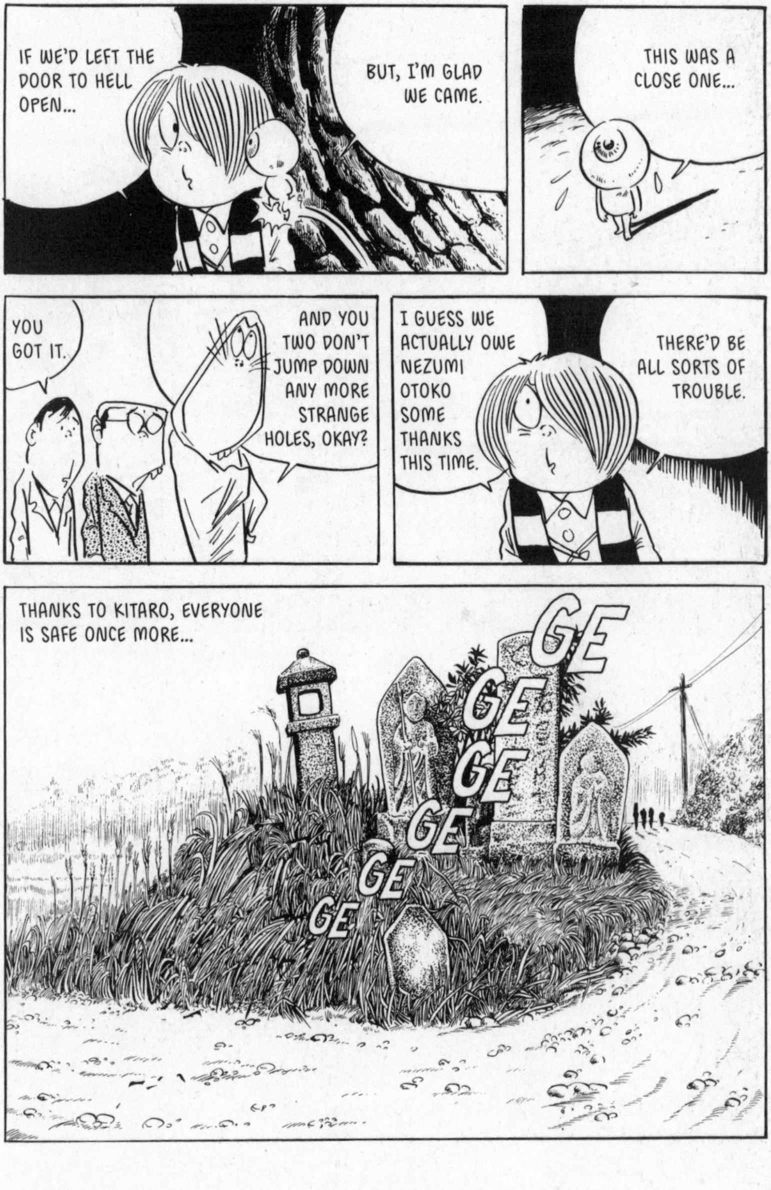
THIS WAS A CLOSE ONE...
BUT, I'M GLAD WE CAME.
IF WE'D LEFT THE DOOR TO HELL OPEN...
THERE'D BE ALL SORTS OF TROUBLE.
I GUESS WE ACTUALLY OWE NEZUMI OTOKO SOME THANKS THIS TIME.
AND YOU TWO DON'T JUMP DOWN ANY MORE STRANGE HOLES, OKAY?
YOU GOT IT.
THANKS TO KITARO, EVERYONE IS SAFE ONCE MORE...
GE GE GE GE GE GE

UMI ZATO

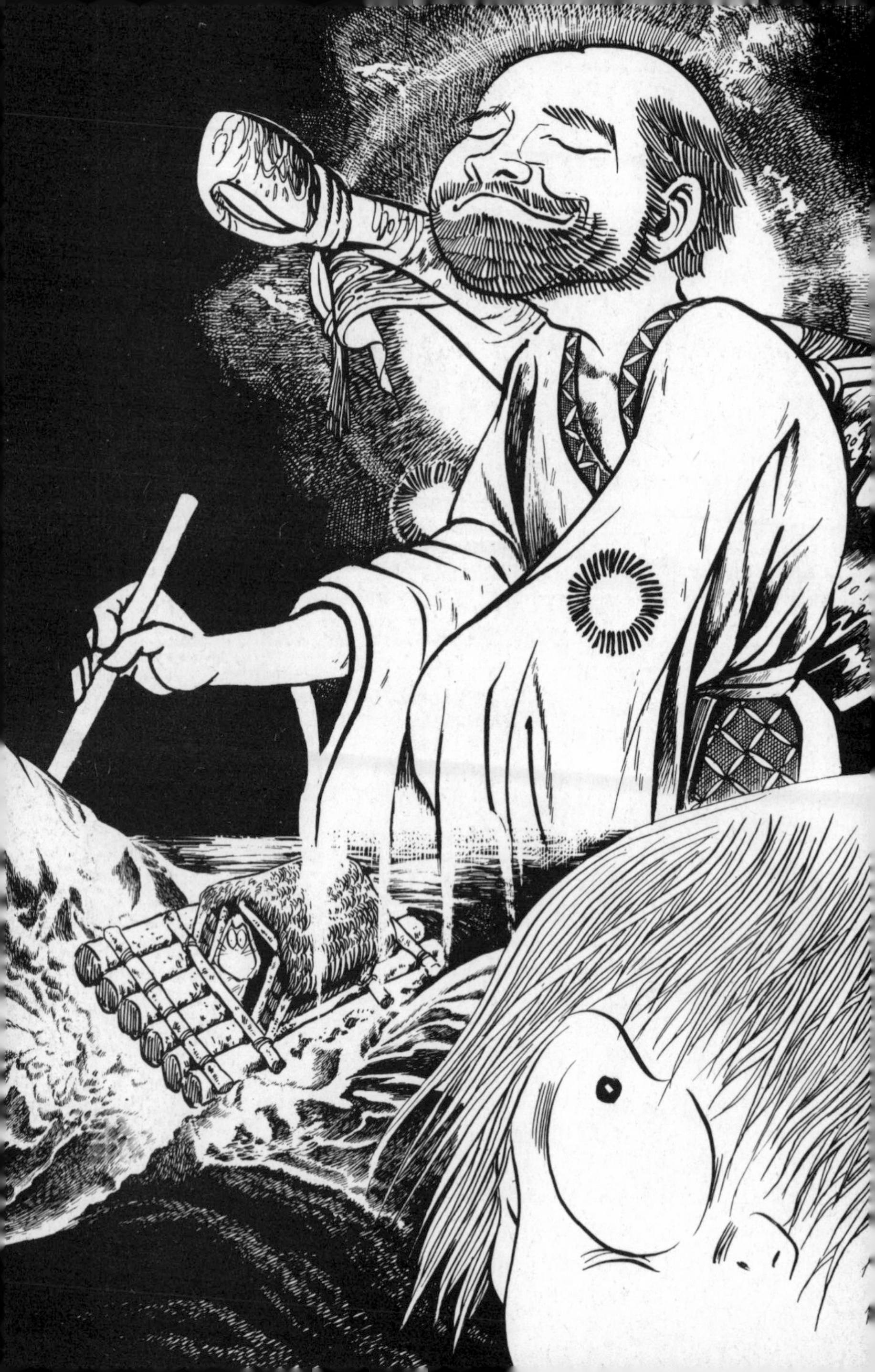

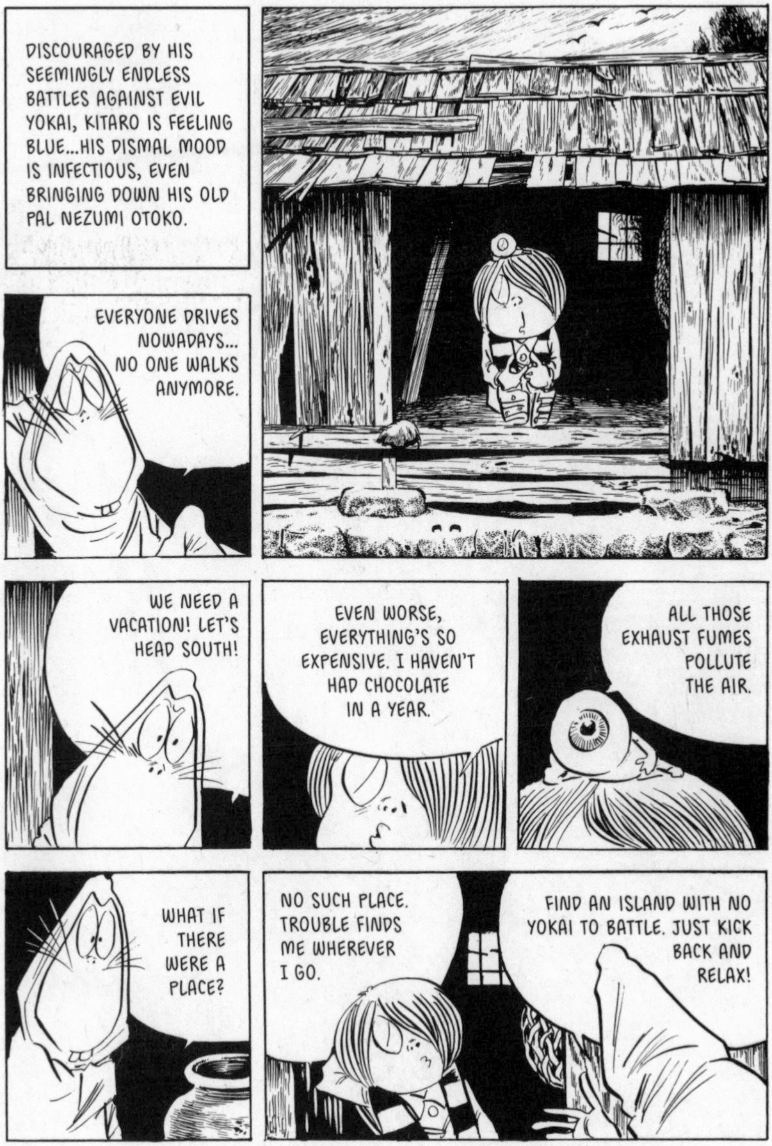

DISCOURAGED BY HIS SEEMINGLY ENDLESS BATTLES AGAINST EVIL YOKAI, KITARO IS FEELING BLUE...HIS DISMAL MOOD IS INFECTIOUS, EVEN BRINGING DOWN HIS OLD PAL NEZUMI OTOKO.
EVERYONE DRIVES NOWADAYS... NO ONE WALKS ANYMORE.
ALL THOSE EXHAUST FUMES POLLUTE THE AIR.
EVEN WORSE, EVERYTHING'S SO EXPENSIVE. I HAVEN'T HAD CHOCOLATE IN A YEAR.
WE NEED A VACATION! LET'S HEAD SOUTH!
FIND AN ISLAND WITH NO YOKAI TO BATTLE. JUST KICK BACK AND RELAX!
NO SUCH PLACE. TROUBLE FINDS ME WHEREVER I GO.
WHAT IF THERE WERE A PLACE?

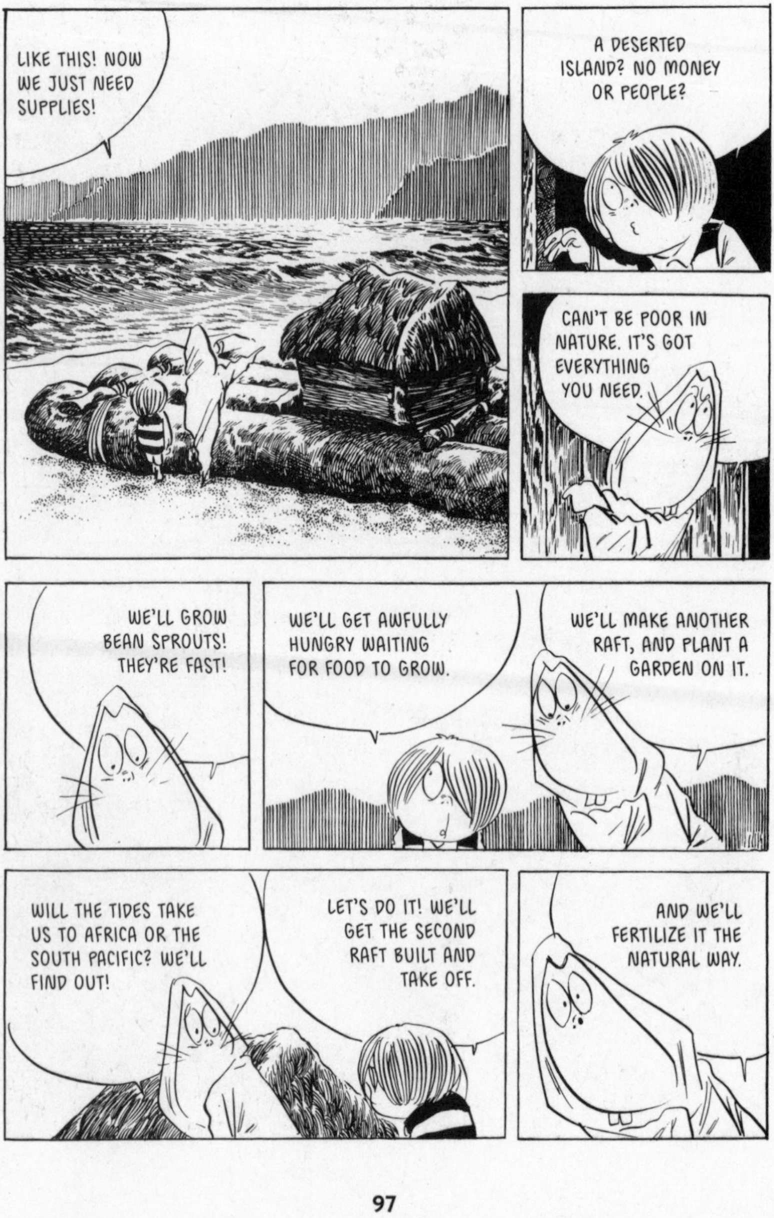
A DESERTED ISLAND? NO MONEY OR PEOPLE?
CAN'T BE POOR IN NATURE. IT'S GOT EVERYTHING YOU NEED.
LIKE THIS! NOW WE JUST NEED SUPPLIES!
WE'LL MAKE ANOTHER RAFT, AND PLANT A GARDEN ON IT.
WE'LL GET AWFULLY HUNGRY WAITING FOR FOOD TO GROW.
WE'LL GROW BEAN SPROUTS! THEY'RE FAST!
AND WE'LL FERTILIZE IT THE NATURAL WAY.
LET'S DO IT! WE'LL GET THE SECOND RAFT BUILT AND TAKE OFF.
WILL THE TIDES TAKE US TO AFRICA OR THE SOUTH PACIFIC? WE'LL FIND OUT!

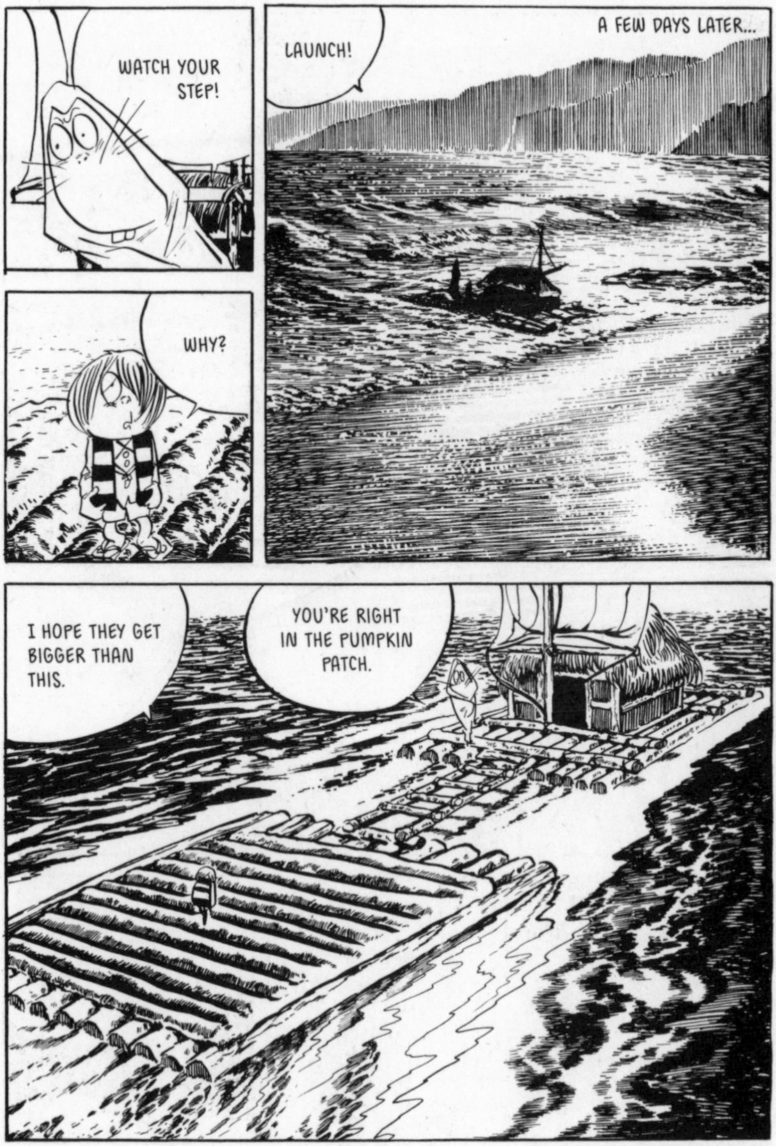
A FEW DAYS LATER...
LAUNCH!
WATCH YOUR STEP!
WHY?
YOU'RE RIGHT IN THE PUMPKIN PATCH.
I HOPE THEY GET BIGGER THAN THIS.

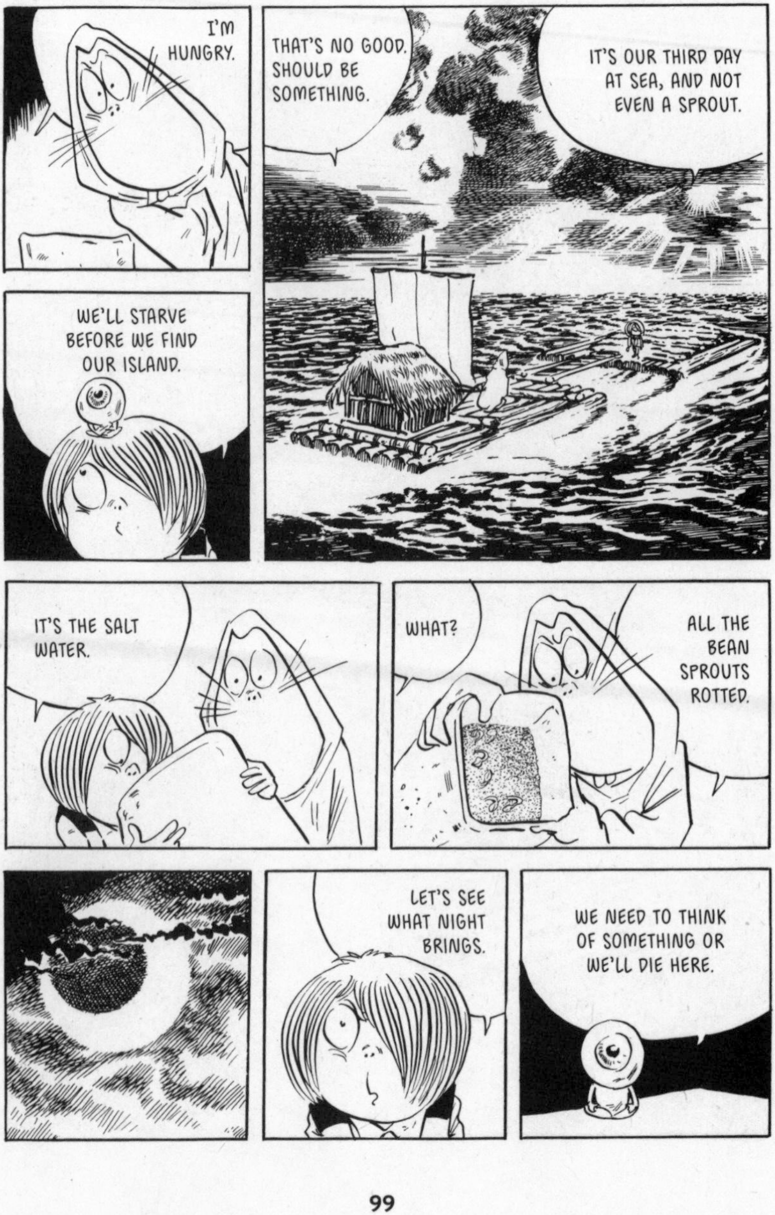
IT'S OUR THIRD DAY AT SEA, AND NOT EVEN A SPROUT.
THAT'S NO GOOD. SHOULD BE SOMETHING.
I'M HUNGRY.
WE'LL STARVE BEFORE WE FIND OUR ISLAND.
ALL THE BEAN SPROUTS ROTTED.
WHAT?
IT'S THE SALT WATER.
WE NEED TO THINK OF SOMETHING OR WE'LL DIE HERE.
LET'S SEE WHAT NIGHT BRINGS.

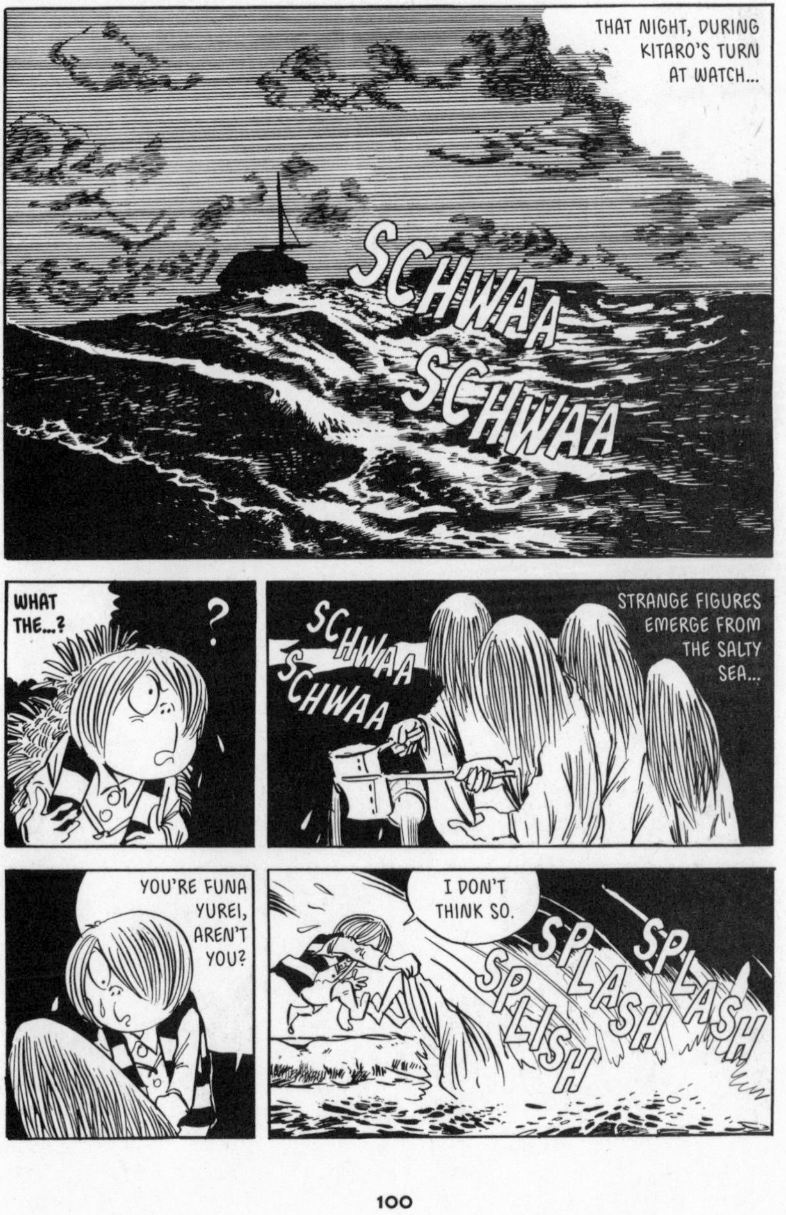
THAT NIGHT, DURING KITARO'S TURN AT WATCH...
SCHWAA SCHWAA
STRANGE FIGURES EMERGE FROM THE SALTY SEA...
SCHWAA SCHWAA
WHAT THE...?
?
I DON'T THINK SO.
SPLASH
SPLASH
SPLISH
YOU'RE FUNA YUREI, AREN'T YOU?

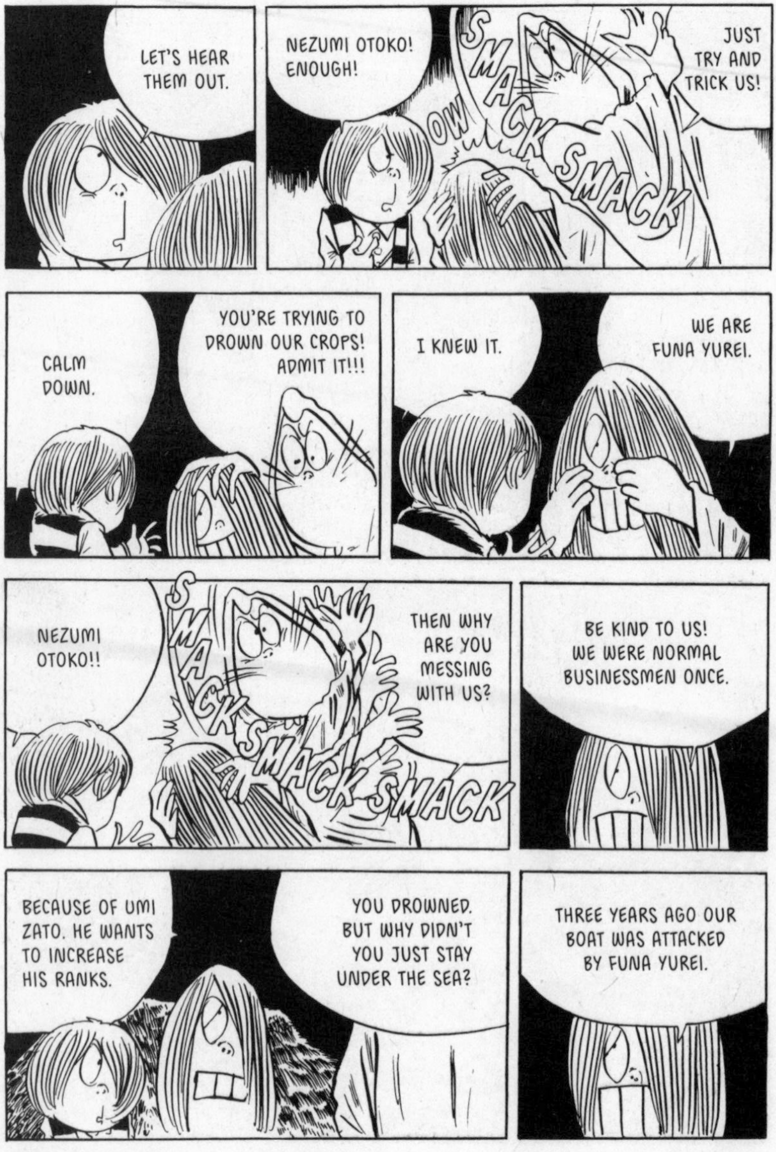
JUST TRY AND TRICK US!
SMACK SMACK
NEZUMI OTOKO! ENOUGH!
OW
LET'S HEAR THEM OUT.
WE ARE FUNA YUREI.
I KNEW IT.
YOU'RE TRYING TO DROWN OUR CROPS! ADMIT IT!!!
CALM DOWN.
BE KIND TO US! WE WERE NORMAL BUSINESSMEN ONCE.
THEN WHY ARE YOU MESSING WITH US?
SMACK SMACK SMACK SMACK
NEZUMI OTOKO!!
THREE YEARS AGO OUR BOAT WAS ATTACKED BY FUNA YUREI.
YOU DROWNED. BUT WHY DIDN'T YOU JUST STAY UNDER THE SEA?
BECAUSE OF UMI ZATO. HE WANTS TO INCREASE HIS RANKS.

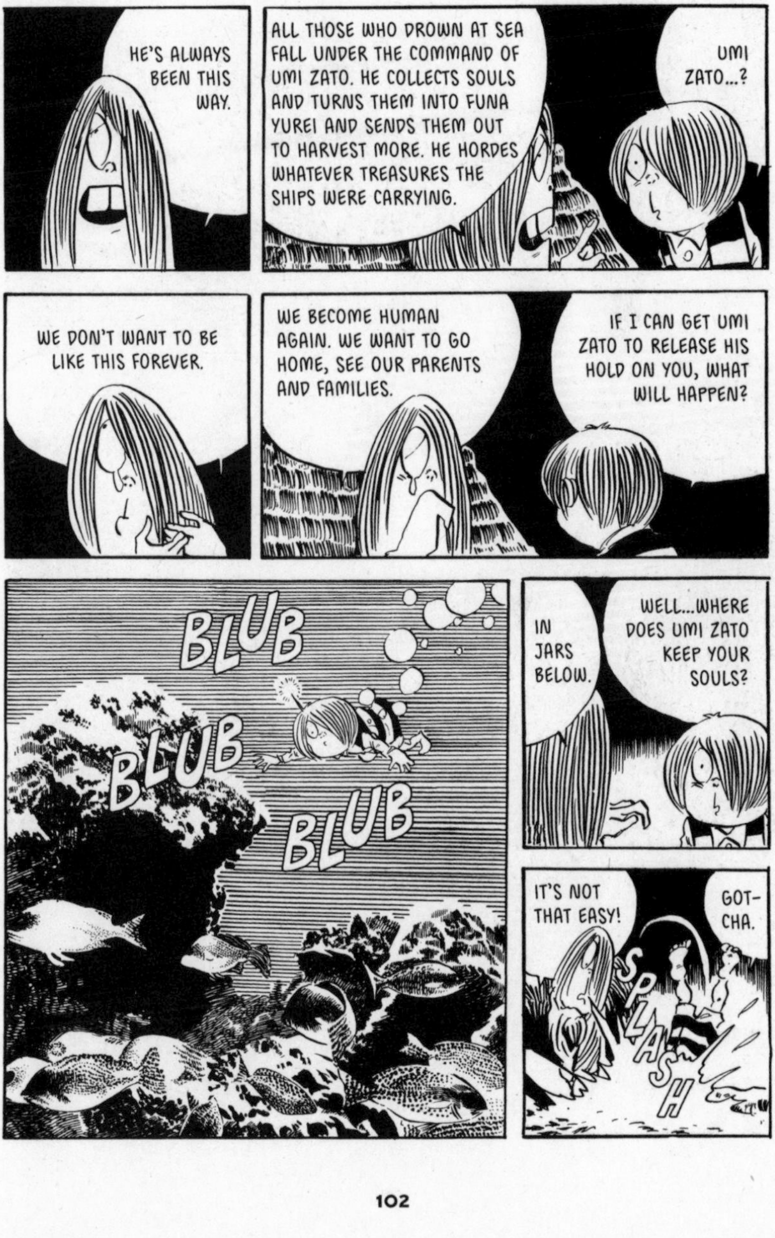

UMI ZATO...?
ALL THOSE WHO DROWN AT SEA FALL UNDER THE COMMAND OF UMI ZATO. HE COLLECTS SOULS AND TURNS THEM INTO FUNA YUREI AND SENDS THEM OUT TO HARVEST MORE. HE HORDES WHATEVER TREASURES THE SHIPS WERE CARRYING.
HE'S ALWAYS BEEN THIS WAY.
IF I CAN GET UMI ZATO TO RELEASE HIS HOLD ON YOU, WHAT WILL HAPPEN?
WE BECOME HUMAN AGAIN. WE WANT TO GO HOME, SEE OUR PARENTS AND FAMILIES.
WE DON'T WANT TO BE LIKE THIS FOREVER.
WELL...WHERE DOES UMI ZATO KEEP YOUR SOULS?
IN JARS BELOW.
GOT-CHA.
IT'S NOT THAT EASY!
SPLASH
BLUB
BLUB
BLUB

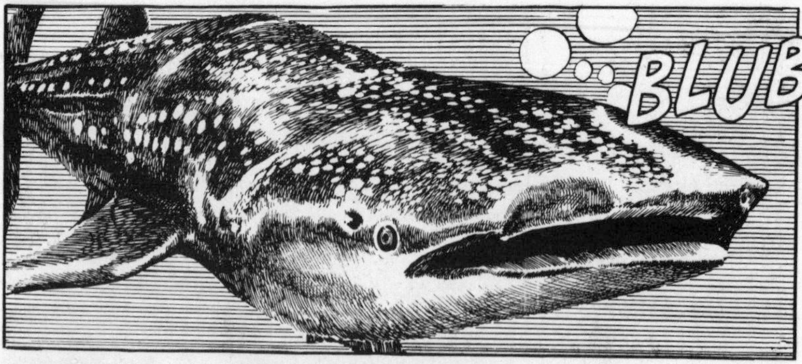
BLUB

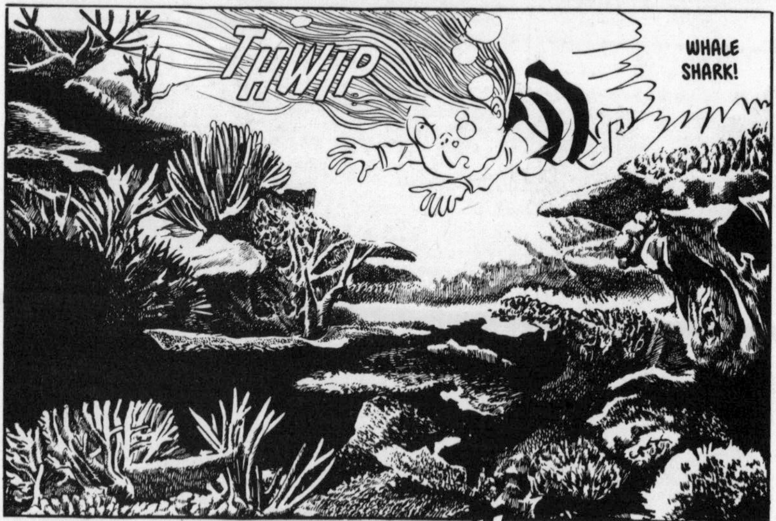
WHALE SHARK!
THWIP

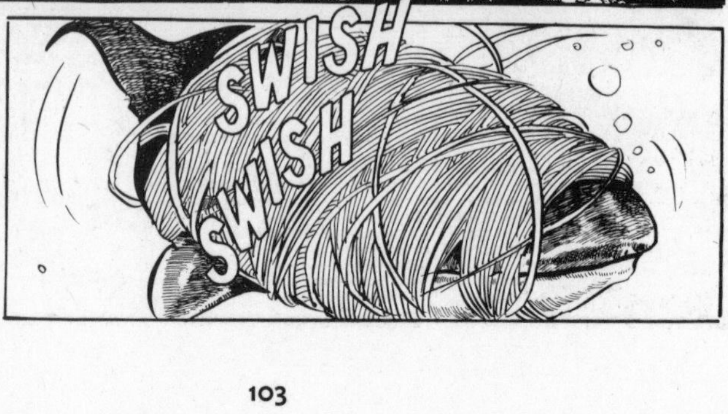
SWISH
SWISH

THE GREAT BEAST GUARDS THE STOLEN SOULS. IT'S STRONG, BUT KITARO'S SPIRIT HAIR IS UNBREAKABLE.

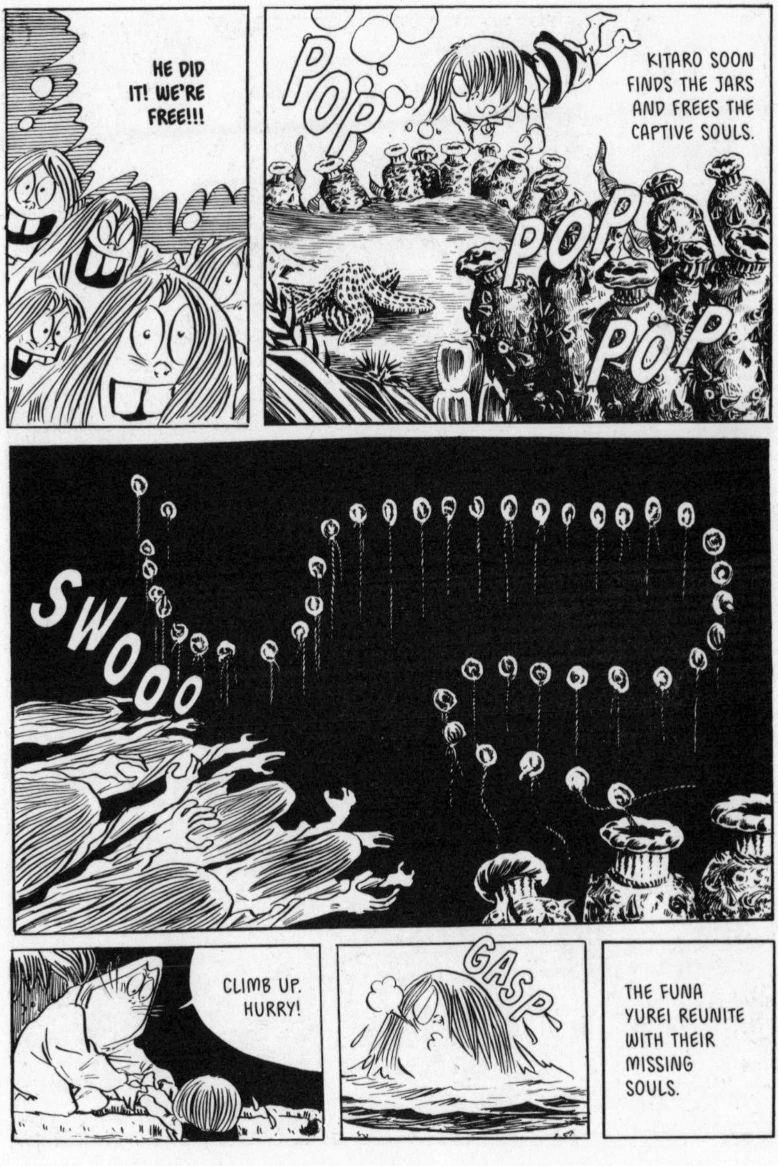
KITARO SOON FINDS THE JARS AND FREES THE CAPTIVE SOULS.
POP
POP
POP
HE DID IT! WE'RE FREE!!!
SWOOO
THE FUNA YUREI REUNITE WITH THEIR MISSING SOULS.
GASP
CLIMB UP. HURRY!

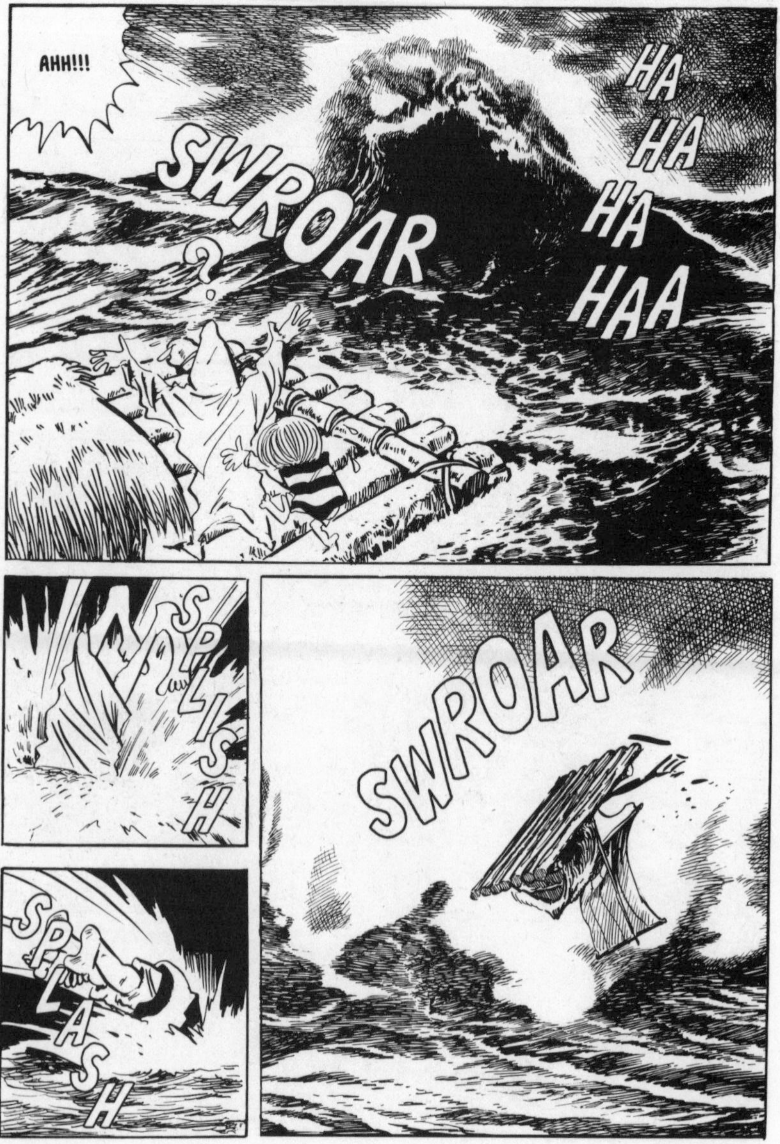
HA HA HA HAA
SWROAR
AHH!!!
SWROAR
SPLISH
SPLASH

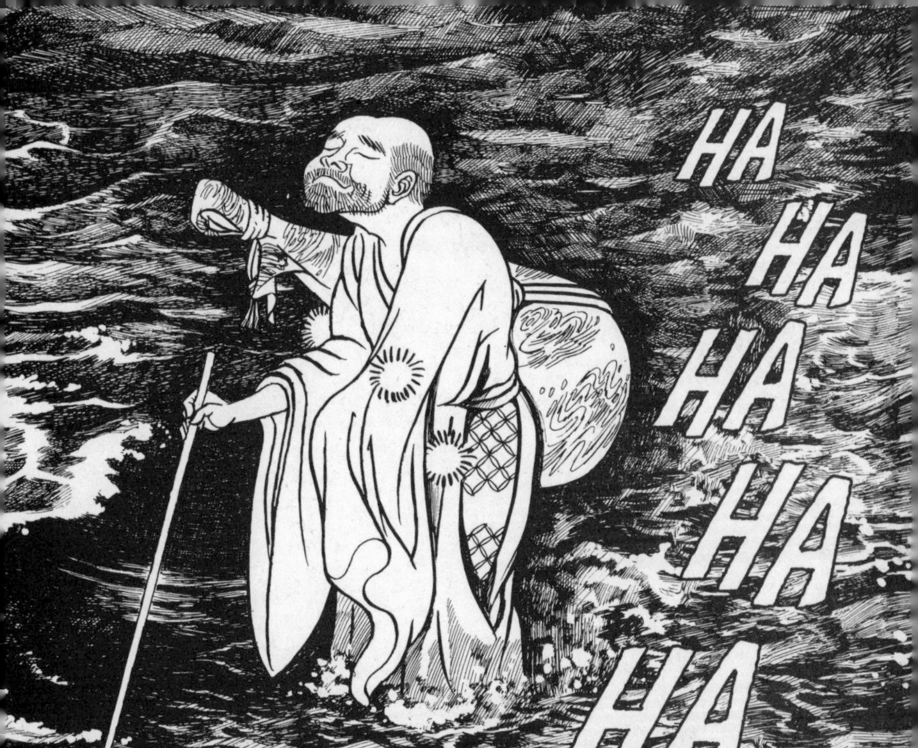
HA HA HA HA HA HA

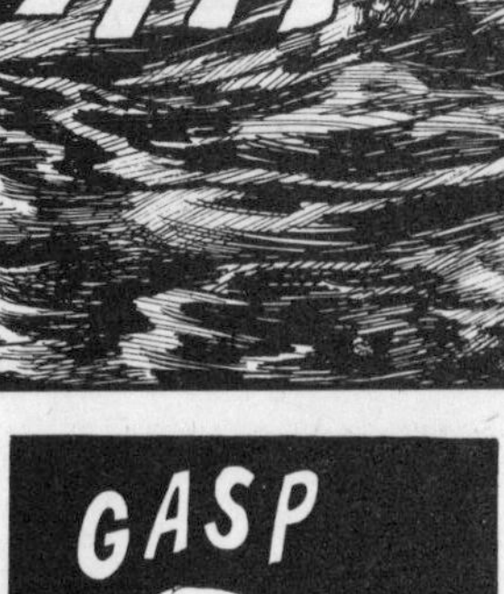
GASP

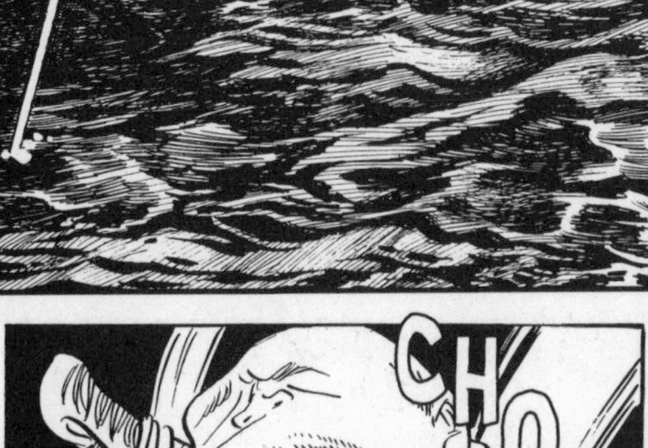
CHOMP

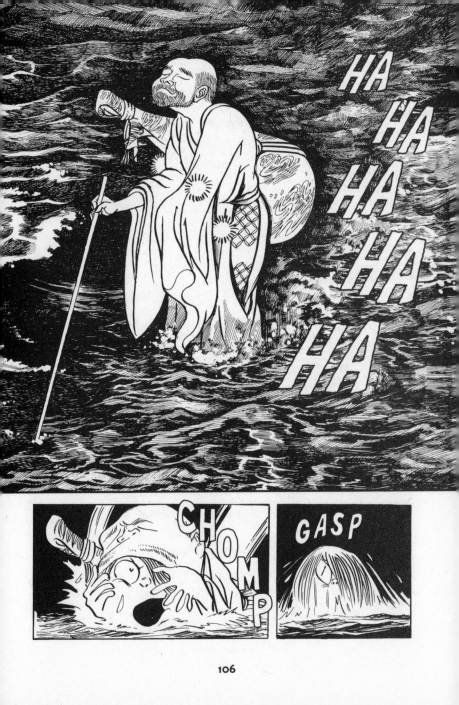

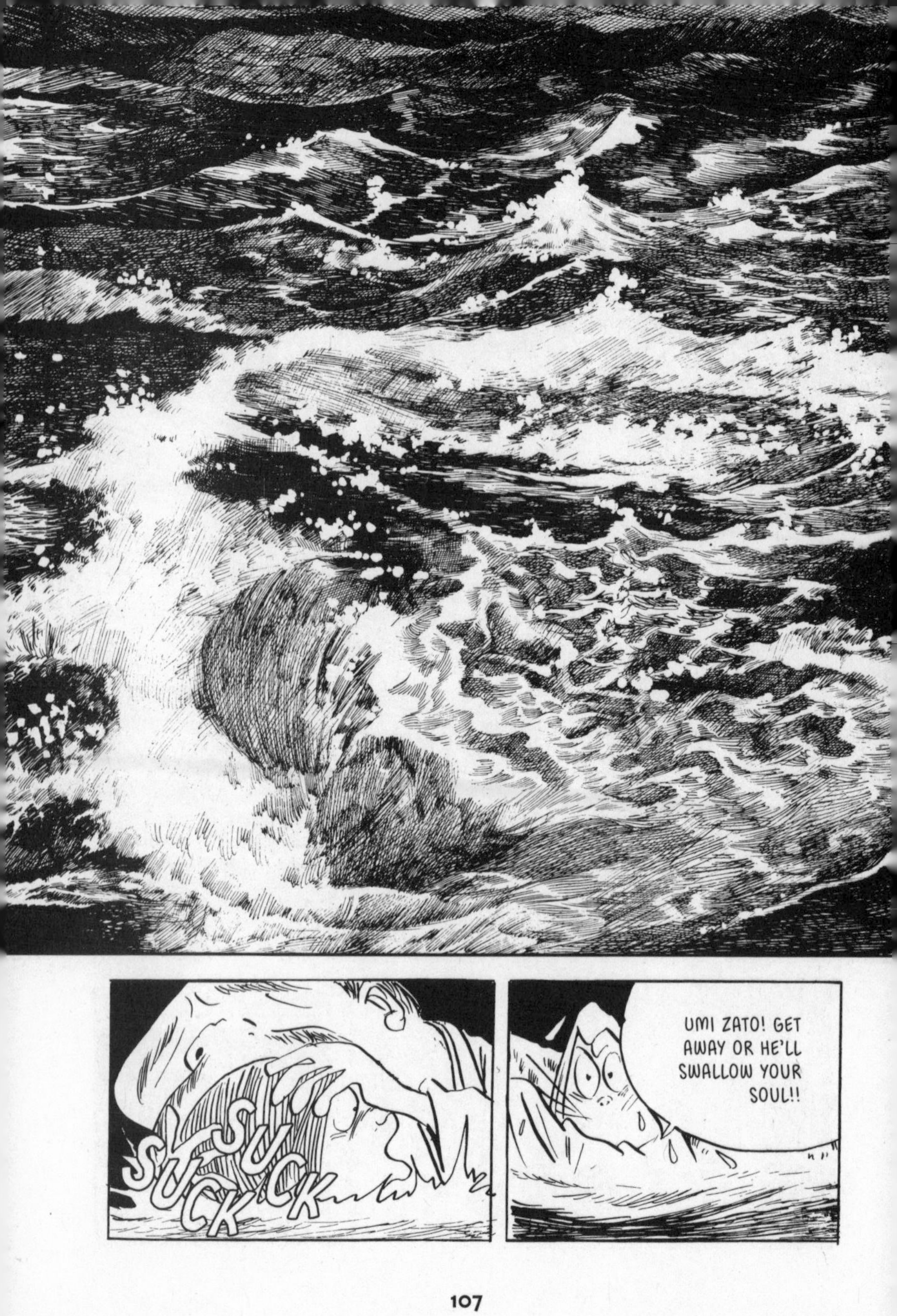
UMI ZATO! GET AWAY OR HE'LL SWALLOW YOUR SOUL!!
SUCK SUCK

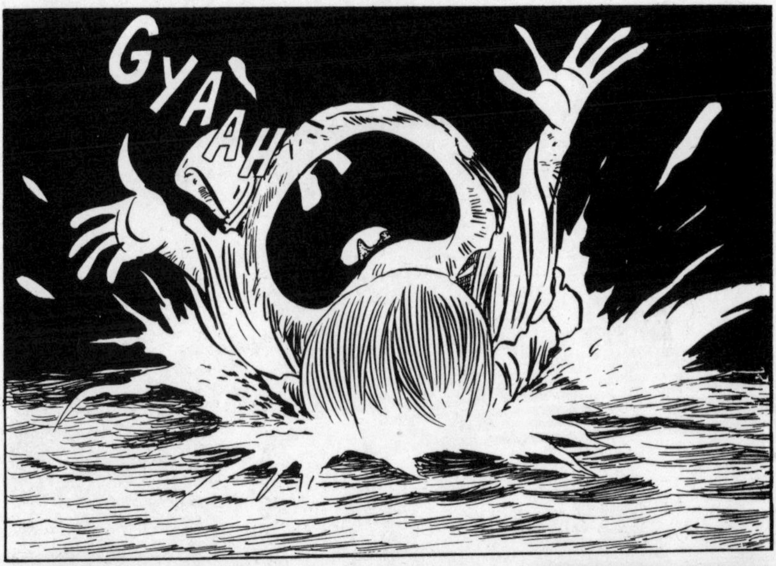
GYAAAH
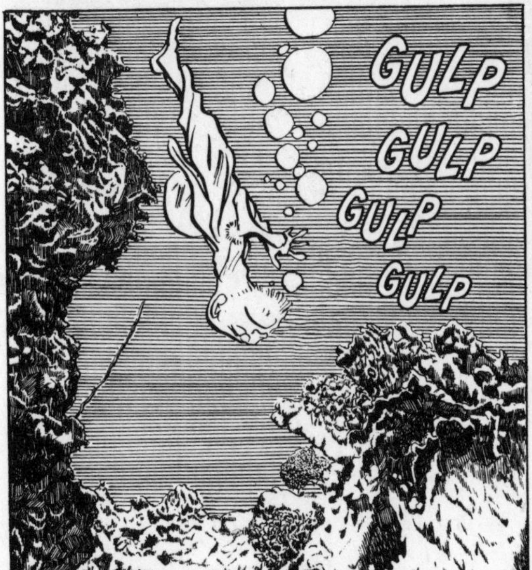
GULP
GULP
GULP
GULP
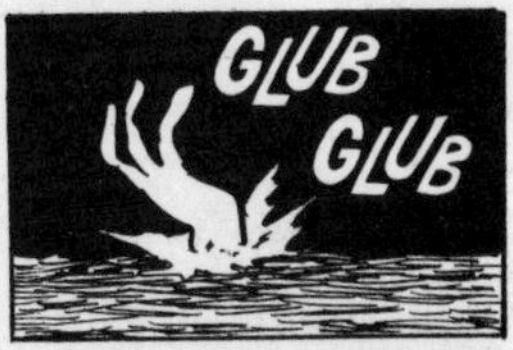
GLUB
GLUB
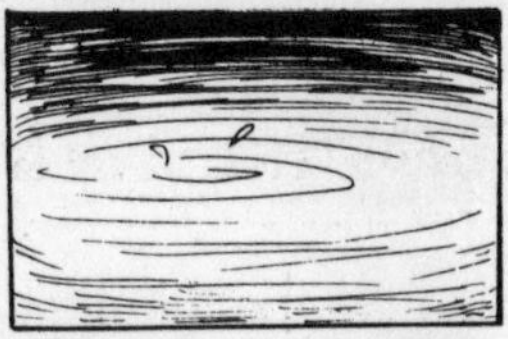
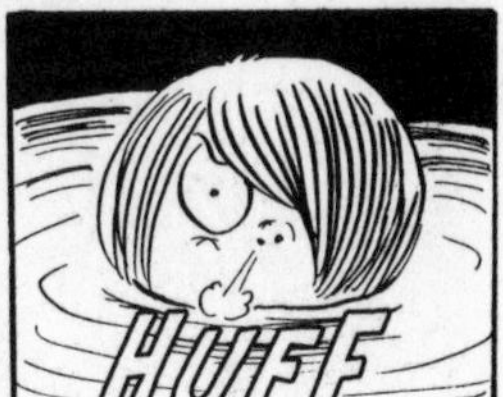
HUFF

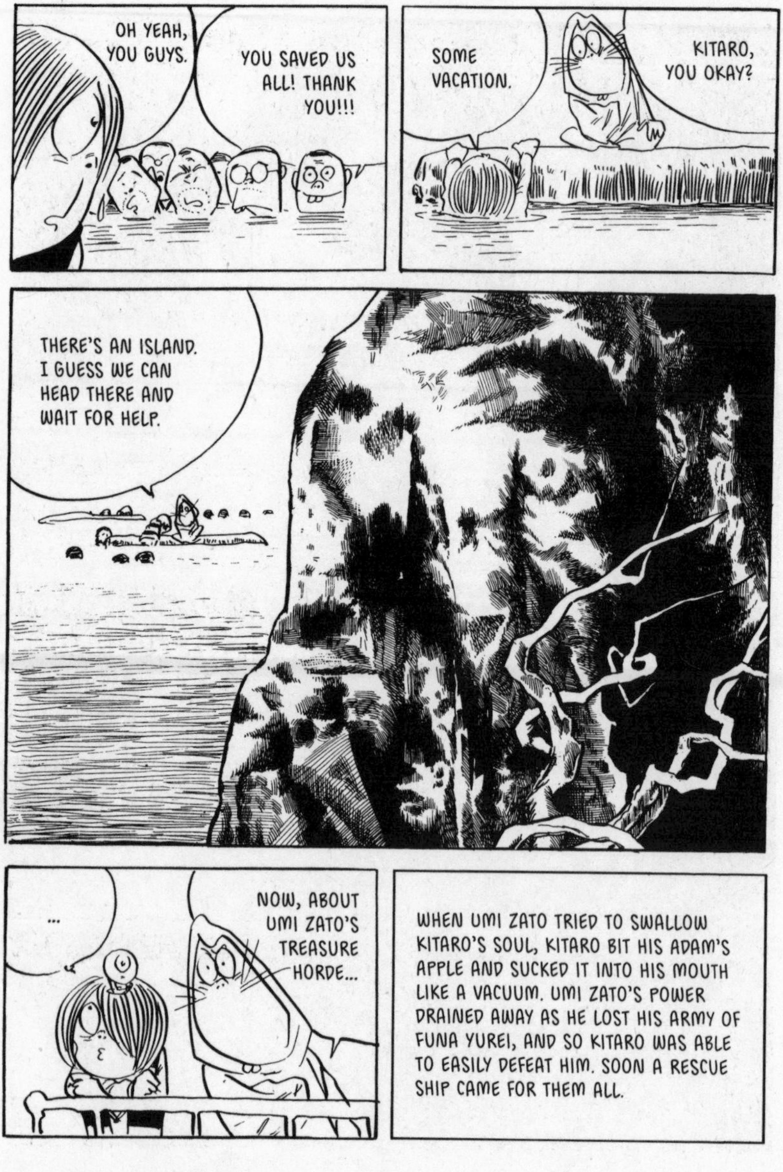
KITARO, YOU OKAY?
SOME VACATION.
YOU SAVED US ALL! THANK YOU!!!
OH YEAH, YOU GUYS.
THERE'S AN ISLAND. I GUESS WE CAN HEAD THERE AND WAIT FOR HELP.
WHEN UMI ZATO TRIED TO SWALLOW KITARO'S SOUL, KITARO BIT HIS ADAM'S APPLE AND SUCKED IT INTO HIS MOUTH LIKE A VACUUM. UMI ZATO'S POWER DRAINED AWAY AS HE LOST HIS ARMY OF FUNA YUREI, AND SO KITARO WAS ABLE TO EASILY DEFEAT HIM. SOON A RESCUE SHIP CAME FOR THEM ALL.
NOW, ABOUT UMI ZATO'S TREASURE HORDE...
...

ODORO ODORO

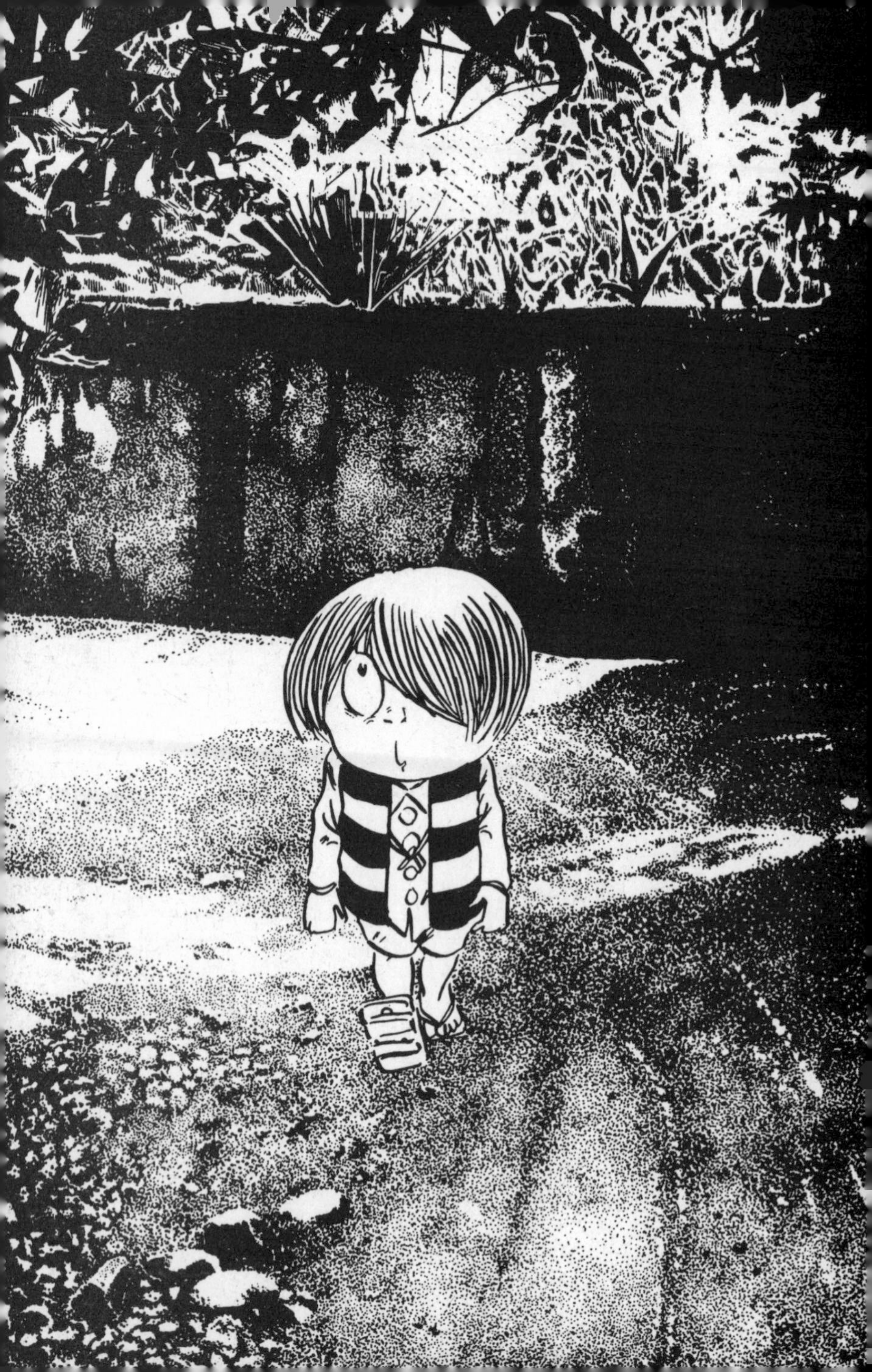

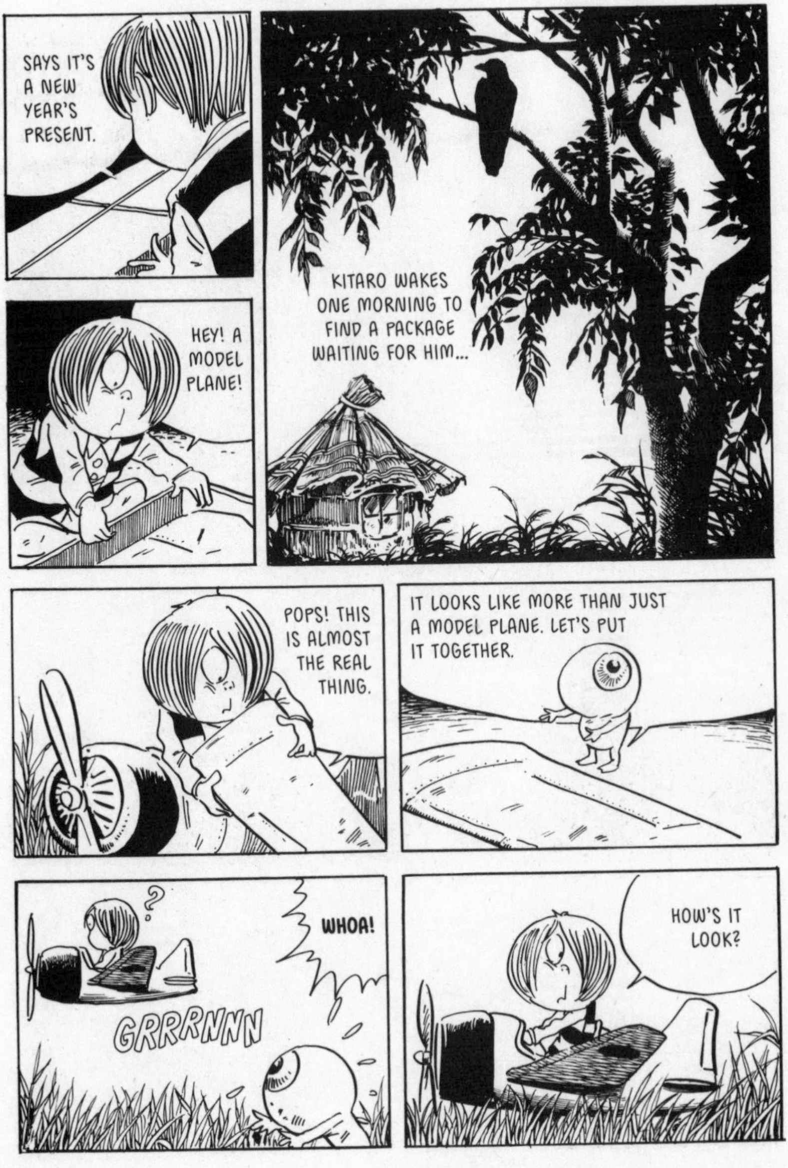
KITARO WAKES ONE MORNING TO FIND A PACKAGE WAITING FOR HIM...
SAYS IT'S A NEW YEAR'S PRESENT.
HEY! A MODEL PLANE!
IT LOOKS LIKE MORE THAN JUST A MODEL PLANE. LET'S PUT IT TOGETHER.
POPS! THIS IS ALMOST THE REAL THING.
HOW'S IT LOOK?
WHOA!
GRRRNNN

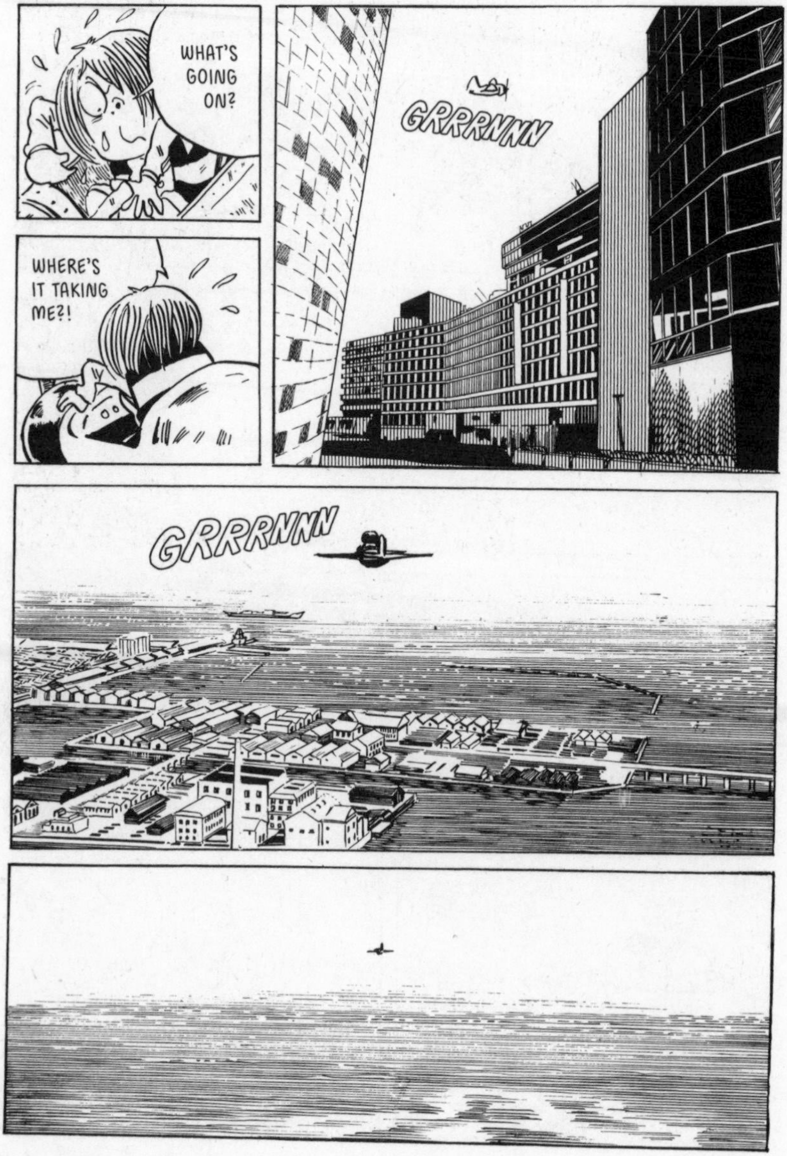
GRRRNNN
WHAT'S GOING ON?
WHERE'S IT TAKING ME?!
GRRRNNN

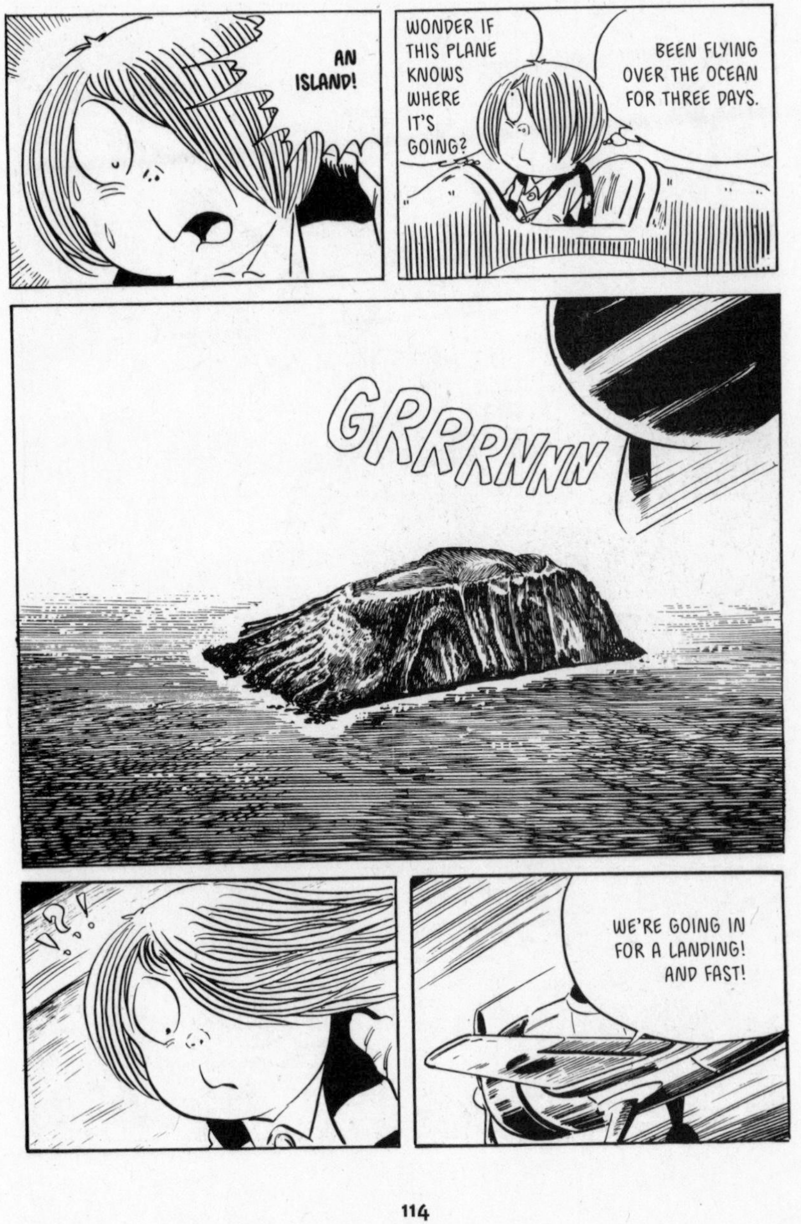
BEEN FLYING OVER THE OCEAN FOR THREE DAYS.
WONDER IF THIS PLANE KNOWS WHERE IT'S GOING?
AN ISLAND!
GRRRNNNN
WE'RE GOING IN FOR A LANDING! AND FAST!

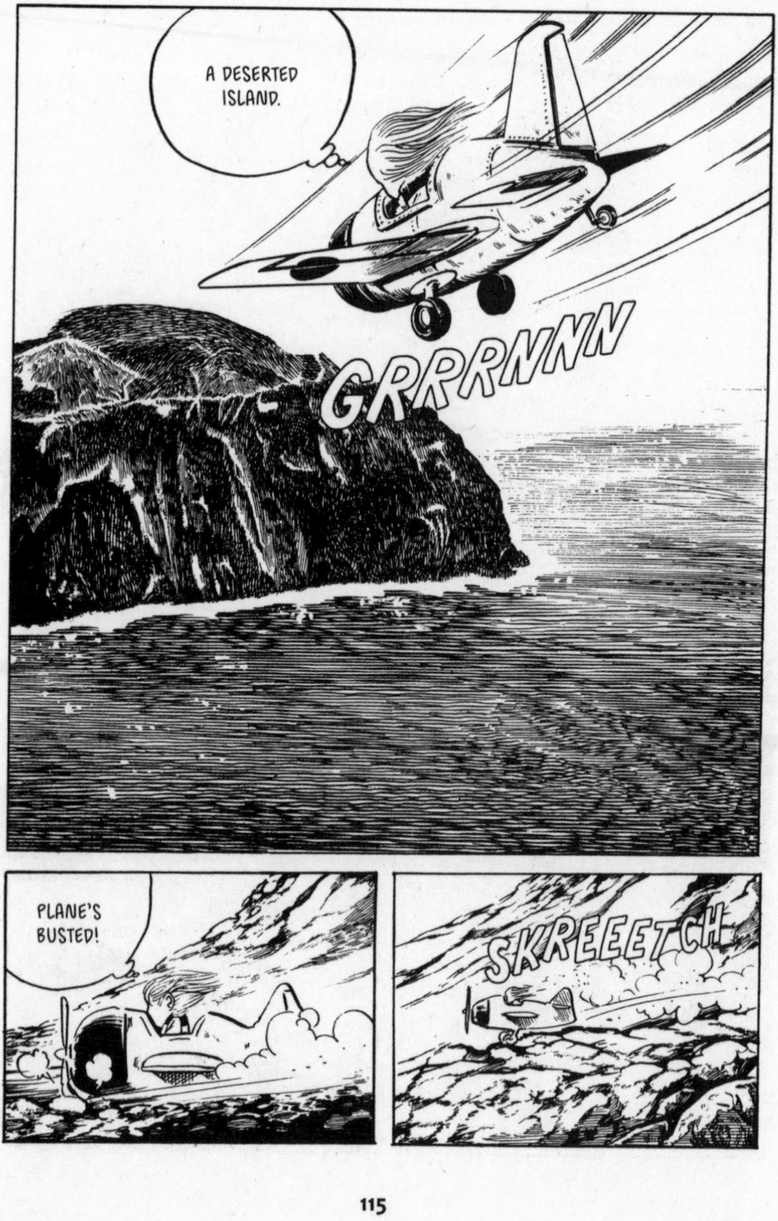
A DESERTED ISLAND.
GRRRNNN
SKREEETCH
PLANE'S BUSTED!

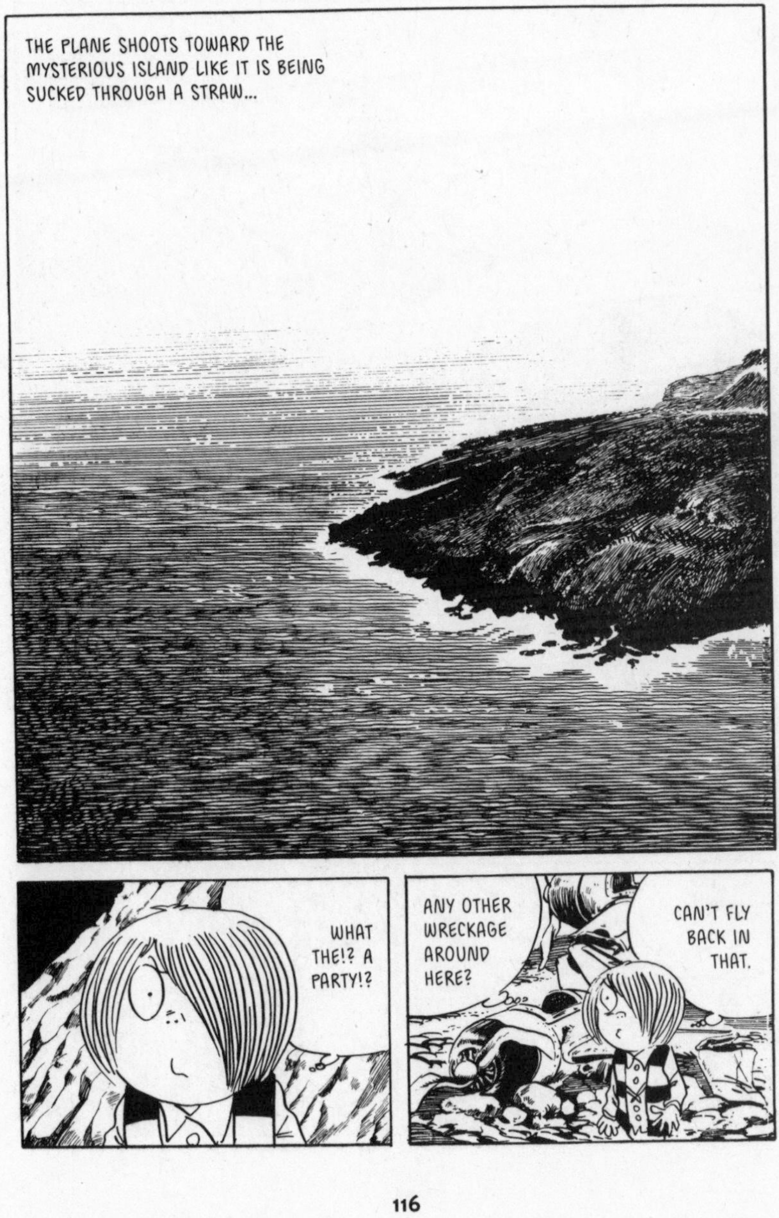
THE PLANE SHOOTS TOWARD THE MYSTERIOUS ISLAND LIKE IT IS BEING SUCKED THROUGH A STRAW...
CAN'T FLY BACK IN THAT.
ANY OTHER WRECKAGE AROUND HERE?
WHAT THE!? A PARTY!?

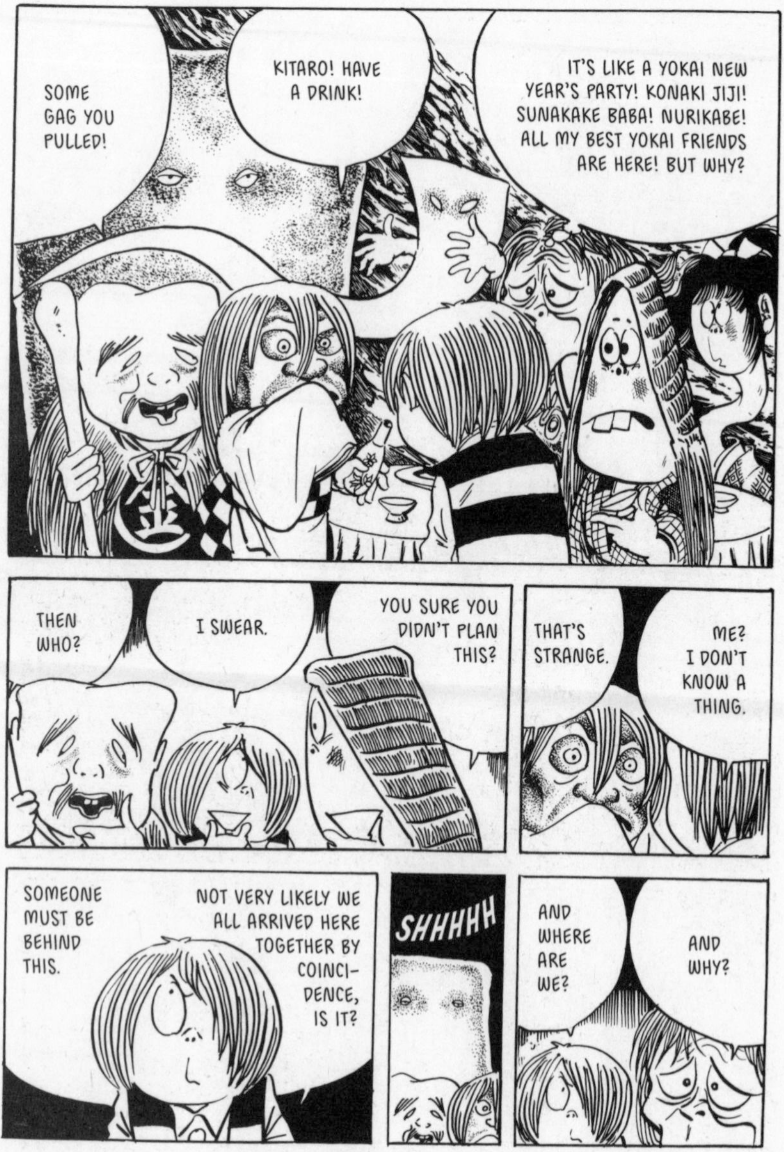
IT'S LIKE A YOKAI NEW YEAR'S PARTY! KONAKI JIJI! SUNAKAKE BABA! NURIKABE! ALL MY BEST YOKAI FRIENDS ARE HERE! BUT WHY?
KITARO! HAVE A DRINK!
SOME GAG YOU PULLED!
ME? I DON'T KNOW A THING.
THAT'S STRANGE.
YOU SURE YOU DIDN'T PLAN THIS?
I SWEAR.
THEN WHO?
AND WHY?
AND WHERE ARE WE?
SHHHHH
NOT VERY LIKELY WE ALL ARRIVED HERE TOGETHER BY COINCI-DENCE, IS IT?
SOMEONE MUST BE BEHIND THIS.

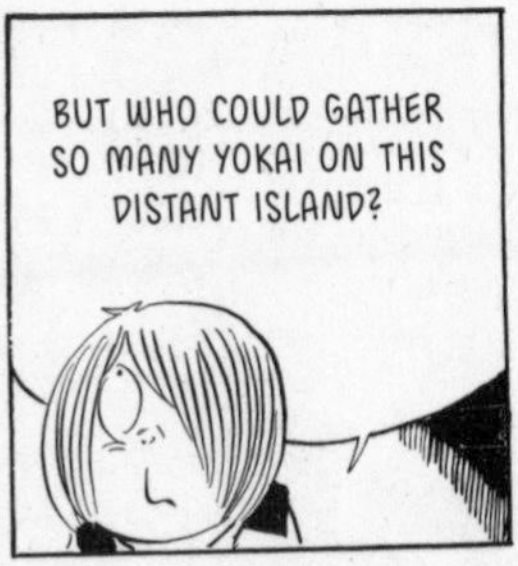
BUT WHO COULD GATHER SO MANY YOKAI ON THIS DISTANT ISLAND?

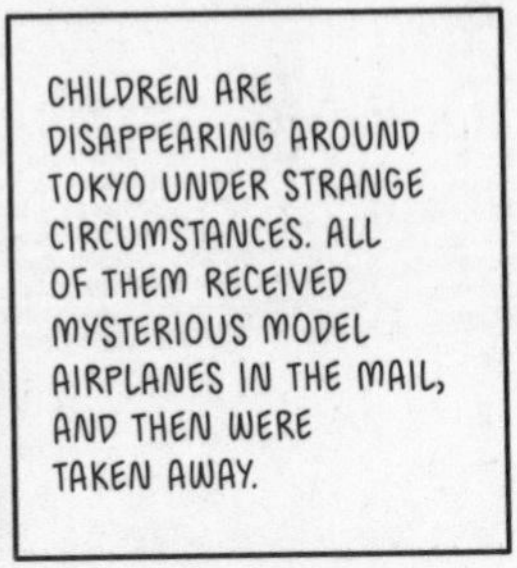
CHILDREN ARE DISAPPEARING AROUND TOKYO UNDER STRANGE CIRCUMSTANCES. ALL OF THEM RECEIVED MYSTERIOUS MODEL AIRPLANES IN THE MAIL, AND THEN WERE TAKEN AWAY.

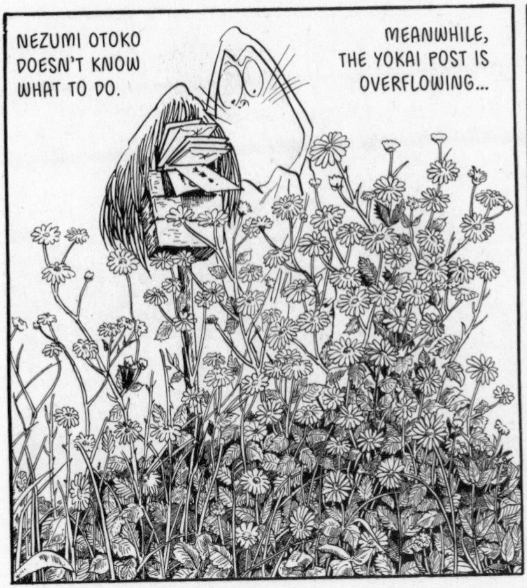
MEANWHILE, THE YOKAI POST IS OVERFLOWING...
NEZUMI OTOKO DOESN'T KNOW WHAT TO DO.

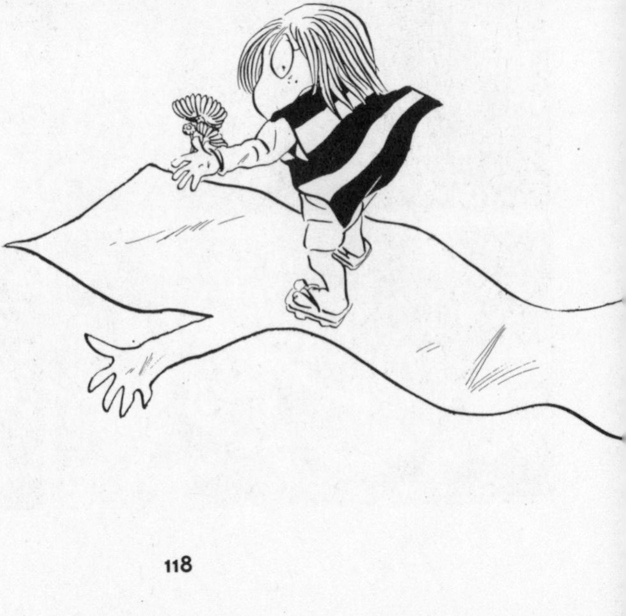

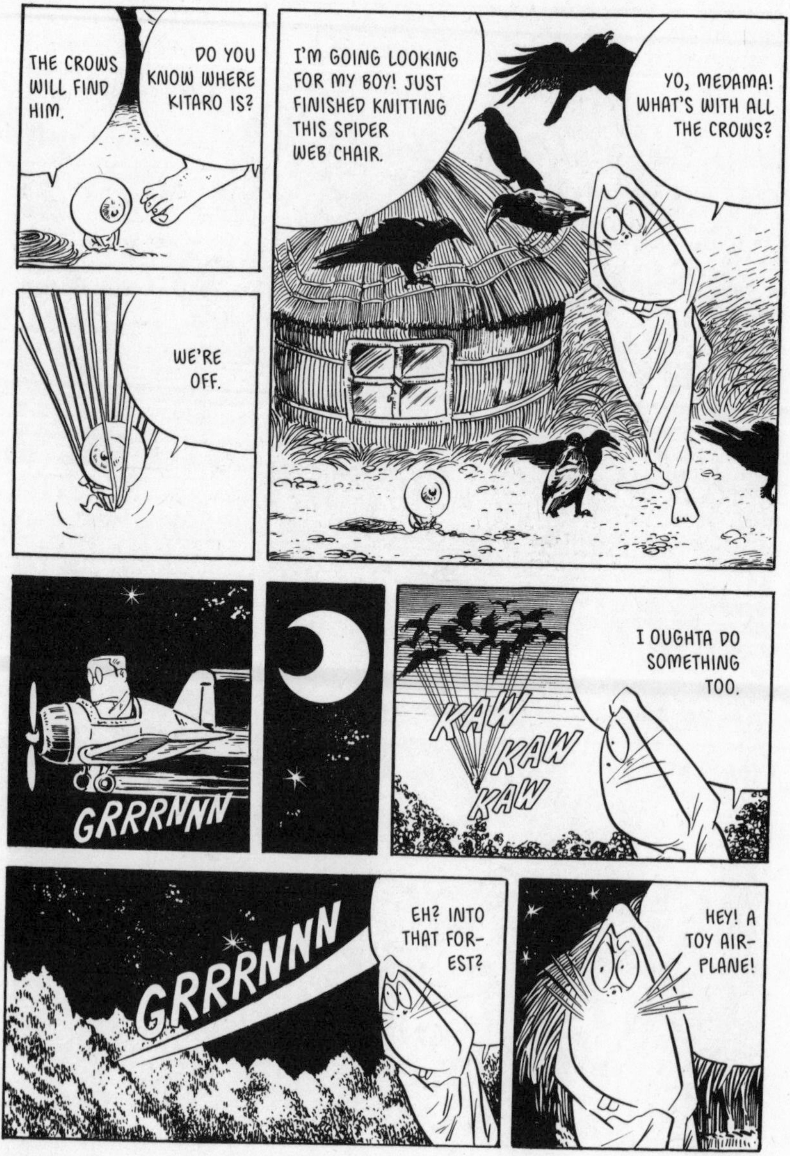
YO, MEDAMA! WHAT'S WITH ALL THE CROWS?
I'M GOING LOOKING FOR MY BOY! JUST FINISHED KNITTING THIS SPIDER WEB CHAIR.
DO YOU KNOW WHERE KITARO IS?
THE CROWS WILL FIND HIM.
WE'RE OFF.
I OUGHTA DO SOMETHING TOO.
KAW KAW KAW
GRRRNNN
HEY! A TOY AIR-PLANE!
EH? INTO THAT FOR-EST?
GRRRNNN

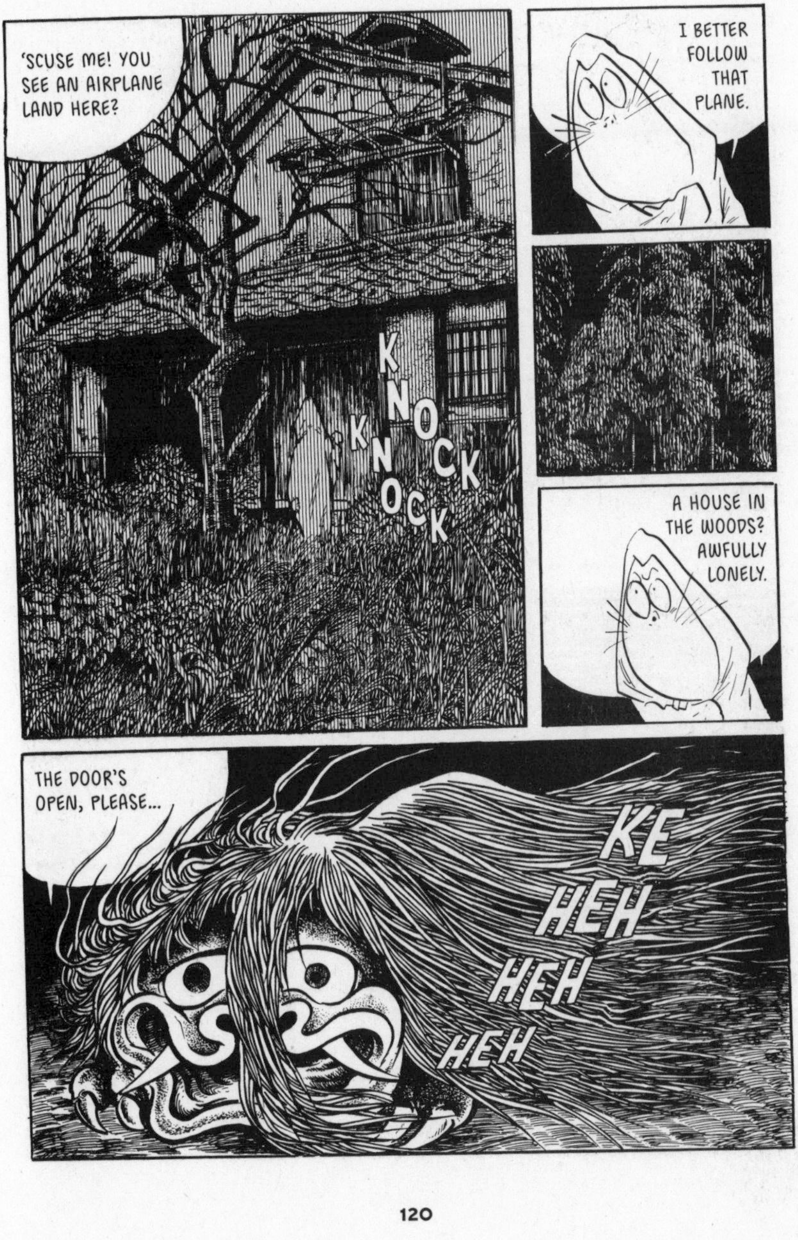
I BETTER FOLLOW THAT PLANE.
A HOUSE IN THE WOODS? AWFULLY LONELY.
'SCUSE ME! YOU SEE AN AIRPLANE LAND HERE?
KNOCK KNOCK
THE DOOR'S OPEN, PLEASE...
KE HEH HEH HEH

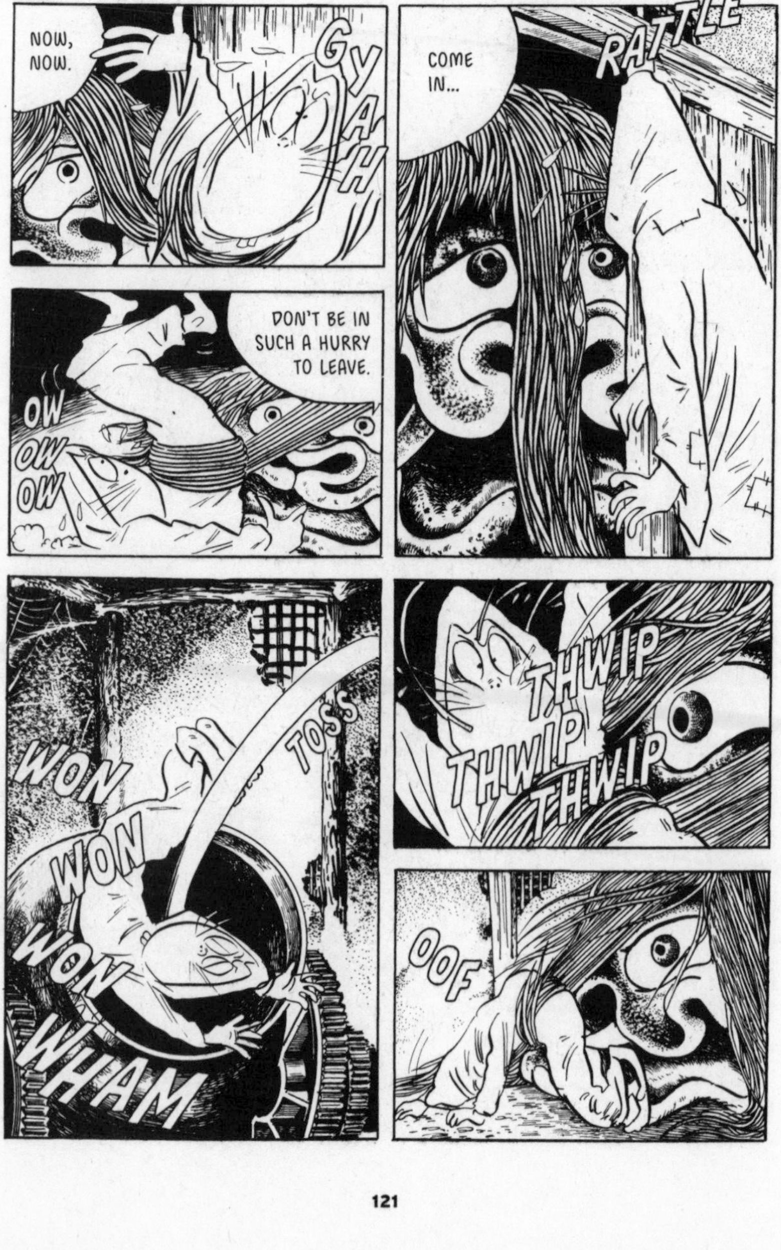
COME IN...
RATTLE
NOW, NOW.
GYAH
DON'T BE IN SUCH A HURRY TO LEAVE.
OW OW OW
THWIP THWIP THWIP
OOF
TOSS
WON WON WON
WHAM

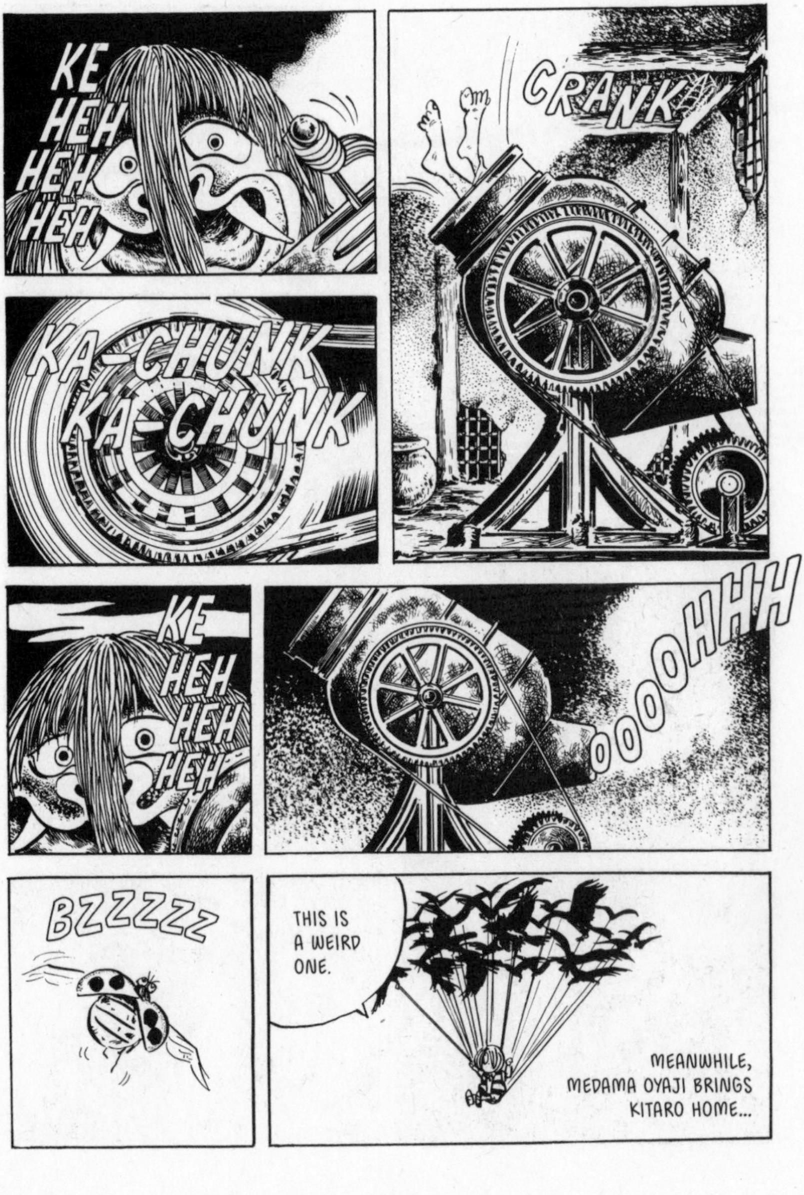
CRANK
KE HEH HEH HEH
KA-CHUNK KA-CHUNK
OOOOOHHH
KE HEH HEH HEH
THIS IS A WEIRD ONE.
MEANWHILE, MEDAMA OYAJI BRINGS KITARO HOME...
BZZZZZ

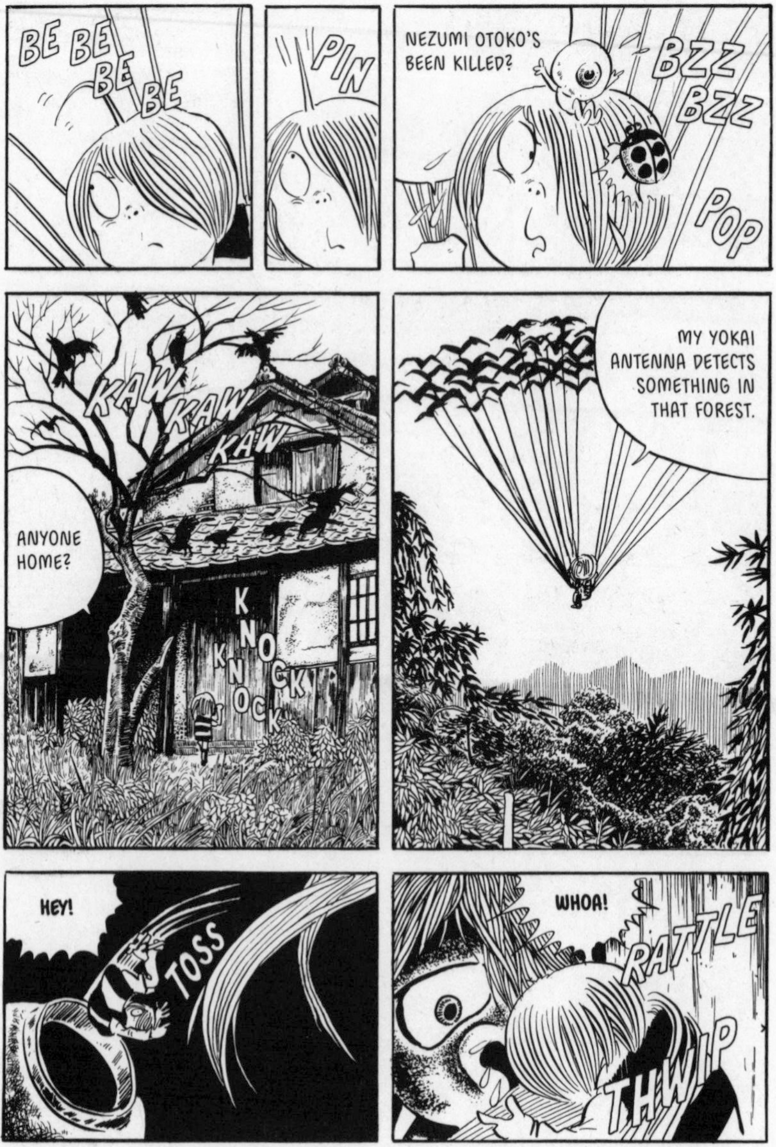
BZZ BZZ
NEZUMI OTOKO'S BEEN KILLED?
POP
PIN
BE BE BE BE
MY YOKAI ANTENNA DETECTS SOMETHING IN THAT FOREST.
KAW KAW KAW
ANYONE HOME?
KNOCK KNOCK
WHOA!
RATTLE
THWIP
HEY!
TOSS

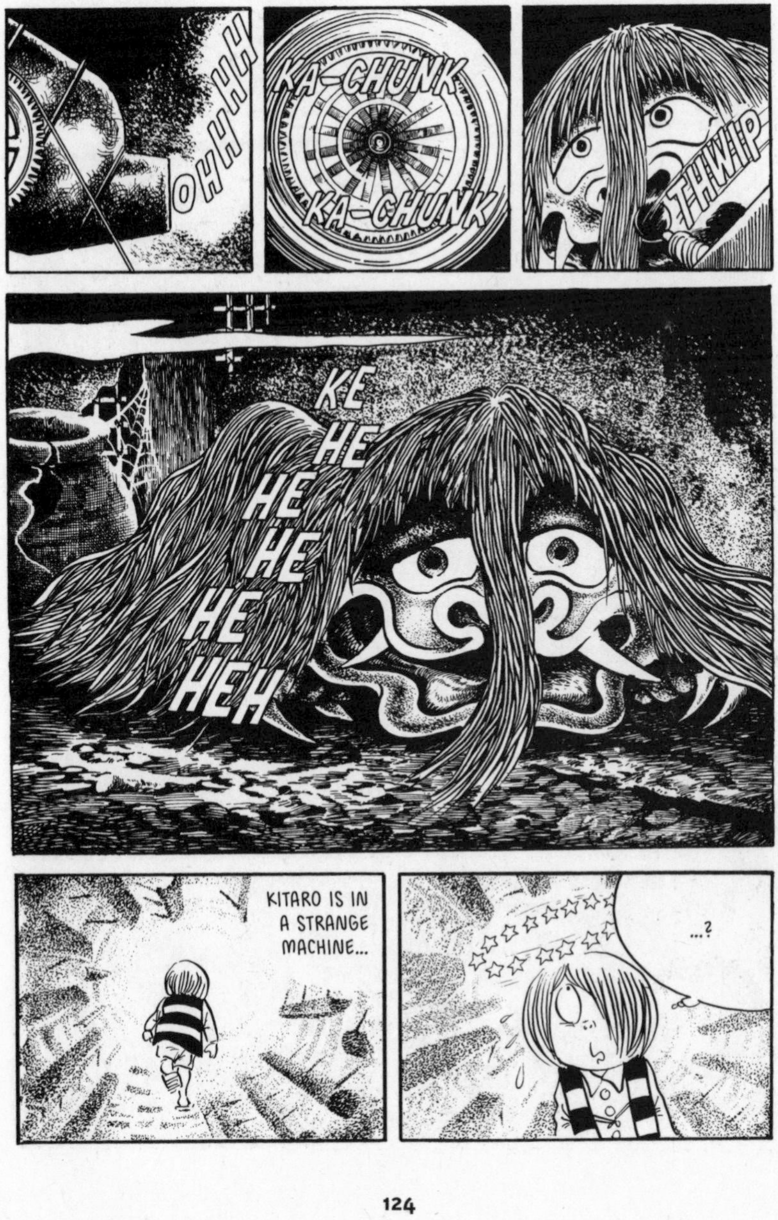
THWIP
KA-CHUNK
KA-CHUNK
OHHHH
KE
HE
HE
HE
HE
HEH
...?
KITARO IS IN
A STRANGE
MACHINE...

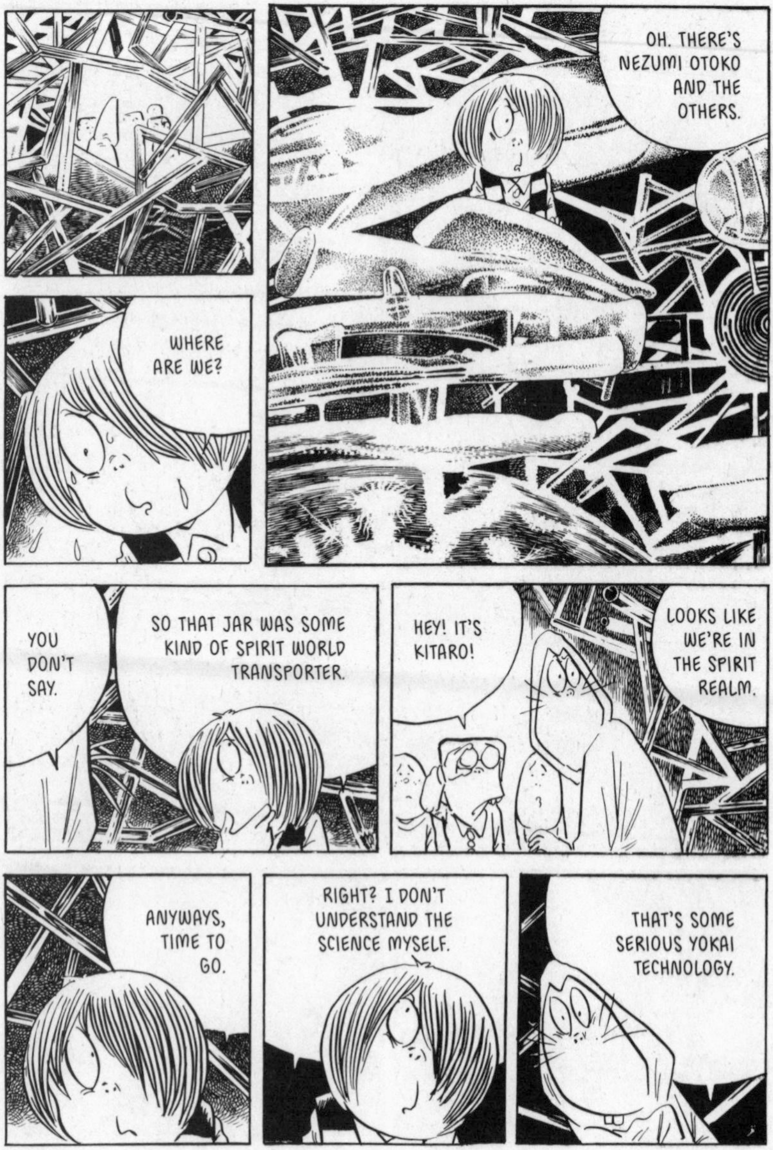
OH. THERE'S NEZUMI OTOKO AND THE OTHERS.
WHERE ARE WE?
LOOKS LIKE WE'RE IN THE SPIRIT REALM.
HEY! IT'S KITARO!
SO THAT JAR WAS SOME KIND OF SPIRIT WORLD TRANSPORTER.
YOU DON'T SAY.
THAT'S SOME SERIOUS YOKAI TECHNOLOGY.
RIGHT? I DON'T UNDERSTAND THE SCIENCE MYSELF.
ANYWAYS, TIME TO GO.

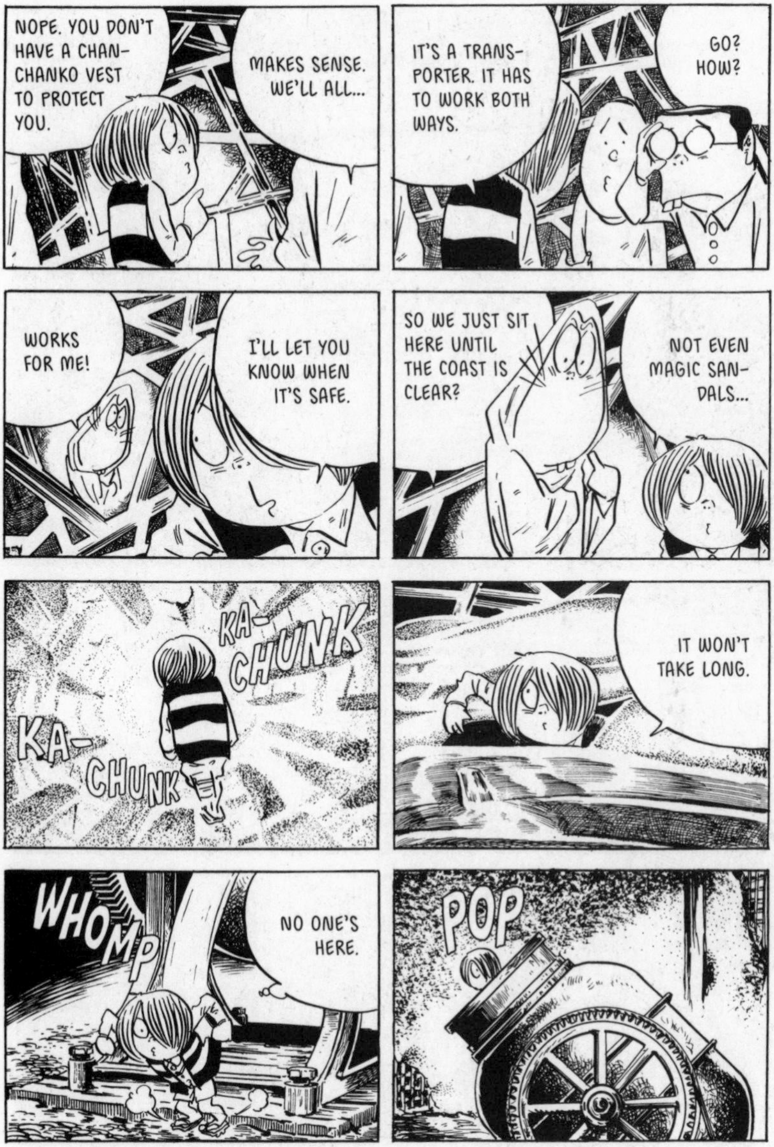
GO? HOW?
IT'S A TRANSPORTER. IT HAS TO WORK BOTH WAYS.
MAKES SENSE. WE'LL ALL...
NOPE. YOU DON'T HAVE A CHANCHANKO VEST TO PROTECT YOU.
NOT EVEN MAGIC SANDALS...
SO WE JUST SIT HERE UNTIL THE COAST IS CLEAR?
I'LL LET YOU KNOW WHEN IT'S SAFE.
WORKS FOR ME!
IT WON'T TAKE LONG.
KA-CHUNK
KA-CHUNK
POP
NO ONE'S HERE.
WHOMP

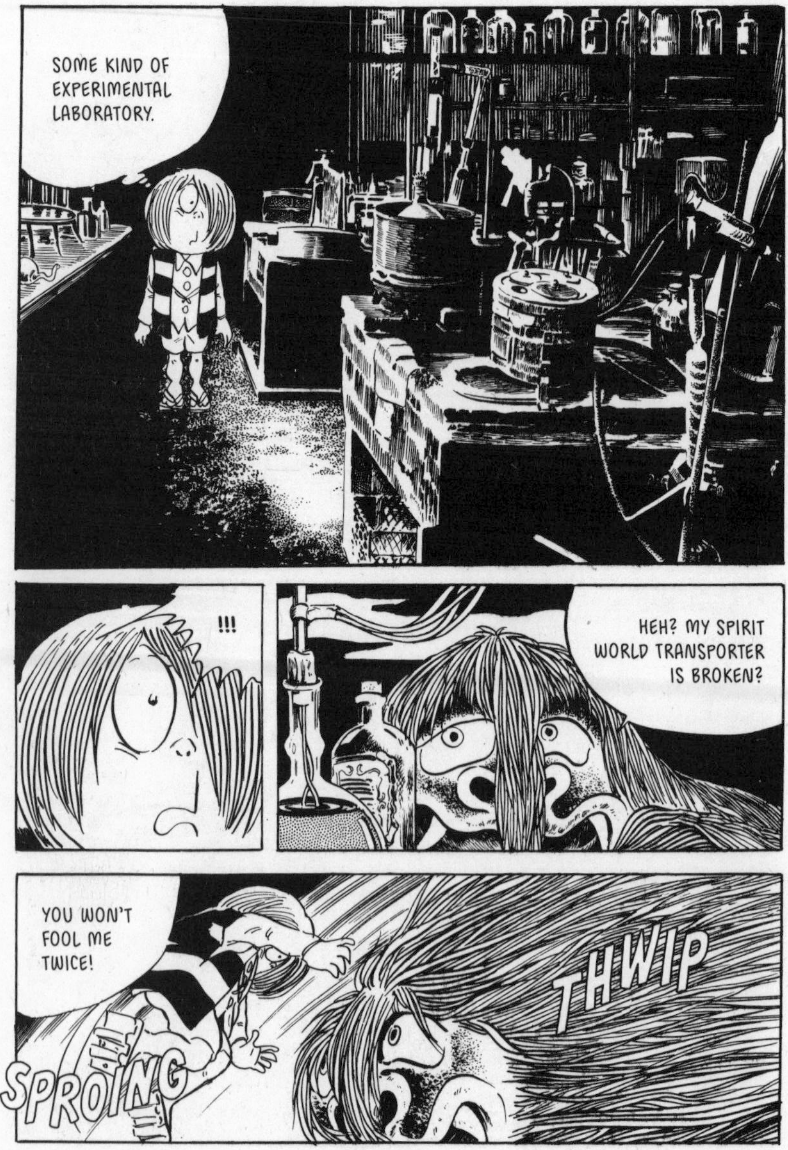
SOME KIND OF EXPERIMENTAL LABORATORY.
HEH? MY SPIRIT WORLD TRANSPORTER IS BROKEN?
!!!
YOU WON'T FOOL ME TWICE!
THWIP
SPROING

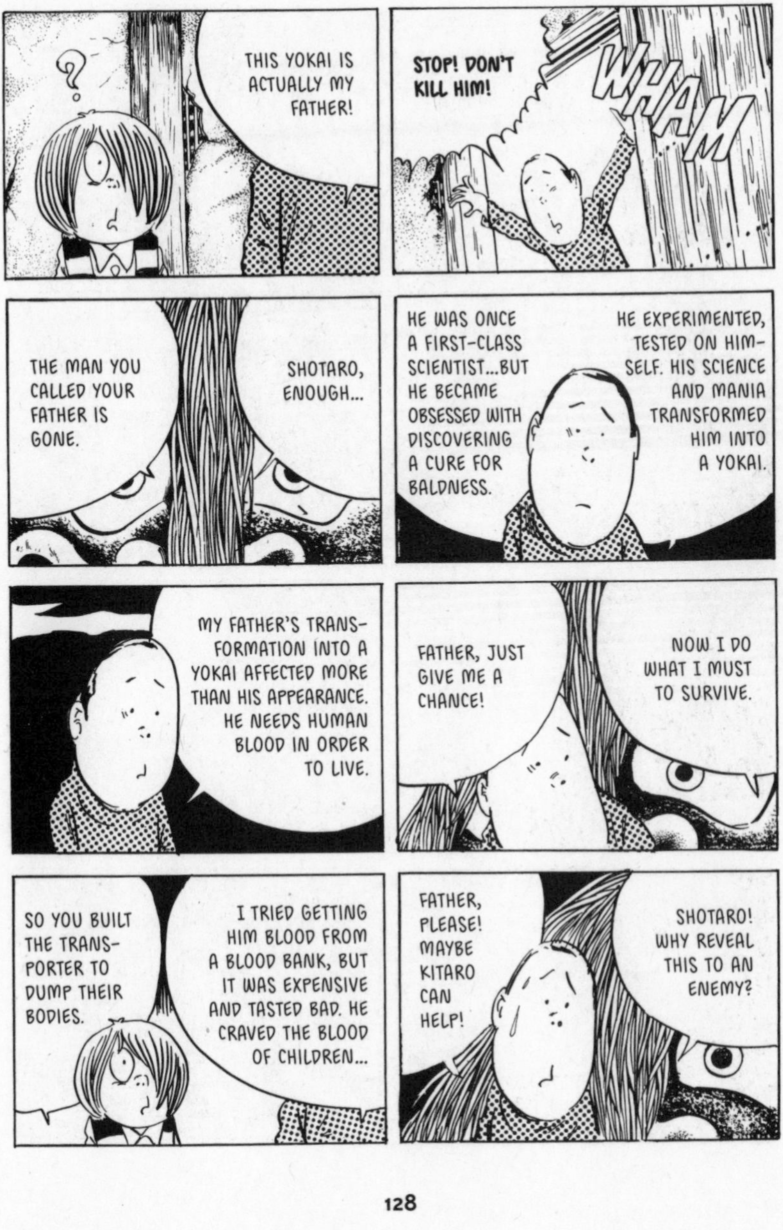
STOP! DON'T KILL HIM!
WHAM
THIS YOKAI IS ACTUALLY MY FATHER!
HE WAS ONCE A FIRST-CLASS SCIENTIST...BUT HE BECAME OBSESSED WITH DISCOVERING A CURE FOR BALDNESS.
HE EXPERIMENTED, TESTED ON HIM-SELF. HIS SCIENCE AND MANIA TRANSFORMED HIM INTO A YOKAI.
SHOTARO, ENOUGH...
THE MAN YOU CALLED YOUR FATHER IS GONE.
NOW I DO WHAT I MUST TO SURVIVE.
FATHER, JUST GIVE ME A CHANCE!
MY FATHER'S TRANS-FORMATION INTO A YOKAI AFFECTED MORE THAN HIS APPEARANCE. HE NEEDS HUMAN BLOOD IN ORDER TO LIVE.
SHOTARO! WHY REVEAL THIS TO AN ENEMY?
FATHER, PLEASE! MAYBE KITARO CAN HELP!
I TRIED GETTING HIM BLOOD FROM A BLOOD BANK, BUT IT WAS EXPENSIVE AND TASTED BAD. HE CRAVED THE BLOOD OF CHILDREN...
SO YOU BUILT THE TRANS-PORTER TO DUMP THEIR BODIES.

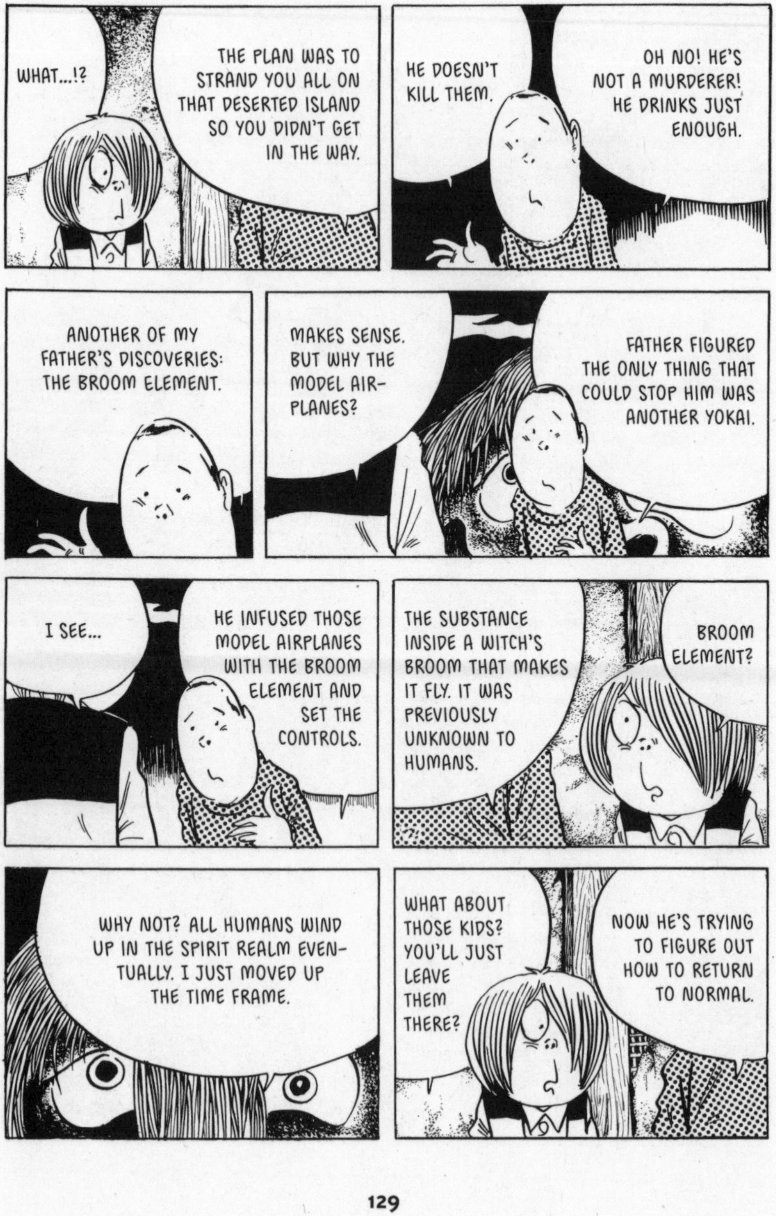
OH NO! HE'S NOT A MURDERER! HE DRINKS JUST ENOUGH.
HE DOESN'T KILL THEM.
THE PLAN WAS TO STRAND YOU ALL ON THAT DESERTED ISLAND SO YOU DIDN'T GET IN THE WAY.
WHAT...!?
FATHER FIGURED THE ONLY THING THAT COULD STOP HIM WAS ANOTHER YOKAI.
MAKES SENSE. BUT WHY THE MODEL AIR-PLANES?
ANOTHER OF MY FATHER'S DISCOVERIES: THE BROOM ELEMENT.
BROOM ELEMENT?
THE SUBSTANCE INSIDE A WITCH'S BROOM THAT MAKES IT FLY. IT WAS PREVIOUSLY UNKNOWN TO HUMANS.
HE INFUSED THOSE MODEL AIRPLANES WITH THE BROOM ELEMENT AND SET THE CONTROLS.
I SEE...
NOW HE'S TRYING TO FIGURE OUT HOW TO RETURN TO NORMAL.
WHAT ABOUT THOSE KIDS? YOU'LL JUST LEAVE THEM THERE?
WHY NOT? ALL HUMANS WIND UP IN THE SPIRIT REALM EVEN-TUALLY. I JUST MOVED UP THE TIME FRAME.

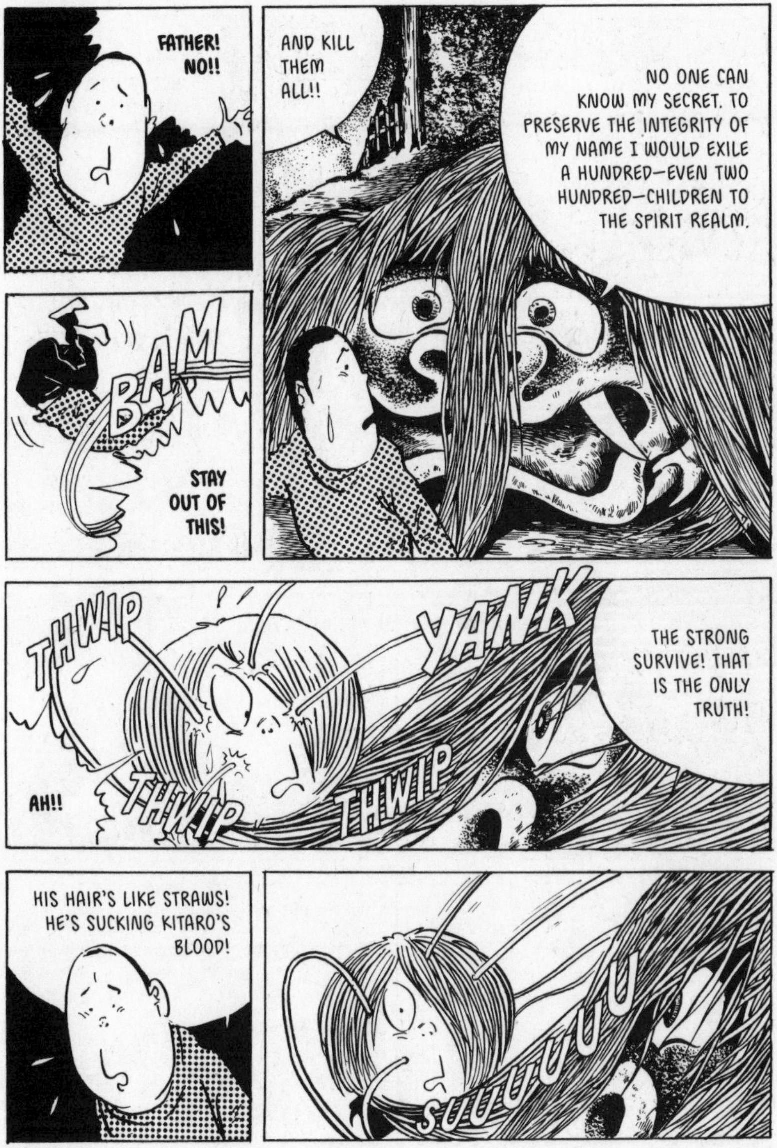
NO ONE CAN KNOW MY SECRET. TO PRESERVE THE INTEGRITY OF MY NAME I WOULD EXILE A HUNDRED—EVEN TWO HUNDRED—CHILDREN TO THE SPIRIT REALM.
AND KILL THEM ALL!!
FATHER! NO!!
BAM
STAY OUT OF THIS!
THE STRONG SURVIVE! THAT IS THE ONLY TRUTH!
YANK
THWIP
THWIP
THWIP
AH!!
SUUUUUUU
HIS HAIR'S LIKE STRAWS! HE'S SUCKING KITARO'S BLOOD!

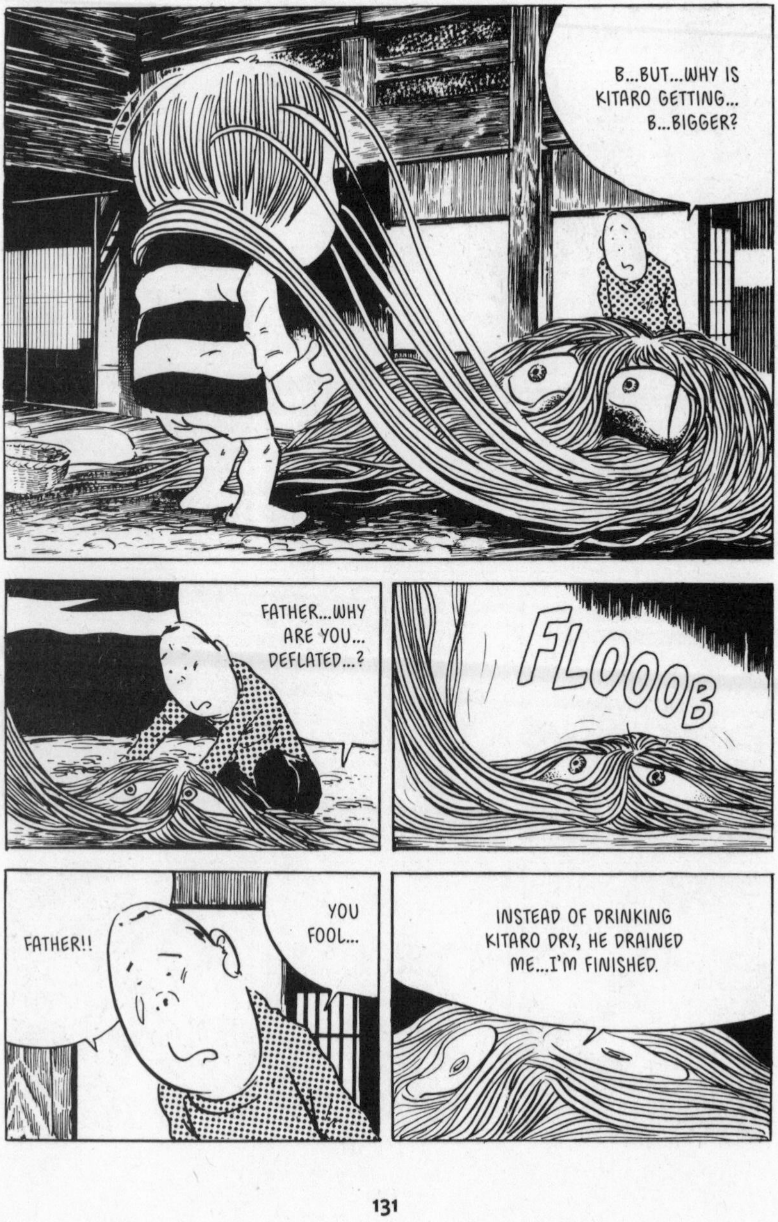
B...BUT...WHY IS KITARO GETTING... B...BIGGER?
FLOOOB
FATHER...WHY ARE YOU... DEFLATED...?
INSTEAD OF DRINKING KITARO DRY, HE DRAINED ME...I'M FINISHED.
YOU FOOL...
FATHER!!

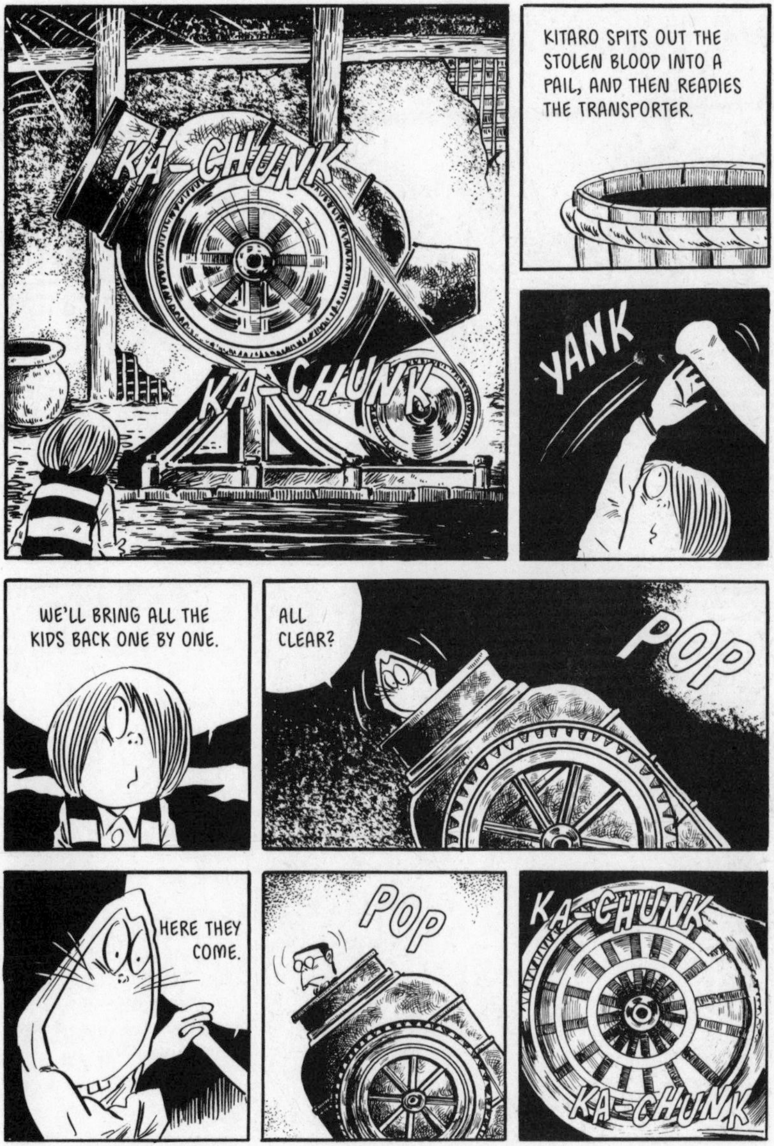
KITARO SPITS OUT THE STOLEN BLOOD INTO A PAIL, AND THEN READIES THE TRANSPORTER.
YANK
KA-CHUNK
KA-CHUNK
POP
ALL CLEAR?
WE'LL BRING ALL THE KIDS BACK ONE BY ONE.
KA-CHUNK
KA-CHUNK
POP
HERE THEY COME.

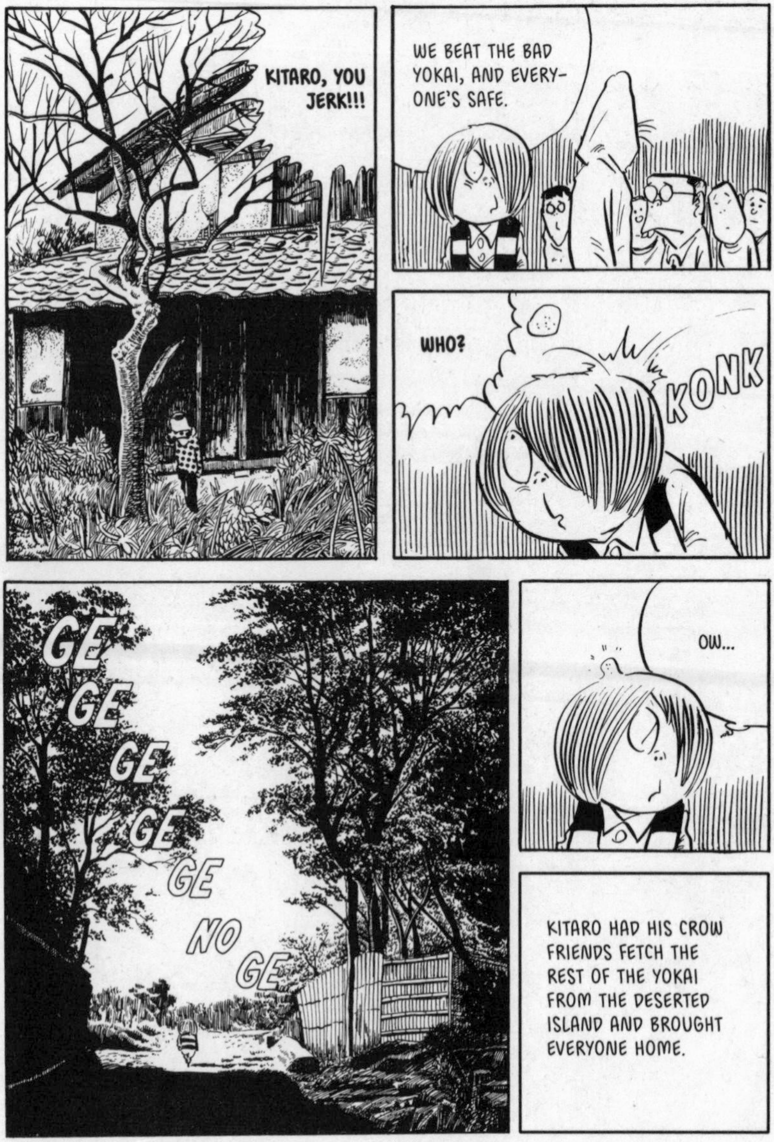
WE BEAT THE BAD YOKAI, AND EVERY-ONE'S SAFE.
KONK
WHO?
KITARO, YOU JERK!!!
OW...
KITARO HAD HIS CROW FRIENDS FETCH THE REST OF THE YOKAI FROM THE DESERTED ISLAND AND BROUGHT EVERYONE HOME.
GE GE GE GE GE NO GE

ODORO ODORO
VERSUS VAMPIRE

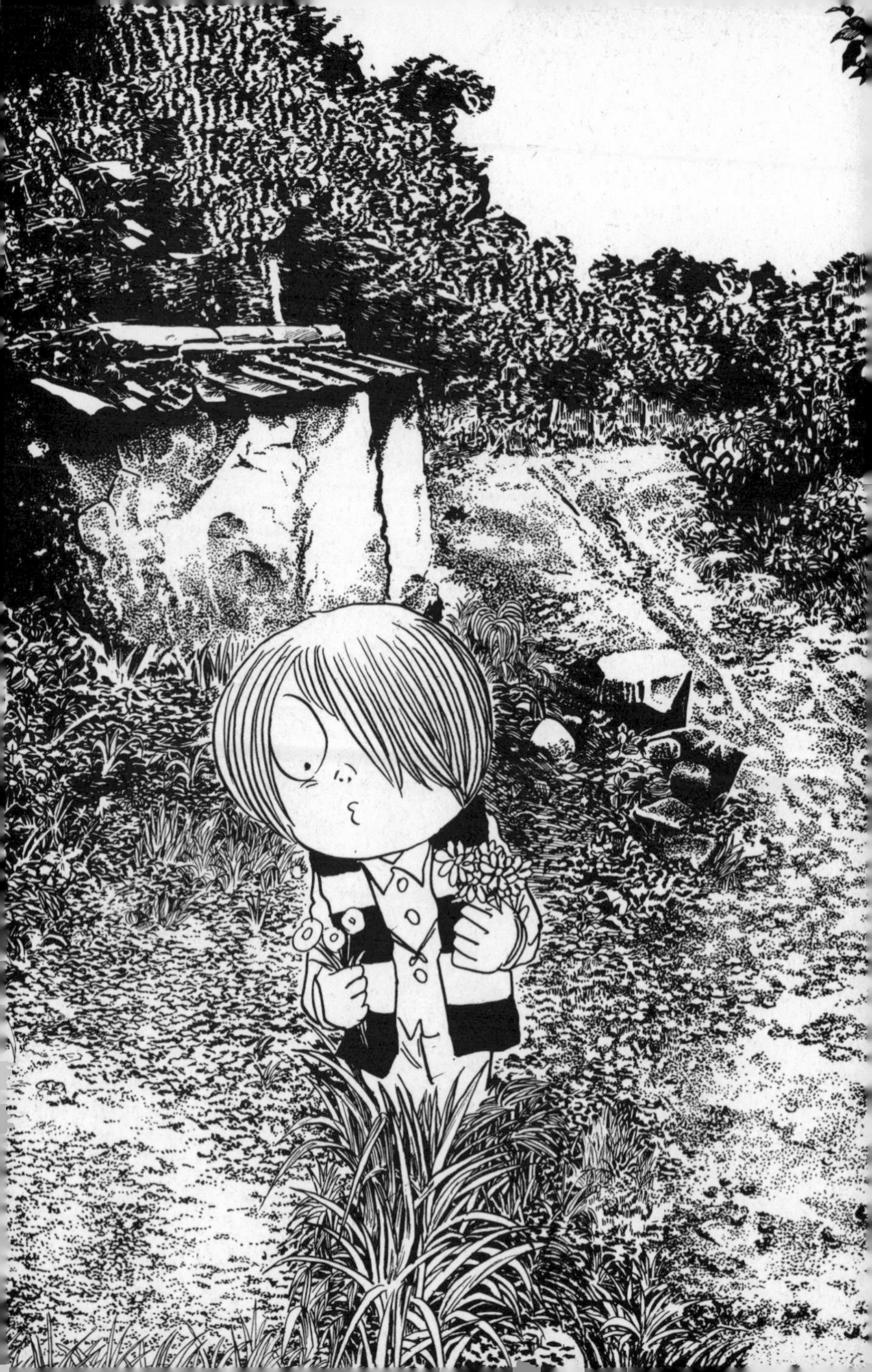

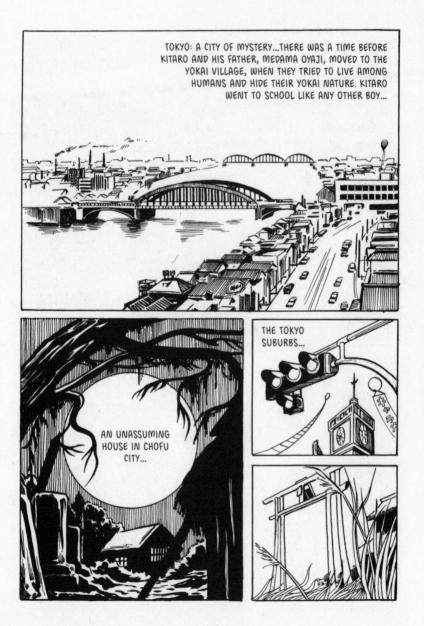

TOKYO: A CITY OF MYSTERY...THERE WAS A TIME BEFORE KITARO AND HIS FATHER, MEDAMA OYAJI, MOVED TO THE YOKAI VILLAGE, WHEN THEY TRIED TO LIVE AMONG HUMANS AND HIDE THEIR YOKAI NATURE. KITARO WENT TO SCHOOL LIKE ANY OTHER BOY...

THE TOKYO SUBURBS...

AN UNASSUMING HOUSE IN CHOFU CITY...

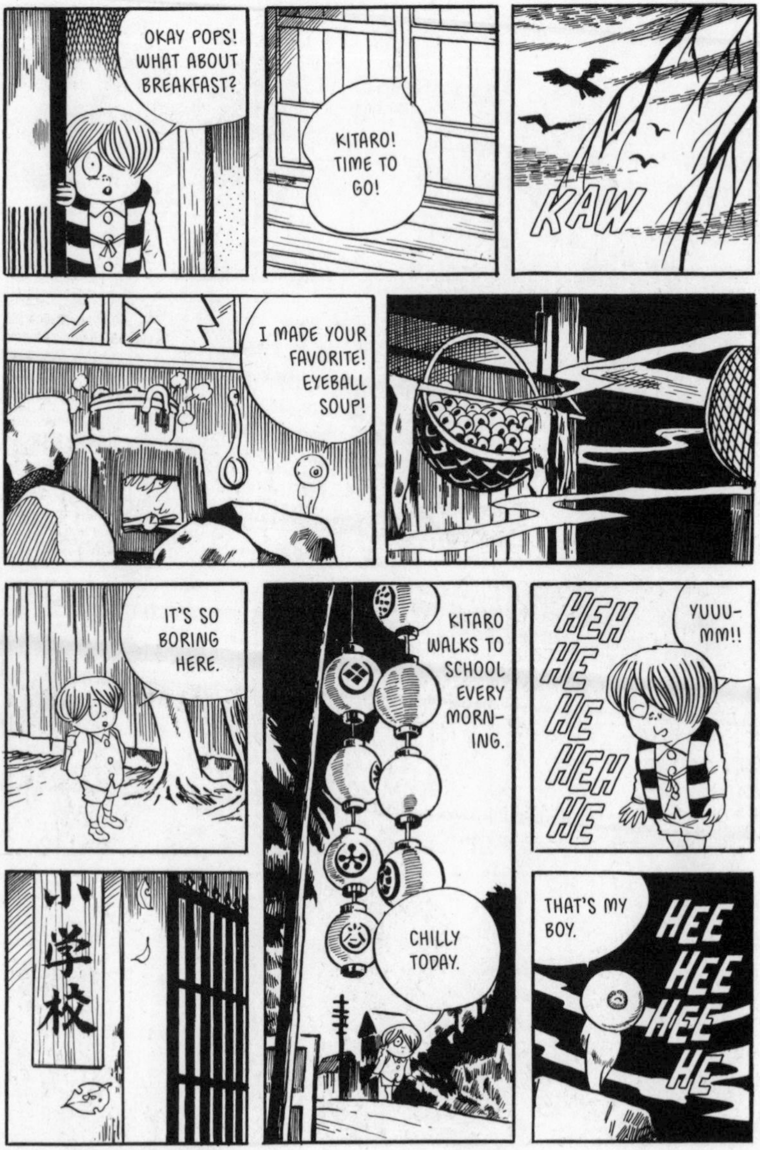
KAW
KITARO! TIME TO GO!
OKAY POPS! WHAT ABOUT BREAKFAST?
I MADE YOUR FAVORITE! EYEBALL SOUP!
YUUU-MM!!
HEH HE HE HEH HE
HEE HEE HEE HE
THAT'S MY BOY.
KITARO WALKS TO SCHOOL EVERY MORNING.
CHILLY TODAY.
IT'S SO BORING HERE.
小学校

SIGN: ELEMENTARY SCHOOL

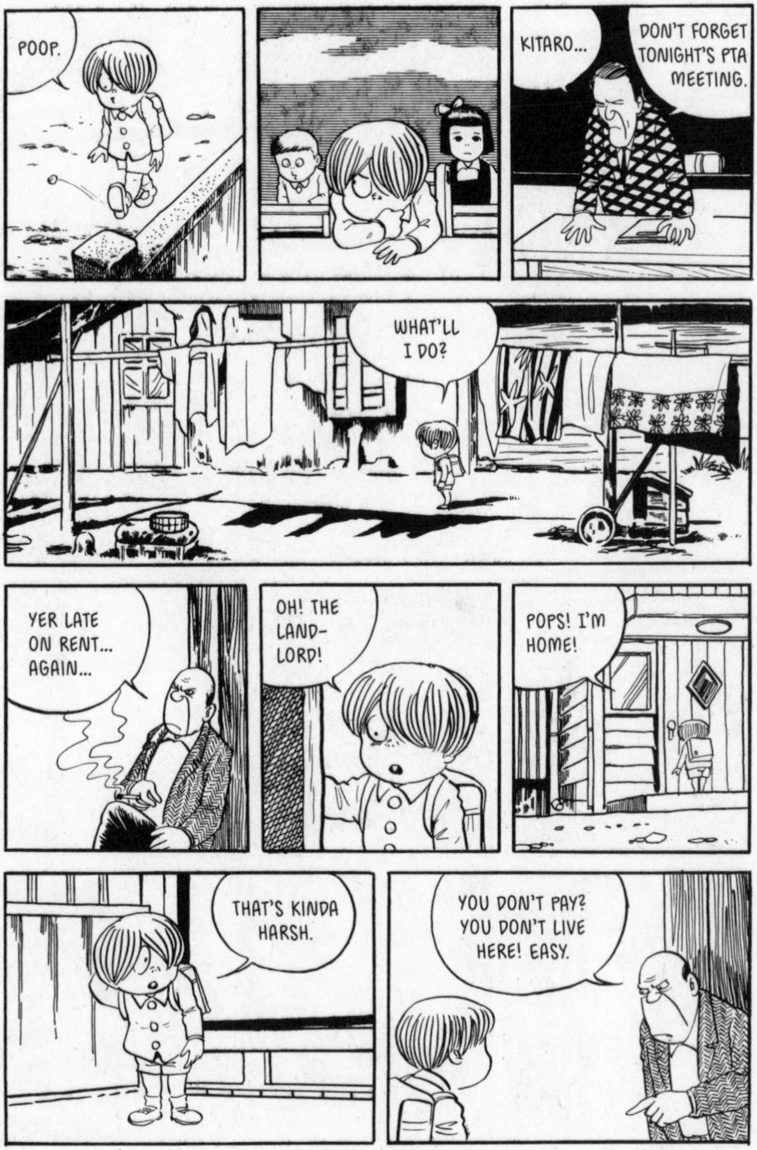
KITARO...
DON'T FORGET TONIGHT'S PTA MEETING.
POOP.
WHAT'LL I DO?
POPS! I'M HOME!
OH! THE LAND-LORD!
YER LATE ON RENT... AGAIN...
YOU DON'T PAY? YOU DON'T LIVE HERE! EASY.
THAT'S KINDA HARSH.

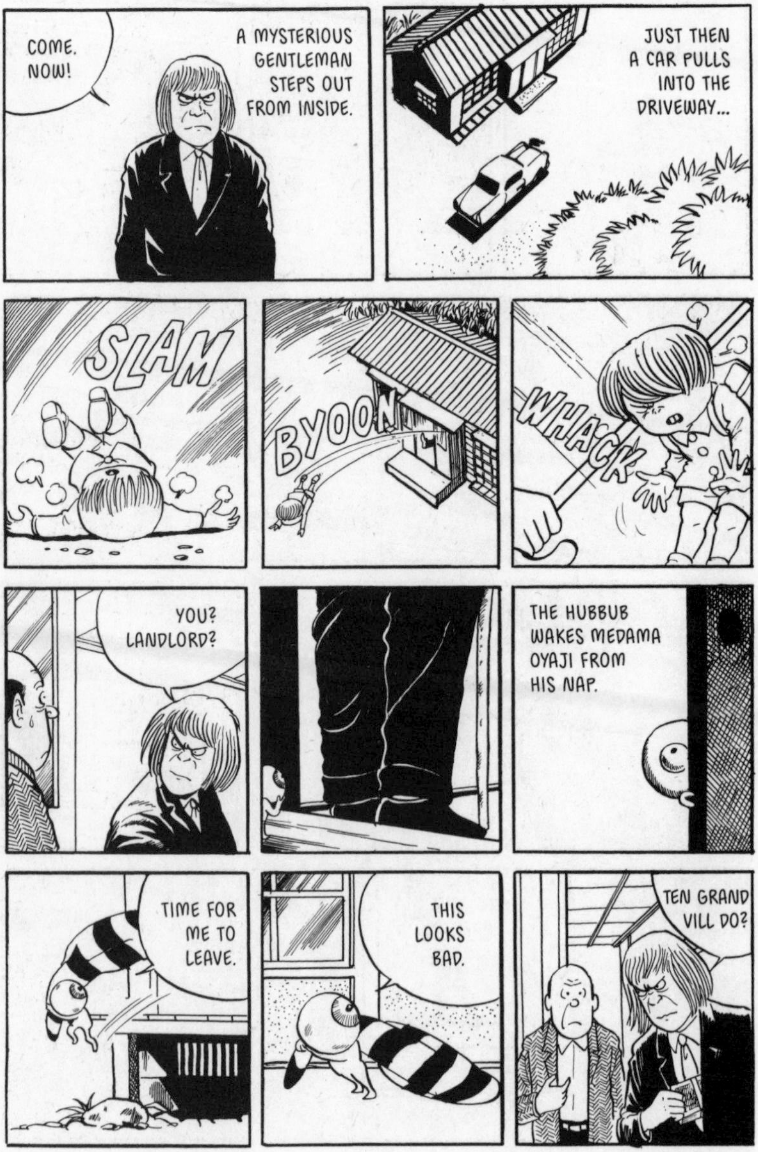
JUST THEN A CAR PULLS INTO THE DRIVEWAY...
A MYSTERIOUS GENTLEMAN STEPS OUT FROM INSIDE.
COME. NOW!
WHACK
BYOON
SLAM
THE HUBBUB WAKES MEDAMA OYAJI FROM HIS NAP.
YOU? LANDLORD?
TEN GRAND VILL DO?
THIS LOOKS BAD.
TIME FOR ME TO LEAVE.

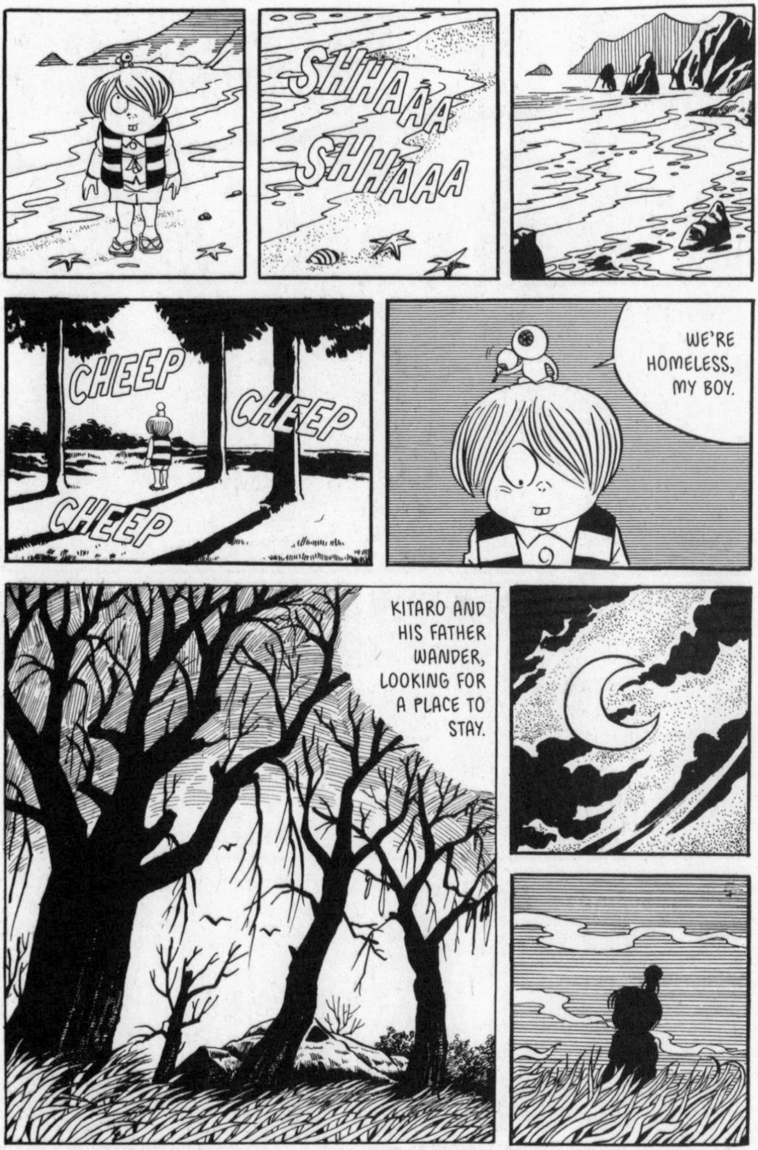
SHHAAA
SHHAAA
WE'RE HOMELESS, MY BOY.
CHEEP
CHEEP
CHEEP
KITARO AND HIS FATHER WANDER, LOOKING FOR A PLACE TO STAY.

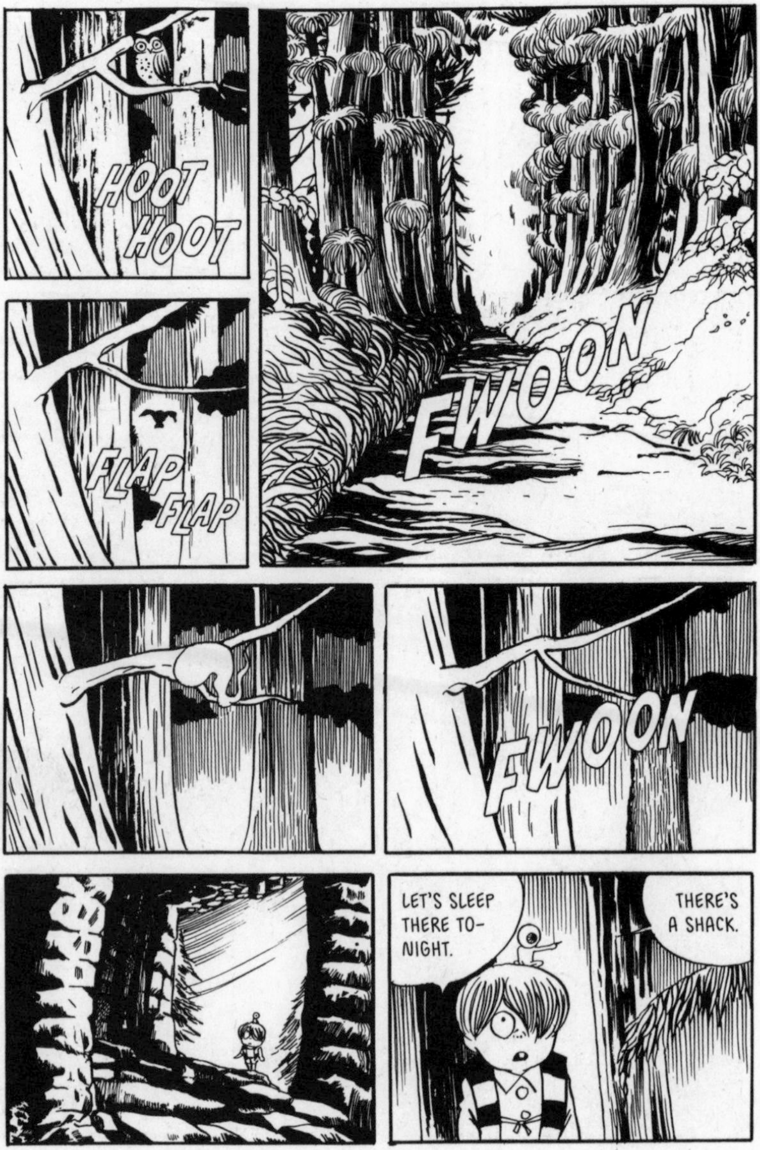
FWOON
HOOT HOOT
FLAP FLAP
FWOON
THERE'S A SHACK.
LET'S SLEEP THERE TO-NIGHT.

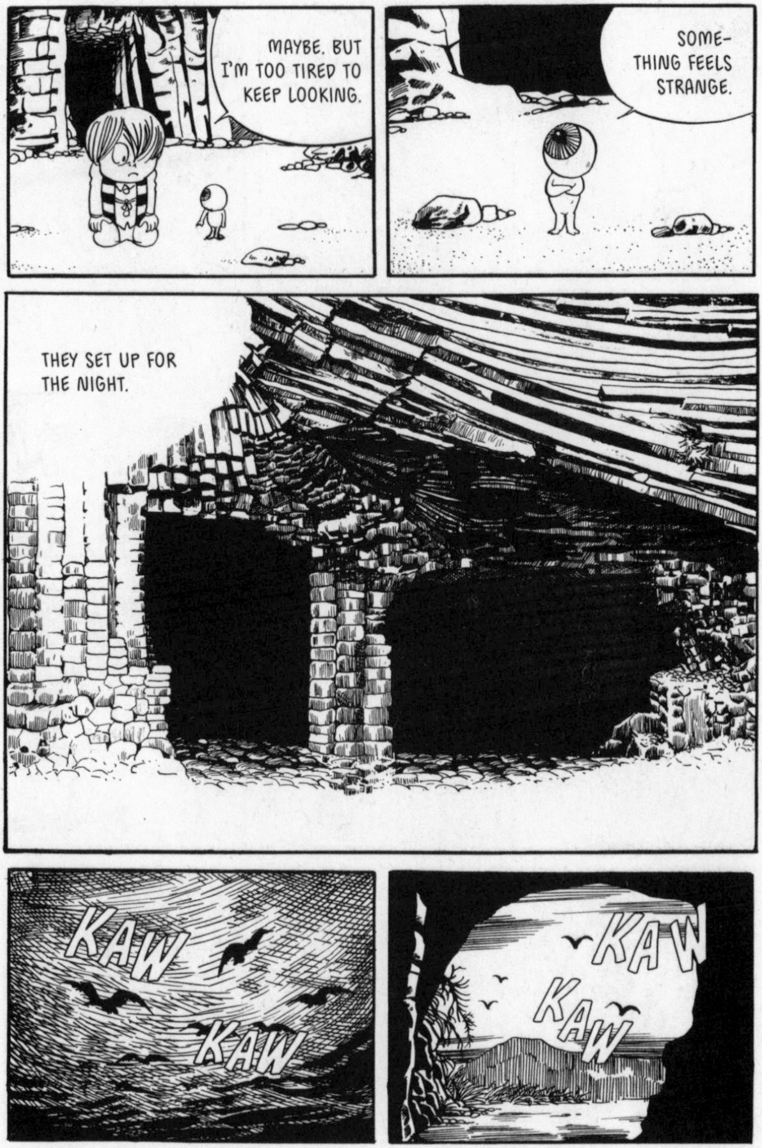
SOME-THING FEELS STRANGE.
MAYBE. BUT I'M TOO TIRED TO KEEP LOOKING.
THEY SET UP FOR THE NIGHT.
KAW
KAW
KAW
KAW

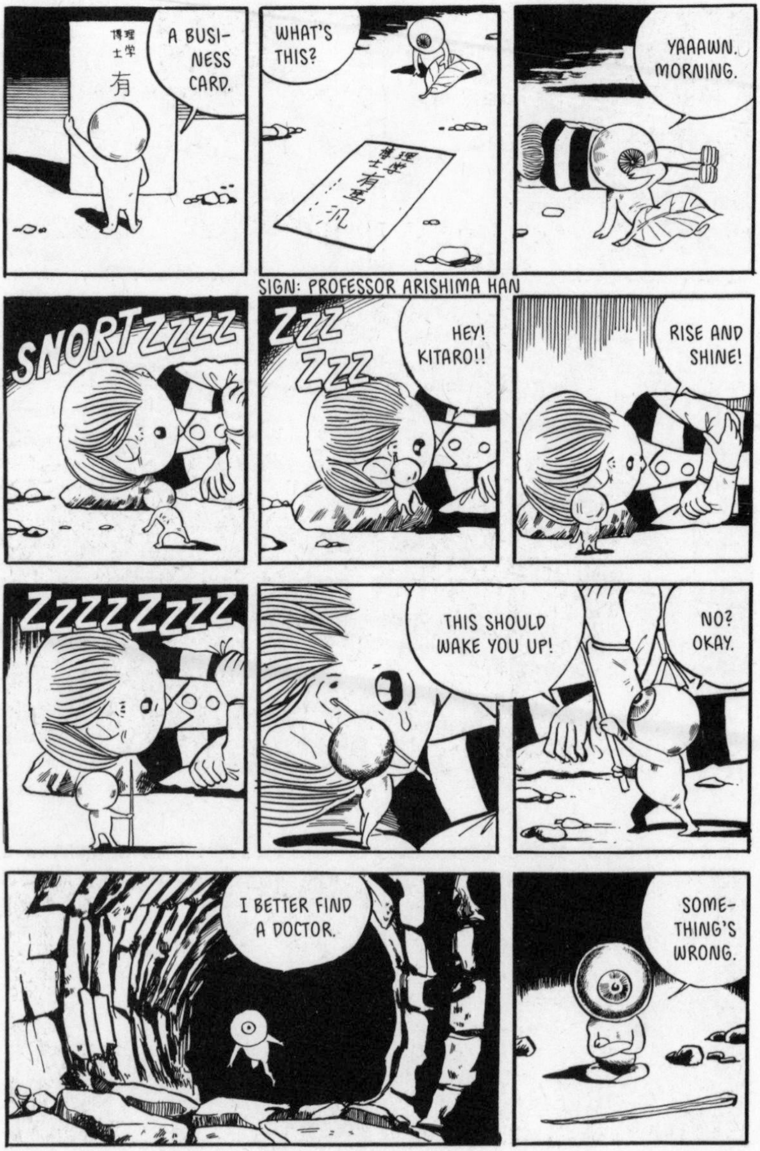
YAAAWN. MORNING.
WHAT'S THIS?
SIGN: PROFESSOR ARISHIMA HAN
A BUSI-NESS CARD.
RISE AND SHINE!
HEY! KITARO!!
ZZZ ZZZ
SNORT ZZZZ
NO? OKAY.
THIS SHOULD WAKE YOU UP!
ZZZZ ZZZZ
SOME-THING'S WRONG.
I BETTER FIND A DOCTOR.

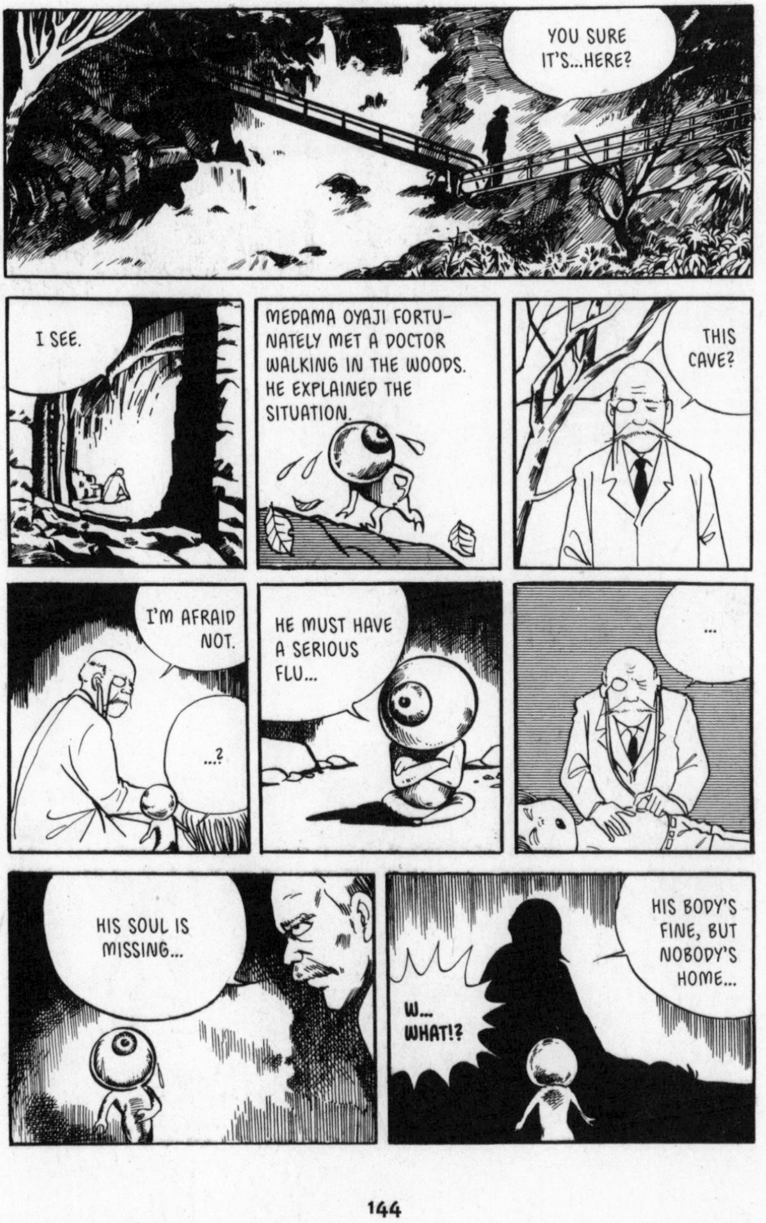
YOU SURE IT'S...HERE?
THIS CAVE?
MEDAMA OYAJI FORTUNATELY MET A DOCTOR WALKING IN THE WOODS. HE EXPLAINED THE SITUATION.
I SEE.
...
HE MUST HAVE A SERIOUS FLU...
I'M AFRAID NOT.
...?
HIS BODY'S FINE, BUT NOBODY'S HOME...
W... WHAT!?
HIS SOUL IS MISSING...

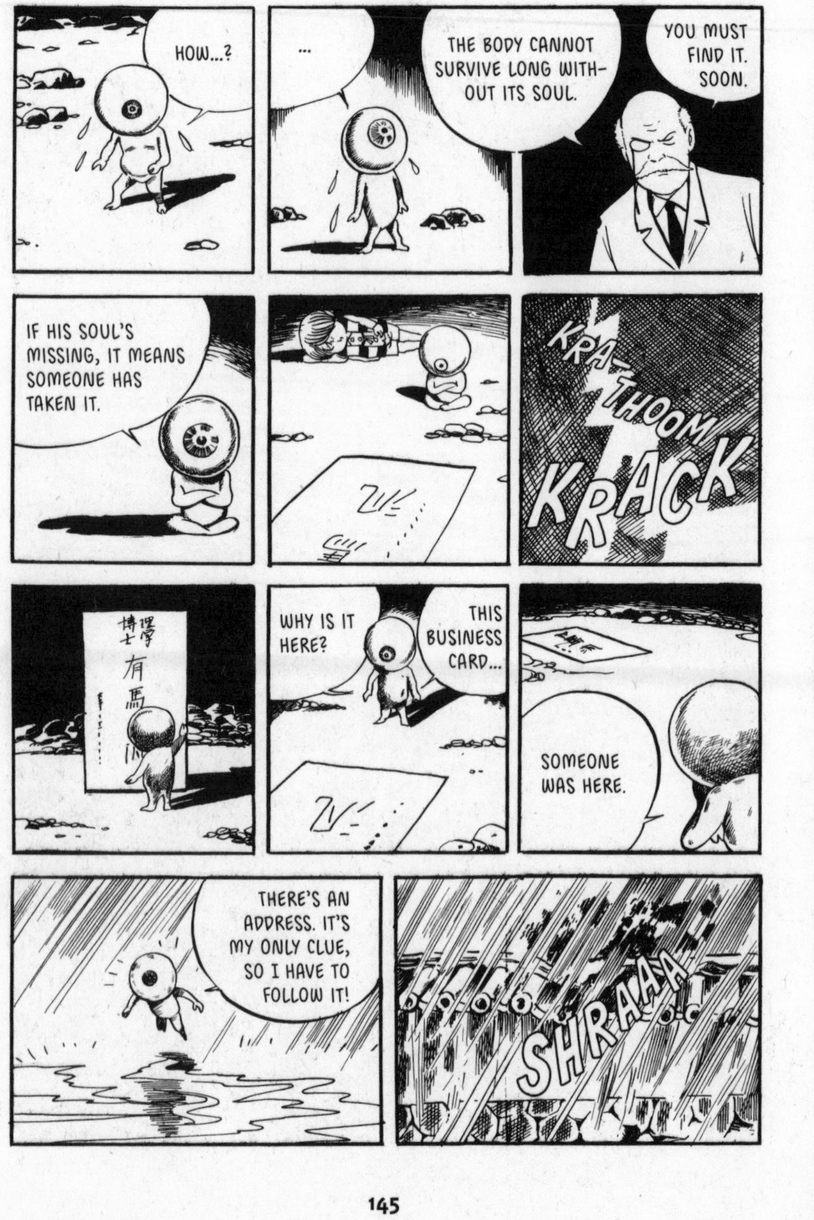
YOU MUST FIND IT. SOON.
THE BODY CANNOT SURVIVE LONG WITH-OUT ITS SOUL.
...
HOW...?
KRA-THOOM
KRACK
IF HIS SOUL'S MISSING, IT MEANS SOMEONE HAS TAKEN IT.
SOMEONE WAS HERE.
THIS BUSINESS CARD...
WHY IS IT HERE?
理學博士
有馬
SHRAAA...!
THERE'S AN ADDRESS. IT'S MY ONLY CLUE, SO I HAVE TO FOLLOW IT!

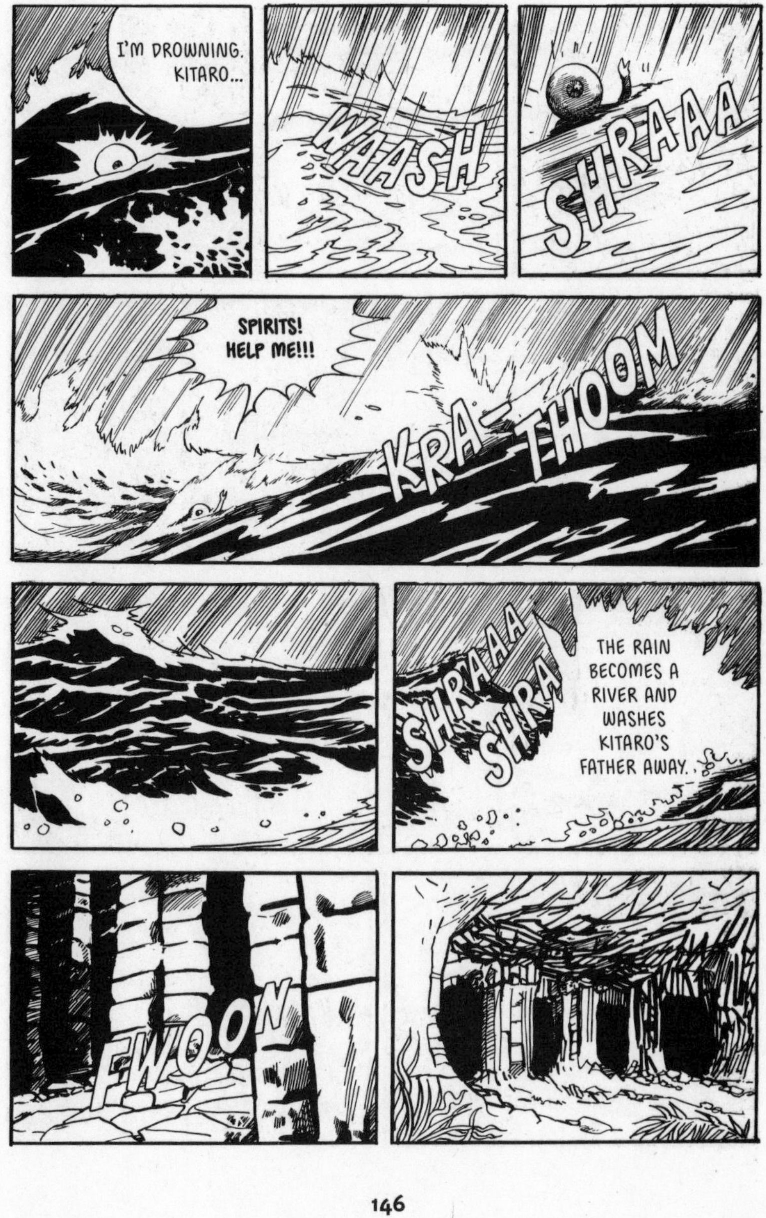
SHRAAA
WAASH
I'M DROWNING. KITARO...
SPIRITS! HELP ME!!!
KRA-THOOM
THE RAIN BECOMES A RIVER AND WASHES KITARO'S FATHER AWAY...
SHRAAAA
SHRA
FWOON

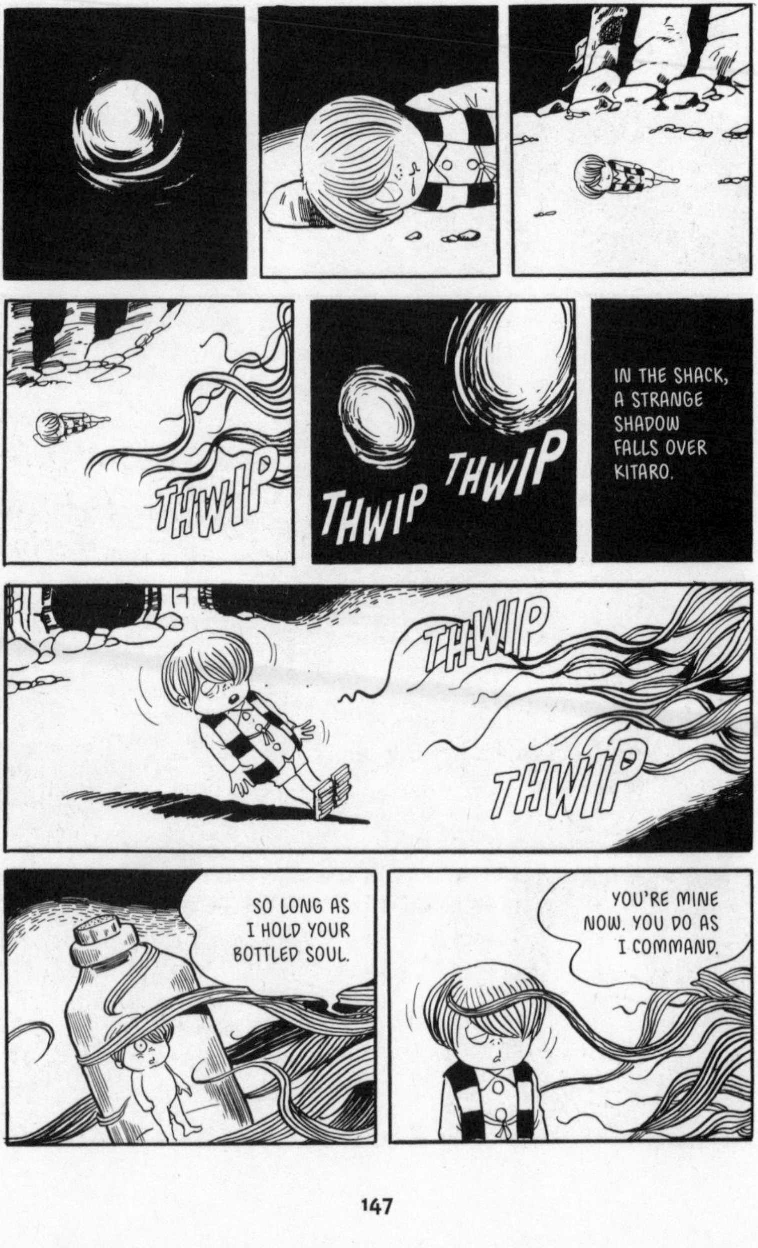
IN THE SHACK, A STRANGE SHADOW FALLS OVER KITARO.
THWIP
THWIP
THWIP
THWIP
THWIP
YOU'RE MINE NOW. YOU DO AS I COMMAND.
SO LONG AS I HOLD YOUR BOTTLED SOUL.

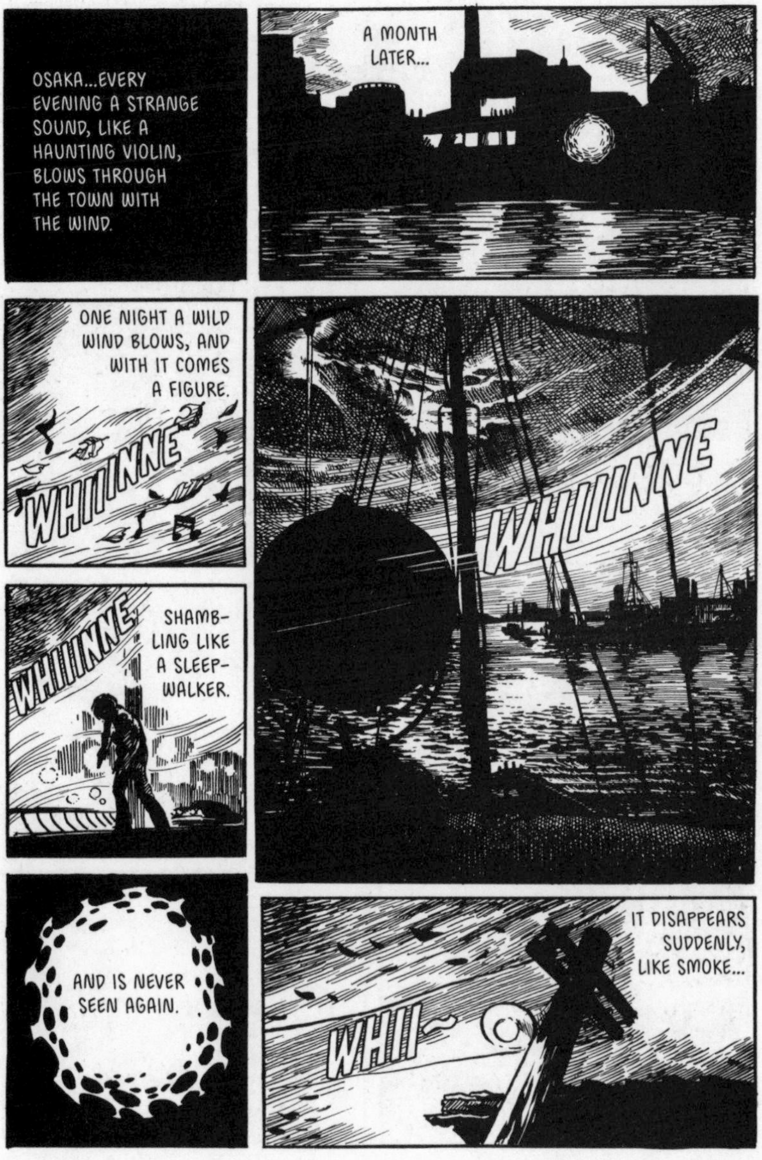
A MONTH LATER...
OSAKA...EVERY EVENING A STRANGE SOUND, LIKE A HAUNTING VIOLIN, BLOWS THROUGH THE TOWN WITH THE WIND.
WHIIIINNE
ONE NIGHT A WILD WIND BLOWS, AND WITH IT COMES A FIGURE.
WHIIINNE
WHIIIINNE
SHAMB-LING LIKE A SLEEP-WALKER.
IT DISAPPEARS SUDDENLY, LIKE SMOKE...
WHII~
AND IS NEVER SEEN AGAIN.

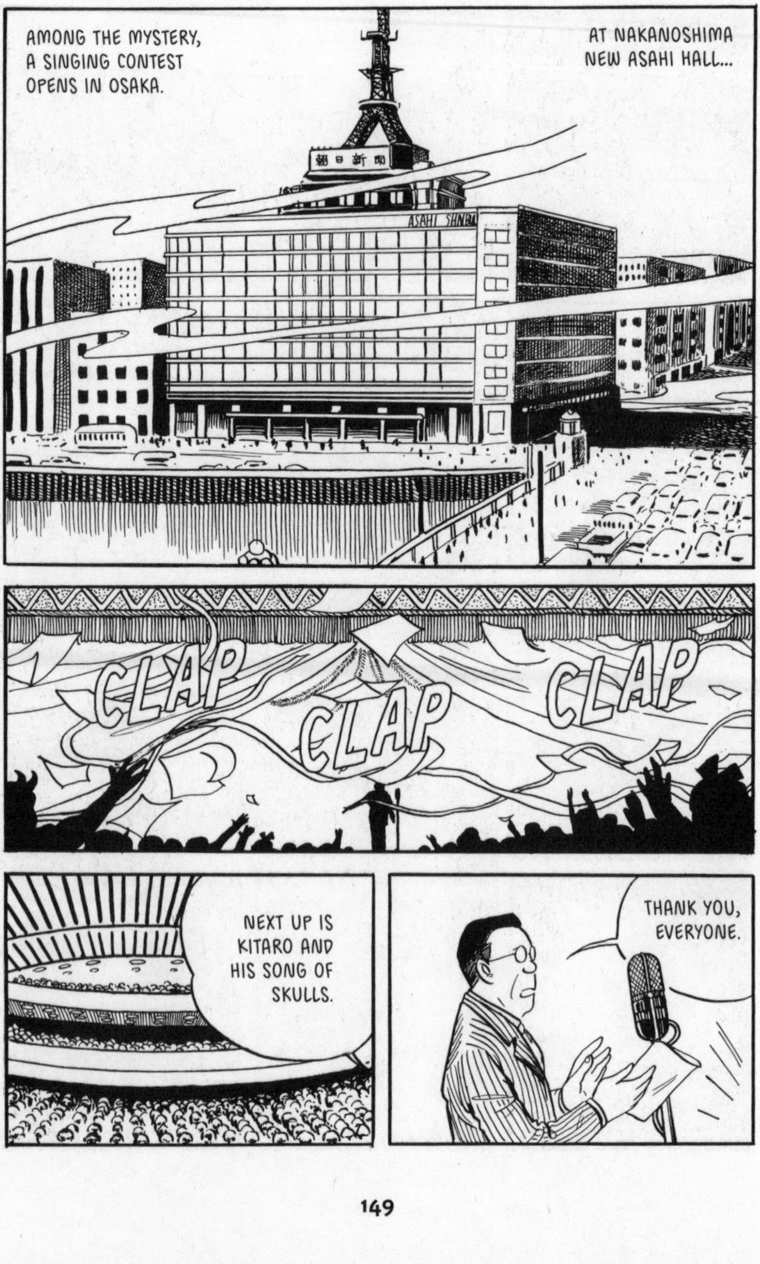
AT NAKANOSHIMA NEW ASAHI HALL...
AMONG THE MYSTERY, A SINGING CONTEST OPENS IN OSAKA.
CLAP
CLAP
CLAP
THANK YOU, EVERYONE.
NEXT UP IS KITARO AND HIS SONG OF SKULLS.

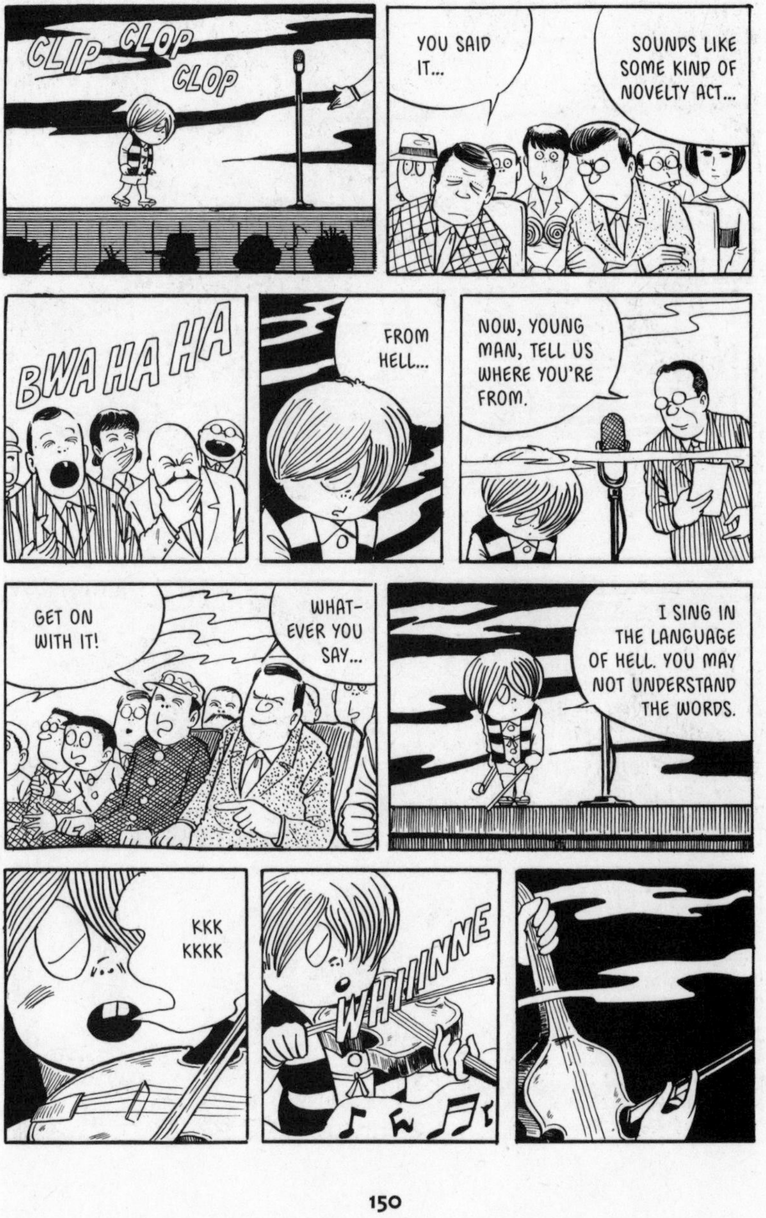
SOUNDS LIKE SOME KIND OF NOVELTY ACT...
YOU SAID IT...
CLIP CLOP CLOP
NOW, YOUNG MAN, TELL US WHERE YOU'RE FROM.
FROM HELL...
BWA HA HA
I SING IN THE LANGUAGE OF HELL. YOU MAY NOT UNDERSTAND THE WORDS.
WHAT-EVER YOU SAY...
GET ON WITH IT!
WHIIINNE
KKK KKKK

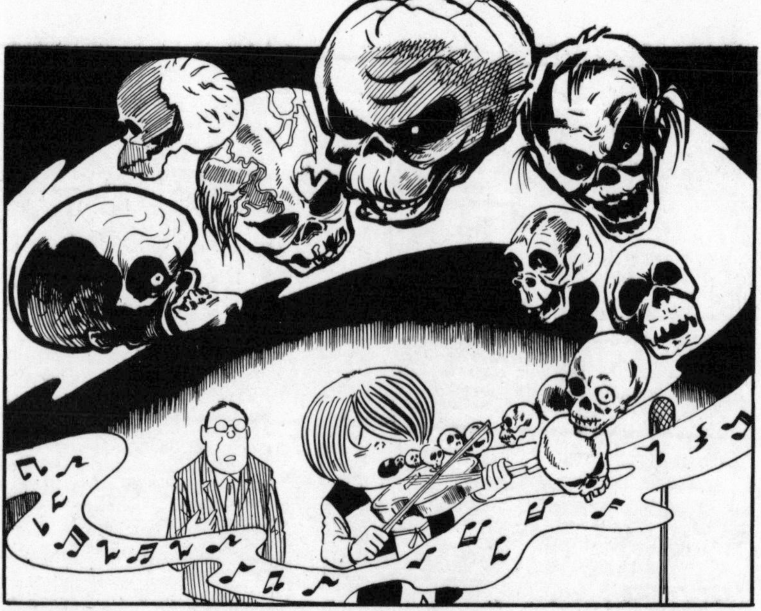

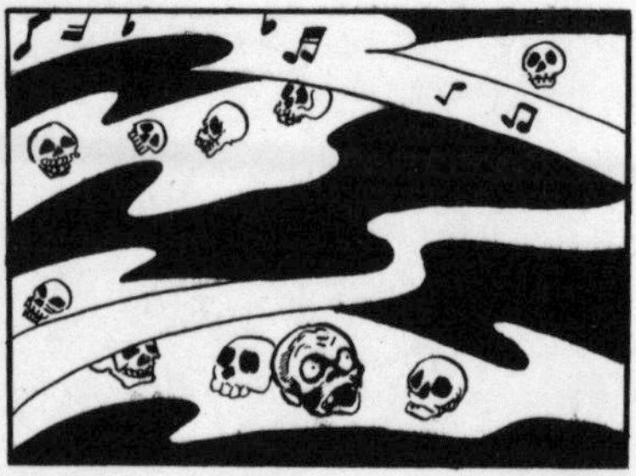

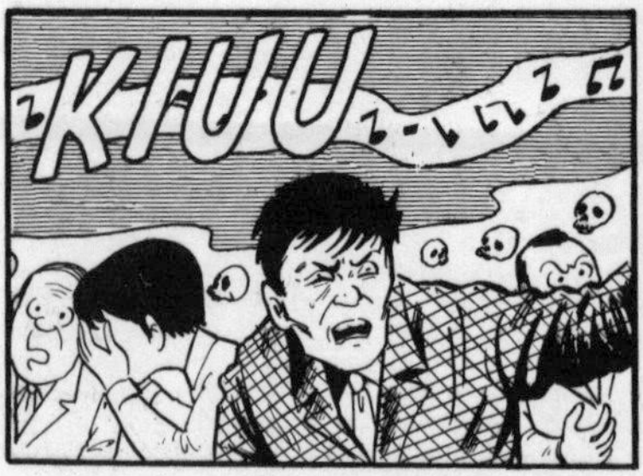
KIUU

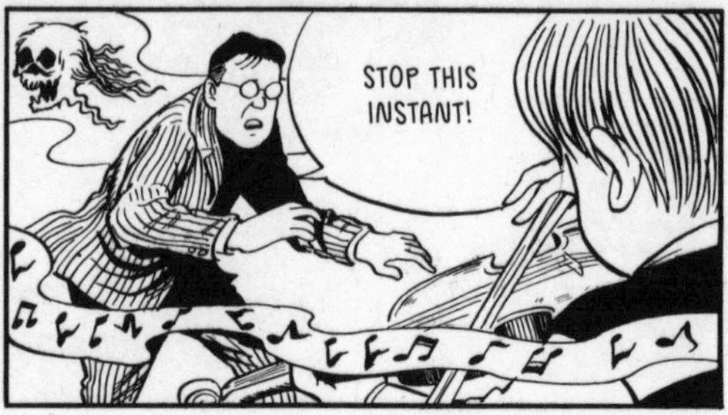
STOP THIS INSTANT!

THE ANNOUNCER CUTS KITARO'S MICROPHONE. THE VIOLIN MUSIC IS THE SAME EERIE SOUND THAT HAS BEEN BLOWING THROUGH TOWN. KITARO KEEPS PLAYING UNTIL THE ENTIRE HALL HAS BEEN CLEARED. EVEN THEN, THE HAUNTING MELODY STAYS WITH THE AUDIENCE LONG AFTER THEY ARE GONE.

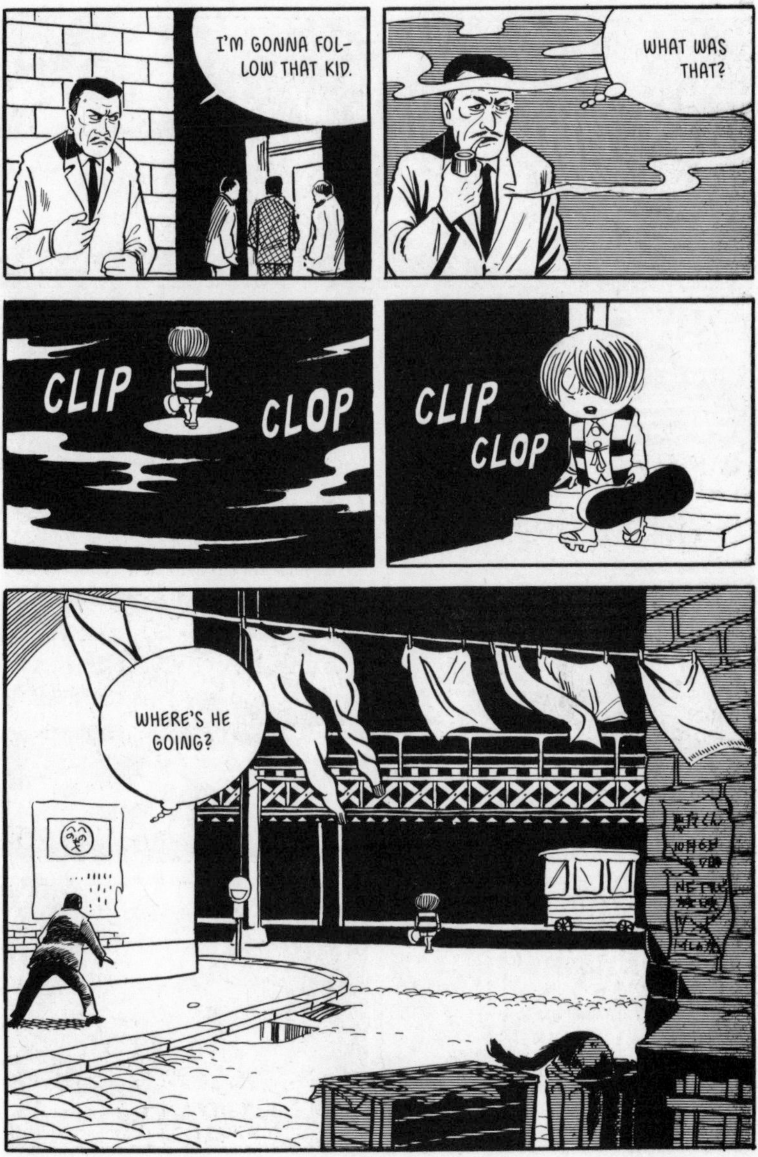
WHAT WAS THAT?
I'M GONNA FOL-LOW THAT KID.
CLIP
CLOP
CLIP
CLOP
WHERE'S HE GOING?

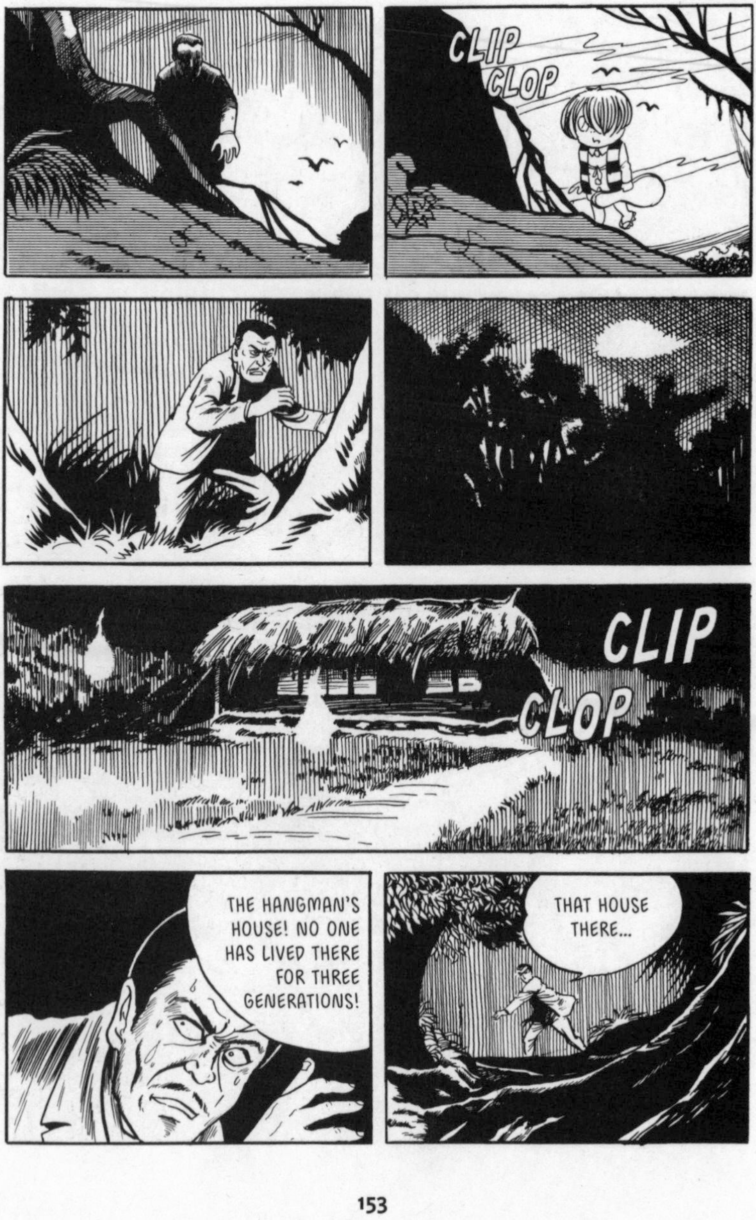
CLIP
CLOP
CLIP
CLOP
THAT HOUSE THERE...
THE HANGMAN'S HOUSE! NO ONE HAS LIVED THERE FOR THREE GENERATIONS!

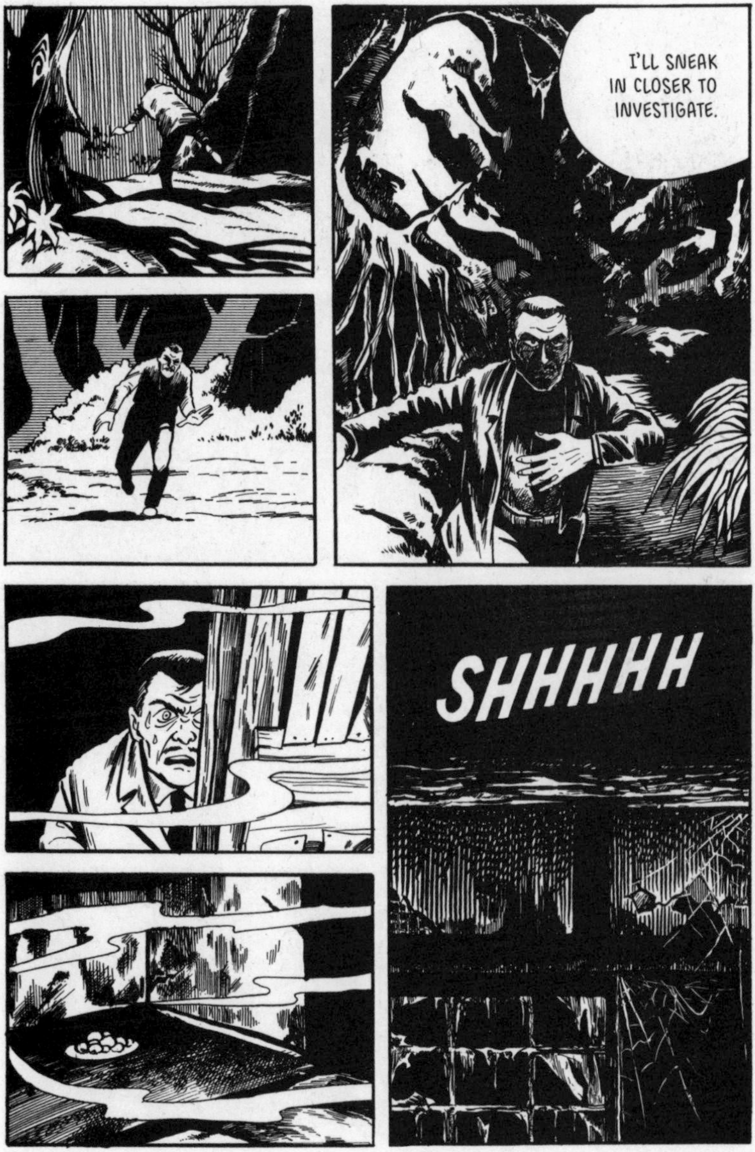
I'LL SNEAK IN CLOSER TO INVESTIGATE.
SHHHHH

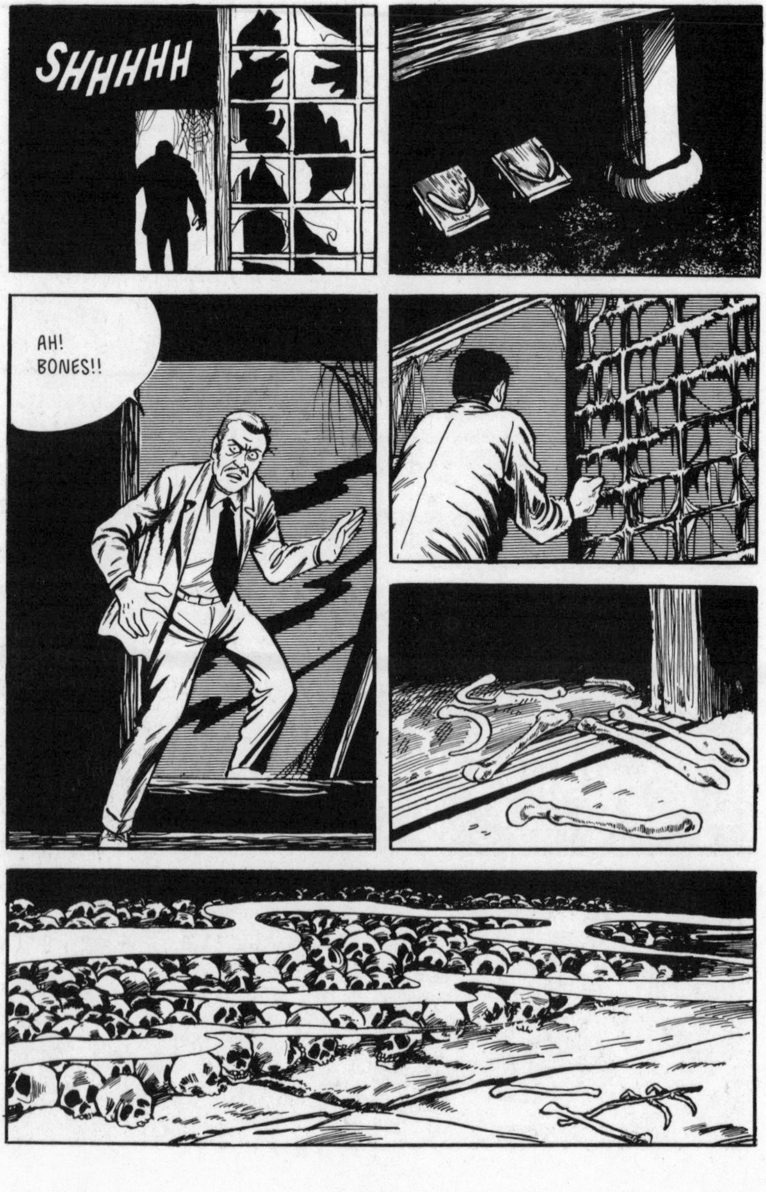
SHHHHH
AH! BONES!!

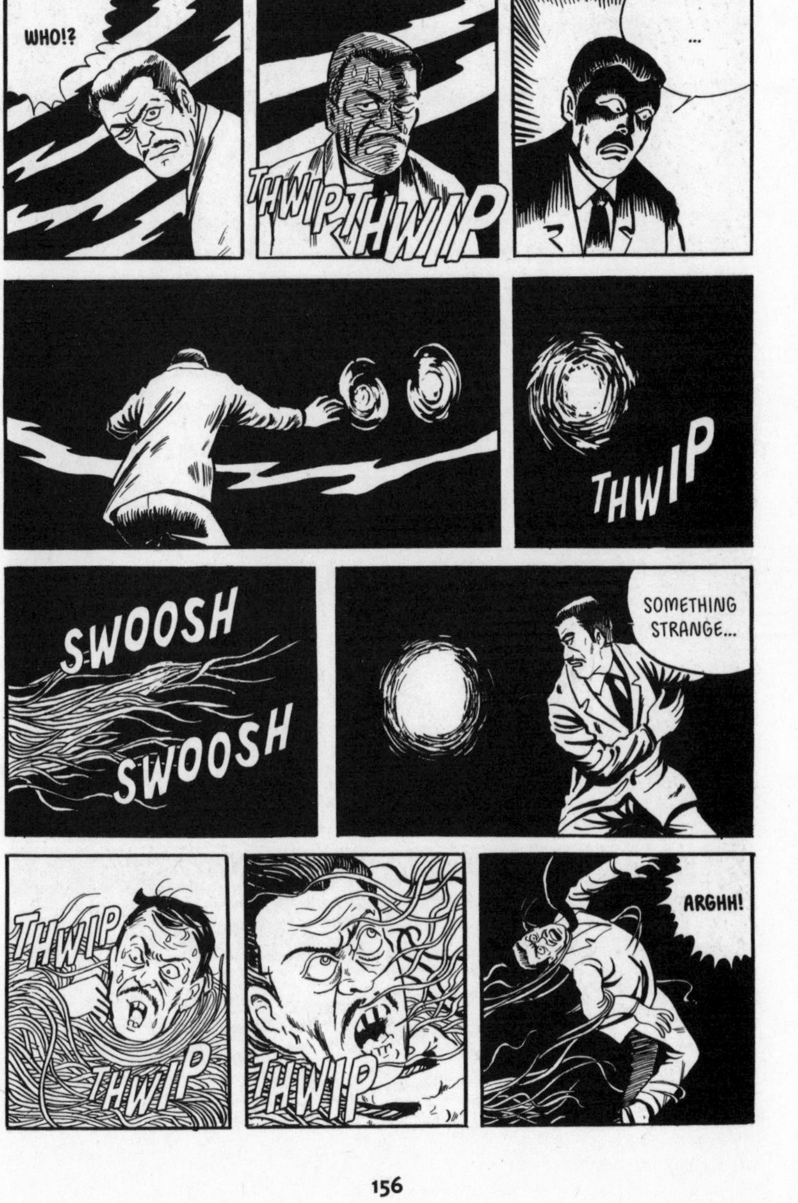
...
THWIP
THWIIP
WHO!?
THWIP
SOMETHING STRANGE...
SWOOSH
SWOOSH
ARGHH!
THWIP
THWIP
THWIP

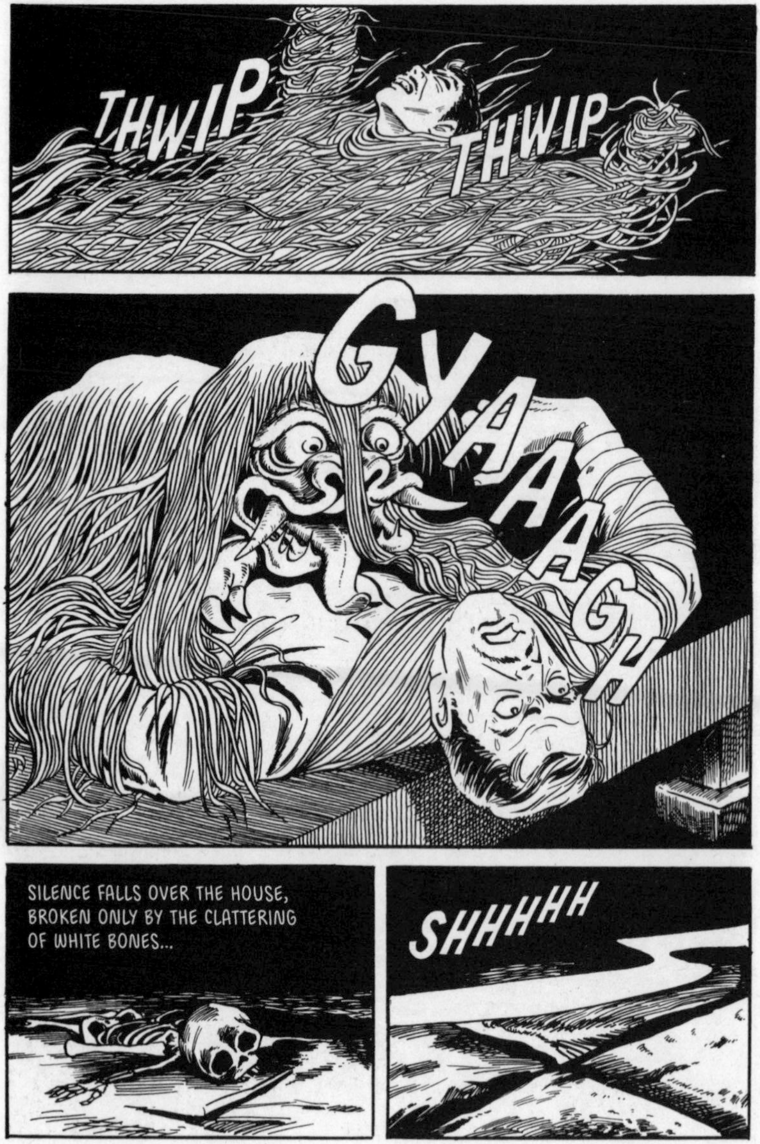
THWIP
THWIP
GYAAAGH
SHHHHH
SILENCE FALLS OVER THE HOUSE, BROKEN ONLY BY THE CLATTERING OF WHITE BONES...

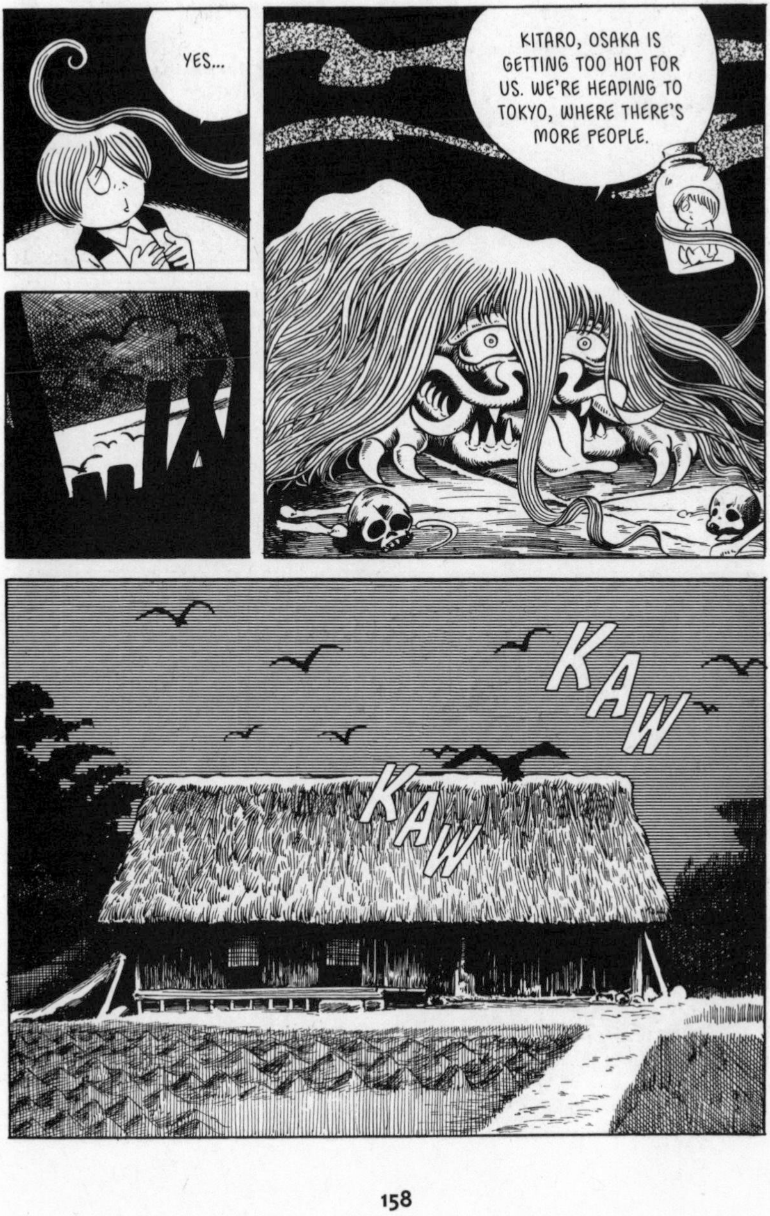
KITARO, OSAKA IS GETTING TOO HOT FOR US. WE'RE HEADING TO TOKYO, WHERE THERE'S MORE PEOPLE.
YES...
KAW KAW
KAW KAW

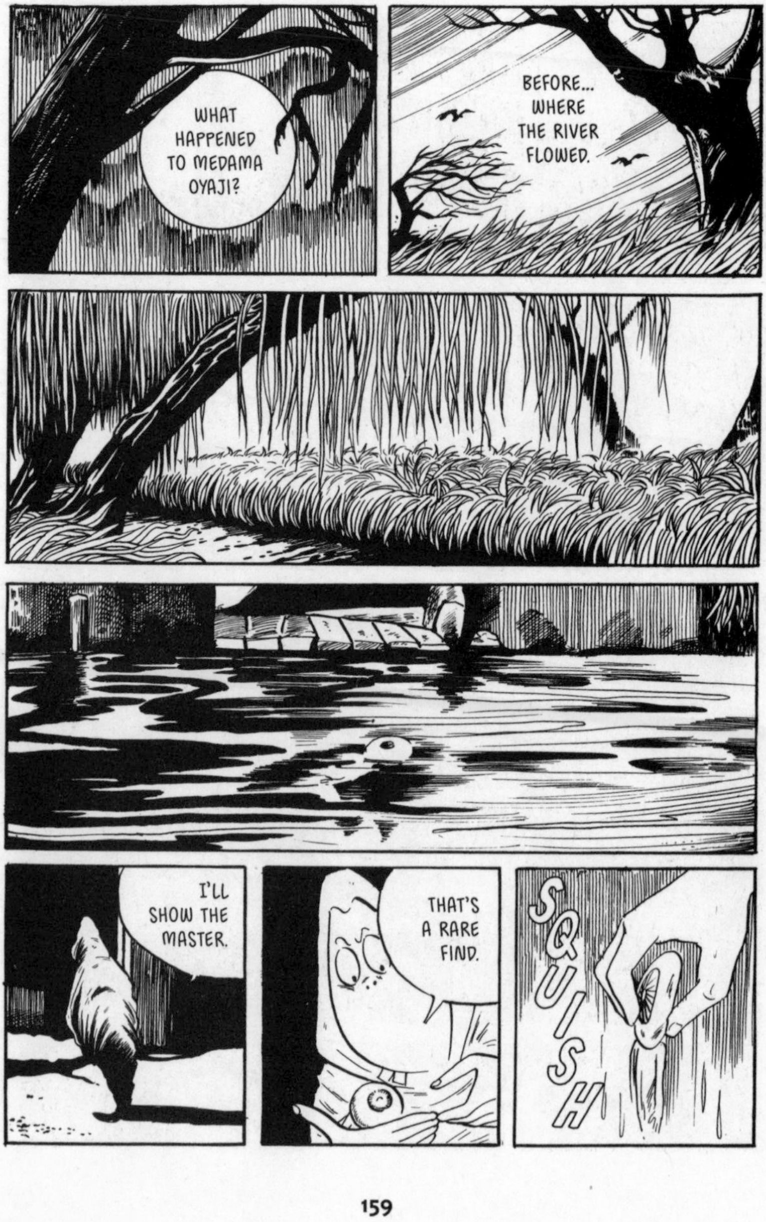
BEFORE... WHERE THE RIVER FLOWED.
WHAT HAPPENED TO MEDAMA OYAJI?
SQUISH
THAT'S A RARE FIND.
I'LL SHOW THE MASTER.

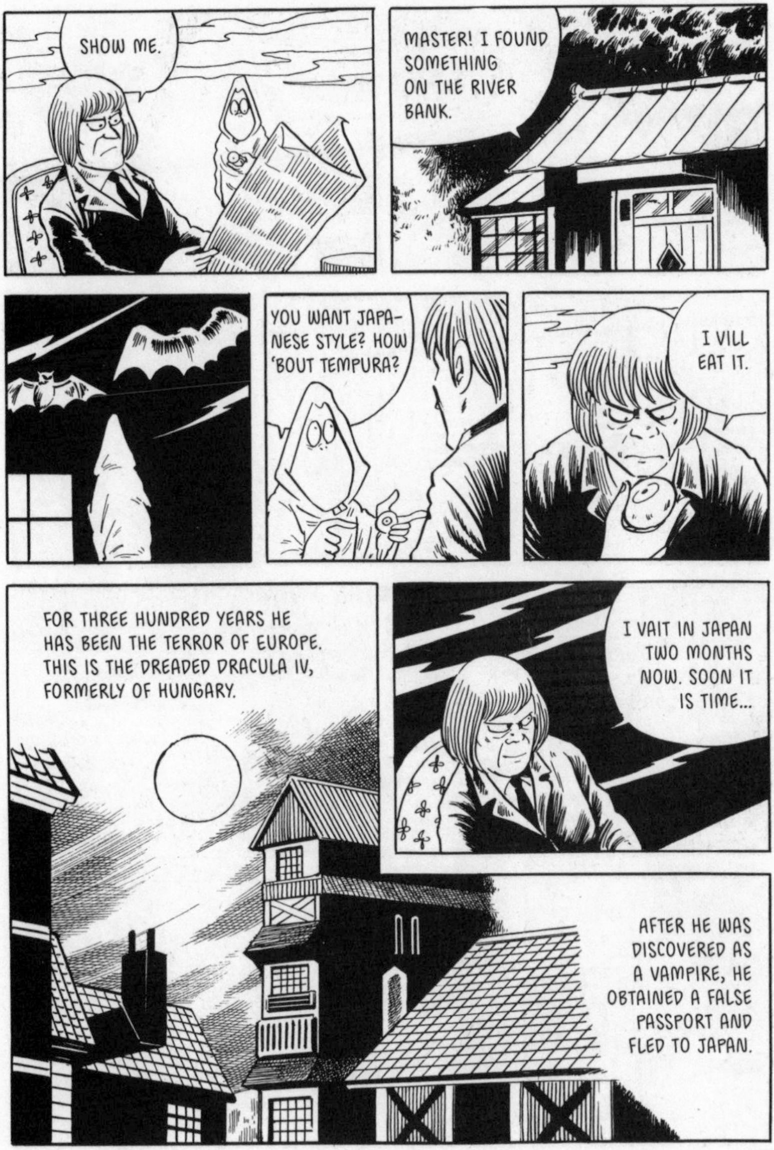
MASTER! I FOUND SOMETHING ON THE RIVER BANK.
SHOW ME.
I VILL EAT IT.
YOU WANT JAPA-NESE STYLE? HOW 'BOUT TEMPURA?
I VAIT IN JAPAN TWO MONTHS NOW. SOON IT IS TIME...
FOR THREE HUNDRED YEARS HE HAS BEEN THE TERROR OF EUROPE. THIS IS THE DREADED DRACULA IV, FORMERLY OF HUNGARY.
AFTER HE WAS DISCOVERED AS A VAMPIRE, HE OBTAINED A FALSE PASSPORT AND FLED TO JAPAN.

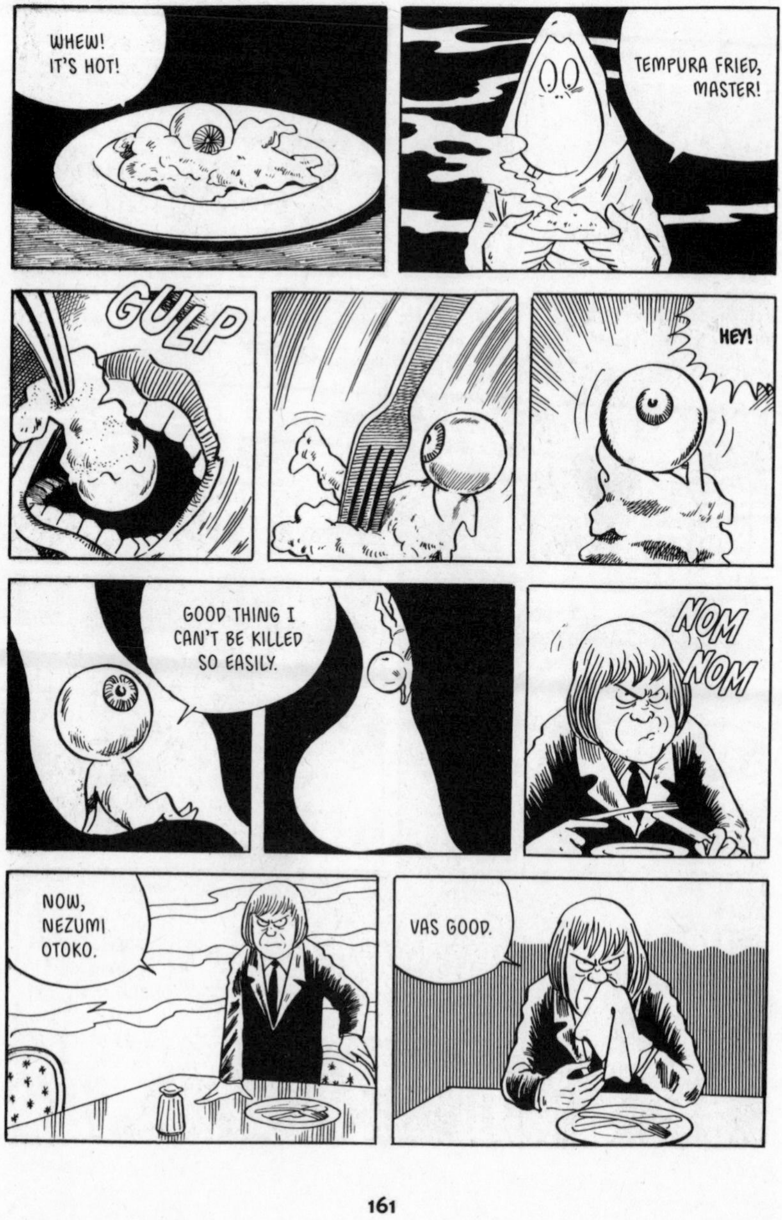
TEMPURA FRIED, MASTER!
WHEW! IT'S HOT!
HEY!
GULP
NOM NOM
GOOD THING I CAN'T BE KILLED SO EASILY.
VAS GOOD.
NOW, NEZUMI OTOKO.

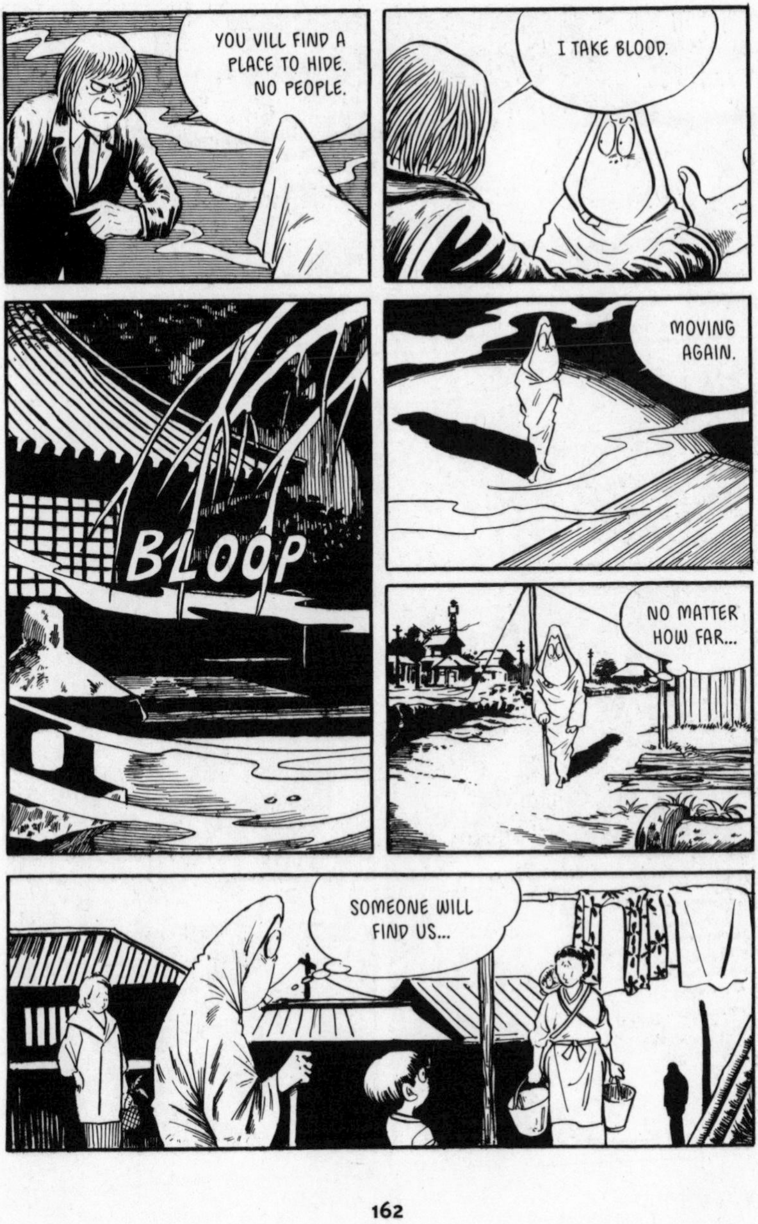
I TAKE BLOOD.
YOU VILL FIND A PLACE TO HIDE. NO PEOPLE.
MOVING AGAIN.
NO MATTER HOW FAR...
BLOOP
SOMEONE WILL FIND US...

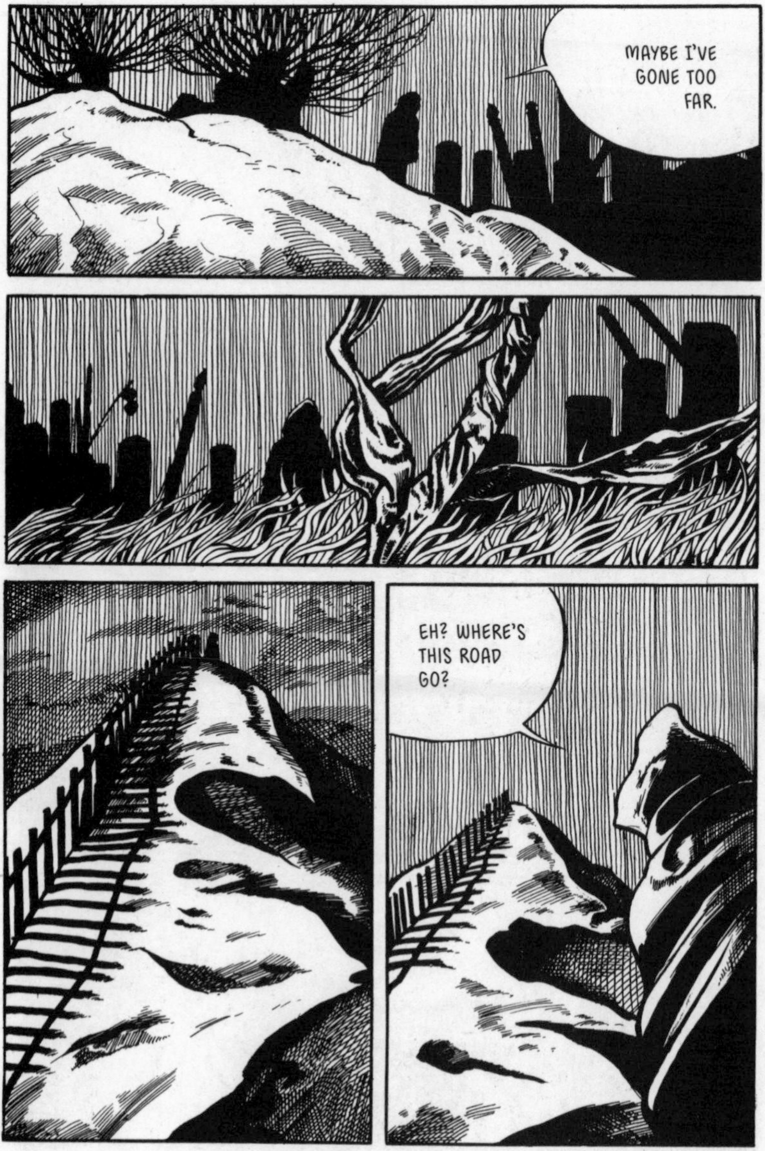
MAYBE I'VE GONE TOO FAR.
EH? WHERE'S THIS ROAD GO?

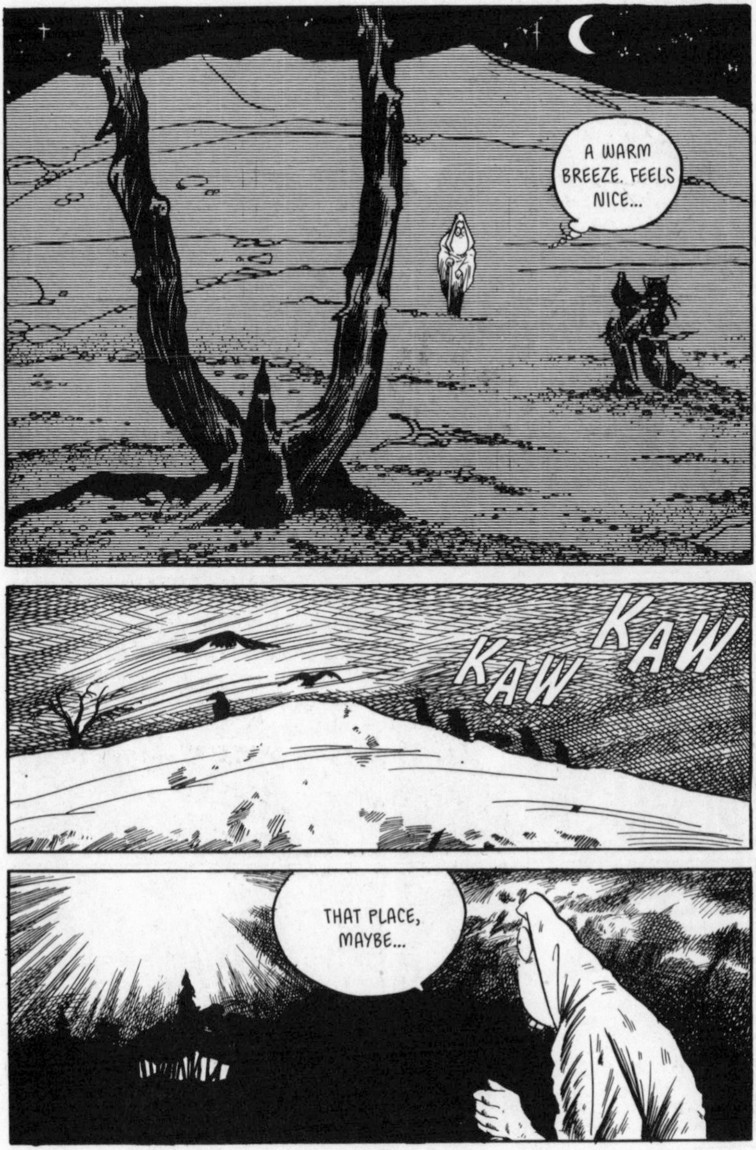
A WARM BREEZE. FEELS NICE...
KAW KAW
THAT PLACE, MAYBE...

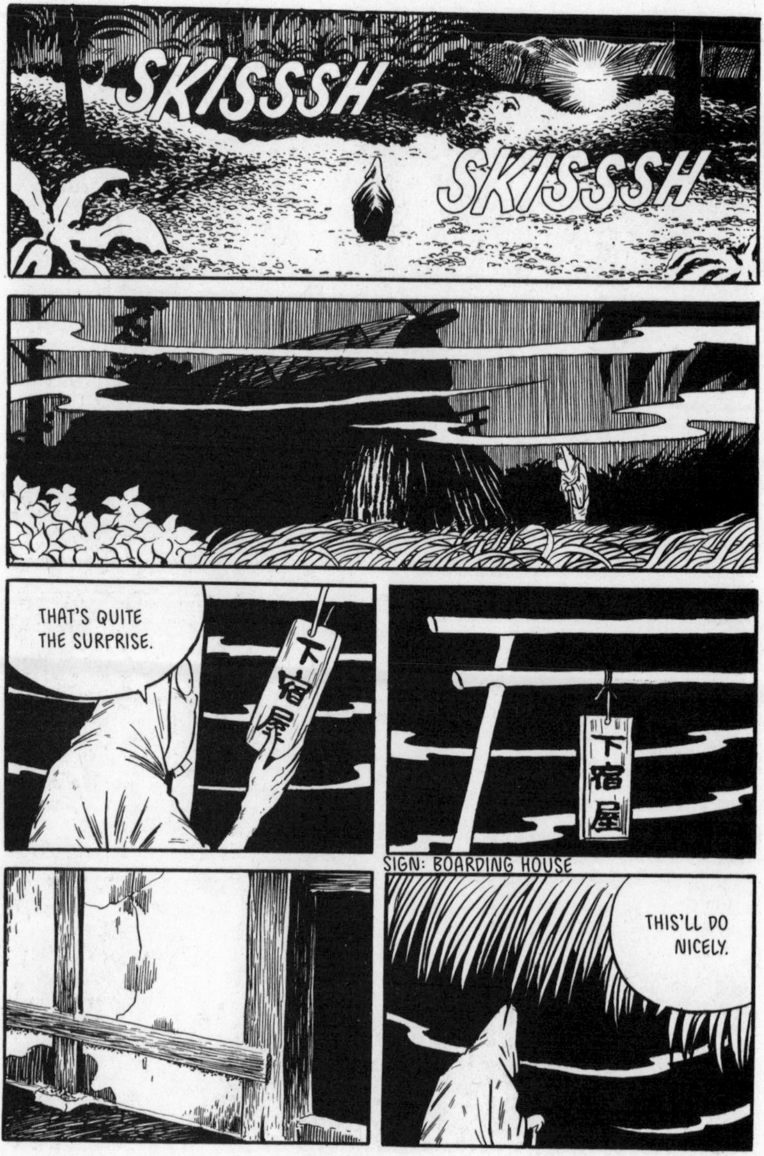
SKISSSH
SKISSSH
下宿屋
SIGN: BOARDING HOUSE
THAT'S QUITE THE SURPRISE.
下宿屋
THIS'LL DO NICELY.

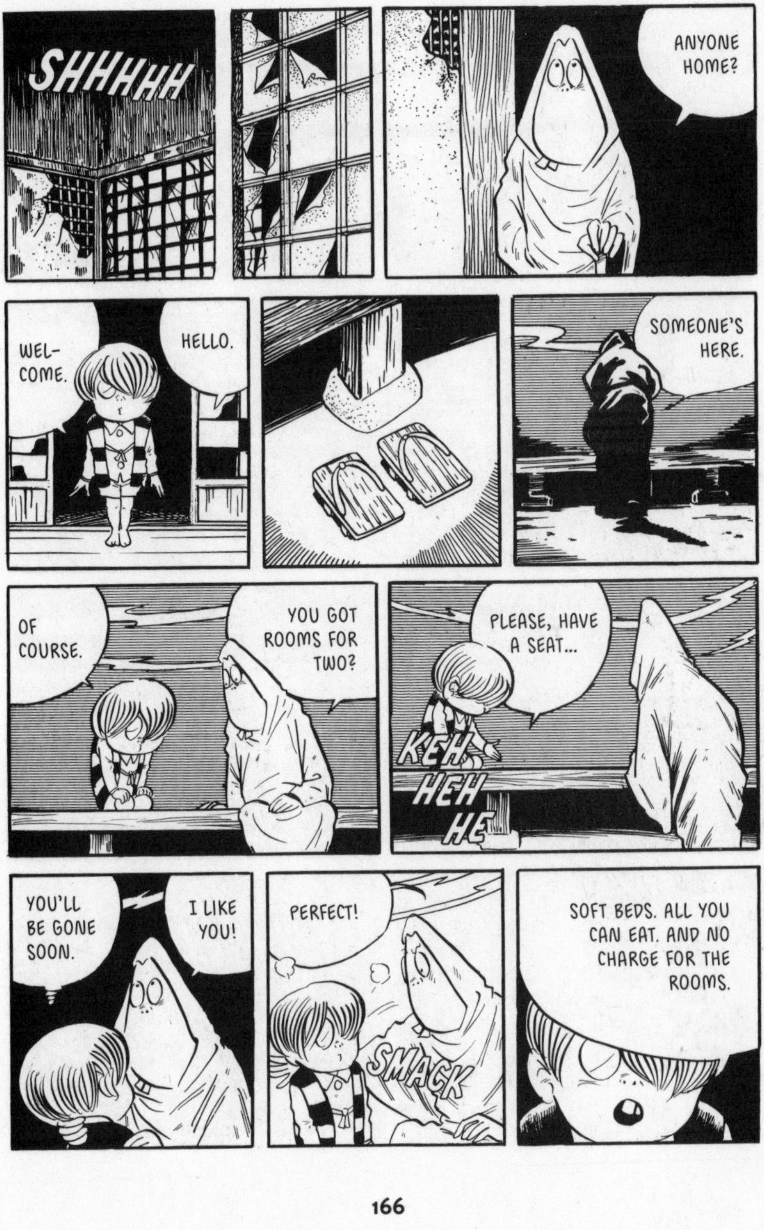
ANYONE HOME?
SHHHHH
SOMEONE'S HERE.
HELLO.
WEL-COME.
PLEASE, HAVE A SEAT...
KEH HEH HE
YOU GOT ROOMS FOR TWO?
OF COURSE.
SOFT BEDS. ALL YOU CAN EAT. AND NO CHARGE FOR THE ROOMS.
PERFECT!
SMACK
I LIKE YOU!
YOU'LL BE GONE SOON.

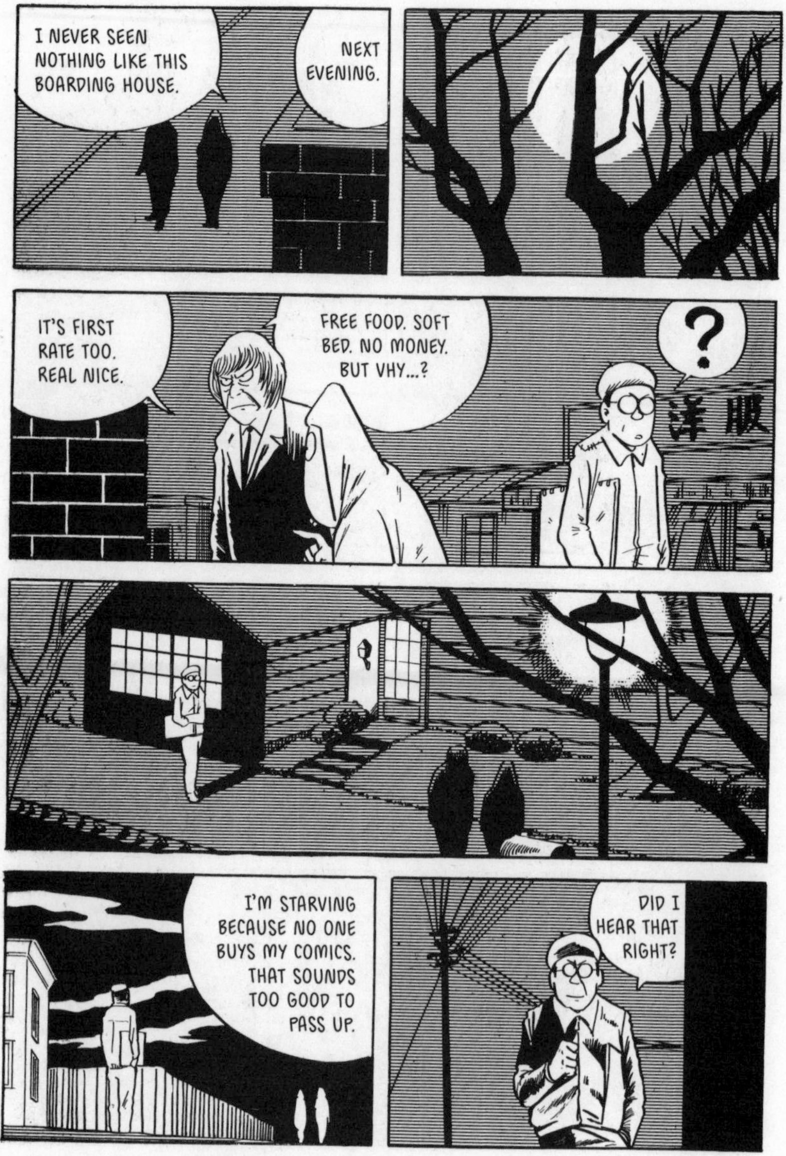
NEXT EVENING.
I NEVER SEEN NOTHING LIKE THIS BOARDING HOUSE.
?
洋服
FREE FOOD. SOFT BED. NO MONEY. BUT VHY...?
IT'S FIRST RATE TOO. REAL NICE.
DID I HEAR THAT RIGHT?
I'M STARVING BECAUSE NO ONE BUYS MY COMICS. THAT SOUNDS TOO GOOD TO PASS UP.

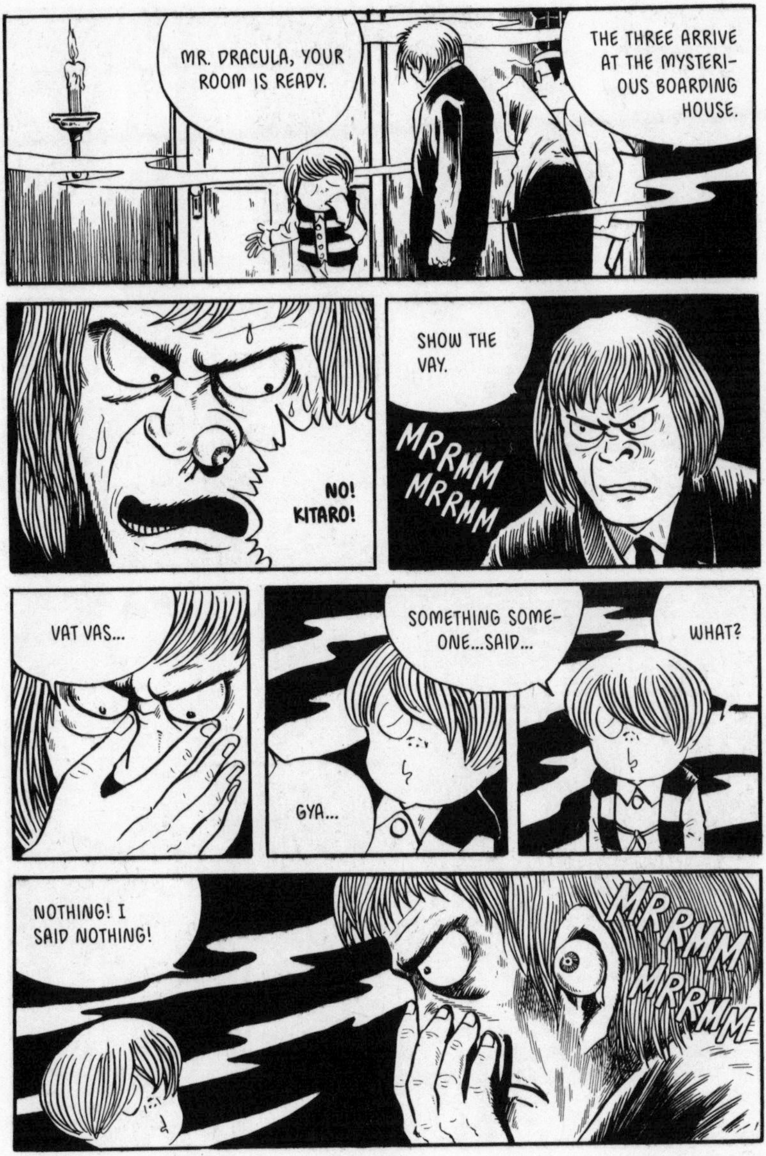
THE THREE ARRIVE AT THE MYSTERIOUS BOARDING HOUSE.
MR. DRACULA, YOUR ROOM IS READY.
SHOW THE VAY.
MRRMM MRRMM
NO! KITARO!
WHAT?
SOMETHING SOME-ONE...SAID...
GYA...
VAT VAS...
MRRMM MRRMM
NOTHING! I SAID NOTHING!

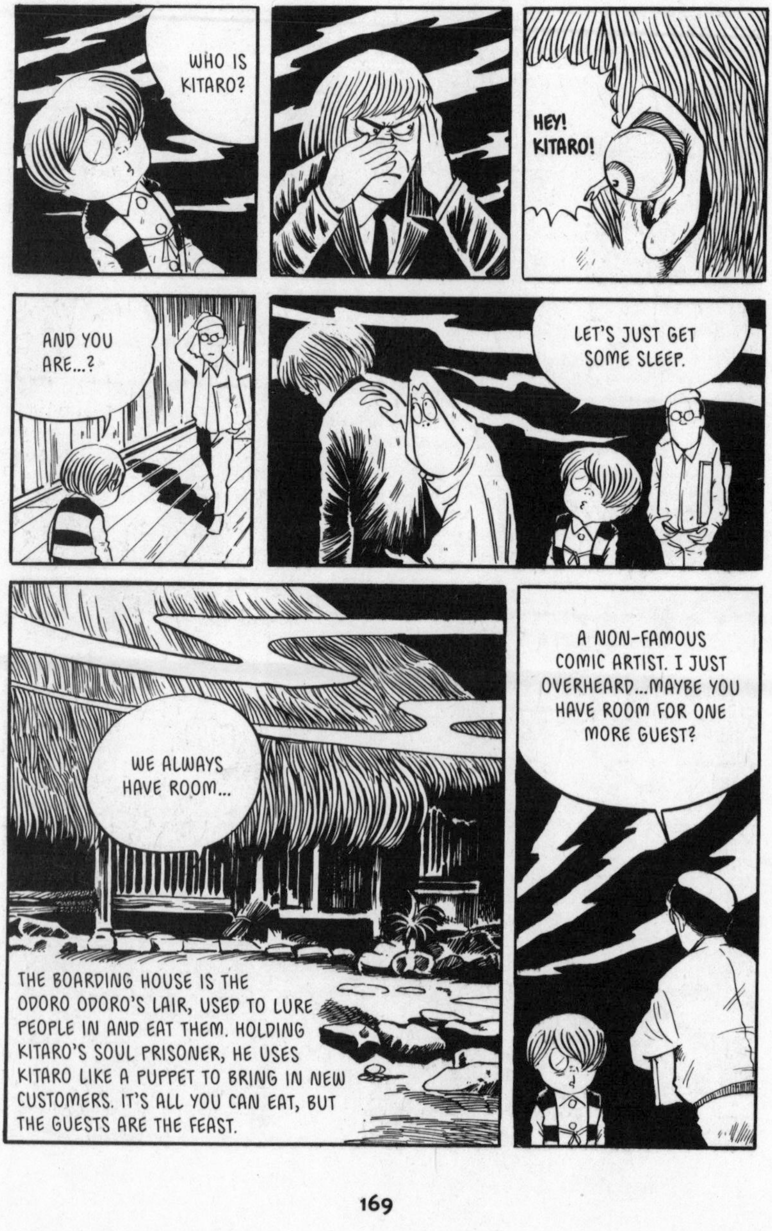
HEY! KITARO!
WHO IS KITARO?
LET'S JUST GET SOME SLEEP.
AND YOU ARE...?
A NON-FAMOUS COMIC ARTIST. I JUST OVERHEARD...MAYBE YOU HAVE ROOM FOR ONE MORE GUEST?
WE ALWAYS HAVE ROOM...
THE BOARDING HOUSE IS THE ODORO ODORO'S LAIR, USED TO LURE PEOPLE IN AND EAT THEM. HOLDING KITARO'S SOUL PRISONER, HE USES KITARO LIKE A PUPPET TO BRING IN NEW CUSTOMERS. IT'S ALL YOU CAN EAT, BUT THE GUESTS ARE THE FEAST.

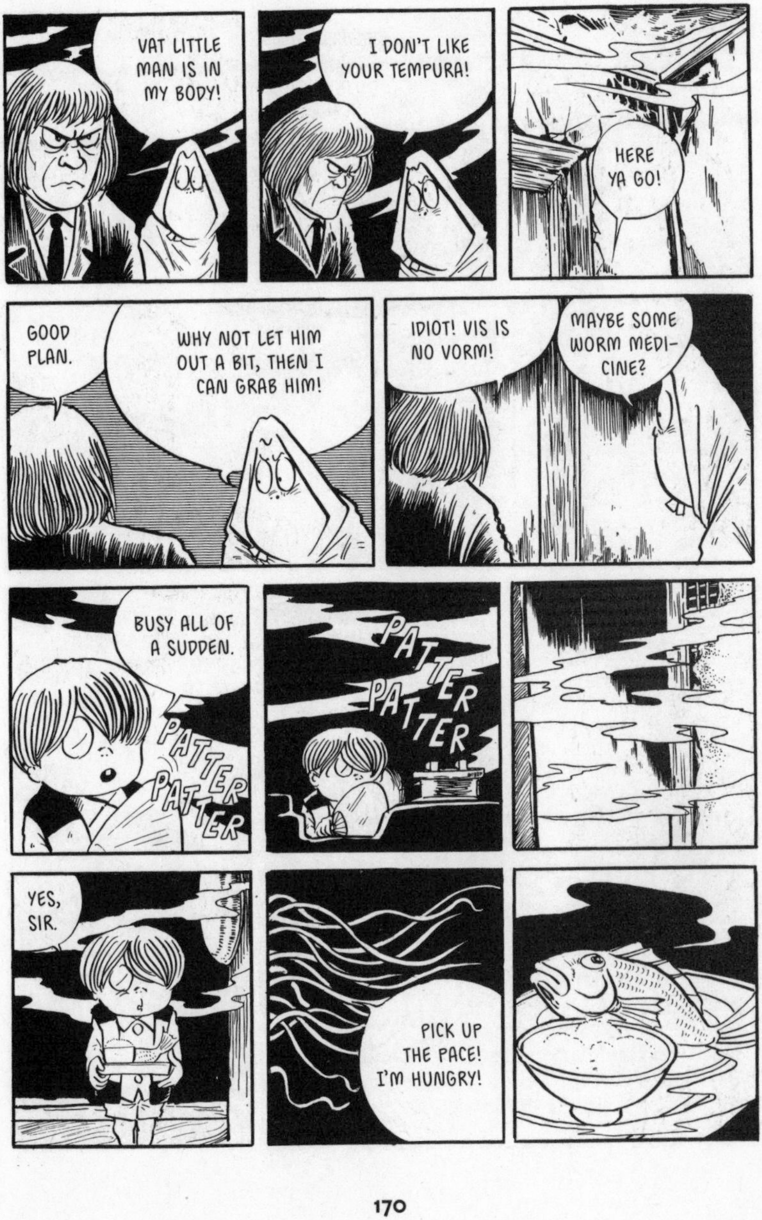
HERE YA GO!
I DON'T LIKE YOUR TEMPURA!
VAT LITTLE MAN IS IN MY BODY!
MAYBE SOME WORM MEDI- CINE?
IDIOT! VIS IS NO VORM!
WHY NOT LET HIM OUT A BIT, THEN I CAN GRAB HIM!
GOOD PLAN.
PATTER PATTER
BUSY ALL OF A SUDDEN.
PATTER PATTER
PICK UP THE PACE! I'M HUNGRY!
YES, SIR.

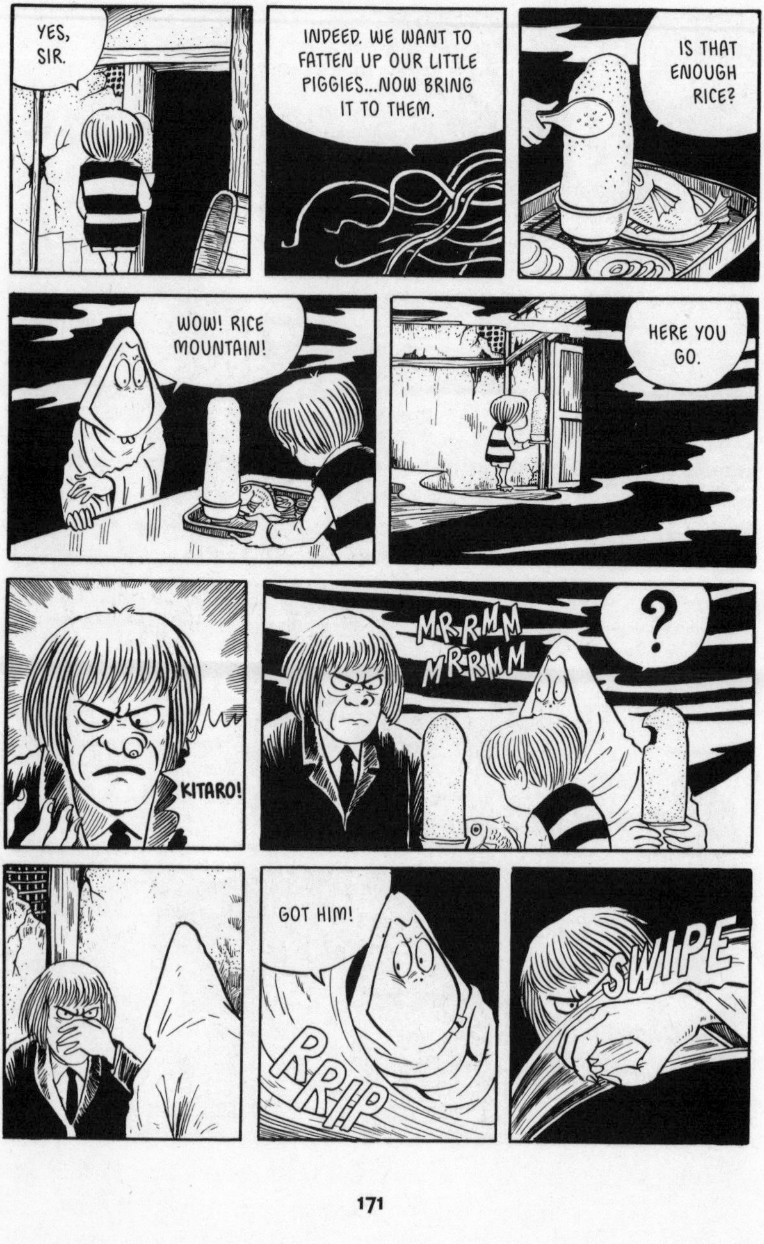
IS THAT ENOUGH RICE?
INDEED. WE WANT TO FATTEN UP OUR LITTLE PIGGIES...NOW BRING IT TO THEM.
YES, SIR.
HERE YOU GO.
WOW! RICE MOUNTAIN!
?
MRRMM MRRMM
KITARO!
SWIPE
GOT HIM!
RRIP

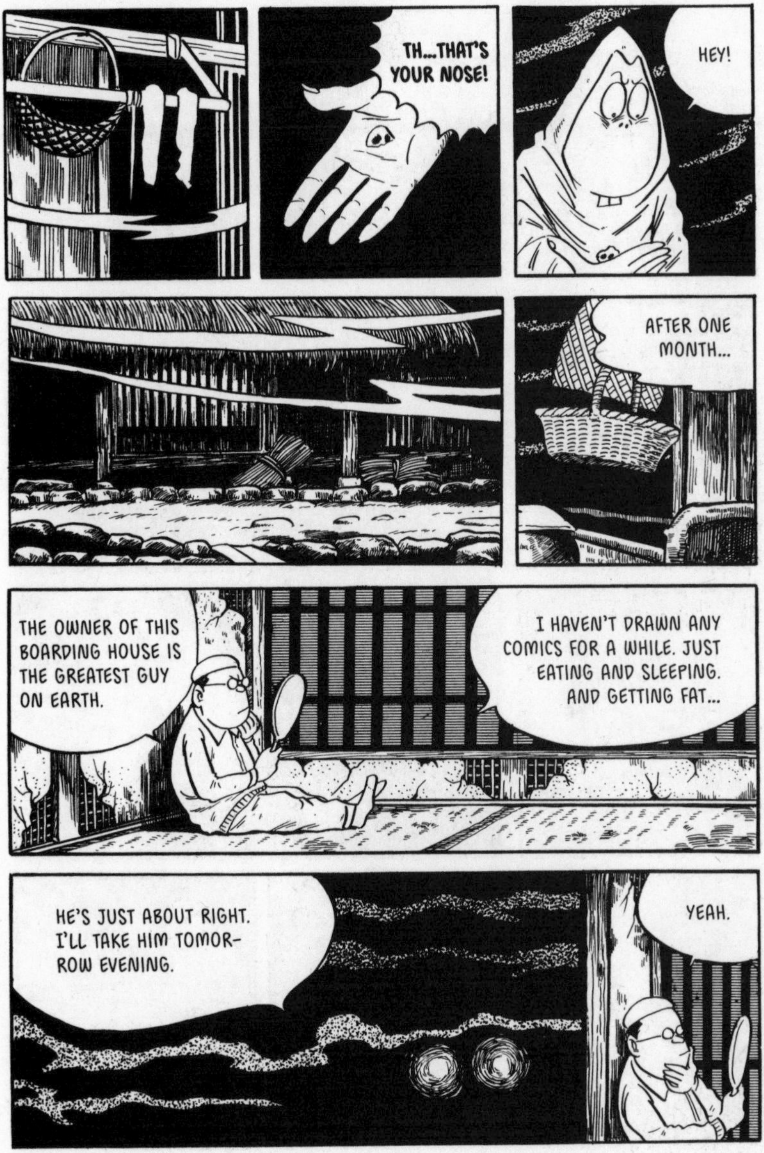
HEY!
TH...THAT'S YOUR NOSE!
AFTER ONE MONTH...
I HAVEN'T DRAWN ANY COMICS FOR A WHILE. JUST EATING AND SLEEPING. AND GETTING FAT...
THE OWNER OF THIS BOARDING HOUSE IS THE GREATEST GUY ON EARTH.
YEAH.
HE'S JUST ABOUT RIGHT. I'LL TAKE HIM TOMOR-ROW EVENING.

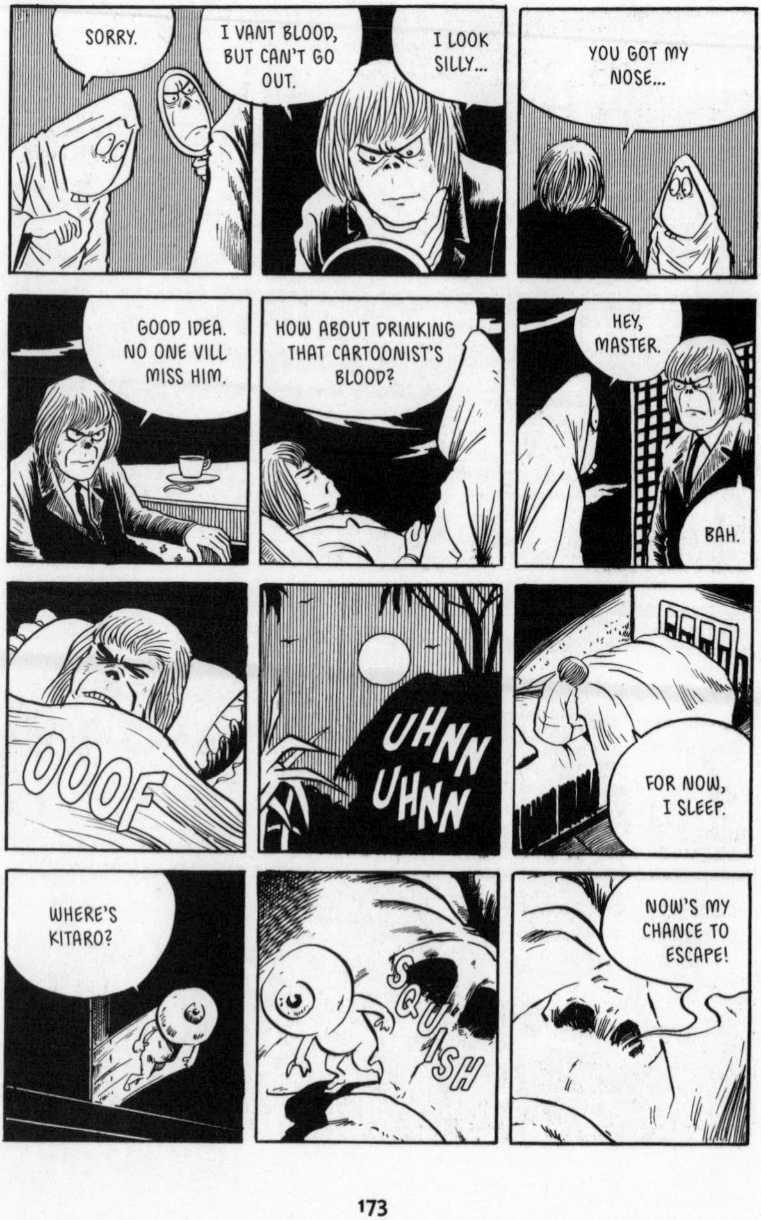
YOU GOT MY NOSE...
I LOOK SILLY...
I VANT BLOOD, BUT CAN'T GO OUT.
SORRY.
HEY, MASTER.
BAH.
HOW ABOUT DRINKING THAT CARTOONIST'S BLOOD?
GOOD IDEA. NO ONE VILL MISS HIM.
FOR NOW, I SLEEP.
UHNN UHNN
OOOF
NOW'S MY CHANCE TO ESCAPE!
SQUISH
WHERE'S KITARO?

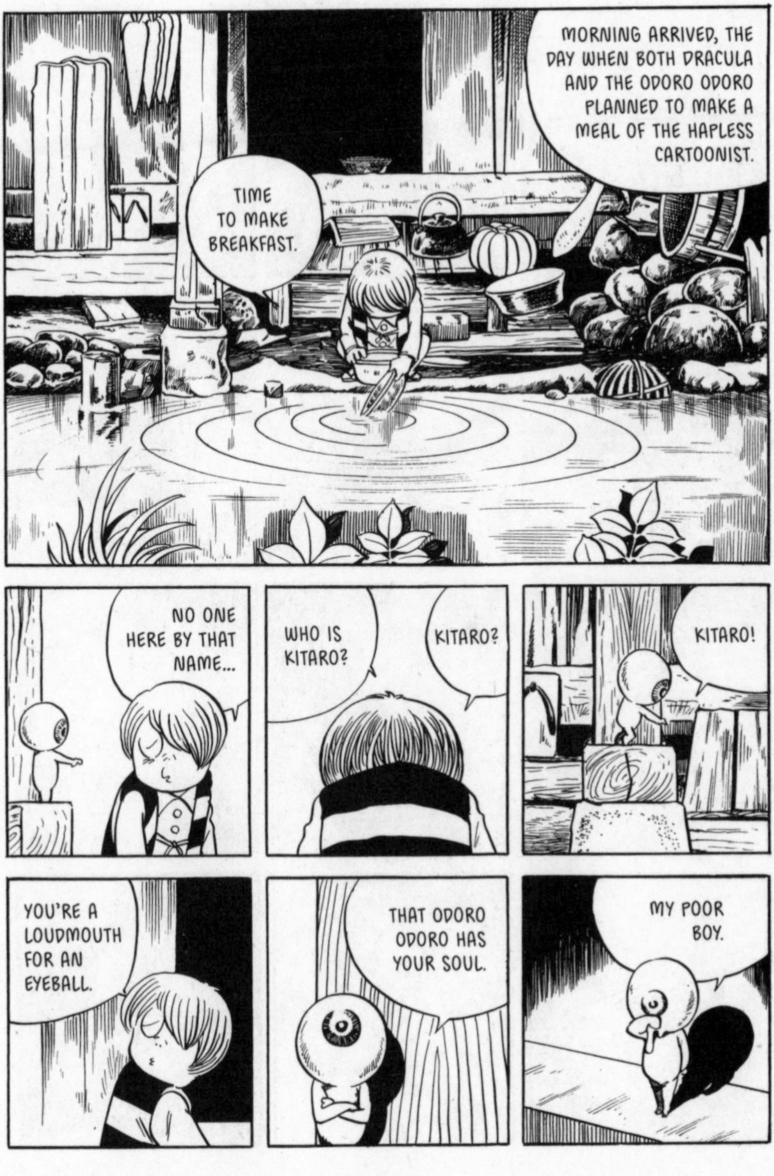
MORNING ARRIVED, THE DAY WHEN BOTH DRACULA AND THE ODORO ODORO PLANNED TO MAKE A MEAL OF THE HAPLESS CARTOONIST.
TIME TO MAKE BREAKFAST.
KITARO!
KITARO?
WHO IS KITARO?
NO ONE HERE BY THAT NAME...
MY POOR BOY.
THAT ODORO ODORO HAS YOUR SOUL.
YOU'RE A LOUDMOUTH FOR AN EYEBALL.

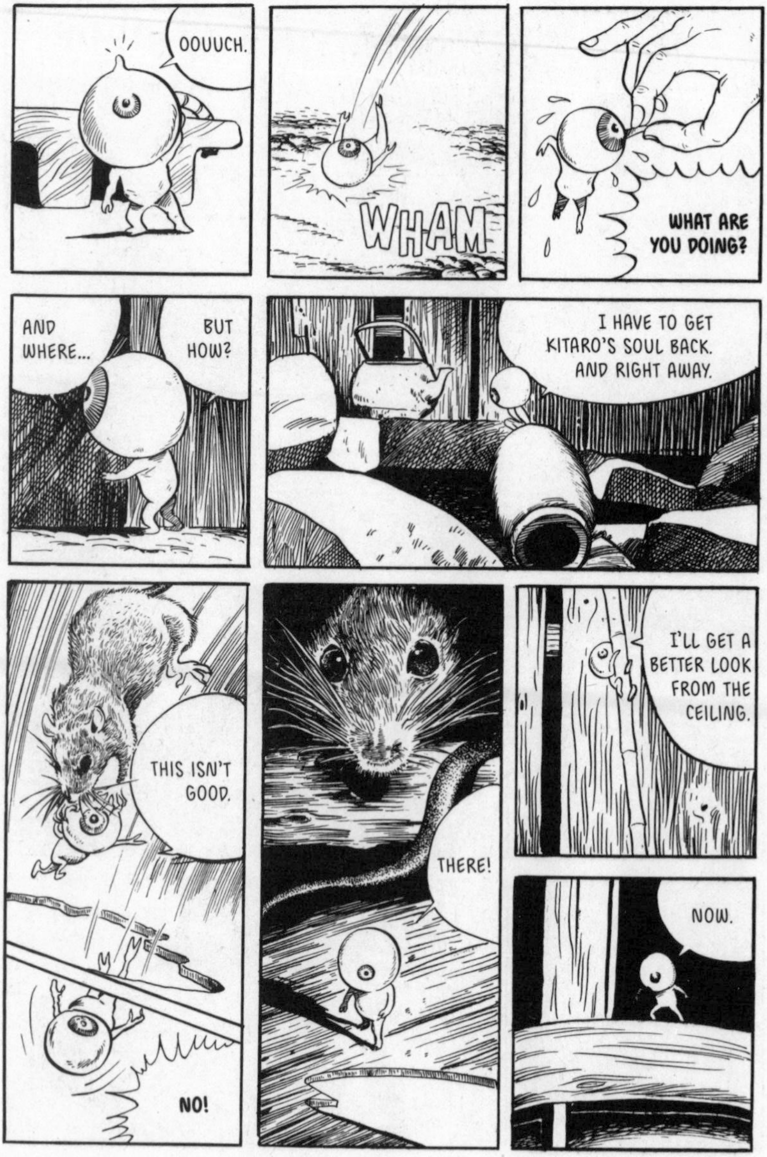
WHAT ARE YOU DOING?
WHAM
OOUUCH.
I HAVE TO GET KITARO'S SOUL BACK. AND RIGHT AWAY.
BUT HOW?
AND WHERE...
I'LL GET A BETTER LOOK FROM THE CEILING.
NOW.
THERE!
THIS ISN'T GOOD.
NO!

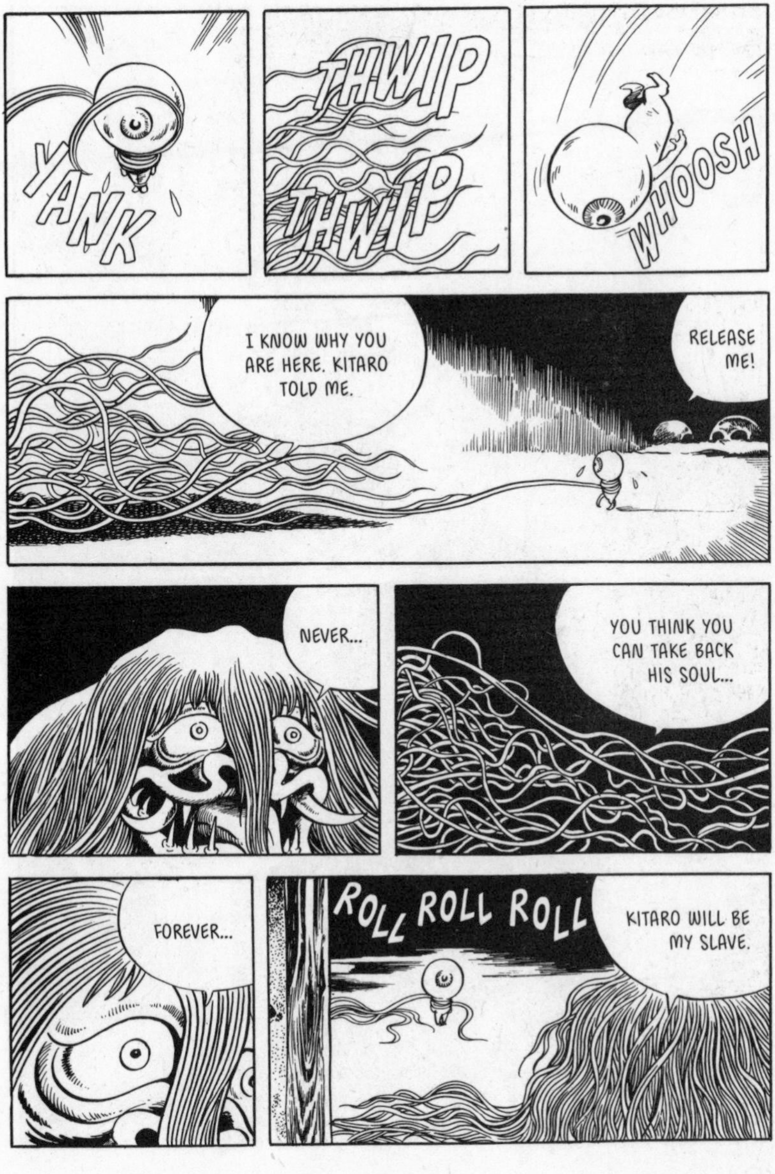
WHOOSH
THWIP
THWIP
YANK
RELEASE ME!
I KNOW WHY YOU ARE HERE. KITARO TOLD ME.
YOU THINK YOU CAN TAKE BACK HIS SOUL...
NEVER...
KITARO WILL BE MY SLAVE.
ROLL ROLL ROLL
FOREVER...

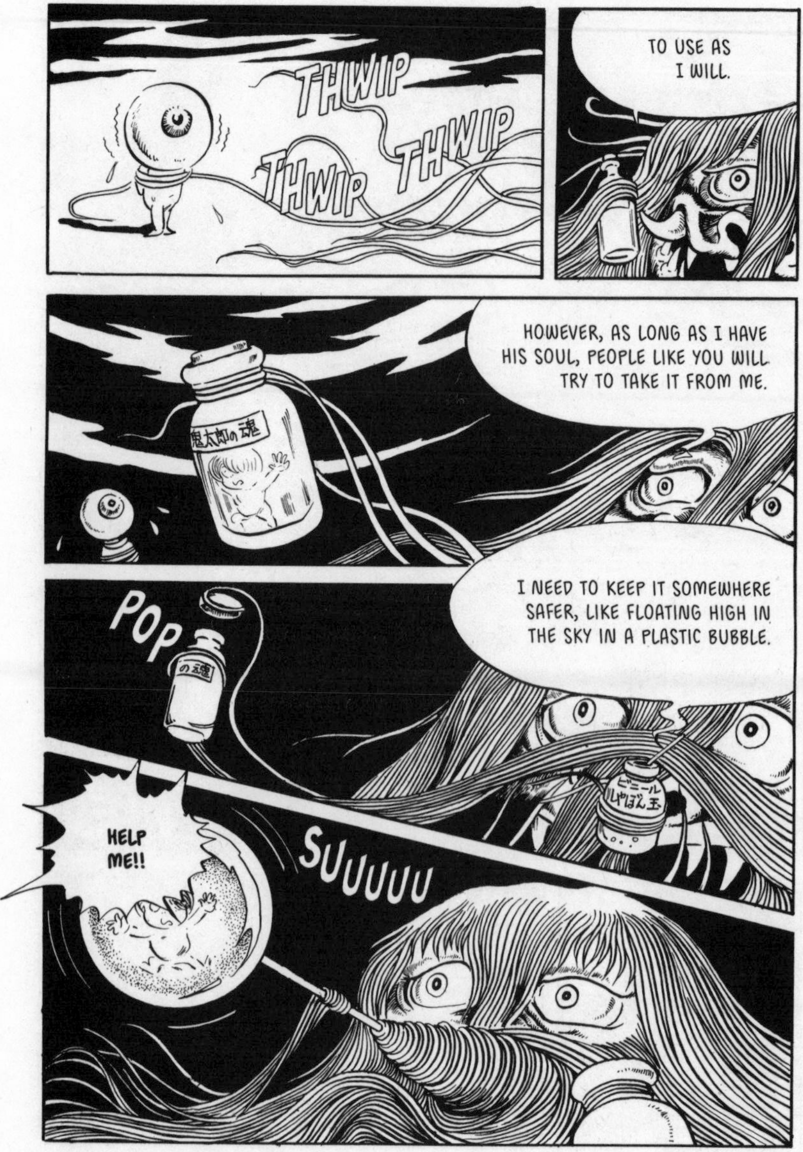
TO USE AS I WILL.
THWIP
THWIP
THWIP
HOWEVER, AS LONG AS I HAVE HIS SOUL, PEOPLE LIKE YOU WILL TRY TO TAKE IT FROM ME.
鬼太郎の魂
I NEED TO KEEP IT SOMEWHERE SAFER, LIKE FLOATING HIGH IN THE SKY IN A PLASTIC BUBBLE.
POP
の魂
ビニールしゃぼん玉
SUUUUU
HELP ME!!

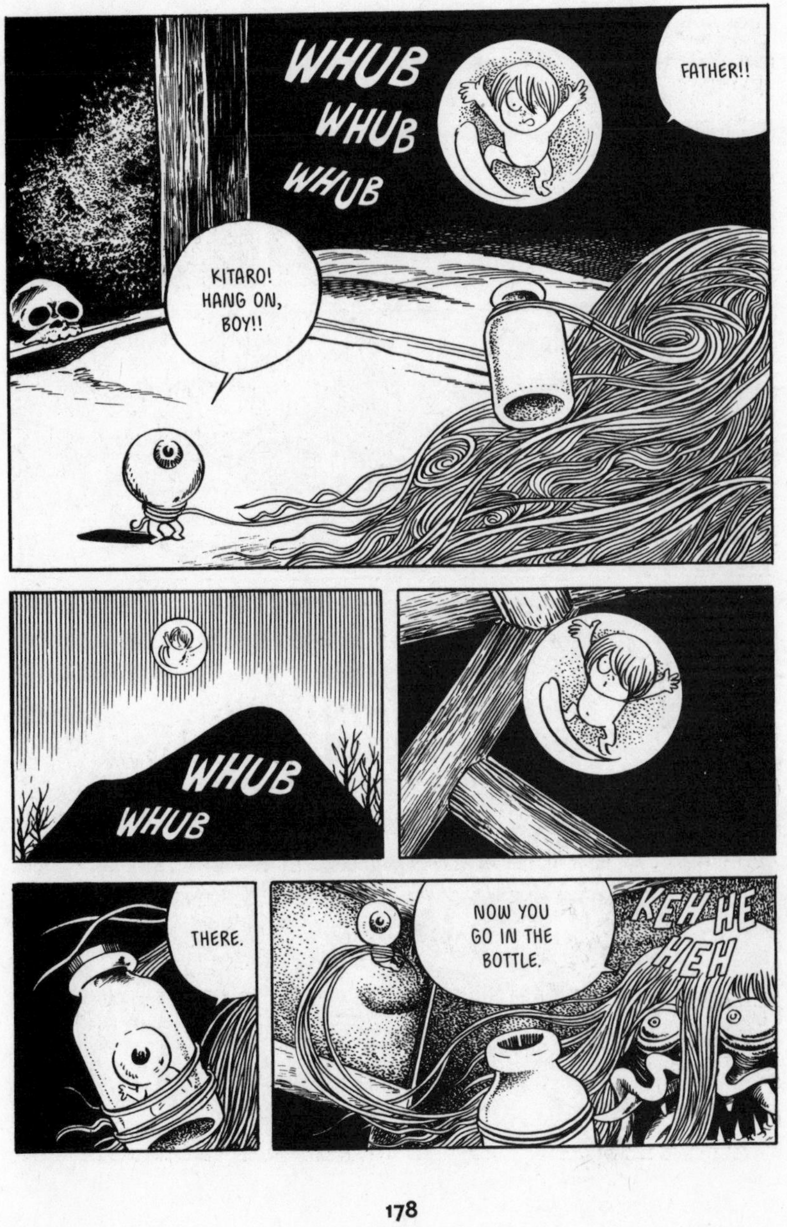
FATHER!!
WHUB WHUB WHUB
KITARO! HANG ON, BOY!!
WHUB WHUB
KEH HE HEH
NOW YOU GO IN THE BOTTLE.
THERE.

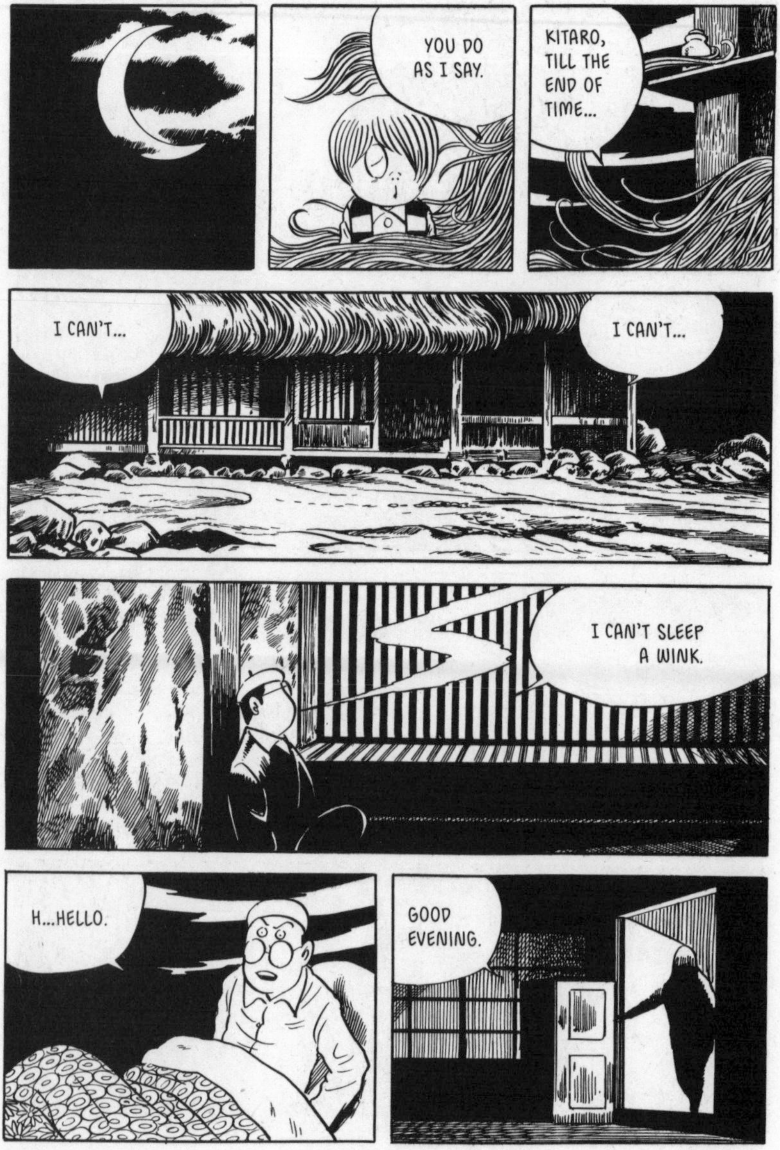
KITARO, TILL THE END OF TIME...
YOU DO AS I SAY.
I CAN'T...
I CAN'T...
I CAN'T SLEEP A WINK.
GOOD EVENING.
H...HELLO.

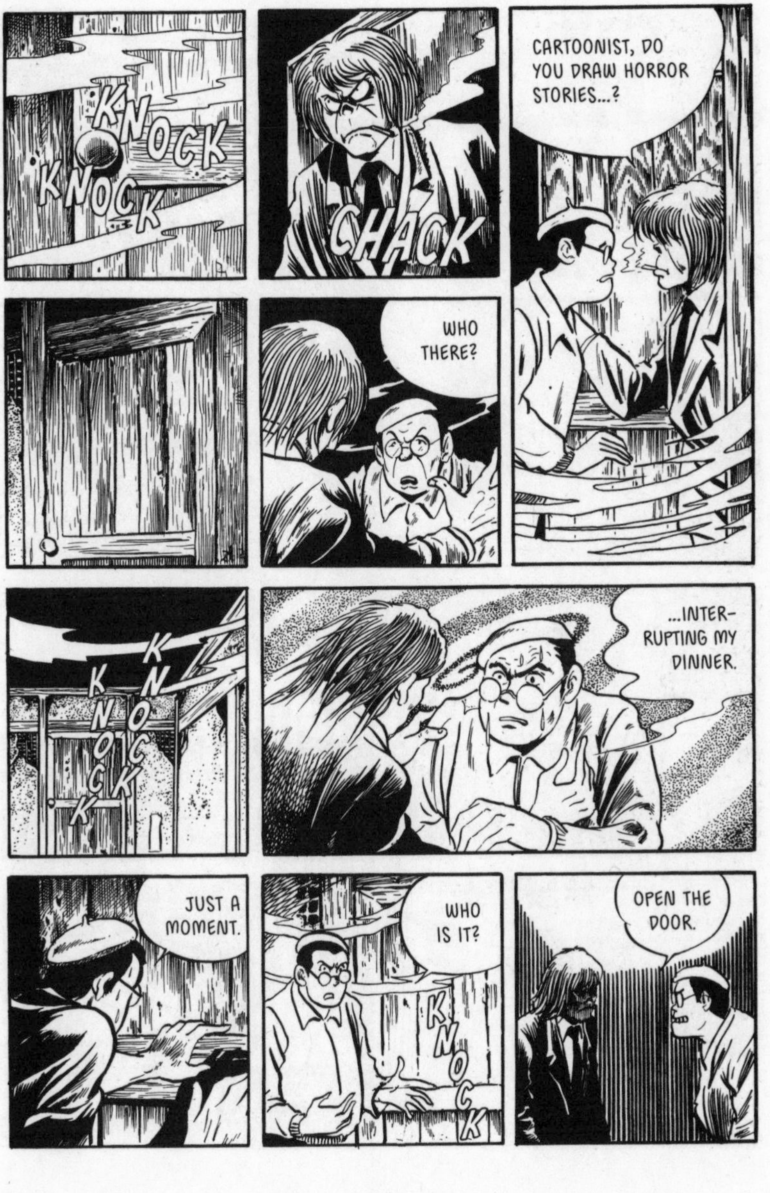
CARTOONIST, DO YOU DRAW HORROR STORIES...?
CHACK
KNOCK
KNOCK
WHO THERE?
...INTER-RUPTING MY DINNER.
KNOCK
KNOCK
OPEN THE DOOR.
WHO IS IT?
KNOCK
JUST A MOMENT.

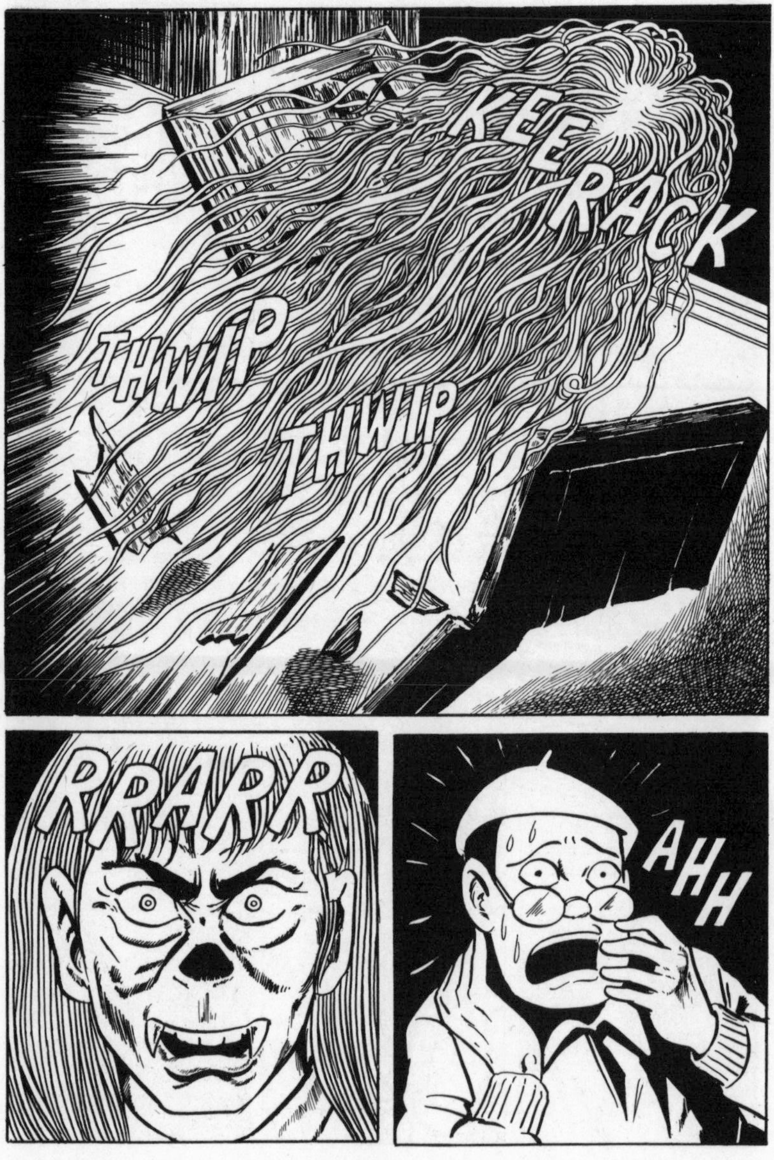
KEE RACK
THWIP
THWIP
AHH
RRARR

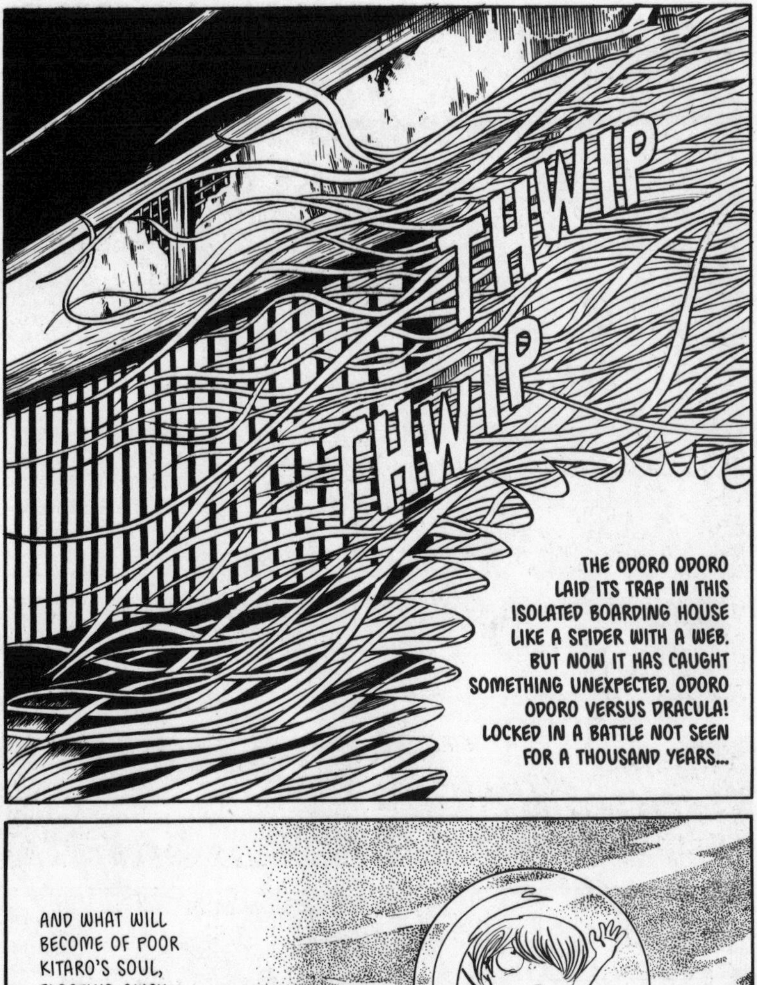
THWIP
THWIP
THE ODORO ODORO LAID ITS TRAP IN THIS ISOLATED BOARDING HOUSE LIKE A SPIDER WITH A WEB. BUT NOW IT HAS CAUGHT SOMETHING UNEXPECTED. ODORO ODORO VERSUS DRACULA! LOCKED IN A BATTLE NOT SEEN FOR A THOUSAND YEARS...

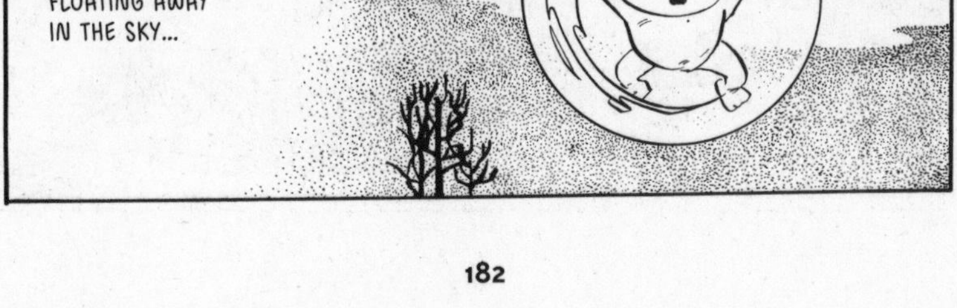
AND WHAT WILL BECOME OF POOR KITARO'S SOUL, FLOATING AWAY IN THE SKY...

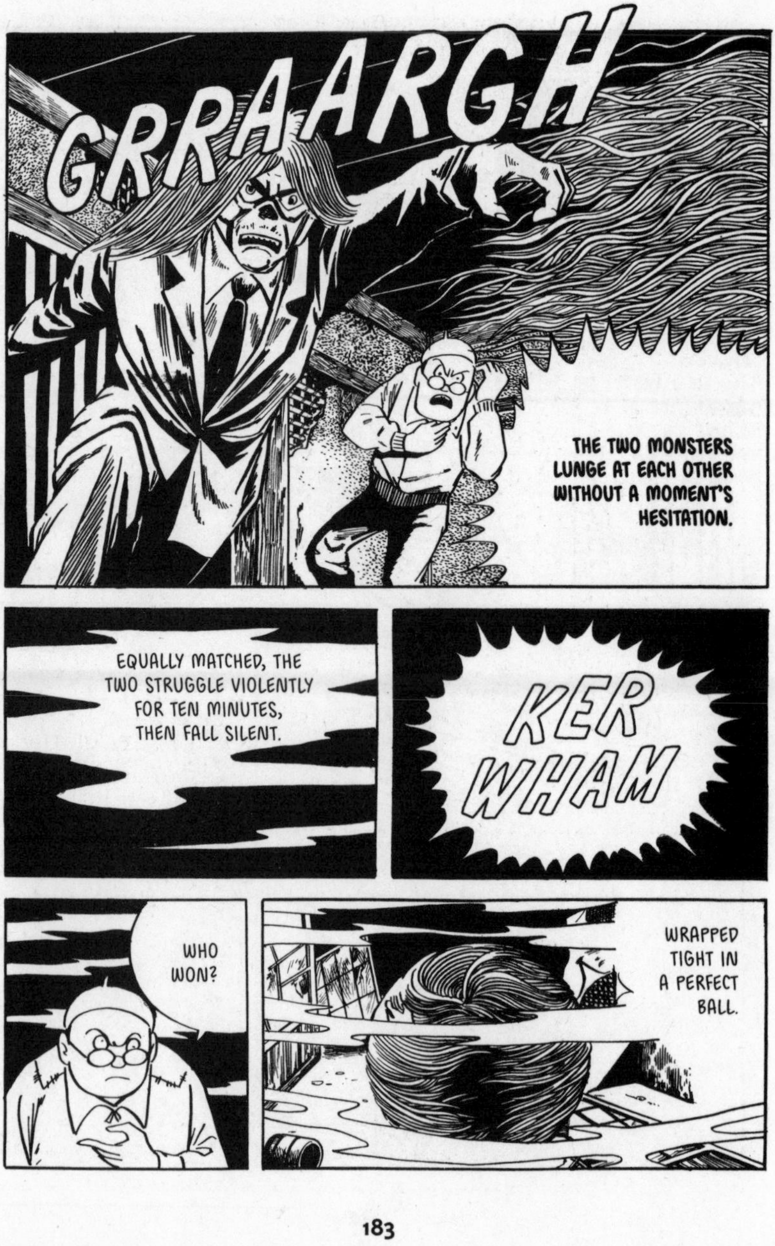
GRRAARGH
THE TWO MONSTERS LUNGE AT EACH OTHER WITHOUT A MOMENT'S HESITATION.
KER WHAM
EQUALLY MATCHED, THE TWO STRUGGLE VIOLENTLY FOR TEN MINUTES, THEN FALL SILENT.
WRAPPED TIGHT IN A PERFECT BALL.
WHO WON?

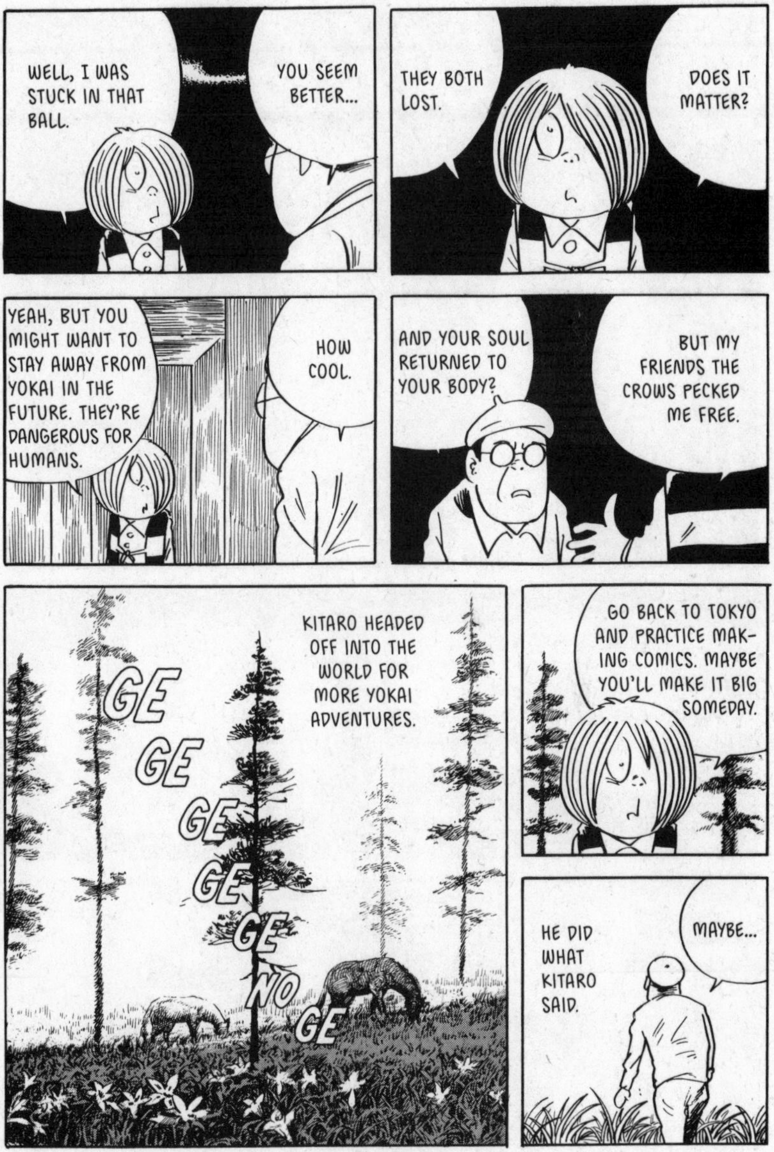
DOES IT MATTER?
THEY BOTH LOST.
YOU SEEM BETTER...
WELL, I WAS STUCK IN THAT BALL.
BUT MY FRIENDS THE CROWS PECKED ME FREE.
AND YOUR SOUL RETURNED TO YOUR BODY?
HOW COOL.
YEAH, BUT YOU MIGHT WANT TO STAY AWAY FROM YOKAI IN THE FUTURE. THEY'RE DANGEROUS FOR HUMANS.
GO BACK TO TOKYO AND PRACTICE MAKING COMICS. MAYBE YOU'LL MAKE IT BIG SOMEDAY.
MAYBE...
HE DID WHAT KITARO SAID.
KITARO HEADED OFF INTO THE WORLD FOR MORE YOKAI ADVENTURES.
GE GE GE GE GE NO GE

YOKAI FILES
BY ZACK DAVISSON

WHAT ARE YOKAI?

You'll meet many different kinds of yokai in the pages of *Kitaro*, but it's not easy to describe exactly what that means. The word is difficult to translate, meaning something like "mysterious phenomenon." Yokai as a term encompasses monsters, spirits of rivers and mountains, deities, demons, goblins, apparitions, shape-changers, magic, ghosts, animals, and all manner of mysterious occurrences. There are good yokai and bad yokai, and some that are in between.

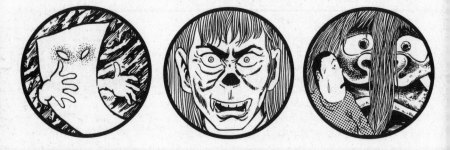

Some yokai are very old, with histories longer than civilization. Some are young, and have only appeared in the past couple of years. Some were once human beings who fell under a curse or otherwise changed, while some—like Kitaro and his father Medama Oyaji—were born yokai and have always been yokai.

Many are from Japan, but others are from China, Korea, India, or countries like Romania, the UK, Canada, the USA—or even outer space. Yokai can be legendary figures from folklore or urban legends, or characters from books or movies. They can come from anywhere. They can look like anything. Yokai can be giant monsters, unnatural plants, winds, or earthquakes. They can be visible or invisible.

Perhaps the best definition is to say that anything that cannot readily be understood or explained, anything mysterious and unconfirmed, can be yokai.

DATSUI BABA blurs the line between common yokai and deities. She is a guardian of hell, and one of the servants of Emma-O, the dreaded king of hell and judge of the dead. Datsui Baba guards the Sanzu River, where the dead cross into the afterlife. With each new arrival, Datsui Baba strips their clothes and weighs them. If the person was poor, they cross a bridge over the river. But if they were rich, they have to struggle across where the river is deepest.

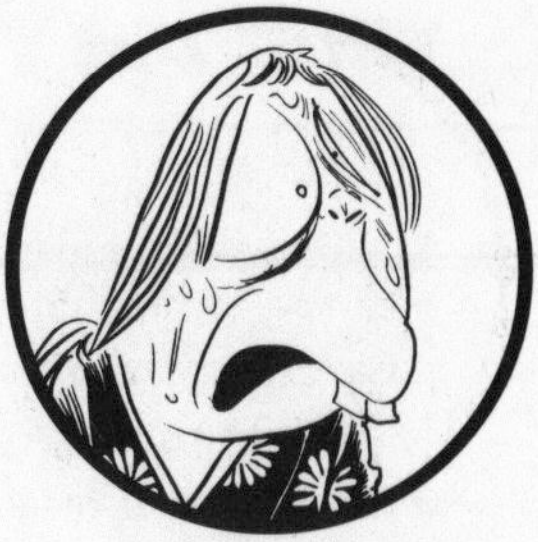

DRACULA IV is a western yokai who comes from Hungary, and is the fourth descendent of the famous bloodsucker, Dracula. He is over three hundred years old, and fled to Japan on a false passport after he was revealed as a vampire in his home country.

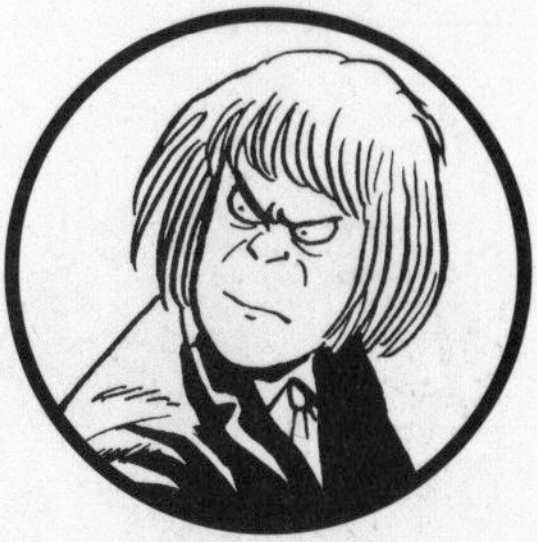

FUNA YUREI are ghosts of people who died at sea. They appear at night, during rain and heavy fog, and try to drag people under the water to join their ranks. Funa Yurei often ask for a wooden spoon, and if you give them one, they fill up your boat to drown you. The best way to escape from them is to give them a spoon with holes in it so they can't ladle water into your ship.

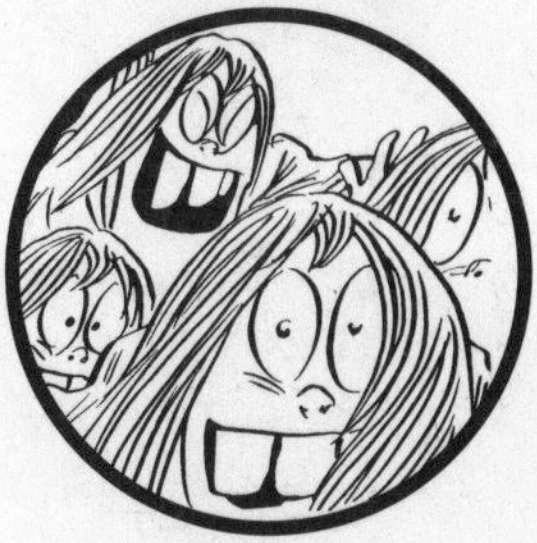

JAKOTSU BABA is also known as the Old Snake-Bone Woman, and is a mysterious yokai from Funkan-koku, China. Legend says when her husband died, Jakotsu Baba transformed into a yokai to stand guard over his grave. Jakotsu Baba is terrible to behold. A blue snake slithers in her right hand and a red snake in her left. Nobody knows exactly what she wants, only that she is one dangerous yokai!

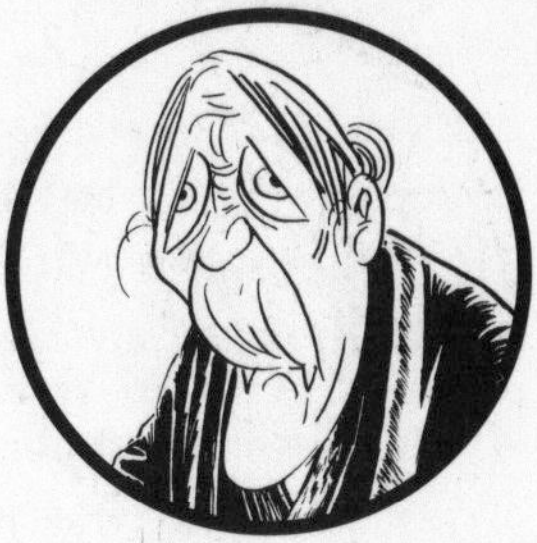

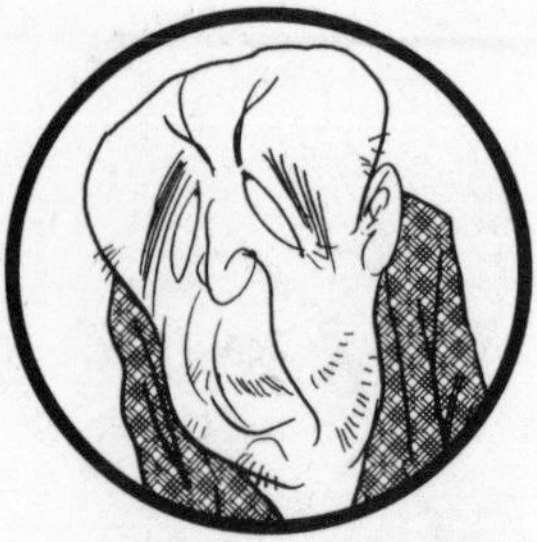

NURARIHYON, a slippery spirit whose true nature is hard to pin down, is the self-styled "Supreme Commander of the Yokai." He is an urban yokai with a mysterious air of authority. Nurarihyon comes into your house and orders you around, acting like an important guest. He drinks all your best tea, eats all your best food, then struts out the door. Only after he is gone and the spell is broken do you realize you have been a victim of Nurarihyon.

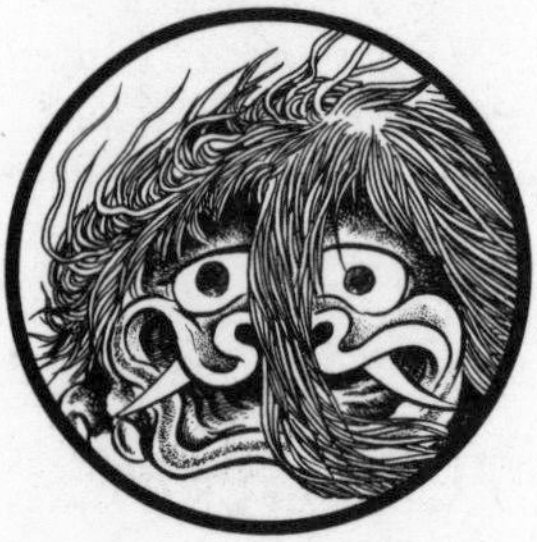

ODORO ODORO hide their terrifying faces under long hair, and only come out when they are ready to strike. They use their hair like long straws to drink people's blood. A rare yokai created by science, the Odoro Odoro was accidently conjured by a greedy man trying to invent a cure for baldness.

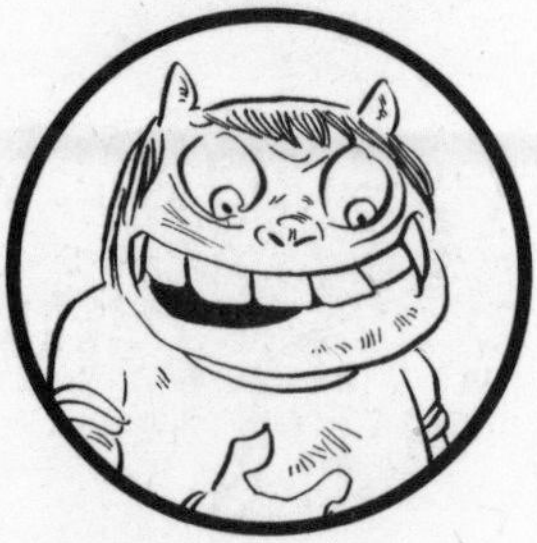

ONI are as old as Japan, and come in many shapes and sizes. The oldest Oni were invisible spirits that caused disease and disaster. In the sixth century, contact with India and monsters called Rakshasa influenced Oni—they gained bodies with red skin and horns. Modern Oni work various jobs in hell. They can be naughty or nice, depending on their moods. Watch out if you ever meet one! You never know what you'll get!

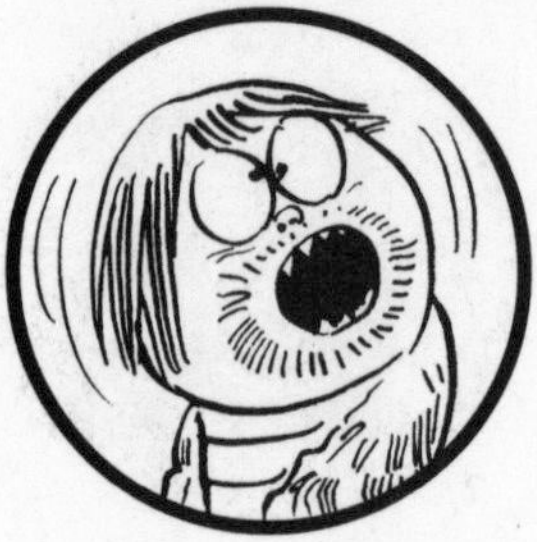

SARA KOZO are one of the many species of Japanese water spirits called kappa. Sara Kozo are dangerous monsters. They are covered in hair and have a mouthful of sharp teeth like a saw. Their most powerful weapon is their plate-like head, which can be fired in attack or used as a lens.

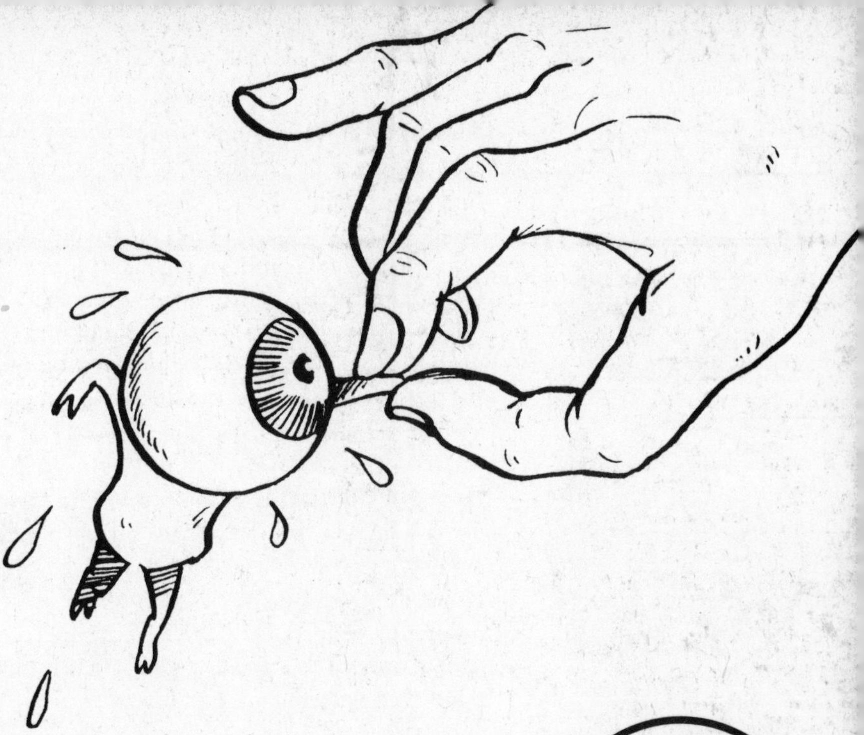

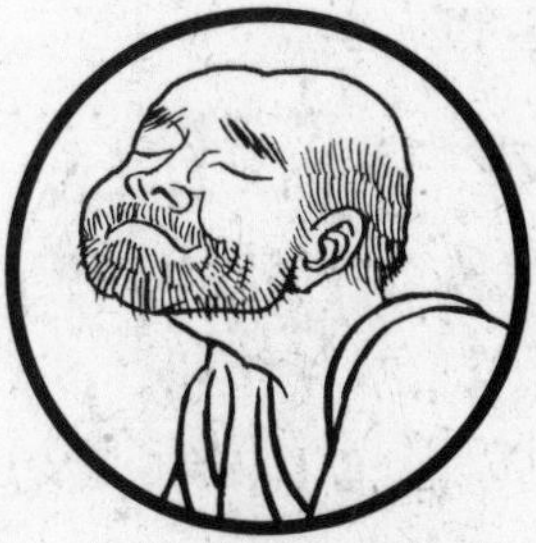

UMI ZATO are giant water spirits who look like the ghosts of blind *biwa* (Japanese lute) players, strolling across the ocean waves. They are generally seen in northern Japan near Iwate prefecture, and appear near the end of each month. Umi Zato attack fishermen and ships at sea. They are sometimes big enough to swallow whole ships in one bite!

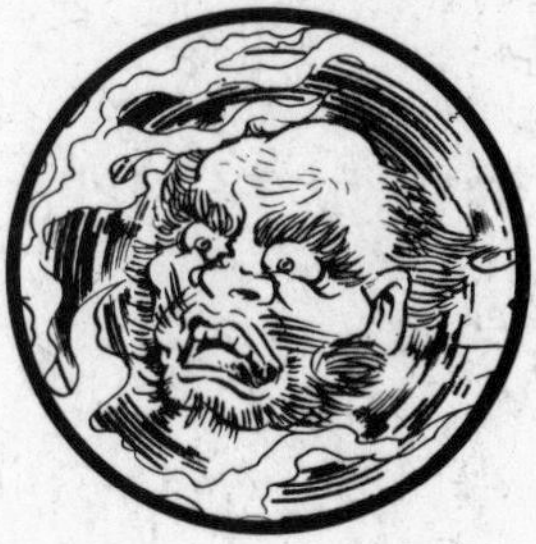

WANYUDO are the spirits of monks who have fallen from the righteous path. After death, they are cursed into to the shape of an oxcart wheel. They roll through the streets of Japan on certain nights of the year, dragging to hell anyone unlucky enough to cross their paths.

Also available from Shigeru Mizuki's Kitaro series: *The Birth of Kitaro* (2015)

 Font design: Kevin Huizenga. Drawn & Quarterly gratefully acknowledges Presspop Inc. and Maki Hakui for their invaluable assistance with the publication of the book. Production assistance by Laura Madden.

drawnandquarterly.com. First paperback edition: October 2016. Printed in Canada. 10 9 8 7 6 5 4 3 2 1

Library and Archives Canada Cataloguing in Publication: Mizuki, Shigeru, 1922–2015. [*Kitaro*. Selections. English] *Kitaro Meets Nurarihyon*. (*Shigeru Mizuki's Kitaro*) ISBN 978-1-77046-236-6 (paperback) 1. Graphic novels. I. Davisson, Zack, translator, writer of added commentary II. Title. III. Title: *Kitaro*. Selections. English. IV. Series: Mizuki, Shigeru, 1922–2015. *Kitaro*. PN6790.J33M5913 2016b 741.5'952 C2015-906031-1

Published in the USA by Drawn & Quarterly, a client publisher of Farrar, Straus and Giroux; Orders: 888.330.8477. Published in Canada by Drawn & Quarterly, a client publisher of Raincoast Books; Orders: 800.663.5714. Published in the UK by Drawn & Quarterly, a client publisher of Publishers Group UK; Orders: info@pguk.co.uk.

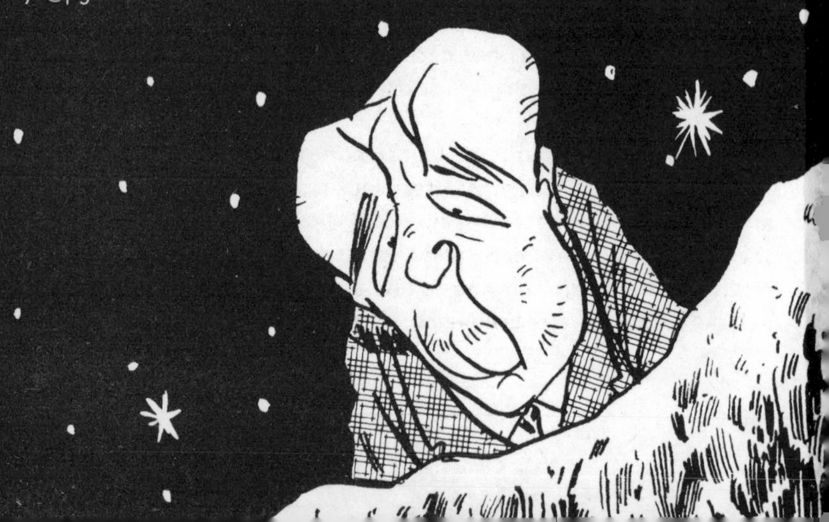

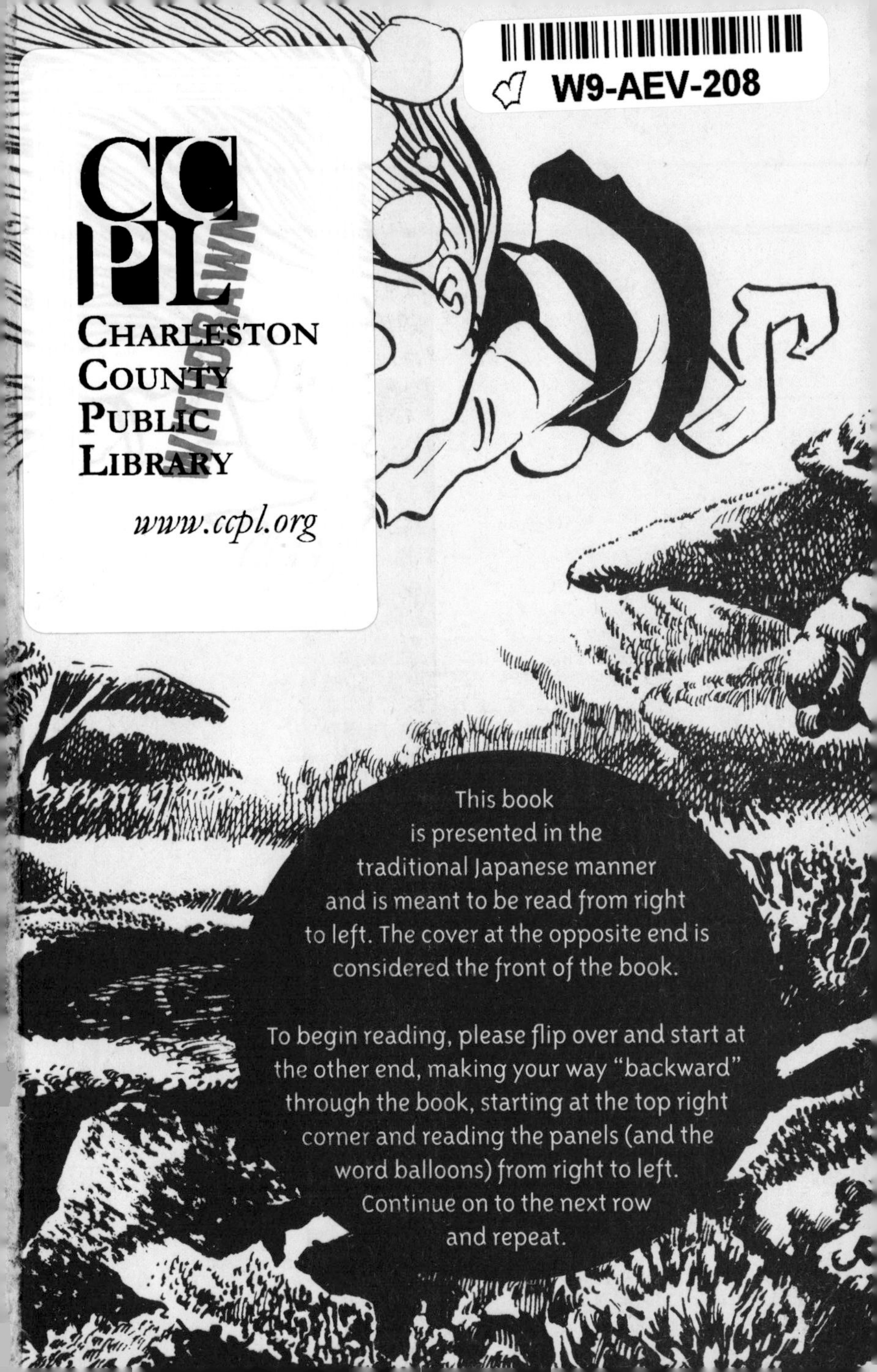

This book is presented in the traditional Japanese manner and is meant to be read from right to left. The cover at the opposite end is considered the front of the book.

To begin reading, please flip over and start at the other end, making your way "backward" through the book, starting at the top right corner and reading the panels (and the word balloons) from right to left. Continue on to the next row and repeat.